PRAIRIE DAWN

By

Karen Dee Musson

Copyright © 2025 by Karen Dee Musson

Edition: First

ISBN: 979-8-89397-586-4

Published by **EliteScribes Book Writing**

This book is dedicated to Liz (Medicine Moon) Martinez, Kimberly Vergonet, Ruth Dennis and my Lord Jesus Christ.

Special thank you to Millie Van Gundy Walke and Millie Musson for helping my dream come true. Could not have done this without you.

Contents

In the Beginning

A blanket of snow is beginning to cover the land that I call home. A cold wind is blowing soft specks of snow on the great windows of the church. I eagerly await as my father ends the church meeting. I reach for my scarf hanging on the coat rack and wrap it around my neck as I wait for my father and my brother Roger to put on their coats. I am eager to get home to our cozy cabin and curl up next to the fire, but first, I must meet up with my beau, Sid Barnes, who will take me home.

"Do not be long, child," my father cautions. "The snow is really coming down."

"I won't, father. Sid will have me home shortly."

I watch them step out into the cold, while my best friend Stella Miller ties her bonnet around her neck.

"We must hurry, Carrie," she says. "It is really coming down out there."

We both pull our shawls into our chests for added warmth as we step outside into the cold, frigid night. We make our way down the main street to meet her father, who is waiting for us at the saloon. I will also find Sid, who has been waiting patiently, drinking his whiskey until I arrive.

Stella is holding onto the back of my coat. The thickness of the snow is making it difficult to see in the dark. We make our way across the street. The warmth of the saloon fireplace is only a few yards away. We approach the alleyway leading to the walkway to the saloon. Stella inches her way in front of me coming to the first step. Relief sets in our frozen bodies, as we are nearly to the saloon door. I stop briefly, as she pushes the door open. I am then suddenly grabbed from behind and pulled into the dark alley. I let out a muffled scream that was only heard by Stella. She rushes into the dark alley, to find me being tossed down behind some crates and quickly being overpowered. She is quick to focus and runs to get some help.

I look up in my struggling, to see that it is Carl Landers. He is the sheriff's brother, who is a loud-mouthed drunk and has been a thorn in my side for years with his obnoxious sexual advances. Carl is a beast and it is taking all my strength to get him off me. I feel his cold hands on my breast. I managed to get my knee free and kick him in the groin. He releases his grip, as he utters out in pain.

"You bitch!" he yells.

Our struggling continues and I am nearing exhaustion when I see Hank, our saloon owner, Sid, and a few other men coming to my rescue. Stella is quick to help me to my feet, as my rescuers proceed to beat the living hell out of Carl. He is left out in the cold, battered and bruised to rot. Hank takes me home where I am welcomed by a very furious brother and irate father.

One month later:

After my ordeal with Carl, I honestly thought that I would be able to put it behind me and Carl would get what was coming to him. Fate takes a turn and after Carl attacked me, my life was never the same. My father and brother are extremely upset with what has happened to me and vowed for justice. My father presses charges with the idea that Carl would be arrested but somehow our sheriff and Sid got all the charges dropped.

They came up with a weak excuse that made me look as if I was soliciting him. This infuriates my father even more and he goes to the county Marshall for help, but somehow again Carl's word is taken over by mine. Despite my witnesses and Hank's testimony,

Carl gets off. It takes no time at all for the news to hit Willow Creek and soon I become the trash of the town.

It is extremely difficult on my father as he is a man of the cloth to hear what the entire town's people are saying and believe about me. The entire ordeal comes between Sid and me, and our relationship comes to a bitter end. I have not spoken to him for several weeks. When we pass in the streets, he avoids any contact with me and looks at me in disgust.

It has been nearly two months since my nightmare with Carl. Holding my head up high and proud has been a challenge. I thank Stella and my family for helping me through it. I have never been the kind of person to wallow in self-pity, and I am not going to start now. For this reason, I brush myself off and go on with my life. I ignore all the stares and whispers, hold my head up, and remain proud.

Chapter One

The Field of Flowers

Three months have passed. Today, I make the short walk into town for a few supplies at the General Store. I notice on the streets a small group of Indians. Willow Creek has always been friendly to the Indians and we trade with them every spring. I assume upon seeing them that is the reason why they are here. As I step onto the walkway leading to the General Store, I smile over at one of their warriors who is watching me walk. Upon entering the store, I noticed how disorderly and full it was. I nudge my way through the door, when I hear.

"Carrie." It is my father.

I excuse myself through the people to greet him. I notice an Indian standing next to him. My father reaches for my hand. I come face to face with the most amazing eyes and features I have ever seen.

"Child," my father starts. "This is Chief White Horse of the Lakota band."

Lakota, I think. This is an honor, for we have never traded with Lakota's.

"Chief White Horse, this is my daughter Carrie." The Chief nods and faintly grins. "I was just telling him that Willow Creek has never traded with the Lakota's and that his people will be warmly welcomed."

"Welcome to Willow Creek," I tell the Chief. "I hope you do well."

The Chief has the most beautiful eyes, I easily got lost in them. He is much younger than I thought a Chief would be. He takes great pride in his appearance. Our eyes connect with each other and until my father speaks neither one of us blinks.

"Oh dear, you must excuse me," he says, as he opens his watch to check the time. "I got so preoccupied in the moment that I forget why I came here to begin with. Please Chief, allow for me to show you where your people can set up and then I must leave and tend to my business."

"Father," I blink. "I can show him," I then feel flushed. I am usually not this direct around the opposite sex. "That is if the Chief would not mind?" I ask.

"Oh, child that would be great," Father turns to the Chief. "Would you mind Chief White Horse? My daughter will see that you are tended to the way you wish."

The Chief nods giving a faint smile. My father excuses himself by giving the Chief a firm handshake, vowing to exchange with him in the future before leaving. I take the Chief through the crowd. Only a few onlookers are curious and hesitate a moment to glance our way. It is not until we make our way to the walkway when I engage in a conversation. I am not sure as to how much English the Chief speaks, so I make our conversation simple.

"Good day for trade?" I say very slowly.

"Yes, we are hopeful," he answers.

I clearly underestimated how well and clear his English is. I smile at myself for my ignorance.

"My father is an ally with the Indians and will see that you and your people are treated well."

"Yes," he answers. "The word of his friendliness to our people is known throughout. That is why I brought my people here to trade."

I had no idea my father was well known for his kindness. We begin our walk to the center of the town, where the trading will be done. I explained to the Chief where his items can be set up. I am amazed at how well Chief White Horse speaks English; it is very clear and well-articulated. I am also impressed at how well he presents himself. He moves in certainty, proud of who he is. He is kind, and gentle, and easy on the eyes. We make our way into the center square where the trading will take place. Chief White Horse is satisfied with it and leaves to go send word to his people that the trade has begun.

I quickly go home to find something I can trade for. I collect some eggs and hope that it will satisfy a decent trade. When I go back into town, everything is set up and the trading has already begun. I see my father finishing a trade for old Mr. Hamilton, who is hard of hearing. I wave to him as I walk to the blanket that holds the items I am most interested in. The Chief sees me approaching and joins me. I stop in front of an old woman who appears very frail and up in her age. I give her a smile and in return she gives me a nod.

"I was not sure if you would be trading with us today," the Chief says. "Yes," I answer. "I had to go home to collect some eggs."

He glances at my basket of eggs that is looped through my arms.

"I hope she will trade with me," I say.

"She will," he answers.

I watch him as he speaks his tongue to the elder. They exchange a brief conversation. The Chief melts me with his dark eyes when he looks my way.

"She asks what it is you would like to trade your eggs for."

"I simply adore her baskets," I say.

He addresses the older woman.

"She says she will trade for your eggs and your hair ribbon."

I feel that is reasonable, and I am pleased that I did so well. I handed her my basket of eggs. To complete my end of the trade, I reach around and remove my hair ribbon from my hair. I catch the Chief's eyes on me as my hair falls free. I sweetly smiled and handed her my ribbon. The trade is complete. I really do not want to leave, as something about the Chief intrigues me, but I feel that if I stay, I will make my crush on the Chief obvious, so I thank them, hoping that they will return one day soon. I then make my way home with my basket, feeling happy and refreshed.

Two weeks later:

The flowers are blooming abundantly in the meadow near my home. Every Saturday for several years, I come here to pick a basket full of flowers. I will arrange them in a vase that I will put on a table in front of the pulpit for Sunday church. It is a weekly routine and my time to be by myself. I come down to my knees to start picking. The recent rain has made the meadow exceptionally thick and high, making my job rather easy. I hear my horse, Sugar Foot neigh.

"What boy?" I say to him, as I walk further into the thick grass to pick more of a variety. I hear a rustle in the thickness not far away. I stopped for a moment to look. Seeing nothing out of the ordinary, I squat down and continue picking. After a few more minutes, I am satisfied that my basket is full.

I step out of the thickness and head to Sugar Foot, who is being more persistent at getting my attention. He starts stomping his foot and snorting. Sugar Foot is normally a very calm horse, seeing his reaction brings me concern. I start looking around to see what is bothering him. I gasp, as not more than a few yards from me are three Indians perched high on their horses. I step back slowly as all eyes are on me. I hasten my stride when I come only a few feet from Sugar Foot. I watch the Indian in the middle step off his horse and come towards me. I run the rest of the way to Sugar Foot. I briefly look back and see the Indian coming in closer. I grab the horn of my saddle and hoist myself onto my horse. I turn my reins to ride off when I stop. I take a closer look at the Indian coming towards me. There is no mistaking that handsome face. It is Chief White Horse. I pet Sugar Foot's neck to calm him down. He is not happy that we are still here.

"It is alright boy," I tell him. The Chief stops next to me.

"Lovely day to pick flowers," he smiles.

"Yes, it is," I say.

"Do you come here often?" he wonders.

"Every Saturday," I answer.

He reaches down and grabs a flower from my basket.

"I will remember that," he says, "until then."

He places the flower in my hair. I am too stunned to move. All I can do is stare at him and disappear in his black eyes. I blink when he turns around and rides off. Riding home, I feel my heart patter and truly hope I do see the handsome Chief again. When I get to my room, I remove the flower from my hair, placing it in a vase on the nightstand next to my bed. I blush as I smile, remembering the handsome man who put it there.

The following week, I make my usual trip to the meadow. I am not there long before I have my visitor. As I am tying Sugar Foot's reins around a tree branch, I see the Chief come.

"Hello, beautiful," he greets as he jumps off his horse.

"Hello," I smile back.

He picks a flower, placing it in my hair.

"Thank you," I blush.

He glances down at my empty basket.

"Please do not let me stop you," he jests.

Shyly, grinning I head into the meadow finding the flowers that I want to pick for the service. The Chief follows me in, finding a place on the ground next to me. He then watches me pick. For several moments, his eyes followed me as he is concentrating on my every move. Finally, the silence is broken.

"Why do you pick the flowers?" he huskily asks.

"I use them for Sunday church to pretty up the pulpit," I answer.

"If you are in this thing called a church then no flowers are necessary, as you are all the beauty it needs," he says.

I feel the heat on my cheeks. I grin shyly as I turn my head away. Knowing that he is making me blush, he smiles and quickly changes the conversation.

"Your father seems like a good man."

"He is. I owe him a great deal."

"In what way?" he asks.

"He is really my uncle. My father died tending to a wounded soldier when I was six years old. He brought me into his home and raised me as if I were his own."

"Where is your mother?"

"She died in childbirth when I was six, along with my brother David. My father was a well-known doctor. When my mother died, she bled a lot, and my father was unable to stop it. He was heavy with grief. My uncle asked him to come and live with him. He would help us. Therefore, we did. My father never got over her loss. He took work that had him go far away, working for the government and tending to the wounded soldiers at the Fort. The Fort was attacked, and my father was killed while he was tending to a soldier."

I glance over at the Chief. His eyes look thick with remorse.

"That is a very sad story," he finally says. "One I can relate to."

"Oh?" I ask.

"I lost my father two summers ago. He was brutally slaughtered when our camp was attacked by Pawnee."

"And that is why you are Chief," I conclude. That explains to me why he is so young.

"Yes," he answers.

I can tell by his long face that it is still very fresh in his memory. Just as I am starting to warm up to him, I hear a caw of a bird. Startled, I stopped picking my flowers and stand up.

"It is alright," Chief White Horse assures me. "It is just my warriors. I must leave." He places my hand into his, gently squeezing it. "I will be back here this time next week," he smiles.

"I would like that," I smile back.

A rich warmth of lust fills my soul as I watch this magnificent man jump on his horse and ride away. The next three Saturdays, I would meet with the Chief.

Over time, I became more relaxed with him. He is so easy to talk to. We relate to each other in so many ways. I feel like I have known him all my life. During his recent visit, he began sharing his beliefs, his religion, and his culture with me. I find it fascinating. The more he speaks, the deeper I am falling for him. I cannot wait until our next visit.

Today's visit I want to make special. It is a beautiful day. Both Roger and my father will be gone for most of it, allowing me plenty of time to be in the meadow. I hope the Chief has the time as well. I have decided to have a picnic. It takes most of the morning to prepare the meal. I finished packing up the last of the food. It is time to head down to the meadow. I take a quick look at myself in the mirror and do some last-minute touch-ups before heading out the door.

The meadow is very close to my home, and it only took me a few minutes to get there. I found a nice place under a tree to set up the food. I know at any moment, the fascinating Chief will show up. I am nearly done when I see him coming.

"Hello beautiful," he greets.

"Hello," I smile. "I have a surprise for you."

"I do not care for surprises, but if it involves you, I am sure I will like it."

He follows me to the blanket and sees all the food.

"I hope you are hungry."

"I am," he answers.

"Allow me to serve you a plate."

I start preparing his plate, as his dark mysterious eyes watch my every move. I start with the meat and work my way around. I reach for a strawberry when he puts his hand over mine. I look up at him. He gently grabs the strawberry and slides closer to me. He then placed the tip of it gently in my mouth and I take a bite. He removes the other half and eats it. Never once did he remove his eyes from mine.

"Come with me," he huskily says. "Let me take care of you."

I am stunned. His offer takes me completely off guard. For a moment, I am speechless.

"I... I... I don't know what to say," I finally say.

"Say yes."

"Chief White Horse...."

"Please, you do not need to address me as Chief. To you, I am White Horse; to everyone else I am Chief." I am flattered.

"White Horse." He gently placed his finger over my lips. "I am a very private man, especially to a woman, but Carrie, you are not just any woman. You are different. Since my Flowering Blossom died two summers ago, I have had no eyes for any other woman."

"You were married?" I questioned.

"Yes. We do not speak of the ones who have passed on, but I feel that it is important you know, so therefore I will tell you."

He continues. "I lost my wife the same day I lost my father. I was out hunting when I saw the smoke. I reached the camp too late; both my father and wife were dead. We went looking for the Pawnee to get our revenge, but they slithered away like the cowards that they are. I mourned heavily for her and I miss her tremendously. I see a lot of her in you. Your skin color and hair are different, but otherwise, you are both a lot alike. I want to take care of you like I did her. That is why I want you to come back with me."

"Oh, White Horse, this is all happening so fast. What about my family?" He takes my hand into his, kissing it.

"You think about it. Now, shall we eat?" he grins.

He takes his plate and begins to eat. He quickly changes the conversation, making it lighthearted and funny. We spent most of the afternoon together before we had to part ways. The following week, I tell White Horse that I will not be following him. I just feel it is too soon, and I still am not sure what to tell my father. He seems to understand, but I can tell he is disappointed. He helps me collect the flowers, and we have a good visit, but like them all, it is time to part.

The following week, I wait in the meadow for his arrival. My basket is full and I am ready to leave. I feel it is odd that he is not here. I start to wonder if he took my rejection as an insult and is not showing up. Disappointed and heartbroken, I head back to Sugar Foot. I am just getting ready to pull myself up on his back when I notice White Horse coming through the field. I sigh in relief. I walk to greet him as he jumps off his horse. He is different from the moment I see him. He is failing to smile. His head is low. I know something is wrong.

"White Horse, what is it?" I ask.

"I am leaving."

"Leaving, but why?"

"The herd has been spotted. We must follow them."

"The herd?" I question.

"The buffalo," he explains.

"I see." I lower my head.

The thought that I may never see him again is weighing heavily in my heart.

"Carrie you must understand. Buffalo is essential to our way of life. We need the herd to survive. It is our food, our shelter. We must follow it."

"I understand." He lifts my head. Our eyes meet. I hear him deeply sigh, as he rubs my shoulders.

"Come with me Carrie," he stresses. "I will teach you my ways. You will want for nothing. You will be me my Queen."

Lord, he is making this so hard. How I want to go. How my heart desires to be with him, but I cannot leave my father. I just cannot get myself to leave him this way.

"I can't," I cry. He pulls me into his arms.

"Do not cry for me," he says. "I understand."

"Will I ever see you again?" I ask.

"I am hoping to return next spring. If I do, I will come for you."

"Take care, White Horse," I sniff. He cups my face in his palms and kisses my forehead.

"Take care, Beautiful," he says, flicking my nose.

He then turns and jumps on his horse. With a tear in my eye, I watch him ride off. My heart breaks as the man of my dreams rides out of my life.

Once again, I am alone. White Horse lies on his pelt at his winter camp. He thinks of the woman with the golden hair, that he reluctantly left only a few months ago. How he has not stopped thinking of her. How he wishes he had done more to convince her to run away with him. Perhaps if he hadn't followed the herd when he did, he would have had more time to persuade her and she would be with him now. He regrets he had not been more forceful and had not kidnapped her, as he originally intended to do. But she is so delicate and the last thing he wants is for her to fear him. He must follow his vision that he had so many months before. He had seen her in a dream. She had called his name. He knows soon he will see her again. Until then all he can do is dream about her and hope that spring will soon arrive, so he can come to her again.

Chapter Two

Willow Creek

Early Spring

Willow Creek is a small town that is nestled back in the woods. It received its name from the beautiful willow trees that surround it and the large creek that flows through it. It's a town that I call home.

Willow Creek is a friendly place. Most of the people here have been living here their entire lives. We receive very little excitement from the outside world. Most people here keep to themselves, but you have the few who have nothing better to do than to spread gossip. One of the worst is Mrs. Forbes. She and her husband own the General Store. It is unclear as to why she does not like me; however she adores Roger and my father. In her eyes, I am the bad apple from the tree. Roger seems to think that it may have something to do with me being such good friends with Stella and Hank.

Hank owns our saloon and hires his saloon girls to "entertain". Stella at one time was one of those girls. Although Hank has never approached me to be one of his girls, I am labeled as one just by the association and now more than ever with this whole Carl episode. Hank is a big man, well over six foot and built like an ox. Many men fear him, but many women love him. I am one of them. Stella and Hank were a couple at one time. When she gave up that life, she gave up Hank. It was a bitter parting and took some time, but now they are the best of friends.

Across the street from the saloon is our doctor's office, run by my brother, Roger. He is the youngest doctor we have ever had, but a damn good one. There is no soul around here who would tell you differently. Roger gives his life to his medicine. He is always keeping current on the newest treatments. He was the one of the first doctors who put a stop to bleeding. He found a more humane method of caring for their illnesses. He has saved many lives because of it.

Next to his office is our post office, run by Stella's parents. Stella works there as well. Further down the street is our barber, our bank, and our restaurant, where they serve the best fried-chicken on this side of the Mississippi. Across the way is our town square where we have our church. A big and beautiful building stands by itself in the center of the square. The front of the lawn is used for our church gatherings, festivals, picnics, and at times our service. My father, Jeremiah Sims, runs the church.

Looking across the lawn of the church is our schoolhouse, next to that is our mill, blacksmith, and stables. One bridge leads in and out of Willow Creek. It is the main path into our town and underneath it swims a stream of fish. Just across the bridge is our cemetery and half a mile down the road, taking the fork to the left, stands our home. My father built it when I was eight and Roger was twelve. It has been our home ever since. We have a barn and a chicken pen. We tend to no fields, even though we have the land to keep them. I have a garden that I take great pride in. My tomatoes are the ripest and juiciest in the land.

As for me, my name is Carrie Rose Sims. I was born on a beautiful summer day to Doctor Zacharias and Rebecca Sims. My father was a very well-known prestigious doctor and my mother was a schoolteacher. I remember very little about my mother, since she died when I was six. I have been told that I am an exact replica of her in every way, all the way down to my golden hair.

I was brought here to Willow Creek by my uncle, shortly after my father died, when he took his calling as Willow Creek's

Reverend. My uncle ran an Orphanage, where I spent two years of my life. It was there that I met Roger. Roger was a runaway that my father found under a porch, after he stole an apple from the General Store. He took a liking to Roger and brought him into his home, where he raised him as his own. To Roger and me, he is our father and always will be.

Roger is a bookworm and incredibly smart. Medical school was a breeze for him. It has taken him a while to earn respect from the town, mostly because of his young age, but he did it. There is not a soul here who does not trust him. Roger and I are very close. Although we are not related by blood, we consider ourselves siblings and carry on as if we are. I hear Roger coming down from the loft as I tend to our morning meal of biscuits and gravy.

"Good morning," he grumbles.

"Good morning," I say.

I watch as he pours himself a cup of coffee.

"Another late night?" I ask.

"Yes, old Mr. Sheppard. I am afraid all those years of smoking has finally caught up to him."

"That bad?"

It saddens me because I have known Mr. Sheppard since I was a little girl. I remember him giving me piggyback rides and taking Roger and I fishing when father would leave town to visit the Orphanage. The misses and him were never able to have children themselves, despite the years of trying. He went quickly downhill when his wife died last winter of fever.

We hear our father come through the front door.

"Good morning, Father," I greet.

He opens the closet door without a word and thumbs around. "Hmmm," he mumbles and closes the door. He thinks for a moment.

"Ah yes," he says and walks into his bedroom.

Roger and I just shrugged our shoulders.

"Come on and eat," I tell Roger, while putting his plate on the table. Father returns from his bedroom, clearly annoyed.

"Now where did I put that silly thing?" he huffs.

"Put what Father?" I ask.

"My fishing pole," he says.

"Going fishing, Pa?" Roger asks.

"No, I am going to trade for it."

"Trade?" I ask.

"Yes."

"With whom?" I wondered.

"Chief White Horse," he said.

I nearly dropped my plate. I haven't heard from the handsome Chief in almost a year.

"Oh, Pa," Roger snorts. "I know what he promised you, but his type never stays around much; they're nomads. You are wasting your time waiting on him."

"Is that so. I would like to have you know that I just saw him and his band a few moments ago coming into town. I helped them set up."

I gasp. My stomach jumps circles just thinking that he may be here. I can still remember our time together, and how he wanted me to go away with him. I have never forgotten him and prayed every night for a month that he would return. This was like a dream come true.

"I believe the pole is in the barn, Father," I answer.

"Yes, of course the barn. Why didn't I think of that?"

"Hmm Father," I begin. "Would you mind if I was to go into town with you? I would love to see what there is to trade."

"Of course, child."

I cannot control my enthusiasm. I have been waiting for this moment for nearly a year. I catch Roger looking at me.

"What?" I ask.

"Why are you so excited?"

"I'm not. What business is it of yours anyway?" I huff and storm off to my room to dress myself up. My father finds his pole and finishes his breakfast just when I come out of my room.

"You look radiant my child," he says.

"Thank you."

"Coming with us, son?" Father asks.

"I will pass, but thank you anyway. I must go see Mr. Sheppard."

"Do give him my best, will you son?"

"Will do," said Roger.

"If you don't mind Roger, can you tend to the breakfast dishes. I do not want to delay father anymore by doing them myself," I say.

"Don't you think you are a little dressed up just to be trading with a bunch of heathens?"

"Roger, you surprise me," my father scolds. "The Sioux may not worship the same God we do, but they are still his children, and you will show them some respect." Roger huffs, as he turns his attention to the dishes.

My father stops the wagon in front of the church. I glance over at the traders, who seem to be doing very well. I immediately see White Horse. We exchange quick smiles and both look away.

"Father what are you trading for?" I wonder.

"Blankets. The Orphanage is in dire need of them."

"How many are you going to get?"

"As many as I can. This pole is worth a lot. It is solid as a rock and has caught hundreds of fish."

There is no doubt about that. I have caught many fish with this pole as well. We make our way to the blankets and both men greet each other with a firm handshake. White Horse and I exchange a quick smile.

"I would like some of your blankets. I am prepared to trade my rod and tackle box for them," my father says.

I recognize the elder woman with the blankets as the same woman who traded the basket with me last spring. The Chief speaks his tongue to the woman. In a frail, soft voice, the woman speaks her tongue back.

"For your pole and box, she will give you four blankets," he says.

"Oh my," father says. "I was hoping to give each child their own blanket."

"If that is the case Father, you will be short two blankets," I say.

"Yes, but it will just have to do. I will replace the ones that are very thin and the other ones will just have to wait."

"If I may make a suggestion," Chief White Horse offers.

He looks so good and remarkably handsome. I am trying not to make it too obvious because of the company, but I am finding it extremely difficult to keep my eyes off him.

"She will trade you four blankets for your pole and tackle box. However, I will trade the other two for your daughter's scarf and bonnet," the Chief says.

Both of us were stunned at the generous offer.

"You are serious?" my father asks.

"When it comes to trading, I am always serious."

My father looks at me and speaks. "I can replace both, child."

"I have many," I state.

"You have a trade Chief," Father says. White Horse grins. "Although I am curious as to what you possibly want with a scarf and bonnet?" Father asks.

"We have many cold winters on the prairie. I am sure one of the children can use them."

I start untying my scarf when Esther Miles, who is the cook in our restaurant, motions for my father to come.

"Carrie," my father says. "I trust you to finish up the trade."

"Yes Father," I tell him.

I am glad to do it. Now maybe I can talk to White Horse alone. My father gives the Chief a handshake before walking away, allowing me to finish the trade. I hand White Horse my scarf and bonnet.

"I will have my warriors put your blankets in the back of your wagon," White Horse says.

"That will be fine," I say.

He glances down at the older woman and then out behind me, making sure we are alone.

"I miss you, beautiful. Meet me in the meadow in two hours," he says. "Can you get away?"

"Yes. I will be there."

I am not sure how he thinks he is going to get away undetected but I do not care. I just want to see him. In two hours sharp, I meet up with White Horse under a tree. He immediately holds my hands.

"I was not sure I would ever see you again," I state.

"I could not stay away. I have never stopped thinking of you," he says.

He pulls me into his embrace. He holds onto me tightly. The smell of his sweet incense fills my soul. How I miss his smell and touch.

"I'm sorry I didn't follow you," I say.

He pulls free from our embrace, gazing deeply into my eyes.

"I understood. What matters is now." With that said, he kisses me. "I must get back before I am missed," he says after our lips part.

"Alright."

"We will meet here to pick flowers," he says.

I smile for how I cannot wait to see his handsome face again.

White Horse leads his people to their camp, satisfied with today's trade. Although he should be happy with the wealth they received today, he cannot keep his mind off the beautiful woman, whose lips taste like honey. He wraps her scarf around his hand, thinking how lovely the neck was that it hung around. He knows he will sleep well tonight with the vision of the woman with golden hair. His best warrior and brother Koawa rides up to his side.

"Forget her brother," he says in his tongue. "She is not for you."

But White Horse is paying no mind. He knows somehow, some way they will be together. His vision told him so. He is adamant. This time he is not leaving her behind. Before the next migration, she will be his.

Chapter Three

The Bear

"Good morning, Father," I greet.

"Good morning, child," he says, as he finishes hooking up the wagon. "There is fresh coffee on the stove," I say.

"There is no time, child. I am on my way to the orphanage to deliver the blankets. I must leave now to make it there before nightfall."

"Do tell Sister Ann I say hello."

"Will do," he assures. "Now child, I will be gone for several days."

"I know, Father."

"I will stay on a few extra days to make some necessary repairs. You can wire a message to Sister Ann in care of the orphanage if you need me."

"Roger and I will be fine," I assure him.

"You always are," he smiles, before giving me a hug and climbing into the wagon. I wave as he rides off.

"Bye, Pa!" Roger yells from the barn.

Father waves as he is riding off. I walk to the barn to greet Roger, who is saddling his horse.

"You are leaving me too?" I whine.

"Marianne Simpson never came by yesterday for her checkup," he states. "She is nearing her time for delivery. She has lost two babies already, and I do not wish her to lose another one. I am going to pay her a visit."

"Do give her my best," I add.

"I will."

Roger's horse is saddled, and he is ready to leave when we see a rider coming in fast. It is Jethro Peters. He farms for Mr. Sheppard in exchange for free room and board. Awkward-looking fellow, but nice.

"D-d-doc," he stutters. "MMMMR. Sh-Sheppard is r-real b-bad."

"This could be it. I must go," Roger says.

"What about Marianne?" I question.

"She will just have to wait. Harold is there if she needs anything."

"I will go and check on her," I volunteer.

"Are you sure?"

"Yes, Roger, I am sure."

It is not uncommon for me to help Roger whenever I can, and besides, it gives me something to do.

"Thank you, Carrie. I will stay with him until he passes on. I am not sure how long it will be. Will you be alright?"

"Yes, it is not the first time I have been left alone for days on end. Now go! I will be fine. If I need anything, I will call on Hank."

He says no more and rides quickly away. I head back inside and finish my chores. I packed a basket of freshly made bread that I made this morning to give to Harold when I arrive. I saddle up Sugar Foot and head to the Simpson house. On the main road it is a good hour's ride. The backwoods will cut down on my time, but considering the terrain is so thick and at times rather steep, I choose the safer way, taking the road as far as I can. I take a right at the bend in the road and head through the prairie for the smoother ride to their home.

Further down the prairie, White Horse and his brother Koawa are out for a ride along the prairie. White Horse is having a very difficult time keeping his mind off a beautiful woman with hair like the prairie grass. Despite his brother's warnings, he wants nothing more than to have her permanently in his arms. He has been thinking all day about how he will do that. Koawa challenges his brother to a horse race. The first one to the trees is the winner. White Horse is always up to a challenge and accepts.

Just in the distance, the Simpson home comes into view. I immediately noticed smoke coming out of the chimney, a sure sign that someone was home. I see the Simpson wagon hitched next to the barn, but I see no horses. I figure Harold is most likely out hunting or went out for supplies without the wagon. I step up to the door and knock. After waiting a few moments with no response, I knock again. Still with no answer, I walk around thinking I may find Marianne perhaps in her garden or collecting eggs. I notice the pigs have been recently fed, as well as the chickens, indicating someone has been here not too long ago. I call out.

"Hello! Is anyone here?"

A woman in her condition should not be traveling far, and I knew Harold would not allow her to ride. I look out towards the fields at the well-maintained crops. I see no sign of them. I walk into the barn. One of the two horses is still here. Marianne must be around. I go up to the porch and knock again. This time through the door I hear a kettle whistling. I knock louder.

"Hello! Marianne. Are you alright?" I hear no response.

I am certain someone is here and worry they may be hurt. Lord only knows, as the wildlife here is abundant. I try the door. I cracked it open just a bit and called out for her again.

"Hello!" I walk in. "It is Carrie Sims. Is anyone here?"

The kettle is loudly whistling. I walk over to it, removing it from the stove. Something is not right. I can feel it in my bones.

"Marianne?" I holler.

"Carrie. I am in here," I faintly hear.

I quickly hurried to the bedroom. Marianne is on the bed in obvious labor. I quickly raced to her side. It is apparent to me from her distress that she has been in this state for some time.

"The baby is coming?"

I grasp my thoughts together and feel her stomach. It is very hard, and her breathing is deep.

"Where is Doctor Briggs?" she asks.

"Marianne, I don't think you have much time." I come down to the end of the bed. "I need to check for the baby," I tell her.

I lift her dress and see that she is crowning. It is time for her to push. "Marianne, I need you to push hard."

"I can't do this by myself. I need Doctor Briggs," she whines.

"Marianne. There is no time. I can see the head. I can do this. Trust me."

I have assisted Roger with numerous births over the years. I know what I am doing. She hears the urgency in my voice. She begins to push. Her pushes continue for several minutes. The air is filled with her bellows as the baby makes its way through the canal. Finally, I can see the end is near.

"Almost, Marianne. One hard push."

On my command, she pushes with everything she has, releasing the infant from its womb. I support the head as the child is born into the world. I sigh with relief when the baby cries. Finally, after several stillborns, Marianne has a healthy baby. I clean and wrap the baby up, placing it in Marianne's arms.

"It is a boy," I say.

Marianne starts to cry. She is overwhelmed with happiness and joy. She knows her husband, Harold, will be overjoyed as well.

"I want to see Harold," she says.

"Harold is not here," I say.

"Are you sure? He left to go get the doc hours ago."

"His horse is gone," I say. "I looked for him when I came here. I never saw him."

"I thought when you came it was because he came for you," she cries. "No. I am here because you did not show up for your appointment yesterday with the doctor. He is with a very ill patient and asked me to come in exchange. Good thing I did. I was needed."

"I do not understand Carrie. He had plenty of time to get to your home. What could have happened to him?"

"Now, I do not want you to worry about that. You need your rest."

"No!" She removes her covers to get up.

"You listen here," I argue, "you need to stay in bed and rest."

"But something is wrong. He should have returned by now."

"I am sure he is fine. Try not to worry," I tell her.

"No! Carrie something is wrong please go find him."

"Alright, but only if you promise to stay in bed until I get back."

"I will, I promise."

I make sure that she and the baby have everything they need before I leave.

"He would have taken the shorter way into town through the trees," she says. I had figured as much, as I had not seen him on the road on my way here. "I will be back," I assure her.

Roger returns home. Mr. Sheppard died just a few hours before. He is hoping to join his sister at Marianne Simpson's when he sees a note attached to the door. He reads the note and realizes his services are needed somewhere else. He walks into the home and pulls a piece of paper out from the drawer. He sits down and writes a quick note.

Dear Carrie,

I had every intention of joining you at the Simpson house. I received a message that there is some sort of epidemic at the immigration camp, and my services are desperately needed. Hope it is nothing serious. I'm not sure how long I will be gone. Holler at Hank if there is a problem.

Regards,

Roger.

He folds up the note and places it neatly on the mantel before heading out the door.

Going through the trees is indeed shorter and slow-moving due to the steep and rocky terrain. I am uncertain which way Harold may have taken, as there are several routes one could take to get back to town. All I can do is take the way that is the most logical and hope I am correct. The woods are full of wildlife, including mountain lions. bears, foxes, and wolves, all of which I do not wish to see.

I spot a squirrel scampering up a tree and a hawk flying overhead. I see a porcupine run quickly to get out of the way of my horse's hooves as we approach his path. I come to a small clearing on top of a hill, looking down at the river that flows through Willow Creek. It is there that I see a hat lying on the ground. I stop in front of it and get off to pick it up. There is an inscription inside the label of the hat that reads, 'To My Dearest Harold.' I can only assume that it belongs to Harold Simpson.

I looked down at the river, thinking perhaps Harold slipped. I gasp in horror when I see Harold lying face down on the riverbed floor; his clothes are shredded, and he is covered in blood. I cup my mouth in horror. Poor Mr. Simpson is dead. It is then that I panic. It is clear to me that a wild animal, perhaps a bear, has taken the life of Mr. Simpson. I then realize whatever it is may still be around, and I could be its next meal. I desperately need to get out of here. I pull myself together and decide I need to go get Hank. He will know what to do. I hoist myself up on my horse and run off as fast as I can. I am running quickly, faster than I should be in this terrain. Sugar Foot stumbles as we go up a rocky ravine. My mind is racing. Poor Marianne, what am I going to tell her? How will she handle it? My heart goes out to her.

I make it to the next clearing that is just before the meadow. I quickly become alert when Sugar Foot spooks and starts prancing around. I hold on tight to my reins when I see a bear come out from behind some trees on its hind legs. Sugar Foot rears up when the bear starts swiping the air with his claws. I shield my face as the beast comes in for his attack. Sugar Foot rears up again. I let out a scream when the bear's claws come down, just missing Sugar Foot's neck. I frantically attempt to control my horse from bucking me off. I am horrified when the bear growls just inches from my head, revealing his razor-sharp teeth. Sugar Foot is snorting and prancing and is just as terrified as I am.

The bear takes another swipe, hitting my arm. The brute strength of the creature forces me off Sugar Foot, and I land hard on the ground. Sugar Foot is bucking at the bear as I crawl to my feet in a daze. The bear turns away and starts charging towards me and rears up. Sugar Foot bucks the bear, bringing it down to all fours. It only stops for a moment and charges at me again. I see its huge fangs and let out a scream. I shield my face as I whimper in fear. I am certain that at any moment this bear will kill me. I let out another scream as I feel the sharp claws ripping open my arm. Sugar Foot is again trying to defend me by bucking at the bear. He backs it off long enough to allow me to get to my feet and make a run for it. I run as fast as I can without looking back. I gain some ground from the bear, but it quickly catches up. I get to a ravine where a shallow brook is running through. I rolled down the hill. The bear is hot on my tail. My heart is racing. I am praying to God above to get me out of this. I hear a roar as I hit the bottom of the ravine and am knocked out.

Chapter Four

Chief White Horse

My head is pounding. It is too painful to open my eyes. Every inch of my body is throbbing. The softness of a blanket and the smell of a fire makes me realize that I am no longer lying in the woods. Where am I, I wonder? I hear unfamiliar voices mumbling nearby. What are they saying? I suddenly feel frightened. I try to focus again, moaning when I do. I feel a hand touch my forehead, delicately repositioning the moist cloth that lays upon it. I attempt to focus again. I hear mumbling, people chanting in a language so different than mine.

"Shhh. You will be alright," I hear.

That voice, I recognize it. A massive pain fills my head when I attempt again to focus. I am left with no choice but to put my faith in the hands of the one who is caring for me. Feeling helpless and in too much pain, I give up and eventually fall asleep. Several hours later, I can open my eyes. The pain is intense as I try to focus. I moan as a sharp pain slices across my temple. I see the silhouette of someone sitting very close to me. I try to focus. A sharp hammering pain shoots behind my eyes. It is so painful, I want to cry.

"Prairie Dawn," I hear. "Do not be frightened. It is I, White Horse."

Am I imagining it? Is White Horse the one taking care of me? But how? How did he find me? It can't be him. I must be imagining, after all, I really did take a blow to the head. I am determined to focus my eyes. I must be sure that it is him. Slowly, his face comes into view. It is him.

"Where am I?" I mumble. I focus, but all is blurry. My insides flip over, and I want to vomit with the pain.

"You are at my Lakota camp. You were brought here a few hours ago." "What happened?" I ask.

"You were attacked by a bear," he answers.

"Now I remember," I say.

I try again to focus. I bellow in pain as I lift my head. White Horse gently pushes me back down.

"You are badly hurt. You need not to move," he says.

"How bad?" I mumble.

"You hit your head very hard. Your arm is torn up from where the bear clawed you. My Sharman cleaned and wrapped it up. You are lucky that I heard your screams. That bear could have torn you to shreds."

"Thank you," I say.

"I want you to rest. I will have someone sit with you until you wake. The medicine that my Sharman gave you will work. You will feel much stronger when you rise." He then stands up.

I hear him speak his tongue. It is then that I realize that we are not alone in the room. I see a flash of light as White Horse pushes open the flap and steps out.

Nightfall is approaching when I wake up. I can open my eyes and look around with little pain. White Horse is correct, I am feeling better. Whatever his Sharman gave me has really worked. I see that I am lying in what I have heard from my father, is a tepee. It is a huge, triangular-shaped hut made from buffalo hide that has a flap for a door. A small fire pit lays in the center. There are several tripods neatly standing around that are holding various items. I am unfamiliar with what they are used for. I am resting on a small mattress called a pelt. It is actually very comfortable. A beautiful geometrical blanket rests over my legs. The smell of sweet incense fills the teepee. A low fire provides much warmth. I feel in my heart that a great deal of care is being made to make sure that I am comfortable. I lean back and rest my head. In no time, I have fallen back asleep.

My eyes open to a new day. The light of the morning sun peaks its head through the open flap on the top of the tepee. I reach up and touch my head. I flinch. It is still painful to touch. My arm is securely bandaged, making me unable to see how bad it is cut up. I raise it up to feel a sting. Suddenly, I turn my attention to the flap when it opens. I grin as I see White Horse walk in holding a cup.

"Good morning," he smiles.

"Good morning," I say.

He sits down in front of me. "How are you feeling?" he asks.

"My head hurts a little."

"I want you to drink this," he says. "Drink it slow. It will help."

He reaches behind me, helping me to a sitting position. He then hands me the cup. As instructed, I drink it slowly. It reminds me of bitter tea, a taste I am not very fond of, but I drink it anyway. After the tea is about halfway down, he takes it from me.

"You feeling hungry?" he asks.

"A little," I answer.

"Good. I will have some food brought in for you."

"Thank you," I smile. He smiles back and then leans in.

"You gave me a fright," he says and then kisses me.

"I will be back very soon. You rest. I will have your meal brought in."

I watch him as he opens the flap and steps out. I barely have my eyes closed when a woman, great with child, places a tray of food down next to me. She smiles at me as she motions for me to eat. On my plate there is cornbread and venison. I will admit, I am a little surprised at how much flavor it has. I eat all of it. I finish the last of the tea as I eat. The woman who is staying with me is very kind and patient. She's communicating with me through hand signs. In front of me, she put a basin of water and a cloth. She then pretends she is washing herself. She wants me to use the water to freshen up. I am happy to comply.

As I am washing up, she reaches inside a bag, called a parfleche, that is geometrically decorated with quill and fringe. It is remarkably beautiful. She pulls out a hairbrush that is homemade. I am assuming the bristles were either out of bison fur or perhaps horsehair. She comes down beside me and touches my hair. She demonstrates that she wants to brush it. I allow it.

She is very gentle. I seldom feel any tugs at all. She seems as if she is admiring my hair. Perhaps it is the color of it. She takes her time brushing it, having her own method of doing it. Besides needing a good washing, it does feel better and less tangled. She goes to the bag again. This time she pulls out the most amazing-looking dress that I have ever seen. She hands it to me. I look at the details on the dress. It appears to be made from two skins. I am presuming deer. The yoke is carefully decorated, forming the upper part. The bottom of the dress is fringed, giving it its fullness. She motions for me to put it on. I am astonished and extremely flattered that I am allowed to wear a dress of such beauty. She smiles widely. She motions for me to stand up and offers to help me to my feet. She is great with child. I do not feel she needs my extra weight; however, I take her hand and come to a stand. She wraps her arm around my waist until I am steady. I feel a little dizzy at first, but it subsides after a few moments of catching my breath. She wastes no time at untying the back of my dress, or should I say what is left of it.

I understand why she wants me out of it. She kindly turns around when the part that makes me a woman becomes exposed. I hold my old dress up to me to cover my breasts as she puts the new one over my head and carefully through my arms, allowing it to fall free. I twirl the dress around, amazed at how well it fits. It is as if it was made for me, although I know that it is not possible. She smiles widely as I admire the dress.

"Thank you," I say.

She looks at me puzzled clearly and does not understand what I said. I smiled instead. I think she understands. She puts her finger up as if telling me to wait. She reaches back inside the bag. She pulls out a pair of moccasins that are made from buckskin. She puts them on the ground in front of me, motioning for me to put them on. It is then that I realize I am barefoot. I put my feet in the moccasins, amazed at the perfect fit. I look up as the woman is holding up her arms, wanting to put a necklace on me.

"Oh no, I couldn't," I protest. "You have already given me too much."

I know she has no idea what I am saying, but she understands that I am declining it. She insists and is not taking no for an answer. I gave up and allowed her to put the necklace on. It is incredibly beautiful and matches the dress, giving it the final look. I feel like a queen. It is then that it dawns on me. White Horse told me last spring, before he left to follow the herd, that if I came with him, I would be treated as a queen. His Queen. I knew he ordered for this to be done. I am flattered and cannot wait to show him how I look. I do not have to wait long before White Horse walks in. Immediately upon seeing her chief, the kind woman leaves.

White Horse takes one look at me and stops dead in his tracks. He gazes up and down at me several times as if in a trance.

"Thank you for the clothes," I tell him. He doesn't say a word.

"Do I look alright?" I ask, thinking perhaps I am wrong, and he is not happy that I am dressed like one of them.

"Yes," he huskily says. "It fits you well."

"I agree. Whoever wore this is about the same size and height as I am; even the moccasins fit well," I state.

"Yes, that they do."

He then pulls himself out of his trance with a blink and grins at me. "How are you feeling?" he asks.

"Oh, I am feeling much better. Thanks to you," I grin.

"I am glad to hear that. Would you like some air?" he suggests.

"I would love it," I answer.

He smiles. Looping his arm through mine, he escorts me to the flap and outside. Stepping out into the sunlight, I see nearly one hundred tepees throughout the prairie, all uniquely decorated and positioned towards the lake. Their horses are running free, except for the few that I see corralled a few yards away. There are children playing. Woman working and some men just leaving camp on horseback. White Horse takes me under a huge tree just to the left of the tepee, looking out towards the camp. He kindly takes my hand, and we sit down together. He perches himself up, resting on the trunk of the tree.

"What do you think?" he gloats.

"You have a big tribe," I say, impressed.

"Our tribe is very large. This is only one band," he corrects.

"I see."

"I have one of the smaller bands. There are larger bands all around us." "Interesting." I wasn't sure if that bothered him or not.

"See that man over there next to the water?" he says. I look over to where he is pointing.

"Yes."

"That is my best warrior, right-hand man, and brother, Koawa."

"I see," I say.

He looks fierce, and he keeps looking my way.

"It is his wife, Running Water, who brought you the dress that you are wearing. She has been sitting with you when you sleep."

"I must thank her," I say.

"She does not mind. When I asked her, she was honored." He looks over to his left to the older woman who I traded with.

"That woman over there is White Fawn, my mother."

"Did she make this dress?" I wonder.

"No. The dress that you are wearing had belonged to my beloved Flowering Blossom. It is all I have left that was not burned." He glances my way. I am sure I have turned pale.

"Do not let it bother you," he says. "I know she would want you to have it."

Before I can say anything else, a small child around the age of six comes running over and plops himself on White Horse's lap. White Horse speaks his tongue as he rubs the boy's head. The little boy giggles. White Horse cuddles the boy in his lap. "Carrie, this is my son, Kikimo."

His son. He never told me he had a son. I should not have been surprised, as I knew he was married at one time. His son looks just like him and how I imagine White Horse must have looked at his age. White Horse speaks his tongue to the boy, and the boy runs off.

"He is adorable," I smile as I watch the little boy run off to play with the others of his age.

"Thank you," White Horse says.

I notice just to the right of me a beautiful woman glaring my way.

"Who is that?" I questioned him. White Horse glances her way.

"That is Minoke. Flowering Blossom's sister."

"She does not look happy that I am here."

"She is not. Many of the women here fear her. You need to stay away from her; if provoked, she would kill you." I gulp.

"Relax, beautiful. Here you are, my queen," he smiles.

"Is that why I am wearing this beautiful dress? Did you not treat Flowering Blossom like a queen?" I wonder.

"It is not our custom to discuss the ones who have passed on, but since you did not know this, I will talk about her. Flowering Blossom's name said it all. She was as beautiful as a flower that was blooming. She was as sweet and delicate as one as well. I gave her everything. She worked among the other women, but I always kept her away from the heavy work. She would not like this, but I was always so afraid she would break. She was with our second child when she died. She lay on top of Kikimo so the attackers would not see him. She saved my son's life."

My heart goes out to him. I can tell it is still fresh in his mind. I reckon it always will be.

"Does Kikimo remember her?" I ask.

"Yes. Although he was very young, he does still ask for her from time to time. Running Water and Minoke take very good care of him. For that I am grateful." He looks over at his son playing in the distance.

"It is time I mourn no more." He then looks at me.

Although nothing was said, I do believe he wants me as his queen. We sit under that tree for hours. He continues to introduce me to his people as they pass by. The one called Koawa keeps a close eye on both of us. I am not sure how to take him and therefore decide to stay away from him. Minoke's glare is intense, cutting through me like a knife. I deliberately do not look her way.

Running Water approaches us, offering us both something to drink. It is some kind of fruit drink. It is very sweet, but very good.

I become intrigued by all I am encountering and am quickly falling in love with the Chief. A woman of my type may be cautious about falling for an Indian, but for some reason it is not bothering me. To me, we are the same. For the most part, I am being looked at as not being any different than them. I am being treated with kindness and respect. Was this a direct order from their chief, or is this normal custom? I cannot help but wonder. After a few hours of sitting there, White Horse takes me for a walk around his camp. He is refusing to take me far, as he feels I am still too weak to leave. I am promised tomorrow, if he feels I am strong enough, that we will venture out. I cannot wait to be alone with him. He shows me where everyone lives, including his tepee, which is the largest of all. He explains what a smokehouse is and how he holds his council there. He explains to me how the village can be moved in less than an hour and demonstrates how to take down and put up a tepee. He takes me over to where a few women are stretching hides and explains what they do with them. It is so fascinating, and I have learned so much. I never knew how hard these people work to survive and how much they use the land. Things that we waste and take for granted they use for survival.

He calls it a day when he sees me rubbing my head. How it is throbbing, but I am too stubborn to say. I think he feels bad, as he walks me back to the tepee where I am staying.

"Rest. I will come check on you later," he says as he kisses my cheek.

It feels good to lay my head down, and in no time I fall asleep. I wake to my head feeling better and my dinner sitting beside me. I sit up and take my plate. It consists of a piece of bread, some turnips, and a piece of meat. I bite into the meat. It is a flavor that I have never tasted before. I know it is not deer or elk, as I have had both. I wonder if it is buffalo. I am going to make a point and ask White Horse next time I see him. I am sitting in front of the fire when I hear a voice outside. It is White Horse.

Daylight has fallen, and a crescent moon is high above the horizon when he opens the flap.

"How are you feeling?" he asks.

"Much better," I answer.

"Did you eat?"

"Yes," which reminds me. What was the meat?" I ask him.

"Skunk," he smiles.

I think he thought that I would be disgusted. He doesn't know me well, as it takes a lot to turn my stomach.

"It was good," I comment. He just smiled. I think it pleased him.

"Feel like a walk?" he asks.

"I would like that."

He offers me his arm, and we make our way towards the lake.

"It is so beautiful here," I say.

"Yes, it is. I walk often at night. It gives me time to reflect and be alone with my spirits, or in tonight's case, a beautiful woman."

"Roger and I walk a lot at night as well."

"Who is Roger?" he asks.

"He is my brother."

"I thought your brother died as a baby," he says.

"Let me explain. My uncle runs an orphanage. When my father died, I was left in his care. Roger was a runaway that my uncle found. He brought us both into his home and raised us as his own. Roger and I are not blood, but we were raised as brother and sister. We are both very close, and I love him very much."

"Your family is probably very worried about you right now. I will be more than happy to send them word that you are here."

"How many days have I been here?" I wonder.

"Two," he answers.

"My father is not back from his trip, and I really doubt that Roger is either. Someone always has him on the run."

"What is it your brother does?" he asks.

"He is a doctor."

"I see."

He cuddles me into his chest as we continue walking.

"And tell me, what would your dear father and brother think right now if they knew you were here?"

"Grateful... Well, at least Father would be. I am not really sure about Roger. He...ah."

I didn't want to insult him by telling him that Roger does not like his kind.

"He doesn't like us," he concludes.

I smiled, impressed he picked it up. "He just doesn't understand. He is a good man; he really is."

"I do not doubt this. And he should fear us. Some of the tribes are not very friendly to your kind. I am the same way at times. But we are just like you. Some of us are good, and some of us are bad."

"So, you would hurt him?"

"I would defend myself and anyone that I care about if need be."

I don't doubt it. I have a feeling that he can be mean if provoked. I just hope I never see it. We stop just to the edge of the lake nestled behind the trees. He turns me to face him and starts caressing my face.

"You do understand that I do not want you to leave."

"But my family," I argue. "After a few days they will begin to worry." "They will just think that the same fate happened to you as it did to the man that we saw by the ravine," he concludes. I know he means Harold. "They will start looking for me," I warn.

"Yes, but they will never find you."

I am not sure how to take that. Is he threatening to hold me captive? Should the man I have grown fond of be feared? Sensing my nervousness, White Horse holds my shoulders, caressing them.

"Do not fear. I will never hurt you or keep you from your family. We are known for doing that, but I do not want you by force." He strokes my hair. "I want you to want to be with me because you want to be, not because I force you."

"White Horse." He puts his finger over my lips.

"Hush," he says. "I do not want to talk right now." He then kisses me. It is the most exciting and breathtaking kiss that I have ever felt. I truly feel my heart pound harder. I wrap my arms around him as the kiss lingers. When our lips part, he looks down at me.

"One more day and I will take you home. I give you my word."

With that said, he puts his arm around me, and we head back to camp. He remains a gentleman, stopping just outside the tepee that has been my home for the last two days. He quickly gives me a goodnight kiss and holds the flap open for me to walk in. I lay on the pelt thinking about tonight. Thinking about going home and not being very certain if this time I want to walk away. My thoughts put me in a deep slumber where I dream.

White Horse feels sure he has made his point. He feels confident that he has shown his tender side to her and she will agree to be his. He tells himself that they will be together. He is not going to let her walk out of his life. He only hopes he does not have to use the force that he is capable of. His loins ache for her. It took every bone in his body to restrain himself from taking her to his pelt. But he did not want to scare her; he did not want her to be afraid to be here. So, he walks to his lodge, leaving his Prairie Dawn behind. He has one more day with her. Yes, tomorrow, he is certain, she will fall in love with him.

Chapter Five

The Fishing Pole

I woke up early from a sound sleep feeling well rested and much stronger. Having an urgency to void, I quietly make my way to the lake so as not to arouse any attention. I find a private spot and relieve myself. I hear the soft, poetic sound of a flute playing nearby. I finish my task and step out of the bushes and make my way to the lake to freshen up. The coolness of the water feels refreshing. The morning sun reflects a glistening ray across the water. This place is so peaceful and calm. I can see why the Lakota call it home.

My mind starts to visualize what it would be like to live here away from all the dust in Willow Creek. What would life be like living among the Lakota? Would I like it? Would I be treated fairly? Knowing White Horse like I think I do, I know I would be. I am already starting to feel like one of them and am loving the feel of my new dress and moccasins that I am graciously allowed to wear.

"Good morning," I am greeted.

I jump when I become startled, as I thought I was alone. I look up to see White Horse.

"I did not hear you come up," I say. "You gave me a start."

"You were deep in thought," he grins.

I look at his hand and see him holding a flute.

"Was that you I heard playing?" I asked in awe.

"Yes, it is my time," he stops a moment to think. "It is, as your people would say, worship."

"Well, it was beautiful; I could listen and watch you play all day." He raises an eyebrow.

"If you are beside me all day, it is not the flute that I would be playing with."

I couldn't help but chuckle. His sense of humor is cute. He chuckles right along with me.

"This is the time of day when I either hunt or fish. Would you like to accompany me?" he offers.

"I would love to," I smile.

I wait for White Horse just outside his lodge. The camp is starting to rise. Running Water smiles my way. Koawa just looks. Minoke crosses in front of me and intimidates me with a glare. I was happy to see White Horse step out. He is wearing over his shoulder a pouch of arrows and a bow. Around his waist he has his knife on one side and his tomahawk on the other. He is carrying a spear and my father's old fishing pole.

"Are you ready?" he asks.

"Yes," I answer.

"Today we will walk."

"Do you usually ride?" I ask.

"It will depend on what I am hunting," he answers. "Fish are light," he jokes.

I chuckle. I truly love his humor. He takes me up a nearby hill, and into the woods we disappear.

"Do you recognize this pole?" he asked me.

"Yes, it belonged to my father," I answer.

"Have you ever caught anything with it?" he asks.

"Yes, many times."

"So, you like to fish?" he asks. He seems a little surprised.

"Roger and I fish whenever we can. He is not very patient with it."

"Yes. I understand. You do need patience," he agrees.

"Do you always carry this much with you?" I wonder.

"I do not usually carry my bow unless I am hunting or fighting in a battle. I always carry my knife and tomahawk wherever I go."

"I see."

"We live off the land. It provides us with everything we need. We only kill when we need to, and we thank our Mother Earth for providing us with the kill."

"That is so sweet," I say.

"It is respect. We do not ever take the Earth for granted. We only take what you need. That is the way I was taught and the way it has been done for many generations."

It all becomes clear to me now. The land is holy to him and needs to be treated wisely. We have walked for nearly an hour when White Horse suddenly stops. He points to a deer grazing nearby. He arrogantly smirks at me.

"Ever touch a live deer?" he whispers.

"No, never," I answer.

He tells me to wait and then slowly steps out where the deer can see him. It perks up its ears. White Horse speaks his tongue. The deer remains cautious. White Horse inches his way in closer to the deer, holding out his hand.

"It is alright, little one; I mean you no harm," he softly says.

He is only inches from the deer. The deer appears as if it is going to prance off. White Horse stops. He speaks his tongue again. The deer appears almost as if it is in a trance. White Horse comes right up in front of it and pets its head. I am in awe. If I had not seen it with my own eyes, I would never have believed it.

White Horse motions for me to come. Very quietly I ease in. White Horse takes my hand as he continues to pet the deer and talk to it in his tongue. He slowly lifts my hand onto the deer's head, and I pet it. Unbelievable, I think. I am truly amazed. White Horse smiles over at me.

"You are amazing," I say.

He smiles widely. The deer barely flinches. The only way you would ever know it is alive is the blinking of its eyes.

"She is beautiful," I say.

"Yes, she is," he says.

I look over at him. He is staring at me. I then realized what he meant.

"I mean the deer, silly," I chuckle.

"Your eyes see what you want. Mine will see what I want," he says.

I blush. Just then the deer jerks, and having had enough, it prances off into the woods. I am disappointed to see it go.

"How did you do that?" I ask him.

"It is something that was passed down to me by my great-grandfather when I was a boy. Koawa can do it too. I will teach my son, when he gets old enough, to remain still and learn patience."

This man is more and more amazing each day. I am still astonished at what I witnessed. We continued our walk. It is then that I ask a few questions that have been on my mind.

"I am curious about some things," I begin.

"Go ahead," he says.

"What happened to the bear that attacked me?" I ask him.

"Koawa killed it," he answers. "The hide is drying behind his lodge. The meat he fed his family with. He shared some with me as well."

"So, you were not there?" I ask.

"Yes. I was the one who carried you back. As Chief, I am well protected. I usually stay close to the camp. That day I was restless and went riding with Koawa."

"So, you are usually here?"

"Yes, when I do venture out, I am watched like a hawk."

"So, we are being watched right now?" I wonder.

"We are close to camp. I can call out if I need something."

"Call out?" I ask.

"I will not demonstrate it because if I do, several warriors will come running, but it is the call of a mockingbird. When we get back to camp, I will show you so you can hear it. That way you will know when I am near."

"Interesting," I say.

"You said you had several questions. What else would you like to ask me?" he wonders.

"Where did you learn to speak English?"

"When I was a mere boy, my father saved an Englishman from raging water. He stayed with us until his passing several years later. My father showed him our ways, and in exchange he taught us English."

"You speak it very well."

"Thank you. My father made me study many days and nights while other boys my age were allowed to play. He knew I would be chief one day, and there would come a day when I would need it. He was correct. I am glad I was taught it. I will teach my son as well."

"Does Koawa speak it too?" I ask.

"Yes, he just does not like to. He uses it as a bluff when someone does not think he understands, when he really does. He speaks it as well as I do."

The view of the river is seen. White Horse and I stop. He hands me the pole. "I do not use a pole to fish. You can have it," he says, as he hands me the rod.

"If you do not use a pole, then how do you fish?" I wonder.

"I spear it when available; if not, I catch it with my bare hands."

"I have never done either."

He casts the rod for me with a worm that he found on the ground. He then hands it to me.

"You may want to sit," he says. "The fish bite hard here and should not take too long, but we may still have a little wait."

I take him up on his offer. I remove my moccasins and sit down on a nearby rock, wading my feet in the water. White Horse then picks up his spear that is lying on the ground and steps out into the water. The fish are abundant in the clear water. I watch him as he concentrates on the water and the fish, having his spear ready to strike. After a few moments, he tosses it in the water, catching a fish.

"You make it look easy?" I tease.

"It is," he says. "Come."

He motioned me over with his hand. I prop up my pole and step into the shallow end of the water. He positions me in front of him. He then wraps his arms around me, showing me how to hold the spear. I feel him cuddle his head into my shoulder as he holds me tighter. I smile at him.

"See that fish?" he finally says. "See how it swims alone?"

"Yes."

"That is the one you want. Keep your eye on it and don't move."

I do as I am told, watching the fish swimming carefree around, unaware of its pending death.

"Now," he orders.

With his help the spear is tossed and the fish is caught.

"I did it," I smile.

He runs out further into the water, picking up his spear and removing the fish. He tosses the fish onto the shore, and we do it again. He returns to the same position, and we repeat. Once again, another fish is caught.

I am having so much fun at the cost of these poor fish. We catch three more before he stops, pulling me into his arms.

"You learn fast," he says.

"Thank you," I smile.

He then leans in to kiss me. His lips are sweet, and his arms are so strong as our kiss lingers. Suddenly, there is a blurb in the water, and my fishing line pulls. I rush to catch the pole before I lose my fish. I reel it in and pull up a decent catch.

"I am proud of you," White Horse says.

He pulls out my line and starts detaching the fish from the hook. I walk a few steps to the shore, glancing up at the horizon, when I become startled. Standing on top of a hill just a few yards away, I see an Indian. I am certain he is not a Lakota. His face is painted with a red handprint on the side. He is virtually bald, except for a small part of his hair that stands straight up on top of his head. I turn to White Horse and point up to the hill. He looks up.

"What is it, love?" he asks. I look back up at the hill, and he is gone. "Nothing. I must have been seeing things." I conclude.

"We have been gone most of the day. You are tired. We should go home." He leans down to pick up the strand of fish. I look back up at the hill.

"Yeah, I reckon you are correct," I say.

I suddenly got a sick feeling in my stomach that we were being watched and am ever so glad to be safe back at camp. The fish are fried up, and a huge fire is brewing outside. A community effort is brought together, and enough meat is made for everyone. White Horse is making the night special and is adding to the entertainment. Several warriors are dancing around the fire, and chants are sung. I watch as the dancers glide along the prairie. After several songs, our dances are done. White Horse stands up and joins his warriors in a last dance. He is stunningly beautiful and elegant as he eases around the fire. Never have I seen so much meaning in a dance.

Running Water and Kikimo join alongside me. I see the admiration in the eyes of Kikimo as he watches his father. I am sure he is memorizing every step so he too can one day have the honor to perform it as well. Running Water smiles at me and then watches her husband, Koawa, as he too dances around the fire. I feel like I belong tonight. Even Minoke is staying away, as she too is busy watching this evening's entertainment. The evening fades fast as a rain cloud appears, threatening to end our night. As the wind picks up, the dancing stops and the night ends. Just as I feel the first raindrops come down, White Horse takes my hand and walks me to the shelter of his lodge. We rush inside, just missing the downpour.

"Make yourself at home," he says.

He kisses my hand and turns to the small fire that is already lit. He starts building it up as I feel a chill come over me. I rub my arms for warmth as I start looking around.

"There is a blanket over there that you can wrap around you," he offers.

I grab the blanket and place it around my shoulders. I watch White Horse as he stands and takes off his tunic. My mouth drops as I see how built he really is. His chest is solid, and his stomach ripples. His biceps are well defined. His long, dark black, silky hair lies freely across his back. I faintly grin, as I recall I do not think I have ever seen a man with a face that matched the body. I feel my face flush just thinking of it.

Chapter Six

Prairie Dawn

The night sky is rumbling with thunder as the sky opens. I find myself in the safe, sweet-smelling lodge with White Horse. The low simmering fire is keeping us warm. A sweet incense smell fills the air as I start looking around. His lodge is very similar to the one that I have been in for the last several days, with the exception that it is bigger and contains more items that I assume he uses as chief.

I can tell he is an adamant hunter by the skulls, bows, and skins he has collected and has nicely decorated throughout. A soft pelt lies neatly in one corner that he uses when he sleeps. A buffalo skin lies on the ground in front of it. He has several storage units made from rawhide and beautiful pottery, all lying neatly in a row at one corner of the lodge. He has his collections of arrowheads, several knives, and his flute neatly placed on a handmade table next to his pelt. All in all, the place is very cozy.

"It is very nice in here," I comment as I watch White Horse lean back on his pelt.

"It is even better when you are in here," he smirks. I blush. "I am not the kind of man who freely opens up my feelings to a woman, but you, my Prairie Dawn, are like no other woman I have met."

"Prairie Dawn," I say, "you called me that once before. What does it mean?"

"Prairie Dawn is the Indian name I have given you," he answers.

"What does it mean?" I ask.

"Prairie, from your hair that is as golden as the prairie grass. Dawn, because you are as beautiful as the morning sun."

"Oh," I am flattered. "That is beautiful."

"No, it is you that is beautiful."

He then leans forward, taking my hand. I came down on my knees in front of him. He reaches up, placing his hand on my cheek.

"Your beauty is not only skin deep. You are beautiful and kind." He strokes my cheek. "Stay with me tonight in my lodge," he huskily says. "Let me hold you; be with me, Prairie Dawn." I am speechless.

He gently pulls me down beside him. He then leans in and kisses me. I am quickly consumed by him and kiss him back. His advances quickly heat up. I feel his hand rub my leg and slowly begin to slide up my dress to caress my thigh. I feel his tongue inching down my throat. A warmth appears between my legs as he inches his hand further up my thigh. I am gently eased back on the pelt as our lips continue locked.

A feeling comes over me that I have never felt before, a longing desire to want more. He gradually lifts my dress and starts to fondle me. I feel a moistness between my legs begin to form. He starts to kiss my neck as he slips my dress off my shoulder.

"White Horse I."

"Shh," he mumbles, "I know."

The moment is intense. I know it is not correct, but there is no way I am going to fight it off. I want this man to be a part of me. I watch him as he disrobes, revealing the part that makes him a man. This is the first time I have ever seen a man fully unclothed. I am not disappointed. He comes down on top of me, slowly caressing and kissing his way down as he undresses me. He meets my lips again as my dress is tossed aside. I feel his hard manhood up against my leg as he gently pushes my legs apart. He then starts kissing and licking his way down my body. He stops at my breasts to suck them, as an infant would suck for milk. My insides tingle, swallowed in his passion.

When he gets his fill, he licks his way down my stomach and stops when he gets between my legs. He will remain there for several minutes, eating me as if I were a piece of meat. I am overwhelmed with excitement as he enjoys his meal. Like a puppy, I whimper out with joy. My womanhood is drenched with the pleasure he is giving me.

I can remember a time when my best friend Stella and I were discussing sex. She told me of the time when she gave Hank a special treat. She explained what that treat was. I lean up, reaching for White Horse. He lifts his head. I crawl to him, picking up his manhood. I start to stroke it up and down. I see him grin and invite me to play with it. I put it in my mouth and began to give him the same pleasure that he gave me. I hear him moan as his manhood heats up. After several minutes of receiving great pleasure, he lays me down on the pelt and comes on top of me. Gently pushing my legs apart, he enters me.

"Now we will go to that special place together," he whispers.

He then slowly and gently pushes himself into me. I bite my lower lip when he gives a hard push and my virginity is lost. He keeps kissing my lips until the pain subsides. When feeling certain that I am alright, I feel his thrusts begin. He is as gentle as can be, starting slow and steady. When I have caught on to the rhythm, his thrusts increase.

I look into his beautiful eyes, just as he closes them out of pleasure. He kneads my bosoms as his thrust continues. I lean my head back out of great happiness, never wanting this moment to end. We rock back and forth. Our bodies become like one. Our hearts are pounding hard; our breaths are heavy. I am taken to flight like a hawk that is soaring in the sky, as our lovemaking becomes intense for several minutes. He grabs my legs, wrapping them around him, allowing him to go in deeper. He remains there, not missing a beat, for several long, enduring minutes.

Our bodies begin to sweat. Our hearts beat like drums. We dance to our own song. I hear him moan as he nears his climax. His thrusts are hard and fast. I reach behind him to squeeze his firm, sinewy buttocks. This arouses him more, and his thrusts quicken. He leans down, tucking his head on my shoulder. The front of his long, dark, silky hair is tickling my breast. We both exchange a moan as he gives one final hard thrust, emptying his white stuff inside me.

We both lie there for a moment to catch our breath.

"You were wonderful," he finally says.

He rolls over and rests on his elbow. He starts to stroke my hair. "My Prairie Dawn. My beautiful Prairie Dawn."

"I like that name," I say.

"Good, because my Prairie Dawn you will always be."

Before the night is through, White Horse and I will make love several more times. Finally, in the wee hours of the morning, we call it a night and fall asleep in each other's arms.

I awake to the morning light with White Horse entwined around me. So as not to disturb him, I slowly lift his arm up that is resting on me. I sit up and reach to grab my dress. I feel his strong arms wrap around me. He kisses my cheek.

"Leaving so soon?" he teases.

"I need to void," I say.

He grins and kisses my cheek again.

"To the left of the camp, you will find a cluster of bushes near the water. You can go there." I give him a kiss before coming to a stand-up. I reach for my dress when he grabs it.

"Hurry back," he smirks. "I am not done with you." I giggle.

He watches me get dressed and open the flap. Except for a lone warrior feeding apples to his horse, the camp is still sleeping. I found the spot next to the water and void. I decided to go to the water to freshen up. I notice Minoke as she steps outside her lodge. I am praying she doesn't see me. I watch her disappear in White Fawn's lodge. Knowing White Horse is waiting for me, I quickly freshen up and make my way back to the lodge. I get up the hill when Minoke is in my face. I jumped, as just a few moments ago I saw her enter White Fawn's lodge. My heart stops for a moment. What am I to do? I remember White Horse telling me to avoid her, so I decide to do just that.

I turn to go another way up the hill. She pulls my dress and whips me around. I then am given the most Godforsaken glare that gave me chills. I gulp, for she looks like she could kill me. I attempt again to avoid her by walking the other way. She pushes me. It became clear to me that despite my efforts, Minoke wants to challenge me. I cannot help but think it is a challenge over White Horse, and the winner receives the prize. If that is the case, I am up for the challenge.

I pushed her back. That is all it took, and the fight is on. She tackles me down to the ground and starts swinging. I shield myself from her blows. I hear Running Water scream. I am hoping it is for White Horse. I struggle with Minoke to get up, but she is strong and giving me the fight of my life. I take a blow to my jaw. Now I am furious and ready for revenge. With all my power, I kick her in the groin. It is hard enough to make her stop, allowing me to get to my feet. It fails to keep her down for long, and it has angered her even more.

She pulls out her knife, waving it in front of me. She then takes a jab. I lunge, and she misses. My heart is racing as she attempts again. I block another jab by only a few inches. Clearly this woman has the upper hand, and I fear she is going to kill me. She lunged at me, knocking me to the ground. She is on top of me and is trying to slash my throat. I wrestled her to keep the knife away from my throat. I am near exhaustion and fearing all hope is lost when I see White Horse running down the hill.

He pulls Minoke off me, and the fight is over. I watch in horror as White Horse pulls Minoke by her hair and drags her to the river. He then tosses her in the river like a rag doll. I think that it is over until I see White Horse come into the water and grab Minoke by the back of the hair. He then pushes her head under water. He repeats this several times until Minoke is in tears. I hear him spouting off in his tongue as he gives her one final push under the water. He then storms out.

Minoke yells at him in her tongue, making White Horse stop dead in his tracks. He turns and runs back into the water. Minoke attempts to swim away, but his long arms quickly capture her. He pulls her out of the water and tosses her down into the dirt. He then lifts her head and smears it on the ground, allowing the dirt to stick on her wet body and mouth. Minoke knows her match has been made and surrenders. In his tongue he spats off to all who have witnessed.

"Let this be a lesson to anyone who defies me again on what will happen if Prairie Dawn is ever harmed." He then walks off and heads to me.

The ground is still. Everyone lowers their eyes and walks off. Running Water runs to Minoke's side and helps her to her feet, walking with her to her lodge. White Horse kneels in front of me. I am not sure how to react. I have seen White Horse at his worst and have witnessed what he will do if he is defied. He warned me to stay away from her, and I did not. What was he going to do to me? I suddenly feared him.

"Did she hurt you?" he asks.

"No," I answer.

"What were you thinking challenging her? She could have killed you," he barks.

"I tried to walk away. I truly did," I defend. He deeply sighs.

"I do not doubt this," he says.

"I am sorry, White Horse."

"No, it is I who am sorry. I knew she was jealous, but I did not think she would fight you right under my nose."

"Jealous?" I question.

"Yes, very much so. She believes that she and I should be together. Just because it was her sister that I was married to, she feels that we should be married. She knows we were together last night, and she did not like it."

"I can understand her being jealous. I am sorry," I say.

"Do not be. She has learned her lesson and has come to terms with it. She will leave you alone now. You have earned her respect because you did what no one else has ever done."

"What is that?" I wonder.

"You stood up to her. You showed no fear, and that, my love, is what a true Lakota does."

I am flattered and greatly relieved that White Horse is not angry with me. We eat our morning meal inside. White Horse and I make love. Afterwards, I am informed that today I will go home.

"If you stay any longer, you will be missed," he says.

It pains me to leave, but I know he is correct. My old, tattered dress has been sewn and washed by Running Water, and it is now time to put it back on. I carefully fold the beautiful, soft, buckskin dress up and lay it neatly on the pelt. Alongside it, I place the moccasins. I take a final look at the lodge and the pelt on which I lay. I pray that one day I will soon return. I step outside, where White Horse is waiting.

"There is one more thing that you must see before you leave," he says.

"What is it?" I question.

He points. I see Koawa walking towards us, leading Sugar Foot behind him. I have forgotten all about him. I ran and gave my horse a hug.

"Koawa found him wandering near to where the bear attacked you," White Horse states. "His foot is cut, and Koawa has been tending to him every day."

I look down at Sugar Foot's leg and see it is wrapped. I look over at Koawa.

"Thank you," I say.

Koawa just looks at me as if he didn't understand. He nods his head and then hands me the reins. White Horse helps me up onto his back. I am allowed to say my goodbyes and thank you to Running Water and give Kikimo a hug. Accompanied by Koawa, the three of us make our way to my home. When we are on top of the hill, I turn and look out at the camp for one final look. I say a silent prayer for my return.

Chapter Seven

Three Men In The Woods

The ride home will take us most of the morning. I am feeling somber and in a daze. I think of everything that has occurred in the past few days. How I have escaped death twice, once with a bear and the other with Minoke. How fond I have become of the Lakota band and how I have fallen madly in love with their chief. I sit and think about what my father and Roger may say if they knew what I had done. I have no regrets about uniting with White Horse. I truly feel we are meant to be together. I only wish that things could be different, as I am certain that neither my father nor Roger would agree with me being with White Horse.

Our lives are so much different, our cultures are miles apart, but deep within us we are the same. Our religions may be different, but we are both spiritual in our own way. A part of me is wanting to turn right around and remain with White Horse, where I belong, but the love for my father is not allowing me to do it. I owe him the explanation as to why I wish to be with a chief whose life is so much different than mine. I must find a way to make him understand that I have found happiness with White Horse.

"You are in deep thought?" White Horse say, interrupting my thoughts. I smiled at him.

"I guess I am," I say. "I'm sorry."

"What is your beautiful mind thinking?" He grins.

"May I ask you a question?"

"Yes."

"Where do we go after today?"

"If you are referring to us, this is a question I have asked myself." "And?"

"I am a man who will fight for what I want and what I need."

"Meaning me?" I conclude.

"You do not need to ask such foolish questions," he grins. I look up at Koawa, who is riding a good distance ahead of us.

"What does he think?" I wonder.

"I am their leader. I think of my people every day. I am prepared to die to protect every one of them. I hear what they tell me and listen with an open mind and heart. They respect me, and I respect them. Koawa is no different than any of them. He spoke to me about you, and I listened. He is a good man. He is fine with it now."

"At first he wasn't?" I comment.

"No, but then he saw in you what I saw, and his mind has changed."

I take that as a good sign and drop the subject.

"We live a very different life," he begins. "I cannot provide you with the life you are familiar with, but I can provide you all of my life if you are willing to accept it."

"I am. I truly am," I say.

"Then where there is a will, there is a way."

"I worry about my father," I begin. "He is a good-hearted man, but I do not think he will accept this."

"As I do not blame him," White Horse says. "Your people and my people have been enemies long before either one of us was born. I have met your father, and I believe he is a peaceful man. We will make him understand that us being together is for the best."

"I wish I had your confidence," I joke.

We are nearing Willow Creek when Sugar Foot begins to act up. I tightened up on his reins.

"Whoa, boy," I say.

White Horse rides in closer to me. "Is he always this anxious?" he asks. "No, last time he did this he heard the bear," I say.

"Give me your lead," he orders.

White Horse holds onto Sugar Foot's reins as he leads us through the trees. Koawa speaks his tongue to White Horse.

"Carrie came between us," he orders.

"Why?" I wonder, as I do as I am told. "What is wrong?"

"It is not a bear your horse smells; it is death." I gulp.

Slowly and silently, we ease our way through the woods. I see, smell, and hear nothing, but Sugar Foot does, and he is beginning to fuss.

"Come slide in front of me," White Horse orders.

He grabs my arm, and I slide on. White Horse eases up on Sugar Foot's reins, letting him lead. When my horse has calmed down, he slides on top of his back and has full control of him. I take over the lead of White Horse's proud possession, Moon Light, his stallion.

I remain in the middle until Koawa pulls ahead. Sugar Foot starts stomping around. White Horse quickly has him under control. I have never seen my horse like this. Something is really bothering him.

"It is alright, boy," I console. "White Horse won't hurt you."

"He smells what we cannot. I feel we are close."

No sooner had White Horse said that when we heard the call of a hawk. "It is Koawa," he says.

We head out in a gallop. We approach a campfire and stop. Sugar Foot is having to be tied to a tree so as not to escape. I jumped down from Moonlight's long, strong back. I follow White Horse. In a matter of seconds, I gasp in horror as two bodies lie dead on the ground. Koawa kicks one over with this foot. On revealing his face, it is apparent that he was killed by an Indian. An arrow is stuck in his heart, and his scalp is missing. The other body is examined as well, with the same fate being found. I become nauseous when I see all the blood. I back up into the trees to get away from the ghastly sight.

Koawa removes one of the arrows. He examines the making before handing it to White Horse. The sight is appalling and making me sick. I back further up to not vomit. When I do, I trip over a stump and fall. Catching my breath, I begin to stand up, and when I do, I see a foot dangling from a tree. I look up to see a man hanging from a branch. I scream! White Horse and Koawa come running. White Horse comes up behind me, putting his hand over my mouth. He looks up at the dangling man. Koawa starts to scale the tree.

"Shh, we must be quiet," White Horse cautions. "These men have not been dead long. They were killed by Pawnee. They may still be close. We leave. Now!"

Koawa releases the rope from the tree, and the man falls to the ground. He then jumps down from the tree, handing the rope to White Horse.

"Pawnee," White Horse confirms. He tosses the rope on the ground. "We leave now!"

Like a bolt of lightning, we are riding hard. All three horses are in full run. Both men are looking around, making sure we are not being followed. It was not until we were at Devil's Elbow, just a few miles from my home, that we stopped and brought our horses to a walk.

"White Horse, I do not understand. Why the haste on leaving? And why were those men killed?" I question.

"Pawnee killed those men," he explains. "My guess is they were in their path."

"Their path to what?" I am in a panic.

By the way we are running, I am certain something is desperately wrong, and White Horse doesn't want to tell me. I watch him look around at the deep canyons that are filled with caves and hollows. A man could get lost in here and never be seen again. That is how it got its name. Legend says that if you are one of the unlucky ones to get lost here, the devil will scoop you up by your elbows and take you to his hell, where you will never be seen again.

"Carrie, these are not just any Pawnee. These are renegades," he finally admits.

"How can you tell?"

"By the arrow that was used to kill them and the rope used to hang them," he answers. How far are we from your home?" he asks.

"A few miles," I answer.

"Good, I need to get you home."

"What do they want?" I ask.

"This is not Pawnee territory, so I am not really sure what they want. It may just be a random act."

I know he is lying. He had us running because he was fearing for our lives. He knows more than what he is letting on. But why? What is he hiding? I see that White Horse is very nervous about this, so I keep still on my questions so as not to agitate him more.

"Carrie, I will feel much better when I get you home. So, we need to hurry before we lose daylight."

I can hear the urgency in his voice. White Horse is nervous, and that scares me, because I don't think this is a man who fears very easily.

The remainder of the ride home is very quiet. White Horse and Koawa are still very nervous and looking up in the hills for any danger. Sugar Foot is riding well, so I, for one, feel very sure that we are safe.

"My home is just on the other side of that hill, through those trees," I tell them, breaking the silence.

"Good," he answers.

We make our way up the hill. My small little home is in view. White Horse looks over at me.

"Anyone home?" he asks.

"I don't see the wagon or the horses, so I am guessing no."

"Then I will come with you and see you safe inside," he states.

As we enter our property, I quickly realize my assumption is correct and no one is home. By the looks of the mess around the henhouse, no one has been home for several days.

"Does everything look alright?" White Horse asks.

"Yes," I answer. "It is not unusual that I am home for days by myself. My father takes frequent trips to the orphanage twice a month. Sometimes Roger will join to check up on the children and their health or spend a day or two at the immigration camp tending to whatever needs they may have. This is most likely what has happened. I expect to see a note on the mantle inside."

White Horse stops just shy of the barn and gets off his horse. He then starts to look around, making sure all is clear. When he is satisfied that I am safe, he steps onto the porch, taking my hand.

"Do you own a gun?" he asks

"Yes," I answer.

"You know how to use it?"

"Somewhat."

"Keep it close to you at all times until your family returns."

"Alright," I say.

He squeezes my hand. I have so many questions about what we saw today and why he is so nervous and adamant that I have a gun nearby. I know he is hiding something from me. But what? And why won't he tell me? For the moment, I refuse to push the matter and enjoy my last few moments with him.

"When will I see you again?" I ask.

"Soon. I promise. And Carrie, for the moment, I do not want you to speak to anyone about what you saw today. Understand?"

"I understand."

He pulls me into his arms and kisses me goodbye. I watch him as he walks to his horse and jumps on.

"Keep an eye on your barn," he says as he turns and rides off.

"Keep an eye on the barn. Now, what is that supposed to mean?" I say out loud.

Sugar Foot has missed his grain and is happily enjoying it as I brush him down. My mind is racing, remembering the stone faces on the men who were viciously slaughtered. I can't comprehend who would do such a horrifying thing. I may brush it off as a random act if it weren't for the change in demeanor that I saw in White Horse. He was considerably nervous and anxious to get me home. I can't stop thinking that he knows more than he is letting on.

"Do you believe it is One Eye?" Koawa asks White Horse as they ride up the hill.

"Yes, I do," he answers.

"That is not good, my brother," Koawa warns.

"I know," he mumbles.

White Horse looks down from the hill at his Prairie Dawn's house.

"Not good at all."

Chapter Eight

Utter Dismay

Darkness is on the land. I have dinner on the stove, expecting to see my father home at any time. I read Roger's note of him being at the immigration camp for some possible epidemic. I thought of riding out there to see if he needed any help but after today's events, I am not sure that I should. I am sitting in my father's chair holding his revolver under my quilt. Today's ordeal is strong on my mind. I begin to grow anxious that neither my father or Roger have returned and have visions of them having the same fate as those three men in the woods did.

I hear a wolf howling nearby. A gust of wind rattles the window. I see the doorknob turn, but no one enters. I perk up as I am certain I see a shadow passing by the window. I cock the revolver from under the quilt. I am suddenly feeling very vulnerable. I am starting to worry, because my father is not home. Where could he be? I let my thoughts consume me. Did the renegades find him sleeping alongside the road? Are they outside watching me?

I shake my head. I am thinking nonsense and giving myself a fright in the process. I push the quilt off me and walk over to the bureau drawer to put the revolver away. I close the drawer when the front door blows open. I scream.

"Child it is I, father."

I take a sigh of relief and rush into his arms.

"Oh, dear child I am sorry to be delayed."

"You gave me a fright," I cry.

"There, there all is fine," he consoles.

"I have kept dinner warm. Are you hungry?" I ask when I come out of his embrace.

"Yes. I am."

I begin to prepare his plate as father washes up.

"I thought Roger would be back by now," I say. "I sure pray he is alright."

"He is fine dear. I just left him," he assures.

"Oh?"

"Yes, at the immigration camp. I met Hank on the road. He told me that he came out here to check on you, but you were not here. He saw Roger's note on the mantle and told me where he was."

"I see."

"Where were you child?" he asks me, as he dries his hands.

I hate to lie, but I have little choice. I quickly think.

"Roger sent me to check on Marianne Simpson. She had her baby."

"Oh, praise the Lord," he said wide eyed.

"A boy," I add.

My father is overwhelmed with joy. I then remember I must cover my tracks, so tomorrow I will pay Marianne Simpson and her son a visit. I will then have to tell her about Harold, if she hasn't already found out. I will have to lie about my whereabouts. I am horrible at lying. I have all night to think about what I will say when I see her.

"Roger will be so proud of you," my father says. "As I am."

He sits down at the table and lifts his fork. "Just think, my daughter a midwife."

"Oh Father," I blush. "Eat your dinner."

I listen to my father as he eats his dinner, filling me in on each child at the Orphanage.

"Did they like the blankets, Father?" I ask.

"Oh yes very much so," he smiles. "It was like Christmas to them. It brought a tear to my eyes."

"I am sure it would have to me as well," I agree.

"Oh, Sister Ann asked about you as well."

"I do miss her. She was like a mother to me those two years I lived there."

"You need to pay her a visit."

"Yes, I do."

The evening comes to an end and my father and I call it a night. I dream of White Horse and what he may be doing tonight.

White Horse sits on the hill perched high on his horse looking down at the home where his Prairie Dawn sleeps. He has been watching her all night. He rode down the hill once and saw his Prairie Dawn through the window. He needed to be sure she was safe. He saw when her father returned home. She is safe for tonight he thinks. Now he can join his other warriors not far away and rest himself.

The morning is on us. Father returns from feeding the horses. I finished gathering up the eggs from the hen house that have been laying there for several days. I have a handful. I am sorting through them and pulling out the ones that I feel are still edible in the basket, as father walks inside.

"Breakfast is nearly ready," I tell him.

"Good, I am hungry," he says, as he begins to wash his hands.

We hear a horse approaching. Father looks out the window.

"Roger is home," he says, as he is drying his hands.

"I will add more grits," I say.

"Hello son," father greets, when Roger steps in.

We watch him hang up his hat and medical bag on the coat rack by the door, before slouching down in the chair.

"What is the problem son?" father ask.

"The Hanson's were attacked last night by Indians,"

Both father and I gasp.

"Their place was burnt to the ground. There are no survivors."

The Hanson's lived three miles out of town, just to the right of the fork in the road. They would come into town once a week for supplies and Sunday service. They were an older couple, but both just as sweet as pie and would never hurt anyone.

"Are you sure son?" father asks.

"Yes, I met the sheriff and his men on my way home. I saw the smoke from the distance."

"Appalling!" father gasps.

I sit down at the table feeling numb by what I have heard and fearing that the three men in the woods was not a random attack.

"Are they sure they were Indians?" father ask. "Why we haven't had an episode here from Indians in many years."

"Yes Pa," Roger says. "Shot through the heart with an arrow."

My eyes grow huge. They died the same way as the men in the woods. I am absolutely horrified.

"Their horses were stolen as well as their cow."

"No," I mumble to myself. "It can't be."

"Child, are you alright?" father asks.

I look up at my father nearly in tears. I want to tell them both about what I have seen but promised White Horse I wouldn't. I know this is not a random act. I fear we are in great danger. I must tell White Horse, but how? I am clueless on where to even look for him and I do not remember the way to his camp.

"I'm fine," I say, shaking my head. "I am just a little scared."

"Carrie. Don't be scared," Roger says. "I am sure they were just hungry and wanting food. They came across the cow and the horse and decided to steal it. Mr. Hanson probably heard their dog barking and came to investigate and that's when they were killed. At least that is what the sheriff believes happened. And it does sound logical, that is how it happened. Believe it or not I think the sheriff is right."

That is a lot for Roger to admit, because it is not a secret that Roger does not like the sheriff or any of his men, since the ordeal with Carl and me.

"I am sure that is what happened as well. Willow Creek has not had any issues with Indians for many years," father says.

I am not so sure.

"I will see to it that they receive a proper burial," father says.

"That would be nice Pa," Roger agrees.

We hear another horse come in. Roger looks out the window.

"It's Hank," he says.

"I wonder what he wants?" I speak.

Roger is quick to get to the door just as Hank is ready to knock.

"Good day," Roger greets. "Please come in."

"Thank you," Hank says, removing his hat as he steps inside. "Reverend," he greets. "Miss," he nods.

Hank is being formal, something is up.

"What is the problem, Hank?" Roger says.

"Coming back from the Hanson's place, little Jimmy Woods came running into town very frightened. He said that he went to the Prewitt house to go see if Ronald could play. He saw the place burnt to the ground, both Ronald and the Mrs. were dead. Mr. Prewitt was hung from a tree. They were attacked by Indians."

I am in total dismay. Now I am certain this is not random.

"Good Lord," utters Roger.

"Dear God!"

Father is beside himself. Father would hire Mr. Prewitt when he needed work done at the Orphanage or here at the house. They had become very good friends. Father is going to take this very hard.

"The sheriff is urging everyone to remain armed and keep watch of their places. He is forming a posse and will patrol at night. I have volunteered to watch your place."

"Well, that is mighty thoughtful of you Hank," my father says. "But I will not need any protection. I am very capable of protecting my own family."

Hank is not known for his generosity. This is a huge deal for him and for father to turn him down must be a huge blow to his ego.

"Father," I say. "Perhaps we should take him up on his offer. No offense, but he is a big man. We could use the strength."

"I see your point child and I do appreciate the kind offer, but I insist on doing it myself."

"As you wish Reverend. I reckon I understand how you feel. If you change your mind, you know where I am at."

Hank then turns and walks out.

"Father, I think we should take him up on his offer," I retort.

"No! From now on, we all come home before dark. Carrie you are not to leave alone on any circumstances," he says. I fold my arms over my chest. "I did not hear you," he says, as he looks over the rim of his glasses.

"Yes father," I whine.

"Good."

"Pa," Roger starts, "perhaps we should secure the door at night from inside."

"Good idea son. I will see to it now."

I am not real fond of the idea of having to be escorted everywhere I go. This is going to make it real difficult for me to get around. I must find White Horse and tell him what all is going on, but how?

Chapter Nine

The Barn

Five days pass, and eight more homesteaders have lost their lives to Indian attacks. Willow Creek is in an uproar. The sheriff has expanded his posse, and they are out around the clock in hopes of catching the attackers in the act. I have been keeping an eye on the barn, as White Horse said, in hopes he will show up. I have seen no sign of him. I am beginning to think that he is aware of the attacks and is scared for his people and has moved them on, or has he been attacked himself and lies somewhere dead?

Since I have been homebound, I have been spending a lot of time in my garden. It is time that has been well spent. With Father gone burying the dead or spending a great deal of his time at the church, Roger has been the man of the house for several days. He only leaves when he is called upon. He is tending to the task of cleaning the barn, as I tend to my garden, when we see Hank ride up.

Hank has been a dear friend of ours and checks on us daily and shares whatever news he has. Lately the news has been good. Giving everyone some hope that the horrifying ordeal is done.

"Howdy," he greets.

"Hello," I greet back. He waves over at Roger.

"Anything new?" I ask him.

"It has been quiet for the last two nights. The sheriff is scaling back his posse. He feels they have moved on."

"You don't sound so sure," I say.

"No. I have dealt with Indians before, and there is one thing I know. You cannot trust them."

That struck a nerve, as I know differently.

"Just keep your guard up, alright?" he warns.

"Alright." Hank is looking unusually tired. "You look very tired, Hank. Would you like to come in? I can make you something to eat," I suggest. "Much obliged, but I need to get back to the saloon."

Hank looks over at Roger. He is making a mess of himself cleaning the barn. Hank grins. "This is your protection?" he laughs.

"He is a doctor, not a farmer," I joke.

"You need a real man," he smirks.

"Do you know of any?" I smart back.

I have known Hank for many years. Even long before I met Sid. One would think we should be courting, but we never have. He would make a good catch. Women fall in love with his looks, but he never slows down long enough to be caught. Hank is too wild for me, and he knows it. Next to Stella, though, Hank is one of my dearest friends. He faintly chuckles and then turns to ride off. He waves over at Roger before galloping away.

Evening is upon us. Father is sitting in his favorite chair. He starts to tell Roger about his day's events. I listen as I begin to expand my father's waistline on one of his trousers.

"I spoke with the sheriff when I was at the restaurant eating my lunch," he begins. "He feels certain that the attacks have stopped, and he has scaled down his posse. Not everyone agrees with him. Of course, Carl is boasting about how he scared them off because he is the one who carries the bigger gun."

"He is so full of himself," I huff.

"I personally feel we will always have Indian problems until they are all moved away or killed." Roger snorts.

"Roger!" I yell. "That is a horrible thing to say. Take it back!"

"Well, it is true. I cannot help how I feel."

"Father," I whine.

"Child, he has a right to his opinion," he argues. "Even though I do not agree. We are all God's children and should be treated as that."

Roger knows his father well enough not to argue. He rolls his eyes and drops the subject. I, for one, thought Father handled it well and smirked over at Roger.

"Have you been to Esther's lately?" father asks.

"No, Pa, I haven't," Roger answers.

"Oh, son, she has a new dessert that is truly divine. You must try it."

"Pa, what have I warned you about eating too many of Esther's desserts?"

"Nonsense, son. I have not been putting on any unnecessary weight."

"Is that why Carrie is expanding your waistline on your trousers?"

"Now son, I said any unnecessary weight," he argues. "Esther's new dessert is necessary. I, as a minister, must give one an honest opinion when asked."

We all laugh. Leave it to my father to find an excuse for why it was necessary for his waistline to expand.

"There, Father," I say as I hold up his trousers.

He comes to his feet and takes the trousers from me, holding them up to his waist. "Perfect child," he says. "As always, you do such fine work."

Just then we hear a ruckus outside by our chickens. Both Roger and Father ran to the window. Seeing nothing, Father reaches for his rifle over the fireplace. "Stay here, children," he warns.

"Do be careful, Father," I rush.

Roger waits by the window, anxiously looking out. I love my brother to death, but he is such a coward. I can handle a gun better than he can. We both anxiously wait for Father's return. We hear a gunshot. We both become alarmed. I ran to the door and swung it open. I stop in my tracks when Father walks in.

"You alright, Father?" I ask anxiously. "We heard a gunshot."

"Yes, but Bessie is gone."

"Oh man, she was my best lawyer," I whine.

"It was a coyote. I am afraid that I am not a really good shot. I missed."

"That's alright, Father; at least you are alright, and it was nothing serious."

"Perhaps, Pa, we should consider getting a dog," Roger says.

"No," my father says. "You know, son, that I am terrified of dogs."

Roger and I both know how terrified our father is of dogs. When we asked him why, he said it had to do with his youth. We both figured that something happened to him, and he has been afraid of them ever since.

"A dog will bark for danger," Roger argues.

"Roger is right, Father. A dog may come in handy."

"I will take care of it, and it can live in the barn," Roger says.

"Let me sleep on it," he says.

"Well, at least that's something," Roger sighs.

Early the next morning, Father leaves for town for the day. Roger decides that he needs to check on some patients that he hasn't seen in a while. I walk out with him to the barn as he is saddling up his horse.

"I made you a bucket for lunch," I say.

"Thank you, Carrie, but I am planning on being back by then."

"You are seeing Mr. Lawson; I know he can keep you." Roger chuckles.

"Yes, let me see what will ail him today." He leans over and kisses my cheek.

"Thank you," I grin.

My heart skips a beat when I glance up at the loft over Roger's head to see, looking down at me, hidden behind some straw, White Horse. He places his finger over his mouth, telling me to hush.

"Are you sure you will be alright when I am gone?" Roger says.

"Yes, of course," I say. "Now you really should be running along."

"Are you trying to get rid of me?" he asks.

"Of course not. I just know that the Lawson homestead is a good ride from here. I want you to get an early start."

"Oh," he says.

I watch him hoist himself up onto his horse, Flash. White Horse ducks down when Roger turns and looks up at the loft.

"Remind me when I get home to take down some straw. I notice the horse's pens are needing a fresh layer."

"Will do." I smile and wave at him as he rides off.

When he has cleared the view of the homestead, I tell White Horse to come down. He jumps down, landing right in front of me. I quickly rushed into his arms.

"I have been up there all night waiting for you to come out," he says. "You slept in the loft?" I asked.

"Yes. I was very comfortable," he smiles.

"I am glad you are here; so much has happened."

"Yes, I am aware of that. I have been watching you and Willow Creek for several days."

"You have?"

"Yes, my love. I fear you are not safe, and therefore I will not leave you. My warriors are keeping watch on your place when I am unable to be here."

"But the attacks have stopped," I say.

"That is what they want you to think, but they will return. I can guarantee you that."

"When?" I ask.

"I do not know, but I fear it will be very soon. For they are still in the territory."

"How do you know this?" I ask.

"My camp was raided a few nights ago."

"Is everyone alright?" I gasp.

"Yes, we scared them off. They were trying to get to the horses and the food. They left before they got anything."

"I must warn everyone."

"No, my love, you cannot do that."

"Why?" I ask.

"I ask that you trust me. You must not say a word to anyone about any of this or of us. For if you do, great danger could come." White Horse is making me nervous.

"Come, my love. Come into my arms. They have been apart from you too long." He takes me into his arms, and we embrace. "We can be together tonight, as I have made my people safe."

"I don't know if I can get away."

"When all eyes are closed, I will come to your window."

"Alright." He flicks my nose. "Until then."

Evening is on us. I excuse myself for the evening around eight and close myself inside my room. I try to read as I keep a watch on my window. I hear Roger go up to the loft. He has the same habit every night. He will lie awake and read for about an hour before going to sleep. Father will already be asleep and snoring soundly. I then heard a tap on my window. I am sure it is White Horse.

I pull the curtain aside and see him standing there. I motion that I will go to the front door and meet him around. I slowly open my bedroom door so as not to make a sound. I crept to the door. I look up to the loft. Roger's lamp is still lit. He has yet to fall asleep. I know he is too involved in his book. I lift the lock and quietly open the door. I run to the back of the house, where White Horse is waiting. We don't make a sound until we get to the creek behind our home. He leans me against the trunk of the weeping willow. We then kiss.

"I have missed these sweet lips," he says. "I have also missed something else," he smirks.

White Horse came tonight for one thing and one thing only. He wants me. I give him no objections. He slips my nightgown over my head. He then lifts me up in his strong arms, carrying me to the creek's bed. It is there that we make love. With the gentle evening breeze and the bright moonlight shining down, White Horse gives one final deep, hard thrust and empties inside of me. It is at that moment that it occurs to me that no precautions were taken, and I am risking it all if I become pregnant.

With White Horse right beside me, it is a chance I am willing to take. Nothing seems to matter; I have no care in the world. I am absorbed in this moment, treasuring every bit of it. Lying nestled in his arms, with my head on his chest, is the perfect time to ask him why he thinks the attacks are not over, but why ruin the moment? A moment that will soon end. Hand in hand, we walk back of the house. He kisses me, vowing to return for me very shortly. Smiling and in complete bliss, I make my way to the front of the house and quietly close the door behind me. I place the board back on the handles to secure the lock. I turn to go to my room when I see Roger behind me.

"Where have you been?" he asks.

"Using the outhouse," I lie.

"No, you were not. I checked. Where were you?"

"I..I....remembered that I left Sugar Foot's stall open, and I went to close it. Then on my way back I went to use the outhouse. That is probably why you didn't see me."

I hate to lie, and I am not good at it, but I had no choice. I sheepishly look at him and brush past him.

"Good night," I say and quickly rush to my room and close the door.

I feel him watching me. I am positive he doesn't believe me. I lie in bed feeling so in love with White Horse, I had to pinch myself and ask myself if it is real. I wish I could scream out for all to hear that I am in love, but I can't, and I love White Horse too much to give it a second thought.

Chapter Ten

The Accusations

Two more days have passed. All is quiet on the prairie. I am beginning to think that White Horse is wrong and the Pawnees have indeed moved on. Willow Creek is completely back to normal. I am once again allowed to leave at will, which I am thrilled about. Roger is tending to patients that have been neglected for over a week. I figure he will be gone all day. Since we are out of danger, Father again has said no on getting a dog. His excuse is it will kill our chickens. Roger and I both know better.

The weather is very pleasant today, and I am anxious to be out in it. I decided to walk to town instead of riding. I collect a basket of eggs to trade at the general store. I need some supplies, and Mr. Forbes, who runs the store, is very generous when he buys my eggs. Mrs. Forbes, on the other hand, is a different story. I know she is out visiting her mother, so I feel confident that I will get a good deal.

"Good morning, Mr. Forbes," I greet as I walk up to the counter.

"Good morning, Miss Sims."

"I have brought you some eggs."

"Well, let me take a look," he says.

"You look busy today," I say as I look around the store. It is not that he has so many customers; it looks more as if he just received his shipment.

"Yes, I will admit it has been nice with the Mrs. gone, but it isn't really nice when it comes to work needing to be done."

"I reckon it is, sir." I agree.

"Would you like cash or credit for your eggs?" He asks me.

"Cash, please, and I need some cornstarch, sugar, and coffee, please."

"Well, alright. You may want to stock up some. I was told today that I will not be receiving any more shipments of supplies."

"Why is that?" I wonder.

"Stagecoaches are refusing to come in until our Indian problem is resolved."

"Indian problem?" I question. "I thought they were gone?"

"So did the rest of us. A stagecoach was attacked by Indians just out of town yesterday; no survivors."

"Oh, my Lord," I gasp.

"Supplies were taken from the coach. I heard it was a gruesome attack." "Where was this?" I ask.

"By Rosy Peak."

Rosy Peak overlooks the meadow. The trail leads to Willow Creek. The meadow is only half a mile from my home.

"Oh, my, that is very close."

"Yes, it is," Mr. Forbes agrees.

"Alright, here are your supplies, and with the thirty cents that you get for the eggs, I owe you five cents."

"Thank you," I smile.

"You have a good day and give your father my regards."

"I will."

I grab my supplies and make my way to the post office, where I am hoping to find Stella. I am walking down the main street when I see Carl standing outside the saloon. He has Rachel, one of the saloon's "entertainers," leaning on him.

Fortunately for me, he is too preoccupied with what he is about to get to pay mind to me. I turn and cross the street to the post office. I stop as the door is being opened for me by a gentleman I do not recognize. He tips his hat to me. I thank him for holding the door open and walk in.

"Good morning, Mrs. Miller," I greet as I step into the post office.

"Good morning, dear," she says as she continues sorting the mail.

"Any letters for us?" I ask.

"Only one. It is for the doctor." She handed me the letter.

"I will see that he gets it."

"Is that my jellybean I hear?"

I smile widely at Mr. Miller, who is in the back room at the desk. When I was a little girl, Stella and I would walk home from school, and every day Mr. Miller would buy us a treat. Stella was always a gumdrop. Mine were jellybeans, thus getting my nickname of Jellybean. Stella's is Gumdrop. I walk to the back room just as Mr. Miller is standing up. I quickly give him a hug.

The Millers are very dear to me. I consider them my second family. There is nothing I would not do for either one of them.

"Keeping busy?" I ask him.

"Hmm," Mrs. Miller says. "Richard busy?" she smiles.

"Busy eating your jellybeans," he teases. We all laugh.

I hear Stella walk in the back door. "Here you go, Pa," she says and hands him a cup of coffee.

"Pa, did you hear about the stagecoach being attacked?" she says.

"Yes, dear. Mr. Forbes told me this morning. Awful, isn't it?"

"I say. Bone-chilling," Mrs. Miller chimes in.

"I heard the sheriff say he thinks he knows who is doing it." Stella says. "Oh, who?" he asks.

"That chief that traded with us awhile back. They say it is his band."

I am speechless. There must be a mistake. The White Horse I know wouldn't do this.

"How can they be certain?" Mr. Miller asks.

"He said that several men have come in to complain that he has been showing up on their property wanting to trade. When they tell him no, he is getting hostile. He said in one case that one of his warriors threatened to kill him and drew their arrows on him. They were so frightened. Mr. Skelov, from the immigration camp, said they had a similar thing happen as well. The sheriff has formed a posse again and says he will find him, and when he does, he will kill him and all his people. He is threatening to bring in the army."

"This can't be," I mumble.

"Here, see for yourself."

She hands me a wanted poster with a sketch of White Horse on it. It read.

Reward.

Wanted Dead or Alive.

"He gave me several of them to hang up. I just haven't had the chance yet," Stella says.

I am numb. I can't believe what I am hearing. I could have cried. I ask myself why. Why would White Horse do this?

"Mrs. Miller, may I take this?"

"Why certainly, dear," she says.

"Carrie," Mr. Miller says. "Have you seen him?" he questions.

I figure my face says it all. I have never been good at hiding my emotions.

"No," I lied. " Not since the trade."

"Good."

I am feeling numb when I leave the post office. There must be an explanation. After all, I was there when those bodies were found in the woods. I saw the arrows. I saw the look on White

Horse's face. He too was nervous. He was just as scared as I was. I know he knew more than what he was telling me. He knows exactly who the renegades are, and I believe he knows why they are here. But why won't he tell? What is he hiding? One thing I know for sure is White Horse is being set up. But by whom and why? I am so confused. None of this makes any sense. I must talk to White Horse. I must find out the truth. I only hope I can handle it.

I cross the bridge and continue my walk home. I hear a rustle in the trees. I turned to look and saw nothing. I brush it off, thinking it is most likely a deer or a squirrel. I continue to walk. I suddenly feel the hair stand up on my back, and I cannot shake the feeling that I am being watched. I hear the rustle again. I see nothing in the trees, but I can't shake the uneasy feeling that someone is following me. I have no intention of finding out if I am or not, so I hasten my stride. I can feel a panic coming over me, as I feel like at any moment I am going to be jumped. I hear a wagon coming up behind me and slowing down. It is my father. He stops, and I jump on the back. I look at the trees as we ride off. I swear I see someone standing in the thicket as we ride off.

Evening is on us. I share with Roger and my father the wanted poster of White Horse. I can see the disappointment in my father's eyes. He liked White Horse and thought he could trust him. I know he too is having his doubts that White Horse is indeed responsible for all the attacks. Roger, on the other hand, is boasting, making it very clear that he warned us both that Indians cannot be trusted.

I am nearly in tears by the time I call it a night and disappear into my room. I lie in bed, not knowing what to believe. Am I being too naive to trust White Horse? Is he lying to me? My head and my heart are in a battle over which one will win, logic or love. The house is in complete silence, as both Roger and Father sleep. As for me, I lie awake, restless, and unable to slumber. I hear a rap on the window. I know exactly who it is. I ask myself, am I really in the mood to see him? I need answers to so many questions, and tonight I am going to get them. I go to the window, acknowledging that I see him. I grab the wanted poster, tucking it in the pocket of my apron. I then sneak my way outside and follow him to his horse that he has waiting near the creek. I watch him jump on. He then reaches his hand down and pulls me up behind him. In the still of the night, we disappear into the woods. We stop when we reach his camp for the night that is boldly less than a mile from the house. He lifts me down off his horse's back.

"I thought we would come here tonight," he says.

He takes my hand, and we walk over to the fire and sit down. I noticed the other warriors off at a distance. I figure it is White Horse's doing of wanting us to be alone.

"So how is my beautiful Prairie Dawn this evening?" he asks.

"Fine," I mumble, avoiding his look.

Taken aback by my rude behavior, he tilts his head to the side to look at me.

"You are different tonight. What is on your mind?"

I gaze out in the darkness. I suddenly feel afraid to confront him. How will he act? If indeed he is responsible for these attacks, what would stop him from killing me? I start to flash back, remembering my time at his camp. Our first kiss, our first night together. Is it all a game for him? Am I just another one of his victims? My insides hurt. My emotions are flying. I want to scream as I feel my anger come out. I bite my tongue to swallow my tears. Not now, Carrie, I say to myself, not now.

White Horse gently reaches forward, turning my chin to face him. I pull it away. My sudden action takes him off guard. I feel his eyes upon me, piercing me through my skin.

"You are frightened of me?" he huskily says. "Why?"

I failed to answer him. I feel the tears coming. I deeply sigh to hold them within.

"Prairie Dawn, you do not need to fear me. I would never harm you. Look at me."

When I fail to look at him, he reaches forward and grabs my chin, forcing me to look at him.

"Why does my Prairie Dawn fear me?"

I reach inside of the pocket of my apron and pull out the poster. I handed it to him. He glances up at me as he opens it up. I watch his expression as he looks at it. For a moment he grows still. I watch him cock his mouth to the side to control his temper. I hear him sigh as he tosses the paper into the fire. He leans back, resting on his palms, and looks over at me.

For several moments he says nothing. I know he is angry and perhaps even a little heartbroken that I would even think he could do this. Finally, he speaks.

"You think I killed these people, don't you?"

"Yes," I mumble.

"Were you not there and see the arrows in the chest of those men?" he snaps.

I only nod my head and shrug. He curls his bottom lip, perhaps to control his anger even more.

"Why would I kill all these people?" he barks.

"Because they wouldn't trade with you," I answer.

"A lot of people don't trade with me. I don't kill them for it."

"But everything that I am being told," I whine.

"Like what?" he growls.

"That you went to trade and you were told no, and one of your warriors drew their arrow on them. They are one of the families that died."

White Horse crossed his legs and leaned forward.

"Let me tell you what happened. Blue Thunder was with fever. He got thirsty. We came across a home with a well. A man came out of the home with a gun. I told the man I meant him no harm, for I had a sick man who was wanting water. The woman gave Blue Thunder water. The man told the woman to back away, and he cocked his gun at me. Koawa drew his bow and pointed it at the man. I slapped the gun out of the man's hand and took it. The woman screamed. We turned and rode off. Koawa was only protecting me. It was a bluff; Koawa never would have shot."

"What about the immigration camp?" I asked.

"We have traded with them before. I thought they would again. We were not welcomed, so we left."

He leans forward and takes my hand.

"Carrie. I am the target because they have no one else. But I am not guilty."

"A stagecoach was attacked the other day."

"I know about it, but we were not there. I give you my word. I am just as concerned about this as you."

"You still feel that we are going to be attacked again?"

"Sweetheart, I am sure of it. There is much I know, but little I will share."

"Why?" I ask.

"I will tell you this. The reason you have not been hit is because they are regrouping, recruiting more warriors. When they return, and it will be very soon, Willow Creek is in great danger."

"What do they want?" I ask.

"I do not know for certain, but I fear for you, and that is why I am camped out so close to your place."

"What do they want with me?" I ask.

"Your home may be in their path."

"I do not understand."

"All your attacks have happened in a straight line. If they continue on this path, they will hit the fork in the road. I do not know which path from the fork they will take. The right or the left. If they take the left, then your home is a target. That is why I am here."

He stops a moment and plays with my fingers.

"I will be here for you to fight if they show up. You and your family are safe." He kisses my hand. "I would die for you."

"You are scaring me."

"You should be. These men are bad. I should know. It is their leader who attacked my camp that killed my wife and father."

My eyes grew huge. "Yes, love, I have a taste for revenge as well," he says.

"Oh, White Horse," I cry, as I throw my arms around him.

"I am sorry I doubted you. Will you ever forgive me?"

"Yes, of course I will. I too would have questioned it." He strokes my hair.

"Until I know for sure that my hunch is correct, you are to tell no one about me. If you do, it could be my life."

"Oh, sweetheart, I won't. I promise."

"Good, I promise you when I know for sure what is going on, I will tell you everything. But I must keep it to myself for now. Try to understand."

"I do."

I knew I was wrong about White Horse. He is being wrongly accused. I now have something else to fear. I fear what will happen if White Horse gets caught. The rest of the night remains light. Neither one of us speaks a word regarding the renegades. As White Horse and I lie next to the fire, Koawa and Blue Thunder are perched in trees standing guard. With our fingers looped together, White Horse speaks.

"When this is all over and done. I want you to come with me."

"I want that more than anything," I smile.

"I understand that you will walk away from the life you live. I cannot provide you with fancy clothes or jewels, but I can give you all of me every day."

"Oh, White Horse." I pushed my head further down in his chest to cuddle him.

"As a chief's wife, you will have many responsibilities, but I am confident that you will be able to handle them. Many women will look up to you, not because they fear me, but because you will be their leader because you are my wife."

"I want them to like me because they want to, not because you tell them to." I declare.

"This will happen. I know my people very well. I assure you. You will want for nothing."

"The problem is my father. It will hurt so much to leave him."

"If you think he will come, we will bring him."

"No, Father would never agree to that."

"If it helps, we will tell him together."

I am so much in love with this man. I never would have thought it possible to fall in love with an Indian chief. When I look at White Horse, I look at what is inside. Not only is he beautiful outside but inside as well. He is intelligent, caring, and has a huge understanding of life. He takes nothing for granted and loves me for who I am. It is his tender side that I am certain few see. White Horse looks like he could kill you in a snap. I believe the warrior still lives inside him, despite his rank, and he thrives on the adventure. Hand in hand, fingers around fingers, I fall asleep and dream of the life that I will one day live.

Chapter Eleven

The Miller's

"Prairie Dawn," I hear. "It is time to wake."

I open my eyes to see White Horse looking down at me.

"There is smoke close to here. This could be it. We need to ride."

In a matter of seconds, White Horse has me up on Moon Light's back, and we are running hard. It only takes me a moment to realize where we are heading.

"It's the Miller's!" I gasp

We reach the Miller's, and my heart sinks. The home is totally engulfed in flames. I hear a woman scream. White Horse quickly has me off his horse and running me to shelter.

"Stay here," he hollers, pushing me to the ground.

I hear Koawa and Blue Thunder give out a war cry. Koawa jumps on the back of a renegade and starts beating him with his club. White Horse starts to run towards the house. A renegade sees him and tosses his tomahawk at him. White Horse is quick to react, dodging out of the way. I scream as it lands hard in a tree trunk just over his head.

My eyes are wide with fear. I see Stella on the ground with a renegade on top of her. I hear her screaming for her life. Blue Thunder comes up behind him and slashes his throat. The renegade falls to his death. Stella and Blue Thunder quickly connect their eyes before he takes off to fight again. I see White Horse grab Stella.

"Come, hurry," he says.

He protects her way, running alongside her until she is beside me. We quickly embrace. Stella is terrified and in tears. We watch in horror as the three Lakota battle their way. Suddenly, Stella and I screamed when a renegade came into the trees and rushed towards us. I see White Horse tackle him to the ground. They begin to wrestle. The knife is just inches from White Horse's throat. I see White Horse push the renegade off him and then slice his throat. The warrior lies dead at our feet. The renegades retreat. Koawa follows them but shortly backs off when he is certain that they will not turn back around.

White Horse is by my side. He cups my tear-stricken face in his palms.

"Are you alright?" he asks.

"Yes," I sob. "I am fine."

I look over at Stella as she stares at the burning house.

"Stella," I say. "Where are your parents?"

"Father went back inside to rescue Ma. He never came back out," she cries.

I lower my head and begin to cry along with her. Our tears are heavy as Stella, and I watch the only home that she has ever known burn to the ground.

The morning arrives. Stella is sitting under the great apple tree that her father planted when she was just a baby. I come down beside her.

"Ma and I were going to pick these apples. We never got around to it," she cries.

"We will pick them together," I say, putting my hand on her shoulder.

White Horse comes up behind me. "We leave now," he says. "We will take the dead Pawnee with us so no one will question you how they died."

"Thank you, White Horse," I say.

He looks over at Stella. "You have suffered a great loss," he says. "I am sorry."

"Thank you," she sniffs. "I owe you my life."

"No. You owe nothing." he looks back over at me. He motions for me to follow him. We walk a short distance away from the earshot.

"The smoke is great still. Soon, it will be seen, and help will arrive."

"I am sorry, White Horse, that we got you involved," I tell him.

"I became involved when my father died. This is something I need to finish, and I will."

"Thank you for everything," I say.

"Carrie, I need to caution you. This is only the beginning."

"Why are they attacking us?" I feel his gentle stroke on my cheek.

"I wish I knew why, but now the Pawnee know that we are involved. I must move my people. I cannot chance an attack on them when my best warriors are with me. You be careful. I will come find you when my people are safe, and I am sure I will not be seen."

"I understand."

He smiles and gently squeezes my hand. He glances over my shoulder at Stella, who is curiously looking on. He strokes my cheek.

"You be safe and do not go out at night alone."

"I won't. Please be careful."

"For you, Prairie Dawn, I will always live another day."

He then gives me a quick peck on the cheek, walks down the hill, and mounts his horse. I then watched the small party of Lakota warriors ride away with the dead Pawnee warriors draped over their horses. Stella joins me by my side.

"We are wrong about him. He is not the guilty one," she says.

"No, he is not," I say.

"You knew that all along, didn't you?" she says.

"Yes, I did."

"Why didn't you tell me?"

"I promised him I wouldn't."

"He is sweet on you. Am I right?" she smiles.

"Yes, Stella. We are sweet on each other."

"What does your father say?" she asks.

"He does not know."

"Carrie, I am surprised. It is so unlike you."

"Stella, you must promise me that you will keep this quiet. No one must know about this. Understand?"

"I promise, but Carrie, if the sheriff finds him, he will kill him."

"I realize that. That is why I need your help in keeping this quiet."

"Carrie, I owe him and his men my life. I will help in any way I can. I promise."

"Thank you."

Stella and I remain sitting under the apple tree for about an hour when we finally see our help arrive. Riding fast up the lane is Hank, followed close behind the sheriff, with his posse, Roger and my father. We are quickly greeted when Father rushes up the hill. Roger is right behind him.

"Heavens, my dear child," my father says as he embraces Stella.

"We saw the smoke." He looks down the hill at the house that is still heavily smoldering.

"Oh, my dear. How mortifying."

"What happened?" Roger asks.

"We were attacked by Indians in our sleep," Stella begins.

Hank walks up the hill and joins in the conversation.

"My father wakes me just as an arrow with flames comes through the window, catching the floor on fire. My father rushes me outside. Ma won't leave without taking her valuables. Pa argues with her to leave. I heard a wall fall. Neither one came out." She starts to cry. "I couldn't do anything. I wanted to, but I couldn't."

Hank is quick to console her and holds her tightly as she weeps. Our sheriff walks up.

"I have to ask you some questions," he says.

"Jesus Christ, sheriff," Hank barks. "Look around. What more do you need to know? Her parents died. Let her grieve in peace."

"I just need to know..."

"Leave her alone!" he yells.

You don't want to anger Hank. He is known for having a short fuse and can be very protective. He has control of Stella now, and he is going to protect her and be beside her, but there is no one who will get in his way. The sheriff knows it and backs off. Hank grabs Stella around the waist and walks off with her.

"Ms. Sims," The sheriff says. "What happened?"

"I came after it was over. I didn't see anything," I lie.

"What made you come here?"

"I couldn't sleep and went out for a walk when I smelt the smoke coming from the Millers. I rushed here, and by the time I arrived, it was done, and the renegades were gone." I am not sure whether he believes me. For a few moments, he just looked at me.

"Well, I reckon I am done then; good day." He is so heartless and callous, a poor excuse for a sheriff.

"The Millers are dead, and that is all you can say?" I snap.

"Pardon me, Miss Sims, but you were the one who chose to stay here until morning for help to arrive, allowing the renegades a full day head start and not take one of the horses and ride into town and get help. Your father will see to their burial, but there is nothing more I can do thanks to you." He then walks off. That man is so infuriating. My father comes up alongside me.

"Child," the father says. "Why did you not run back to the house and wake me."

"I was too frightened to leave, father. I did not know where the renegades were. I knew by staying here they would not return."

"My heavens child, you have suffered so," he says before embracing me. I look over at Roger. I know he doesn't buy my story.

"I am going to help Hank recover the bodies. See, your brother gets you home." Roger's eyes are thick on me.

"Odd how you would walk a chilly night through the woods without your shawl and the only protection on your feet being your slippers."

"I told you it all happened so fast."

"Yes, that is what you said," he says.

I have had enough of Roger's bellyaching. I hasten down the hill and jump into the front of the wagon. I watch Roger as he climbs in and takes the reins. I feel his eyes on me the entire ride home.

The Miller's bodies were found in the ashes later that day by Hank and my father. They were laid to rest under the great apple tree that Mr. Miller took such pride in. I promised Stella that when she is ready, I will help her pick as many apples as we can and make as much jam, cider, and pies as she wishes.

Hank gave her back her old room upstairs in the saloon, free of charge. He pampers and protects her. Her visitors are limited, and he requests that they be light.

Several days have passed, and we have lost more homesteaders due to the attacks. They are getting bolder and more violent. I have not seen White Horse since the night that Stella's parents died. The search for him has intensified with our posse and his bounty has increased. I am very worried for him, and it is starting to show in my moods. I am more withdrawn and keeping to myself. I visit Stella daily, but next to that, I remain in my own thoughts.

Today, Roger thinks it would be nice to pick some of the apples off the Miller's tree and make a pie with them to give to Stella. He has asked me to go with him. We are nearly done filling our baskets.

"I think this is exactly what the doctor ordered," Roger says.

"Yeah. I suppose," I say.

Roger is quiet for a moment as he watches me pick. He pulls an apple off and tosses it in the bucket.

"I remember a time, Carrie, when you would tell me anything," he finally says. Perplexed by his strange comment, I looked over at him.

"What do you mean by that?" I wonder.

"You are different, Carrie. Something is bothering you?"

I pulled an apple from the branch. "I am fine."

I hear him chuckle under his breath. "I know you well, Carrie. You are not. You are hiding something?"

I am in no mood to hear his third degree. I glare over at him as I pick an apple off a branch. I snap the branch when I free the apple. It swings, nearly hitting Roger on the head.

"Are we here to pick apples, or do you just want to badger me?" I snap.

Roger is silent and picks several more apples. He then starts up again.

"I saw Marianne Simpson the other day."

I paused. I completely forgot to go visit her and cover my tracks. Roger just caught me in my own lie.

"She is staying in town until the attacks stop," he says.

I reach and pull down an apple, tossing it in the basket.

"That's good," I say.

"They found Harold. He was mauled by a bear."

"How awful," I coldly say.

"She asked me why you didn't return for her the day the baby was born."

Roger holds the branch away from me, not allowing me to pick any apples.

"Why didn't you return?" he questions.

"I..I,, didn't find Harold, so I came home. I figured he was on his way back home and I just missed him."

Roger releases the branch and takes a few steps towards me. He points his finger in my face.

"You are lying, Carrie, and you lied to Pa the night the Millers died."

"I am not," I hiss.

"Where were you, Carrie?" he badgers.

"I told you I went out for a walk."

"What are you hiding?"

"Nothing," I huff.

"Come on, Carrie, this is me you are talking to," Roger says, frustrated.

"I have nothing to say!" I yell.

I toss the basket down on the ground, and all the apples fall out.

"How dare you corner me." I bark. "You didn't bring me here to pick apples for a friend; you brought me here to badger me like a child, and I will not tolerate it!"

"Carrie, please," he begs. "What is bothering you?"

"Leave me alone!" I yell.

Having enough of his bellyaching, I turn to walk down the hill when I nearly faint. Roger grabs me and gently sits me down.

"Slow breaths," he says. He feels my forehead. "I knew you were not right," he says shaking his head.

"I am fine, Roger. I'm just feeling flushed."

"I have some water on the wagon."

I watch him run down the hill to the wagon. Sometimes, he can be so infuriating and treats me as if I were a child. I watch Roger return with the water and kneel in front of me.

"Slow sips," he says. I do as I am instructed. "I need to get you back to the clinic where I can check you out thoroughly."

"Roger, I am fine. It is just a little warm today and I got over heated," I argue. "I am fine. Really."

I know he is not happy that I have refused, but he pursues it no further. He picks up the apples that have fallen from my basket and helps me to my feet. He then takes me home and orders me to rest.

Chapter Twelve

The Confrontation

Four days have passed. The attacks are happening every night and one or more homesteads are being hit. The town is in an uproar. Several townspeople have packed up what belongings they can and are leaving the area. Many are leaving in groups of three or four families, thinking there is safety enough numbers. My father has been offered several times to leave as well, but like Roger and I, he is refusing to leave.

Father has opened his door to the church for anyone who wishes to have a safe place to sleep at night. All stagecoaches have stopped, leaving our supplies very limited and making Willow Creek a ghost town. A huge sign has been posted just outside of Willow Creek warning all who travel here of the danger. A telegram has been sent out advising everyone to stay clear of Willow Creek. All who remain have been advised to do so at their own risk.

The sheriff's posse is strong, the strongest that I have ever seen. There is constant patrol around the clock within a ten-mile range. Despite their constant effort, there have been no sightings of any renegades. I am more and more concerned about White Horse. It has been ten days since I have seen him. I am sick with worry. For the last few days, I have not been myself. I have vomited the last two mornings, and my stomach is turning circles. I am blaming it on my nerves. I refuse to tell Roger how I feel, for I know he will make a big deal out of it. I suck on some lemons and hope for the best.

Stella and I are in the church preparing cots for anyone who may need them. We spent a great deal of time together, and it was a good distraction for both of us. She is the only one I feel I can talk to about White Horse. She never starts the conversation, but when

I make a comment about him, she is always there for support. I know I can trust her.

"The sheriff's posse has gotten so strong," I tell her.

"Yes, I rarely see Hank at all these days."

"I worry about White Horse," I say.

"Do you think they got him?" she asks.

"No. If they had White Horse, we would know about it."

I look out the window and see Sid, our deputy, returning to town.

"No. White Horse is alive. I am sure of it."

"He is probably unable to come for you."

"I suppose you are right."

I close the curtain, walk over to a pew, and sit down.

"Can I ask you something?" I say.

"Always."

She puts the blanket down on the cot and joins me in the pew.

"When you were pregnant with Hank's baby, how did it feel?"

She seems taken aback by my question. Her conceiving a child over a year ago by Hank has been a dirty little secret just between the three of us. Hank found someone who terminated her pregnancy early on. It is a topic that we have seldom discussed in any way until now.

"Carrie, could you be pregnant?" she asks.

"I am not sure."

"Well...tell me how you feel?"

"I get real sick in the morning. I feel nauseous all the time and I am late for my monthly."

"How late?" She wonders.

"A few weeks."

"Oh, Carrie."

I am almost in tears with the thought that I may be and not knowing where White Horse is. Before much more can be said, we both hear yelling outside for the sheriff. Stella and I both step outside to see Mr. Skelov from the immigration camp running up on his horse. He jumps off in front of Sid.

"Something is wrong," I say. Stella and I make our way down the street.

"They are gone," he says. "They take all of them, my Sarah too."

"Who is gone?" Sid asks.

We met up with Roger and Hank on the edge of the street.

"Our children. They are gone." We gasped.

"They took them. The Indians, they took them."

"Alright. Slow down," Sid says. "Tell me what happened."

Mr. Skelov catches his breath and begins. "We were sleep. Children were taken from their beds. We fight, but too many. Our children are gone."

"Any deaths?" Roger asks.

"That is what is strange. They come quietly like a snake. No one is seriously hurt. They only come for children."

He is right; that is strange, I think.

"Let's go," Hank says.

Both men get on their horses and quickly ride off. Word spreads quickly about the children. Although the children are not ours, regardless, we consider our neighbors to be friends, and friends help friends. Everyone has an opinion on why the children were taken and rumors around Chief White Horse's band are still to blame. I still find it impossible to believe that the man I have fallen in love with is responsible for so much death, and I wish I knew what to do to clear his name.

I now have another problem on my hands. I am almost one month late for my monthly. My morning sickness is progressing, and fatigue is setting in. I am beginning to think that I am indeed with child. The question is, how long am I going to be able to hide it. Roger is already suspicious. He caught me the other day as I was leaving the outhouse after I just finished vomiting. I avoided any questions or comments he was making and quickly walked away.

Roger left early with my father to help in town as most of our men are out looking for the children and White Horse. Father will most likely be gone all day, however Roger is never gone for more than a few hours and I expect him home soon. I go out to the chicken pen and start to collect eggs. I noticed the gate is ajar.

"Oh, Roger, when will you learn," I grumble. I started to collect the eggs. I usually collect a dozen. I count nine.

"Hmm," I think.

I look behind the house and under the straw hut find no eggs. I then look to see if by chance there are any eggs lying around outside the hen house. I see one just to the left of the gate.

"Ok that is odd," I say. I go and pick up the egg. I look around for two more. "What the...," I see another egg outside of the house by the barn. I walk over to it and pick it up.

"How did you get over here?" I wonder.

I am still missing an egg. I turn to walk back to the chicken house.

"You missed one," I hear.

I turn around and standing inside the door of the barn smiling widely, is White Horse. I put down my basket and ran to him, swinging myself into his arms.

"I am so glad you are alright," I cry.

"I have missed you, my Prairie Dawn," he says.

"White Horse, you shouldn't be here. Roger could come home at any time."

"I needed to see you," he huskily says.

"So much has happened. I am so scared."

"I am aware of many things, and I have many things to tell you. Meet me in the meadow in one hour."

"Is it safe?"

"For the moment. My men are detouring your posse. For now, I am safe."

"I will be there," I say.

He kisses my hand and sneaks away into the woods.

I left Roger a note on the mantel telling him that I was going to see Stella. I know she will back me up if questioned. I then saddled up Sugar Foot. It is time to leave and meet up with White Horse. I start my way down the road when I see Roger coming home.

"I left you a note. I am going to see Stella."

"I just left her. Hank is treating her to dinner at Esther's," he says.

"Oh, well I am sure she won't mind. I promised her I would visit her today and we will make some apple strudel."

"She never said anything about meeting you," he argues.

"Maybe she forgot," I snap.

Roger knows I am lying. I never have been any good at it.

"Carrie, stop it!" he says. "I know when I am being lied to."

"No, I am not."

"Come on, Carrie," he argues.

"I don't have time for this, I am leaving."

I hit my horse's ribs to get him going. Roger quickly grabs the reins from me.

"Roger gives me the reins," I snap.

"Not until you tell me what is going on," he barks.

I attempt to pull Sugar Foot's reins from Roger's grip. Both horses are turning as Roger and I fight for the reins.

"I'm going to find out. So, you might as well tell me," he warns.

Damn it, Roger, give me the reins!"

I am furious with him. I smack Sugar Foot's rump. Sugar Foot takes off, making Roger let go of the reins or fall off his horse. I bring Sugar Foot to a full run, leaving Roger in the dust. Roger is not the sort of man who angers easily, but his sister's actions get him boiled. Certain that she is hiding something and fearing that she is in harm's way, he follows his gut, turning his horse around and following his sister.

I find White Horse in the meadow. Koawa is standing next to him. Both men are heavily armed. White Horse helps me down, and we quickly hug. Koawa takes Sugar Foot's reins, and we head uphill to go into the woods.

"Carrie, stay away from those men!" we hear.

We all quickly turn around.

"Roger!" I yell. "Get out of here."

Roger is off his horse, has his gun drawn, and points it directly at White Horse.

"Do you know this man?" White Horse asks.

"Yes, he is my brother," I answer.

Roger cocks his gun as he walks closer to White Horse.

"You stay away from her," he boldly says.

"Or what," White Horse growls.

Roger is standing on his ground while he is soiling his pants.

"I don't want to hurt you. I just want my sister," he says.

In a blink, I am snatched by Koawa, pulled behind both men and shielded.

"Your sister is staying with me," White Horse snarls.

Roger gulps. "Just give me Carrie, and I won't tell anyone that I saw you."

"You got that right," White Horse barks.

"I mean it! Give me Carrie."

I have never seen Roger so scared. I admire his tenacity to stand up to both men, but I honestly feel that soon his braveness will be challenged as White Horse is edging in. Both White Horse and Koawa are pouncing back and forth ready to strike. Roger is trying to remain firm but is weakening at the knees. His hands are trembling making the gun shake back and forth in his hand.

"Don't make me shoot," Roger begs.

"You want your sister; you have to go through us," White Horse threatens.

"Leave him alone," I beg White Horse. "He is my brother."

White Horse pays me no mind. I try to step around both men, but Koawa is persistent in blocking me in.

"You cannot take us both," White Horse says. "You kill me, and he will kill you. You kill him, and I will kill you. Either way, you die."

"Roger, go home. Please. You are no match for them," I beg.

I fear for Roger's life. I know it would take nothing for either one of these men to kill him.

"I won't leave you," Roger tells me.

"Yes, you will," White Horse says.

Roger is scared to death and desperate.

"I will kill you if I must. Now give me Carrie!" Roger screams.

In the blink of an eye, White Horse slaps the gun out of Roger's hand. He grabs Roger by his collar, lifting him off his feet. He then shakes him.

"You hear me," he growls. "You ever pull a gun on me again, and I will forget you are her kin. If you value your life, you will leave and tell no one you saw me."

Roger's eyes are the size of a saucer as he is looking down into the eyes of solid ice. It is very clear to Roger that White Horse is no match for him. He is terrified as White Horse stares him down.

"Roger, just go. I love him. I want to be with him," I blurt out.

Roger looks surprised. He clearly was not expecting to hear what he did. He looks up at White Horse's piercing eyes.

"You heard her," White Horse growls. "Now go."

He releases his grip, and Roger falls flat on his behind. Roger looks over at me. I am pleading with him to go. He then looks up at White Horse, who is still towering over him. He starts to leave by skidding backwards on the loose dirt. Roger then comes to his feet. He takes one final look at both of us before he quickly goes to his horse. Roger is devastated. He looks over at me just as White Horse comes to my side. He then turns his horse around and gallops off.

"How could you be so mean to him? He is only worried about me," I yell to White Horse.

White Horse picks up Roger's gun from the ground.

"Relax," he grumbles. "I would not have hurt him. I was only scaring him."

"Geez, White Horse, you scared the hell out of me."

"Carrie, I told you I will do anything, and I mean anything, to anyone who tries to take what is mine."

As we walked up the hill and disappeared into the woods, it all became clear to me. White Horse already considers me his, and therefore, he will protect me. If he knows that I am carrying his child, I fear it will make him worse. I pity anyone who gets in his way.

Chapter Thirteen

The Pawnee Squaw

I am taken to a remote place in the woods thick with trees. We come to a small clearing. We stop at a shelter made from trees that are covered with a thick bed of leaves and pine needles. A small fire is lit. I assume this is where White Horse and his warriors have been staying for the time being. He offers me a seat beside him.

"It is not the most comfortable," he adds.

"It's fine," I say as I brush away what pine needles I can with my foot before sitting down.

Koawa, who is heavily armed, remains on guard while we talk.

"I do not have much time," he says. "Your posse is close. I was nearly caught yesterday." I gasped.

"I am alright. I saw them before they saw me."

"White Horse, I am scared," I say.

He takes his hand into mine.

"I know you are."

"They kidnapped the children at the immigration camp," I say.

"I know."

"How do you know?"

"I have seen them," he says.

I gasp again. Where?" I anxiously say.

He sighs deeply. "Sweetheart, you and Willow Creek are in grave danger."

"How?"

"A few of my men and I are riding along when we see the Pawnees and the children in a valley. The children were resting. We went in as close as we could without being seen to hear what they were saying. We overheard them telling each other that they were going to blow up Willow Creek and kill everyone around the town."

"But why?" I wonder.

He pauses a moment as if thinking about what he was going to say.

"Someone in your town has done a Pawnee wrong. It must be a member in their tribe that has great importance for them to have such a thirst for revenge."

I stop to think who it could be. As no one in the town really has that much power.

"I know who their leader is, and therefore, it gives me a hunch," White Horse says.

"Who is it?" I ask.

"His name is One Eye. He is the son of a Pawnee Chief. One Eye is not his real name; he got this name after a battle with Santee when he lost an eye to one of their warriors. He had a sister who mysteriously disappeared a few years ago."

"What does this have to do with us?" I ask.

"I do not understand everything, but I will tell you what I know. This sister is a Chief's daughter and is connected somehow to Willow Creek."

"How can Willow Creek be connected to a Pawnee?"

"I am not sure, but somehow it is, and these men are after revenge because of it," he states.

"But it has been two years. Why so long?" I ask.

"As a Chief myself, if one of my children had disappeared, I would never stop looking, and I would seek revenge to the highest. What you need to understand is that a chief of a tribe is like their father, and if someone does their father wrong, many will pay. This is the case for you."

"But who could it be?" I wonder.

"In order for the revenge to be on the town as a whole and not just on that person, it is either one of two things. Either they do not know who the one person is, or that person has such high power that they consider this person as a Chief, and therefore, the whole tribe will pay. In Willow Creek's case, your whole town is the tribe."

After he said that, there is only one person I could think of.

"The sheriff," I say. White Horse nods in agreement.

"Oh, my Lord," I gasp. "I knew he was scum."

"Sweetheart," he begins as he strokes my fingers. "I fear for you. These children are just scapegoats and are only being used as an example."

"Are they going to kill them?" I speak.

"I don't think so. When we saw them, several women are caring for the children. That is why they stole your livestock. They will use meat from the cows and the chickens. They will use it to feed the children. They want the children alive. They are no use to them if they are dead."

"What do they want them for?" I ask.

"This I am not certain on. My logical guess is they are going to sell them."

The thought of those poor little children, many who do not speak English, are going to be sold to complete strangers made me cry. I lower my head as a tear rolls down my cheek. White Horse wipes away the tear with his thumb.

"I must save them. I am sure they are terrified," I cry. "I cannot allow those beautiful children to suffer because of what someone has done."

"Carrie, these men are extremely dangerous and heavily, heavily armed. They do not care who they hurt to get what they want. You are not able to get those children by yourself."

"I can't just sit back and do nothing," I argue. "White Horse, I have to find a way to stop them and bring those children home."

White Horse places his hands into mine.

"There is another reason I have come to you," he states. "I am leaving. I am going to go back to camp and regroup, and then I am going to find the children and bring them back to you. But I need something from you while I am gone."

"What is it?" I ask.

"I need for you to find out whatever you can on your sheriff. Ask around some of your old timers because this may have been going on for many years, and it is just now catching up to him."

"Alright."

"If I cannot bring the children back, then I will leave someone behind to watch them and come back and let you know where they are, and you can send your posse to get them. The reason I say this is that I cannot afford to let One Eye know that I am helping you because it could make matters worse, not only for you and your people but mine as well. So far, my people have not been touched, and I want to keep it that way."

"Do you even know where to start?" I ask him.

"I know they are going to the border where they will drop them off, and from there, they are in the hands of someone else. They will be travelling slowly and often resting, so the children will remain quiet. Most likely, they will cover the most ground at night when the children are at their least restless."

"The closest border must be at least a seven-to-ten-day ride."

"Yes, and that is riding almost nonstop. They will rest often, so they will only cover maybe twenty miles a day, if lucky."

"Thank you, White Horse," I say.

He grins and strokes my cheek.

"I may be tough outside, but inside, I am soft. Especially to you," he jesters. I smile widely, as I am certain that I am one of the few, if not the only one, who sees the soft side of White Horse.

"I love you," I say. He smiles widely.

"And it is our love that keeps me going." He then kisses me.

Koawa whistles. "I need to go. Your posse is close. Koawa will see you back to the meadow."

That is good because I am clueless about where I am. He kisses me goodbye before tucking into the woods. I cup my hand over my mouth, stopping myself from crying. I am so worried about him and am afraid to let him go. Koawa comes up to me, holding Sugar Foot's reins. He does not say a word to me, but with his eyes, he assures me that White Horse will be alright. I faintly grin. He holds my horse, helping me get on. He then leads me to safety.

He has a tender spot for Sugar Foot, petting him often and coaxing him through the woods with berries that he holds in his hand. I know very little of Koawa. He is quiet and never smiles. I am not certain if this is just an act to appear tough or if he is always this way. He is a very nice-looking man, resembling White Horse in many ways. He is smaller in stature and wears his hair in a shorter cut. I can see the family traits as he and White Horse could almost be twins. There is something about him that I like, perhaps because he resembles White Horse in so many ways; it is something that I hope one day I will figure out.

Later that same day, I go visit Stella. I figure now is the time to find out what I can about the sheriff. I am not really sure where to begin, and I hope Stella will think about it. Little did I know that she held the key all along. She pours me a cup of tea, and I fill her in on my visit with White Horse and his encounter with Roger. I tell her about the children and his theory on the reasons for the attacks. She, in return, has a story to tell me that blows me away.

"I remember a time," she starts. "When I was working for Hank. I was hired by Carl to entertain him for the night."

The thought sickens me. Stella agrees.

"He is not good, but anyway, he was drunk as usual and started bragging. He told me about a murder that the sheriff did to an Indian squaw."

My eyes grow huge. "He said that they were out looking for horse thieves when they came across an Indian squaw picking berries. He said the sheriff had been drinking a lot and was." She stopped for a moment. "Well, looking for something," she quoted with her fingers. "Anyway, the woman was protesting him, and the sheriff started messing with her in a very crude way. The more she fought him, the more excited he became. Carl bragged that he, too, was trying to get in on the fun and forced her to do things that a woman should not be forced to do. Like putting her mouth on something."

I can tell she was using her own words and left out what I was sure were graphic details. "Apparently, the woman bit the sheriff, and it angered him. He smacked the woman and, according to Carl, made her disrobe at gunpoint. He then humiliated her by forcing her to do very explicit sexual behavior. Carl said he joined along with them. He said Sid was refusing and wanted to leave, but the sheriff held a gun to him and told him he couldn't leave or he would kill him. He had no choice but to either watch or get involved. Carl said Sid refused to and turned his back. Carl and the sheriff then had their way with the woman. I guess afterwards, as the woman is lying there, he realizes what he did and knows if he got caught or if the woman told her people that he would be killed, so to keep her quiet, he killed her. He made Carl help bury her body. He told Sid that if he told anyone, he would make sure that he took the fall as well."

I am dumb struck. I am hearing something that I would read in a horror story, nothing that I would imagine could happen in real life. I always knew there was a hidden reason why the sheriff was always so protective of Carl. I never imagined it was this.

"Why didn't you ever tell me this?" I question her.

"You know Carl. He talks a lot, especially when he is drunk. I never took him seriously. It wasn't until you mentioned this that I even gave it a second thought," she says.

"You don't suppose that Carl is blackmailing the sheriff, do you?" I ask.

"What do you mean?" she asks.

"When Carl attacked me. You don't assume that Carl blackmailed the sheriff in some way?"

"By telling him, he would tell everyone what he did if he didn't drop the charges on him, which would make you look bad," she added. "I wouldn't put it past him."

"Exactly," I say.

"Too bad. The thing about it is that there is nothing we can do about it. It is pure speculation," she says.

I thought a moment back to a time when I was with Roger when he had to stitch up the sheriff. He told us he cut himself with a knife. It had made perfect sense, so Roger never questioned it.

"Roger," I say.

"Roger?" she questions.

"Yes, I remember an episode regarding the sheriff sometime back."

I stand up. "I need to check something with Roger."

"Good luck," she huffs. "After what happened to him today, White Horse may be a touchy subject."

"I don't care. I cannot ignore the situation, so I might as well face it and let him say what he has to say. It won't change my mind about White Horse. After he hears what I have to say about all this, he will change his attitude. I know Roger very well."

"Ok. Keep me posted."

"Thanks again, Stella."

I make my way down the main street and to the clinic, which is where I am certain Roger went after leaving the meadow. I know I am most likely walking into a hornet's nest, but I am ready to hear what he has to say and then he is going to listen to me.

Chapter Fourteen

Anna Johnson

Roger is at his desk with his head buried in a medical book when I walk in. He briefly looks over the rim of his glasses at me and resumes back to reading. He turns the page. I know him well enough to know he is stewing and not reading. Roger is very easygoing and well-tempered. It takes a lot to anger him, but after what happened today with him and White Horse, I know that Roger's blood is boiling.

"Roger," I calmly say.

"I forbid you to see him," he growls.

"You can't do that," I huff.

"I will tell Pa," he snaps, looking up at me.

"It will do you no good. I will still go with him."

He slams the book closed, pushes his chair back, and comes to his feet. He stomps around his desk, coming to my face. He points his finger at me.

"You listen here!" he says. "That man is a murderer and a thief. He killed the Millers. How in tarnation can you even comprehend that this man is good for you?"

Roger needs to vent, so I quietly just stand there and let him precede. He starts to pace the room. I know his heart is racing with rage. I cannot remember the last time I saw Roger so angry. He quickly turns around and looks at me.

"He has corrupted your mind into thinking he is good when he is not."

"He loves me," I state.

"That man is not capable of love. He is not even a man. He is barbaric, a savage, a heathen." Roger sits back down at his desk. "He deserves whatever comes to him. They all do."

"Shut up!" I yell. Roger struck a chord, and now he angered me. "You call yourself educated. Spending your day behind a book filled with foreign words. You are nothing but a pompous, self-centred, egotistical hypercritic," I bark. "You wouldn't know reality if it slapped you in the face."

I come over to Roger's desk and lean myself over it to get into his face.

"Now, if you want to go run to Father instead of being a man and facing what is coming, then you go right ahead. But I will be damn if I am going to sit back and watch another family die, and an innocent man be blamed for it. This heathen, you call him, is out risking his life and the lives of his warriors to help us. He is searching for the children, and unlike you, Roger, he doesn't judge a person by their color."

Roger grows still. I knew I had struck a nerve.

"Feel better?" he snaps.

"Yes," I say.

"Good, because I am telling the sheriff what I saw."

"No, Roger, you can't."

"Carrie, he has you so confused."

"Damnit, will you listen to me!" I yell. "You can't tell the sheriff because it is the sheriff who has gotten us in this mess to begin with."

"That's nonsense," he huffs.

"Is it? Well, let me tell you a little story that may change your opinion of our dear old sheriff."

Roger sits back in his chair and folds his arms over his chest.

"It seems a few years back, our sheriff met up with a Pawnee squaw. He had been drinking way more than he would normally. He saw the opportunity in a poor, innocent Indian woman. He raped and murdered that woman and had Carl and Sid help bury her. That is why the Pawnee are here. They are seeking revenge. That woman was a Chief's daughter, a very powerful Chief." Roger just rolls his eyes. I know he does not believe me.

"The sheriff is many things. Hell, I don't like him either, but he is no murderer or rapist."

"No? What about that time when you had to stitch him up when he claimed he was cut on a knife."

"What about it?" he snorts.

"That same day, Anna Johnson came into your office all bruised up and distraught. She claimed she was thrown from her horse. A few months later, she became pregnant and was so humiliated by Carl and the sheriff that she left town. When you asked her who the father was, she clammed up. She was too scared to say a word. Roger, think about it. She was raped."

Roger thinks for a moment. "Yes. I remember it. She had scratches on her and blood on her fingernails, which are not normal for falling from a horse. I remember she was very nervous when the sheriff came in."

Roger walks to his file drawer. He thumbs through it until he comes to the file he wants and pulls it out. He brings it over to his desk and opens it up. Roger is adamant about keeping good records. There is no patient who walks through his door, and he does not have a record of that.

"Here it is," he says. "I noted extreme bruising and swelling on the face and extremities. Several scratches and abrasions are seen on the upper thighs and abdomen. The patient seems distraught and nervous. Eyes are red and swollen due to heavy crying. Wounds are atypical to claims of fallen from a horse. The patient refuses any further examination." He closes the file. "I can remember Mr. Johnson coming into my office demanding who the father was. I had no idea. She was very quiet about it and very emotional when I tried to council her options."

He removes his glasses, takes one end of the earpiece, and puts it in his mouth, a common habit of his when he is trying to remember something or is deep in thought. "I remember now," he says. "When I questioned the sheriff on how he got cut, he didn't answer me. Carl was the one who told me he cut it with a knife. In fact, Sid was with them as well, and he was unusually quiet towards me. This was around the time you and him were courting."

"She left very quickly, if I remember. Didn't she?" I ask.

"Yes. It hit Mr. Johnson very hard. Anna was his only child. Eve died giving birth to her. That was before I became a doctor, but I remember when it happened."

"Roger, do you suppose that Mr. Johnson could help us out with any of this?"

He shakes his head. "Theodore refuses to talk about it. He just sits in that big house by himself. He will not let anyone in; not even Father can get him to open the door."

"We have to try?" I plead. "He may know more that will prove our suspicions are correct."

"We can, but be prepared to have the door slammed in your face."

"Roger, I am sorry I called you all those bad things."

"Carrie, I still do not trust the Chief, but I think he may be on to something that is worth investigating further."

"Roger, I have not been completely honest with you?"

"I never would have guessed," he jokes.

"Remember the day you sent me to Marianne Simpson?"

"Yes."

"Well, I delivered the baby."

"I am aware of that."

"After the baby was born, Marianne grew very anxious about where Harold was, and she had me go look for him. I found Harold by the creek bed."

"Carrie, you found him, and you said nothing?"

"I was on my way into town when I ran into a bear, and I was thrown off of Sugar Foot."

"Oh, my Lord Carrie."

"I tumbled down a hill to get away and, hit my head and was knocked out. When I came to, I was at Chief White Horse's camp."

"What!" he barks.

"Roger, he healed me back to health. He took care of me."

Roger is dumbfounded.

"See, look." I roll up my sleeve to reveal the scar on my arm that I received from the bear. Roger stands up and grabs my arm.

"When I was strong enough, he took me home. On our way home, we found three men camping out in the woods with arrows sticking out of them. One man was hanging in a tree. White Horse was quick at getting me out of there and getting me home. I could see the fear in his eyes. The night that the Miller died, I was not out taking a walk; I was with White Horse. We saw the fire and went running. White Horse and some of his warriors fought off the renegades. That is the only reason that Stella survived. You see, Roger, I have seen them personally. White Horse has nothing to do with it, and I am really scared for him."

For a few moments, Roger is speechless.

"Carrie," he finally says. "Why didn't you tell me this?"

"Because I gave White Horse my word that I wouldn't." He sighs deeply.

"Roger, he is out there right now looking for the children. He doesn't have to, but that is just the kindhearted man he is."

"Oh, Carrie," he sighs.

"The thought of him being out there looking for the children and being hunted down like a dog from our posse is so heavy in my heart because I love him, and I am so worried for him."

Roger opens his arms and we embraced. "I am sorry Carrie. I am sorry that you felt you couldn't come to me."

"I know Father is not going to accept this."

"Not right now. He may when we can prove to him that White Horse is innocent and the sheriff is guilty."

"But how do we prove it?" I cry.

"First, we talk to Mr. Johnson," he says.

"You said so yourself that he most likely will not talk to us."

"I know what I said, but after what you just told me, we must try."

The Johnson home is just outside of town on a huge hill overlooking Willow Creek.

At one time, this home was breathtakingly beautiful and Mr. Johnson was the wealthiest man in town. When Anna was forced to move out of town, he mentally shut down and now lives as a hermit. The once magnificent home is in need of desperate repair. Roger and I step onto the porch and knock on the door.

"Mr. Johnson, it is Doctor Briggs," Roger says through the door. We hear a rattle of locks and the door crack open.

"I am not in need of your services. Now go away," Mr. Johnson says.

"Mr. Johnson, we are hoping you will allow us in."

"Why?" he asks Roger.

"I need to ask you some questions about the day that Anna was attacked."

As Roger predicted, the door was closed in our faces as soon as Anna's name was mentioned.

"Mr. Johnson," Roger says through the door. "We want to get the person or person responsible for hurting your daughter."

"Go away," he roars.

"But Mr. Johnson," I beg. Roger grabs my arm.

"Give it up. He will not talk. We need to try something else."

We do as Mr. Johnson requests and leave. For the remainder of the day, we press on asking any old timers that may remember anything. We came up empty handed. By the time evening arrives, and dinner is cleaned up, I am exhausted.

Five days have passed; we have suffered more attacks and more deaths. Just as White Horse had predicted, the attacks are getting closer to town and are nearing the fork. Remembering what White Horse said about the fork in the road, I am becoming increasingly nervous as I know White Horse is not here to protect us; if God forbid, we are attacked.

Today, I woke up with severe nausea and have vomited three times just since breakfast. Although Roger and I are closer than ever at this moment, and he seems to be warming up to the idea of me being with White Horse, I still have not told him that I am pregnant. I am hoping I will be gone with White Horse before I show. I feel it is better this way that no one is told, as I know it will cause more hardship with Roger and my father when the town finds out, and we have enough to worry about as it is.

Stella and I visit her parent's grave site nearly every day. She seems to be doing better, and for that, I am grateful. Today, she tells me, as we are sitting under the apple tree, about a visitor she had the previous afternoon.

"I was sitting on my knees between my parents and talking to them when the warrior who rescued me from the Pawnee that night came up. He startled me. I wasn't sure what he wanted, but he handed me a flower and then knelt beside me. I put the flower down on the grave. He sat with me for a little bit and then left. I thought it sweet but then strange in a way."

It had to have been Blue Thunder, as I know Koawa is with White Horse, but I thought he would take Blue Thunder as well. Does this mean that White Horse is near? If so, why doesn't he come for me? It makes me curious yet at ease, as I am certain that Blue Thunder was left here to protect me.

"That is sweet," I say.

"He is sort of cute too. In a strange way."

I chuckle. Stella can be very flamboyant at times. I blame it on her past life when she was one of Hank's saloon girls.

"Say something to him," I suggest.

"He doesn't speak English."

"That does not mean he does not understand you. He is reaching out to you, trying to be a friend. I think that says a lot about him."

"Is that what attracted you to White Horse?" she wonders.

"No, White Horse is different. I can't explain it. He just makes my insides tingle. He gives me chills every time I look at him. He is tough and hard on the outside but so gentle and kind on the inside."

"You are in love with him, aren't you?"

"Very much so."

"Does he know about the baby?"

"No, only you, and it better stay that way," I warn.

"I will not say a word. I told you that already."

"You are a good friend, Stella. You truly are."

She looks out at the hills.

"Carrie, look," she says as she points.

I smile, as not standing far away I see Blue Thunder. We stand as he comes towards us. Stella and I walk down the hill, as he jumps off his horse. I know nothing about Blue Thunder, but I assume he does not speak any English. We stand there and watch him, as he approaches.

"Chief White Horse?" I ask him.

He understands and shakes his head no. Disappointed, I leave Stella and him alone and go home.

Chapter Fifteen

Devil's Elbow

Willow Creek is virtually a ghost town. Many businesses are closed, school is canceled, and our population is nearly down to nothing. Father keeps the church open and spends a great deal of his time there. Between burying the dead and preaching to the ones who remain about keeping our faith, he is incredibly busy. Roger and I are both concerned about him, as he appears more tired and is not taking care of himself like he should be. Our posse is gone all the time. Shifts are done so the men can rest. Hank is keeping the saloon open, although there is no business except for the men on the posse when their shift ends. Hank, for the most part, stays in town as he feels someone has to be here to protect the women if they should be attacked.

I mentioned the fork in the road to Roger and what White Horse thought may happen, and because of that, we, too, are staying in town as well. We rented a room at the boarding house along with several other women and their children whose husbands are part of the posse. It is crowded, but we are making do. Roger and I are having no luck finding out anything further about Anna Johnson or an Indian squaw. We are both certain that Anna was raped and had conceived because of it. We are both certain that the child was the sheriff, and he somehow scared her enough or bought her off and got her out of town. Roger also believes that Carl was most likely involved, as he was the one who brought the sheriff in. We have said nothing to father about any of this, as I am not going to chance that White Horse's name will come up.

So far Roger is keeping my secret. I personally feel it is not for me, but that he fears White Horse and feels he will carry out his threat if he tells. My morning sickness is not any better and I am so tired all the time. So far, I am able to avoid Roger with my sudden urge to run to the outhouse, but with the dark circles that are starting to form under my eyes it is harder to avoid his to questions on how I am feeling.

Stella goes to her parents' graveside every day, and lately, she has refused any company. This does not make Hank happy. I am certain as for the reason why she is refusing to have anyone go with her is because she is meeting up with Blue Thunder. I am resting in my room when I hear a knock on my door.

"Come in," I say.

The door opens, and Stella comes in.

"I have to talk to you," she says, rushing in and closing the door behind her.

"Come sit down."

She joins me at the foot of the bed.

"I have a confession," she says.

"Yes."

"For the last three days, I have been meeting Blue Thunder under the apple tree."

"I figured as much," I smile.

"I knew you did, but today, when we met, something happened."

"What?" I ask.

"I saw White Horse."

My eyes grow wide. "Are you sure?" I ask her.

"Yes, Carrie, and he told me to tell you to meet him at Devil's Elbow at dusk and come to the apple tree, and Blue Thunder will show you the way."

"How does he look?"

"He looks tired. He did not stay long, and neither did Blue Thunder. I hope I didn't get Blue Thunder in any trouble with his Chief. I would feel terrible if I did."

"I don't think you did." I think for a moment. "Dusk," I say. "Hmmm. That may be tricky."

"What do you mean?" she asks.

"No one is to leave Willow Creek after dusk. How am I going to get away from Roger?"

"Tell them that you will be with me in my room. I will back you up, and when you return, come to my room so it looks legit."

"I hate to lie. I have already lied so much to both Roger and Father."

"You want to meet White Horse, don't you?" she asks.

"Yes, of course."

"Then you are going to have to do this."

"How am I going to get out of town without being detected? Hank is watching all of us."

"Not me. If I tell him I am going to my parent's grave along with you, he won't give it a second thought. We will take the wagon, so when I come back, if someone questions it, I can tell them you got tuckered and you are asleep in the back."

Stella always thinks of everything and has always been quick on her toes when it comes time to covering up a lie. Unfortunately, Stella is a very good liar and has had a lot of practice with it.

"That will work." I give her a hug. "You are a great friend."

"I know," she smiles. "And a sly one, too," she giggles.

She stands up, ready to leave.

"Oh, I nearly forgot. He told me to tell you to bring your shawl."

"Ok." I think it is odd that he requests that I bring it, as the evenings are quite warm.

Stella's plan works without a hitch. She loaned me one of her shawls, and we made our way to the apple tree. Blue Thunder is waiting for us when we arrive. He helps me onto his horse, then brings himself up behind me. He grins at Stella. I am certain that the two of them are sweet on each other. I just hope Stella is careful enough and doesn't allow Blue Thunder to get caught. They exchange their own flirtatious grin before we walk off.

Blue Thunder says not a word. His whole concentration is on the task at hand. He has a job to do for his Chief, and he is taking it seriously. He is quick and guides his horse with ease, in total control, up the steep rocky hills. He takes the steeper and longer way into the canyon. Darkness has come upon us, and the little moon shining is making the ride very creepy. I hear the wolf's howl. They sound very close. Blue Thunder pays no attention and continues.

We are in the canyon. Looking out, I can see the top of Devil's Elbow. We are very close. Blue Thunder starts to climb the canyon, pushing his horse with several kicks to move up the steep rocky incline. We come to level land and ride further on. He then climbs again getting on top of the summit. He then stops his horse and jumps off. He takes my hand and I slide off. Grabbing his horse's reins, we then continue the rest of the way on foot. It is so dark I can barely see him only a few inches from me. We walk what seems like miles. The terrain is extremely rocky and I am very nervous about slipping, making my walk very slow. Blue Thunder stops briefly allowing me to catch up. We walk a few more minutes when we stop.

He then speaks his tongue. I see Koawa climb up the steep hill as if it were nothing and walk up to us. They exchange their tongue back and forth. Blue Thunder then takes his horse and guides it down the incline. I am left alone with Koawa.

"Come," he says.

I follow him. Despite what White Horse has told me about Koawa, I fear him more than I fear Minoke. He is harsh, stone-faced, and has eyes that pierce your heart. Clearly, White Horse inherited all the charm. He takes me a short distance to the side of the canyon. I watch him lean over and remove some brush, revealing an opening to a cave.

"I will be damn," I think. "Very clever."

"Go," he orders.

I of course go, hoping that White Horse is in there. Koawa places the brush back up against the opening of the cave, leaving me in complete darkness.

"White Horse," I call out. "Are you in here?"

"Over here, my love," I hear, a good distance away.

"Where?"

"Follow my voice," he says.

"It is so dark in here."

"Place your hand on the wall and follow it down."

I do as I am instructed. The walls are wet and slimy. The cave is damp and cold. "I am doing it," I tell him.

"Good," he says. His voice is closer. "Just keep coming."

"How far?" I ask him.

I then feel a hand on top of mine.

"Not much further," he says.

I smile because he is right in front of me. I take his hand, and he guides me further until I see a light from a fire. We come to a much larger and more well-lit area of the cave. I can clearly see White Horse. I rush into his arms, and we embrace tightly.

"Come," he says, motioning for me to follow him. "Sit."

He takes me to a pelt made from an elk, where I sit down. I spot a chicken roasting over his fire. It appears as if it is done. White Horse checks it and removes it from the fire.

"Care to join me?" he asks.

"No, honey, I am fine. Thank you."

"Forgive me. I am usually a better host, but I have not eaten for two days, and I am very hungry."

"Why haven't you eaten in two days?" I ask him.

"It has not been safe enough to start a fire, so I go without."

"And your men? I saw no fire when I arrived."

"They will start one soon, and then they too will eat."

He starts ripping the chicken off the stick and eating it. By the way he inhales it instead of chewing it, he is indeed very hungry.

"How long have you been here?" I ask him.

"Since last night. I went to your barn to find you, and I slept there, but you never arrived. Blue Thunder told me you are staying in town, which is good. He told me about meeting your friend at the apple tree. I went with him this morning in the hope of finding you. She told me she would tell you."

He looks over at me. "You can trust her? Right?"

"Oh yes, White Horse. Like you do, Koawa."

He nods his head and bites off another big piece of meat; this time, he chews.

"Good," he says when he swallows. "I have been very worried about you," he continues. "I left Blue Thunder here to watch over you and your family in case your home was attacked."

"They are getting close to the fork."

"Yes. I am aware of that?"

He nearly devours the whole chicken in about five minutes. I have never seen someone eat so fast or so hungry.

"Did you find out anything?" he asks me.

"Yes."

I filled White Horse in on Anna Johnson, the conversation with Roger, and the episode of the sheriff getting his stitches. He said it all makes sense. He is certain the target is the sheriff, and since he is considered the Chief of Willow Creek, all of us are falling victims.

"Pretty clever," he comments. "One Eye is no fool."

"White Horse, what about the children. Did you find them?" I ask.

He takes his final bite and pulls the remainder of the chicken, which mainly is the head and feet, off the stick and tosses it into the fire. He leans back against the damp wall. It is then that I see how tired he really looks. I hear him sigh deeply.

"We make it to the border," he huskily says. "We find a handful of Pawnee camped out. They are small enough to take. We went in, hoping to get the children, but they did not have them."

"Oh no," I cry.

"I get one of them to talk. He tells me that they hid the children and came to the border to get the men who were going to buy them and bring them to them because the children were moving too slow, and your posse was getting too close."

"Did he tell you where they were?" I wonder.

White Horse nods his head yes.

"The other men were killed. I took him with us so he could show us where they were. He attempted to escape during the night. Koawa caught him. The snake closed his mouth and spoke no further. I had no choice; I couldn't risk another escape and him finding his leader and our lives being in jeopardy or my camp being attacked when my best warriors are gone, so I had him killed."

"Oh," I mumble.

"Red Hawk, who is a member of a neighboring Lakota tribe, did the honors."

"So, you do not know where they are at?" I ask.

White Horse nods. "Red Hawk told me that the warrior knew he was going to die and gave him a clue where they were."

"Where?"

"Carrie, they are right under your nose. A day's ride from here."

"Where are they."

"It took us a while to find exactly where they were. Red Hawk remembered a place that he had found while on a vision quest. He said it is a cave a lot like this one, only much bigger, and the opening is very well hidden by big rocks. He said he went in there and followed it for a very long time until he saw a light. When he came to the light and stepped out, he said it was the most amazing thing that he had ever seen. Green trees everywhere and a river with many fish and springs. A huge waterfall came rushing down. He started walking around and came to the waterfall. He went behind it and sat for the longest time until he had a vision.

We went and checked it out. He was right. It is huge. Very steep for our horses. We had to ride a single file for a good distance. We came to the light." He faintly grins. "Carrie, I have never seen such a sight. The earth touched the sky. This place is paradise. We see signs of recent activity almost immediately. I pick up a small doll that I am certain belonged to one of the children. I knew they were close. We all just start looking for anything that may open to another cave. Koawa finds a sharp rock sticking out behind the waterfall. He thought it strange as it didn't look like the others. He pulls and is amazed when the wall opens."

"It opens?" I gasp.

"It opens," he smiles. "All of us were surprised when we saw it open.

Running Bear refuses to go in. He said it would be filled with bad spirits if a mountain just opened. But Koawa and I went in. At first, we see nothing, but then, as we turn to go down another corridor, we spot the children. They are dirty and hungry, but otherwise, they are well. It took me some time, but one little girl who speaks a little English recognized her doll and wanted it back. I told her who I was. She told me that some bad Indians had taken them and she wanted to go home. I told her we would be back very soon.

I saw food trays and a water basket, so I am certain that someone is feeding them. We left them and remained there, hidden, to see if anyone showed up. We waited until dark when we saw a woman return with food. We watched her leave and followed her. We follow her to a camp where we see One Eye and the other warriors. We left before we were spotted. Running Bear is staying back along with his warriors to keep an eye on the children and One Eye."

"Why didn't you bring them back?" I ask.

"For several reasons," he explains. "If I was to take them, One Eye would have come after us, leaving the children at risk of getting hurt. By leaving them there, it allows us more time to make up a plan to rescue these children and stop the attacks. The children are safe for the moment. It will take One Eye a little time to realize that the men he sent on are not coming back. He has already started his plan to come to Willow Creek. It will take him away from the children long enough for us to get them and bring them back. By the time he realizes the children are gone, you will be ready to fight them off."

"How will we know when that time comes?"

White Horse picks up a stick and draws a circle in the dirt. He draws several circles inside the larger one.

"Here is Willow Creek," he points out. "Here is your home, and here is the fork. One of two things will happen. They have already come to the fork. If they stop their attacks, then that is bad because that means he is regrouping a very large number of warriors, and the attack on Willow Creek will be catastrophic. If the attacks continue the same path, I believe the right side of the fork will be hit."

I live on the left. I am relieved. "The reason I think this is you have two very large buildings to the right of the fork that are on that path."

He drew two X's. "Your saloon and your church. When these are hit, that is your warning. You may have a day, or you may have longer. It will all depend on how soon he realizes the children are missing."

"So, it is good if we have more attacks."

"Yes, because that will mean that they are not onto us, and that will allow us more time to get ready."

"I see," I say.

"Now, you must understand this man is ruthless and incredibly smart. You must know his mind if you are going to stop these attacks. You will not be able to run from him because he is on a mission, and he will not stop until he is dead or everyone in Willow Creek is."

"How do we stop him?"

"You will have to have a plan to outsmart him."

"And you have that plan? Don't you?" I smirk.

"Yes. I can stop him, but not by myself."

"What do you need?" I ask him.

"I need many things, but mainly, I need to get into Willow Creek."

"White Horse, they will kill you."

"In order to stop these attacks, we must be one step ahead of them, and for that to happen, I need to get into Willow Creek. Next to your brother, who do you trust that will listen to you when you tell them about me?"

"There is only one who has always been there for me when I needed help, and that is Hank."

"Tell me about him," he says.

"Hank owns the saloon. He is also on the posse. He is the only man that the sheriff fears. Hank does not really like him, especially since..."

I stop myself. I do not feel this is the time to tell White Horse about Carl.

"Well, let me just say Hank does not like his judgment, and they butt heads about it all the time."

"And he will listen to you?"

"Hank will do anything for me. I am certain he will."

"Alright. Then you need to talk to him and tell him everything. Then you have him meet me in the meadow. He is to come unarmed and alone. My men will be watching him. He tries anything, and he is a dead man."

"I will let him know."

"There is one more thing that I will need from you."

"What?" I ask.

"I will need for you to give me a detailed map of Willow Creek."

"Ok, that should be easy enough," I say.

"Good," he smiles.

I lean my head back, pulling my shawl closer around me. I close my eyes. I am feeling so overwhelmed, frustrated, and exhausted. White Horse strokes my cheek.

"You alright?" he asks.

I open my eyes to look at him. I look around at where he is staying. He is living like an animal that is being hunted. It is too much to absorb, and I start to cry.

"No," I say.

"Why is your heart so heavy?" he consoles.

"I am so worried about you. I can't sleep. I can't eat. I am so frightened of you being killed."

"I am fine, my love." He wipes a tear from my Eye.

"You are living like a wild animal being hunted. And for what? Because of some filthy bastard who likes to play with women."

He takes me into his arms. "Shh," he consoles. "It will be all over soon, my love. I promise, and then you and I will be together."

I cling to White Horse. I need his strong arms wrapped around me to feel secure. I worry so much for him, fearing what will happen if, God forbid, he gets caught. White Horse is good, and with Koawa, he is even better, but is he good enough to stay hidden and alive? I wonder if perhaps I should tell him about the baby, but quickly decide against it for fear it would distract him. I need his mind and thoughts to remain clear. Now isn't the time to think of me. What would I do if I lost him? Where would my child and I go? I know I cannot stay here, and I hardly think the Lakotas will take me in. I cannot lose him. Oh, dear Lord, just keep him safe

Chapter Sixteen

The Confidant

Once again, I find myself leaving White Horse. It is getting harder and harder to tell him goodbye. His reassurance that soon everything will come to an end and we will be together forever makes the ride back to the apple tree more bearable. I walk along the road to meet Stella, passing our homestead along the way. Our home so far has been spared, and everything is untouched. There are signs that either Roger or my father have been here, as the chickens have been fed, and there is freshly laid hay for the horses.

A tiny tear begins to form, as I think that one day soon, I will be leaving this home to never see it again. I look at my garden growing diligently. I have always taken great pride in it and wonder if Father and Roger will keep up with it. I wish I could stay here for the little time that remains, but I know I am not safe and quickly walk on by.

I head into Willow Creek, just passing the Johnson home, wondering if Mr. Johnson will ever stop missing his daughter and come outside. I cross the bridge and enter the main street. The town is eerily quiet, almost appearing as if it is haunted. I am literally the only one on the street. I make my way into the saloon. I stop short when I see Sid and Carl at a table playing cards. Sid focuses back on his cards. Carl just smirks with a snarl in his mouth. I race past them and go to the back, where I will find Hank.

"Howdy," he says.

I close the door behind me. There is no way I am taking a chance of being overheard. I quickly got to the point of my visit.

"I need your help," I tell him.

"What is on your mind?" he asks.

Hank is watering down his whisky, something he has done for years. I have always known he did, but have sworn to keep his secret, now I am hoping he will keep mine.

"You may want to sit down for this," I suggest.

"This sounds serious," he says.

"It is," I answer.

"Well, alright then."

He finds a chair for both of us, and we sit down. I sigh deeply as I think about where to begin. Hank is very easy to talk to, but when I am about ready to tell him, I am not sure how he will behave. He sees my hesitation.

"Just tell me?" he coaxes.

"I just don't know where to begin," I say.

"Just spit it out."

"I'm pregnant," I tell him.

He about falls out of his chair.

"Are you sure?" he finally asks after getting over the initial shock.

"Pretty sure," I answer.

"Whoa," he says. "I was not expecting that."

"Me either."

"May I ask who the father is?"

"Well," I curl my lip. "It is Chief White Horse."

Hank comes unglued. I honestly thought he was going to toss his chair through the window.

"Did that son of a bitch rape you!" he yells.

I didn't want Carl or Sid to overhear. I quickly go to the door and peek out, surprisingly they are gone and Hank and I are alone. I close the door behind me.

"Hank, calm down. It is not what you think," I say, placing my hands on his broad chest and gently coaxing him to sit back down.

His nostrils are flaring just with the thought of what he assumes has happened.

"I told you this for a reason. I need your help, but you must keep this quiet. No one must know about my condition."

"You have some explaining to do," he bellyaches.

"And I will." I reach up on the counter and hand Hank a whiskey.

"You may need this," I tell him.

He starts to drink it as I begin my story. I begin to tell Hank everything, starting with Marianne Simpson and working my way up. I tell him about my secret courtship with White Horse, my bear attack, the three men in the woods, the night the Millers died, the Pawnee squaw, Anna Johnson, and my conversation with White Horse in the cave. By the time I am finished, he is completely convinced that White Horse is innocent and the sheriff is a dirty lying snake.

I told him about Roger and our theory on why Carl was not arrested when he attacked me. He agrees. He also agrees to meet with White Horse and tells me he will make the sheriff agree to allow him in. He promises to keep my secret about me being pregnant and my love for White Horse. Relieved that he agrees to help me, I give him a huge hug.

"Thank you, Hank," I say.

"It appears it is the Chief that we need to thank."

"Remember, you go alone and unarmed," I caution him.

"I know."

We both come to a stand. When I do, I become extremely dizzy and faint. Hank is quick to react and carries me, rushing me to the clinic. I wake in the comfort of the clinic's bed. Roger and Hank are both looking down at me. Roger has his stethoscope on my chest.

"What happened?" I ask, still dazed and confused.

"You fainted," Roger said.

I remember and look over at Hank. What has he told Roger? He slightly nods his head, reassuring me that my secret is still safe.

"Now that I know she is alright. I have something to attend to," he says.

By the look he gives me, I know he is going to the meadow to meet White Horse. I slightly grin at him. He then excuses himself and leaves the room. Father quickly rushes in and is down by my side. He takes my hand into his.

"Child," he says. "Are you alright?"

"Yes, Father, I will be fine. I just got a little dizzy."

"Oh? Why would you be dizzy?" He turns to face Roger. "Is this serious, son?" he asks.

"I do not think so, Pa," Roger reassures. "But I will need to examine her further to be sure."

"Oh, Roger, really," I protest. "That is not necessary. I am feeling much better."

"Nonsense child. I insist you have your brother check you out. You have been looking very tired lately."

"But Father," I argue.

"Enough," he states. "There will be no argument. You will allow your brother to examine you, and that is final."

Father is a genuine, kind, and loving man who has never raised his voice at us. He never had to, as we always got his point across by his tone of voice. No matter how much I really don't want Roger to examine me because I know my condition will be known. I do as I am ordered and agree.

"You will keep me posted." Father isn't asking Roger. He is telling him.

"I will be right outside," he tells me and then leaves the room.

Roger draws the curtain behind him.

"Look, Roger, you can just pretend for Father's sake that you have examined me and…"

"Shut Up!" he barks.

"Excuse me?" I say.

"How long do you think you can play the game?"

"I am afraid I do not understand."

"You can fool Pa, but Carrie, you know better than to try to fool me."

"I assure you I do not know what you are talking about."

"His protection for you, you sneaking around; tell Carrie, are you his love slave, or are you just his whore?"

I am appalled and surprised to hear him consider it.

"You bastard," I snap." Who the hell do you think you are?"

"Why else would you sleep with him?"

"What makes you think I have?" I argue.

"Excessive fatigue, fainting; I have seen you rush to the privy, no doubt to vomit. Tell me, Carrie, when was your last monthly?"

"That is none of your business!" I snap.

"I can find out. A simple vaginal exam will answer my question."

"You will not!" I snap.

"What are you afraid of?" He snaps back. "I am a doctor, and you are my patient."

"I am your sister," I tell him.

"No. You are afraid of the truth."

He leans over on the bed and into my face.

"That's right, I forgot you do not know what truth is anymore. All you do is live in a lie." I kicked his elbow with my foot.

"You pig," I glare.

"No," he argues. "Your Chief is the pig. I should."

"What, Roger," I egg on. "You should go run for help. You are nothing but a coward. You won't tell anybody about this or about him because you are too afraid of what he will do to you."

I have struck a nerve.

"You don't scare me, and you sure in the hell don't scare White Horse."

He lowers his head and starts scuffing with his chin, a habit he has when he is trying to control his temper.

"Yes, Roger, I am pregnant." I glare. Just the word makes him shiver.

"And when these attacks are done, I will leave with him. Father will not find out about this. I will tell him about White Horse in my own way, on my own time. He will never know about this child because I will be long gone before there are any signs that I am pregnant."

"Not necessarily Carrie. A woman of your stature will most likely show early on," he argues.

"Within a few weeks, I will be gone, and no one will be the wiser. Father won't have to deal with the humiliation of seeing me pregnant. The town will go easy on him if he tells them I have simply moved on."

"Have you told the Chief?"

"No," I answer. "Not yet."

"What makes you so sure he will accept this and not toss you with yesterday's trash or kill you because now you are no use for him."

"He will never do that. When all this is done, I will leave with him with welcome arms. It is then that I will tell him I am carrying his child. Everything will work out just fine."

"For your sake, Carrie, I hope you are right. Because if Carl finds out about this, it will be hard not only on you but also on Pa."

He leans forward on the bed. "You see, Carrie, he is a man of the cloth, and his reputation matters a hell of a lot more than yours. He is in no condition to deal with this. For his sake, Carrie, you need to leave town as soon as possible."

"Why, what is wrong with him?" I ask.

Roger doesn't answer. He stands up and opens the curtain.

"Roger, what is wrong with Father?" I demand to know.

"Just leave Carrie because I can't deal with this anymore."

"Roger, what is wrong with him?"

"You are welcome to stay here where you can rest because that is what you need right now. I will be back soon." He turns to walk away, ignoring my question. "And Carrie," he says. "You are wrong. I am not afraid of White Horse. I am keeping your dirty little lie for Pa's sake, not because I care what happens to you. You messed up your own life, Carrie. There is nothing more I can do."

I have never seen Roger so cold. I know he is hurt and angry. I was cruel to him, and for that, I am wrong. I love my brother, and I know he loves me. He just needs time. I roll over to my side and close my eyes. His callous words hit me hard. I wipe a tear from my cheek. I hear the door open, and Roger walks out.

"She is resting," I hear him mumble to my father.

 "Is she alright, son?" he asks.

"She is fine." I then hear the door close and the sound of both their boots walking off.

Hank makes his way to the meadow. He quickly stops when he sees three heavily armed warriors standing on a hill. Hank puts his hands up as he dismounts his horse. His eyes are thick on the two warriors that are pointing a gun at him. Koawa grabs Hank's reins.

"Carrie sent me," Hank says to the Chief, who hasn't moved a step.

"Are you Hank?" White Horse asks.

"Yes, and I am unarmed and alone."

White Horse speaks his tongue to Blue Thunder. Blue Thunder then proceeds in making certain Hank is unarmed. When he is cleared, it is then White Horse orders his two warriors to put down their weapons.

"Be warned," he says. "You only see two men; if you are to betray me, many more will come out of the trees, and you will meet their wrath."

"Understood," Hank says. "Carrie says you can help us."

"That I can. She assures me you can be trusted."

"I am only here because of her," Hank assures him.

"Then we have something in common. Come, we will smoke."

Hank follows the Chief up the hill and into the woods. He glances around and wonders to himself just how many warriors are indeed watching him. Can he trust the Chief? Has Carrie been too naive to think she can? He is left with little time to wonder as the warrior holding his horse is nudging him along. He follows the Chief to a secluded area well tucked behind some trees. He is ordered to sit across from the Chief on the ground with his two warriors surrounding him. He is then offered a pipe that the Chief just inhaled out of. It is then, after the smoke, that the Chief gets to the reason for the visit.

A few hours later, I heard a rap on the door. The handle turns, and Hank comes in.

"How are you feeling?" he asks.

"Better. Roger knows the truth."

"How did he take it?"

"Not well." Hank sits down in the chair.

"I am sorry for this," he says. "I have something to say that may cheer you up."

"What?" I ask.

"I met with the Chief."

"How did it go?"

"Very well. We passed his peace pipe back and forth several times, and then we talked."

"What do you think?"

"I think his idea on stopping these attacks is brilliant."

I am relieved. "So now, what do we do?" I ask him.

"I will get him into Willow Creek."

"How are you going to do that?" I wonder.

"I told the Chief that I will meet him and his warriors in the meadow this time tomorrow, and until then, I will be speaking with the sheriff and persuading him that it is in the best interest of the town to speak with him."

"You make it sound so simple." I still doubt that Hank can pull it off.

"I have my ways of making people reason with me," he smiles. I smile back because I am certain he does.

"You didn't tell him about me? Did you?" I question.

"I wasn't sure if he knew, so I didn't say a thing."

"Thank you, Hank." I take his hand. "Thank you so much." I start to cry.

"Now, woman, stop your tears. I can't stand tears," he says.

"I can't help it. Roger said something that is bothering me."

"What did he say?"

"That Father is in no condition to deal with my problems right now."

"He is just angry. He knows how close you are to your father and is trying to just scare you. Your father is fine."

"Are you sure?"

"Of course I am sure," he grins.

Hank has the cutest smile that few ever see. Sometimes, I wonder what life would have been like if Hank and I were a couple. At times, I envy Stella because of it, but I am happy now and grateful that fate took its own path and gave me White Horse.

"Roger told me he wasn't scared of the Chief and that he is only keeping my dirty little lie for my father's sake." Hank just looked at me.

"Carrie. I have yet to meet a man that I feel I could go Yella on until today. I would not want to anger that man. Roger is full of shit."

"Do you think I am wrong to trust him?"

"Chief White Horse?" he asks. I nodded my head yes.

"I do not know the man well enough to answer that, but I will tell you this. When I asked him why he was endangering his life and the life of his warriors to fight these renegades, he told me because of his Prairie Dawn."

I smiled. "He had to explain to me who that was. Afterward, I knew under that tough skin there is a man of compassion, not only for you but for the children."

Hank keeps me company for a little while longer until the sheriff rides into town. He said that it was his cue to leave and excuse himself. From the clinic window, I watch Hank walk by and make his way to the sheriff's office. I briefly close my eyes and pray for the dear Lord to be with Hank, as Willow Creek's fate lies in his hands.

Chapter Seventeen

The Stand Off

I woke up from a well-deserved nap with a knock on the door and my father stepping in, holding a plate of food.

"Hello, my child," he greets with a smile. "Feeling any better?"

"Oh yes, Father," I say, sitting up in bed. "Much better."

"That is good news. I thought you may be hungry."

"I am," I say.

"Roger told me to keep it light because your stomach is upset, so I had Esther make you a bowl of her chicken noodle soup."

Esther is a cook at the town restaurant. She is one of the few that has refused to leave. Her husband Clyde works at the livery.

"It smells delicious," I rave.

"Is there ever anything that our dear Esther makes that is not delicious?" Father says as he places the tray with the soup on it over my lap.

He removes the lid and picks up the crackers.

"Father, I can feed myself," I smile.

"Oh, dear me," he blushes. "I reckon you can."

I chuckle to myself. I then became somewhat sad. How on earth am I going to get myself to leave him? I catch him watching me as I lift my spoon. I gulp back any tears that may be surfacing and dip the spoon in my bowl.

"I saw Hank on my way here," he says.

"Oh?"

"Yes, he said that he would be by shortly and that he had something to tell us. He asked Roger to join us. Sounds serious."

I am assuming Father does not know what Hank is up to and unless Roger told him, he is also unaware of Anna Johnson as well.

"Father, have you spoken to Roger?"

"Yes, he told me about your suspicions on Anna Johnson and the reason behind the attacks. I remember when Anna abruptly left town, and I thought it was odd that the sheriff bought her a ticket and escorted the stage out of town. I knew something was off with it, but I never imagined what it was."

"So, you believe it could be true?"

"Yes, I do believe it is."

"And what about the Pawnee Squaw?"

"I believe he did that as well and that Carl was there and blackmailed him, and that is why the charges were dropped when he attacked you."

"And the entire town is paying the price for his deception."

"It looks like that way."

"And are your thoughts on the Chief?"

"I believe he can help, but I question as to why he would."

I sip some soup when the door opens, and Roger and Hank step in. Roger pays no attention to me and walks over to Father, sitting down in the chair beside him.

"I have brought you all here because I just got done talking to the sheriff," Hank says.

"What did he say?" My father asks.

"He didn't admit to anything. However, he did agree to speak with the Chief."

"Well, that is a start," Father says.

"Yes. He agrees to allow Chief White Horse and his warriors into Willow Creek."

"You think he can be trusted?" I asked Hank.

"We are talking about the sheriff, but I do believe that the sheriff is realizing that he is over his head and is accepting help."

"He could have just called the Army in," Roger states.

"Apparently, he tried, but the Army is not interested in helping. They said that they have more important matters to attend to and that they do not consider stolen children an urgent matter."

"Something does not add up there," Roger says.

"I know," Hank agrees.

"Sounds like he does not want to raise suspicion on himself and chance an investigation."

"He would rather allow the people he is sworn to protect to die to save his own ass," Roger says.

"Good Lord," Father huffs. "When are you bringing the Chief here?"

"Tomorrow morning. And I would like you both here just in case."

"I wouldn't miss this for anything," Roger smirks.

"What I do not understand," Father states. "If the Chief knows where the children are, then why did he not tell us or bring them back here himself?"

"I asked him the same question, Reverend, and he told me that the place is so well hidden that he could not possibly explain to anyone where it is, and he couldn't bring the children back because he could not risk them getting hurt."

"I see. The thought of the children out there with those monsters is chilling."

"He has assured me that they are safe."

"I think Mr. Skelov should be here tomorrow," Roger suggests.

"I think he will appreciate that," Father says.

"I just came from there, and they are just sick and worried about their children," Roger declares.

"I don't blame them. I would be too," I comment.

"Well, children," my father says, coming to his feet. "I need to set up the church for tonight in case we have any visitors."

"May I help you, father?" I ask.

"Thank you, my dear, but I want you to rest more."

"I am feeling much better, Father." He looks over at Roger.

"She needs her rest," he mumbles. Damn you, Roger, I think.

"Doctor's orders," my father says. He leans down and kisses my cheek.

"I will be back before you sleep tonight to check on you."

One by one I watch the men leave. Roger looks across the room at me and just shakes his head before closing the door behind him.

Another day is on us. I wake to the morning sun with a quick run to the outhouse, where I vomit. My stomach is in knots. I am so nauseous I can hardly stand up. Esther brought me breakfast. It is huge and looks divine, but with the way my stomach is today, I cannot eat it. The smell is sickening. I again make another run to the outhouse. So far, this is the worst morning sickness I have had. I crawl back into bed and close my eyes. Within a few minutes, I fall back asleep. I am awakened when I hear a commotion outside. I crawl out of bed and look out the window. The deserted town begins to emerge with people, and all eyes are on the bridge.

I slip on my slippers and robe and step outside. When I open the door, I immediately discover what the commotion is. I see Hank on horseback coming across the bridge, and behind him,

I see White Horse and several of his warriors. We make brief eye contact when he rides past me.

The crowd starts to follow Hank and the warriors down the streets to the center square, where the sheriff's office and jail are located on one of the corners. I follow along as well. I spot Carl just outside the saloon. He steps down off the platform and walks alongside the warriors as they pass. He has the most God-awful look on his face that I do not trust. I followed close behind him. I glance across the street and spot Sid, who is keeping exact steps with Carl from the other side of the street. I become very nervous as I am certain they are up to something.

Hank brings the warriors to a stop in the middle of the street. The sheriff comes down to the bottom step as Hank dismounts.

"Sheriff, this is Chief White Horse," Hank begins, "of the Lakota Sioux tribe."

"I know who he is," he growls. "What do you want?"

"He has come to help," Hank states.

"We need no help," he snaps.

Hank is through with being formal. His demeanor instantly changes. His patience is gone.

"Now you see here, we made a deal," he growls.

"No!" the sheriff yells.

He comes down off the step. I glanced across the street at Sid. So far, he is doing nothing but watching. I look up the street and find a way to Carl. He isn't looking as innocent. I spotted out of the corner of my eye a horse tied to a post with a rifle in the gun boot.

"My mind has changed. I have nothing else to say."

The sheriff looks over at White Horse, who is sitting high on his horse.

"Heed my warning and leave our territory before every one of you is killed," he hisses.

That hit a nerve with White Horse. I can see him grinding his teeth. Hank is furious.

"You gave me your word," he growls.

"I gave you nothing. You have five minutes to leave with them, or all of you will be shot where you are sitting."

I see Carl unlatch his holster along with Sid.

"I assure you sheriff," Hank snaps," unless you want more bloodshed, you may want to think twice about that. Look around sheriff."

Hank points. Our eyes turn wide when we see a fair number of Lakota warriors perched on top of buildings and hills all around us. This is when Sid gets smart and releases his grip on his gun. Carl is not as wise. I glance at the rifle again in the gun boot and then over at Carl. He is now releasing his gun and has it drawn. I gasp. I have to do something before this damn idiot gets us all killed. I see him point his gun at White Horse. I quickly ran to the gun boot, removed the rifle, and stepped out into the street. I point the rifle at Carl. My actions take everyone off guard.

"Drop it!" I yell at Carl.

Carl snorts a laugh. The warriors act fast, withdrawing their bows. The quickness made everyone gasp. In a blink, we are all cornered.

"I said drop it!" I ordered him, coming in closer to him. He cocks his gun.

"You son of a bitch drop it!" I scream as I cock it.

"Come on bitch shoot me," he growls, turning the gun on me.

In an effort to keep peace and keep me from harm, White Horse places his hand out, ordering his men to put down their weapons. Except for the ones on horseback, everyone else follows his orders. White Horse slowly slides off his horse, slouching down under his belly, ready to pounce if need be. Hank has now removed his gun and has it pointed at Carl.

"Leave her alone!" he growls.

"Come on bitch shoot me," Carl eggs on.

"Carl!" The sheriff yells.

Carl is glaring at me, just waiting for me to shoot him. Hank suddenly turns and points his gun at Sid when he sees him draw his gun.

"Drop it, asshole," he says.

Sid does as he is told. Hank then turns his gun to Carl. The situation is rapidly getting out of hand. I am desperate. I look over at the sheriff.

"You son of a bitch. You owe me!" I yell.

He grows still. "For once in your pathetic life, do something right," I bark.

"Carrie!" I hear.

Roger steps down from the platform across the street. He makes his way to the center of the street and to my side. He glares over at Carl.

"You harm her in any way, you asshole and I will see to it that you hang from a noose if I have to do it myself."

Roger is not intimidating. Carl turns his gun onto Roger. I am livid. I am not feeling well. I am ready to vomit and in no mood for Carl's shit. I take a shot at Carl, hitting the water bucket next to him. Water starts squirting out. You could hear a pin drop in the street. Not a person there was expecting me to shoot. My action startles Carl long enough that he drops his gun. Sid redraws but quickly rethinks when he sees Koawa turn his bow to him. Sid calls defeat, dropping the gun to the ground.

"Give me the rifle, Carrie," Roger says.

"I want to kill him. I want to kill them both."

"I know Carrie, but you are better than them. Let us handle it. Drop the rifle."

"You said so yourself. You want Carl dead."

"Yes, but not this way."

"My children," we hear our father say. He steps out to the street, sizing up the situation. Mr. Skelov is with him and remains bewildered on the platform.

"Carrie, what in tarnation are you doing with that rifle?" He looks over at the water bucket and then at Carl.

"You didn't?" he smirks. He looks over at the sheriff.

"I reckon you have lied to us again and gone back on your word."

"I have not," he denies.

"Well, I can assure you that my children have had enough of your lies, as I am sure everyone else has. You obviously only care for yourself because if you were half a man, we would not all be standing here, and my daughter wouldn't owe you another water bucket."

"She tried to kill me, Reverend. Your daughter tried to kill me," Carl cries. "She crazy she is, simply crazy."

"Oh, I assure you, Carl," he says. "That was a warning. Carrie seldom misses."

With no hesitation, Father grabs the rifle out of my hand.

"I, on the other hand, never miss." He points it at Carl. Carl's eyes grow huge. Father can't hit the side of a barn door, but no one else knows that.

"Now, sheriff, do I need to demonstrate my marksmanship skills, or are you reconsidering your decision? I do believe you do not wish for any scandals in an election year."

That hit home, a thought that I am certain the sheriff had never considered. After several moments, the sheriff gets wise and reconsiders.

"Hank, bring them into the saloon. We will talk there," he mumbles.

"I knew you would do the correct thing," Father says.

The drama is over and the street begins to clear. Carl glares over at us and walks away. I look over at White Horse, he has the most peculiar and bewildered look on his face. I gave him no expression as my father and Roger take me back inside the clinic. I watch through the window, Hank taking our guests and disappearing into the saloon.

Chapter Eighteen

Confessions

It is well into the afternoon and the saloon door is still closed. The suspense on what is going on is enough to drive anyone crazy. Life goes on as normal as it possibly can to help time go by. Roger and Father are allowed in at the secret meeting, along with Mr. Skelov. They are the only outsiders that are allowed. Even Carl and Sid must wait outside, which makes Carl very edgy.

I still am not feeling well and just woke up from a short nap. My morning sickness has somewhat improved, but I am still unable to hold any food down today. I carry on like it is nothing, attempting to pay no mind and keeping myself as busy as I can. I decided to help the time pass; I would go clean the church for my father. After nearly an hour, I finished dusting the last pew. I wanted to take the time before I left to pray. I come down in front of the pulpit, place my hands together, bow my head, and start to pray.

The door to the saloon opens. Stella is in the post office when she sees Hank, alongside the Chief, come walking in.

"Showing the Chief around," Hank says. "I need to show him your back room."

"Certainly," she says.

The men come behind the counter and to the back room. She notices Hank has a map. Chief White Horse looks around.

"Is there a door to the back alley?" he asks. Hank nods his head and opens the back door.

"Yes." Hank then makes a big red circle on the map, and the men leave the back room.

"Have you seen Carrie?" Hank asks.

"She is awful upset about today," she answers. "I saw her go into the church a little while ago."

"Thanks."

Both men then leave. Hank takes White Horse to the church, showing him every building along the way.

"You go ahead. I will keep watch," he tells him.

White Horse opens the church door. He steps into the foyer, where he sees me praying up front. He quietly finds a place in the back pew and sits down. He has never understood the White Man's religion, but he knows it is important to his Prairie Dawn, so therefore, it is important to him. He sits and waits; he doesn't care how long, and he will wait forever for his Prairie Dawn. He watches her as she quietly prays. Her beauty lightens up the room. He grins, just picturing how lovely she looks and how much he loves her. He can't wait to take her home as his bride. He thinks how happy they will be and makes a promise to himself that she will always be treated as his queen. She will want for nothing. He thinks of the many children that they will one day have. He will make them happy and make them proud. He watches her stand and wipes some tears from her eyes. He wonders as to what has made her heart so heavy.

He remembers seeing her come out of the medicine man's lodge; the word to her is a clinic. He wonders why? He remembers her words to the sheriff, saying that he owed her. What was it he owed? He remembers how upset she was at the man named Carl. He knows nothing about him but already despises him for drawing a gun on his precious woman. He notices how protective Hank is of her. Why? He wonders. He knows something isn't right. Is this why his Prairie Dawn is crying? If she is sad or frightened of something, he wants to know. He wants to help. She doesn't need Hank anymore to protect her or her father. She has him, and he will never allow anyone to hurt his Prairie Dawn. Tonight, he is planning on telling her how much she means to him. He is a private man and does not share much with anyone, but he will with her. To his Prairie Dawn, he would give his life. He stands when he sees his loveliness turn around.

"White Horse," I say. "I wasn't expecting you."

He walks up to her. "I did not want to disturb you, so I waited," he says.

"How long have you been here?" I wonder.

"Long enough," he answers. I am feeling sheepish and a little embarrassed by my actions today.

"White Horse," I begin, "about earlier…"

He grabs my shoulders and smiles down at me. "You have fire in those beautiful bones of yours," he teases. "I like that."

I blush. He grins. "I need to see you tonight. We must talk."

"Alright."

"Hank will cover for you. He will take you to the meadow tonight. I will meet you there. Bring your horse."

"Alright." He flicks my nose and then opens the foyer door. I watch him leave with Hank, disappearing in the saloon.

Being with Hank makes my absence from town go smoothly. We take Stella along. Hank thinks that by taking both of us, his excuse of escorting us to see Miller's gravesite will not be questioned. He will drop me off in the meadow and then take

Stella back to the apple tree, where they will light a fire and wait for White Horse to bring me back. He assures both of us that we are safe traveling at night, despite the raids all around us, now that the Lakota are allowed in town. He tells us that my father offered all the warriors a place to sleep in the church, and Esther offered them all the free food, but White Horse insists on camping just outside of town.

We arrive at the meadow and are greeted by Koawa, who is on his horse. He looks over at Hank. His eyes are harsh.

"My Chief is your friend, but I am not," he takes my reins. "You betray him, and it is not the Pawnee you will need to fear."

Hank grows motionless. I do not believe he is frightened of Koawa, but I do believe he gets the message. Koawa turns us around and takes me into the woods. He releases my reins, and I stride alongside him. Koawa's English was very clear to Hank, just as I had remembered White Horse telling me. I know nothing about Koawa except for what White Horse has told me. I need to get to know him; after all, one day, we are going to be related.

"You are very protective of him?" I say.

Koawa just looks over at me briefly and then faces forward again.

"Your wife is very beautiful," I say.

I figure small talk is the best way to earn his trust. I am waiting for a response but get no answer.

"She is with child. Will that be your first?" I ask him.

Again, no response. He is a hard one. They are so different than White Horse but so alike. I wonder why he is so cold. What secrets lie in his past to make him despise us? Is it the same reason that my people despise them?

"You talk too much," he growls and pulls ahead of me.

"You are not the first to tell me that," I smile. "My brother tells me that all the time."

"Your brother is a fool."

I curl up my bottom lip. "Are you always this friendly?" I sarcastically say.

"Yes."

He then trots forward, entering the campground. I immediately see White Horse resting under a tree. He comes to his feet when he sees me. Koawa slides off his horse and makes his way to the fire, leaving me on my horse. White Horse smiles up at me as I release my foot from the stirrup.

He reaches up, lifting me off the horse and moving me into his arms. We embrace. My horse is tied loosely around a branch. He then takes my hand and escorts me into the camp and off to a remote corner where we can be alone. We are tucked under some trees in complete darkness, with only the light of the moon and the small nearby campfire. He has already prepared for my visit by making a soft, warm area out of leaves and shrubs for us to sit on.

"I have missed you, my Beautiful," he huskily says as we sit down. He kisses my hand. "My nights are lonely without you."

"I have missed you too."

"Very soon, my love, this will be all behind us, and we can start our lives together."

"I dream of this," I blush.

"There is much to tell you," He begins. "But first." He leans over and kisses me. How I have missed his lips, and the smell of his sweet incense, and the way he holds me when we kiss.

"We have much to discuss," he says. "But most important are the children."

"How was your talk with the sheriff?" I ask.

"He is still not cooperative but has agreed to allow me to show him where the children are. We leave first thing in the morning."

"That is good, but I worry for you when you are out there alone with him that he will turn his back on you."

"Oh, trust me, I have thought of that. For that reason, I do not ride alone. Koawa and Hank will be with me. I feel like I can trust him."

"You can," I reassure.

"Your sheriff is bringing along Carl." I just rolled my eyes.

"He is leaving his deputy back in case he is needed."

"You watch your back with Carl, White Horse," I warn. "He is not to be trusted."

"That is why I have Koawa," he says. He leans back, resting on his palms. "There will be travelers."

"Who?" I wonder.

"You."

"Me?" I question.

"After what I saw today, I am keeping you with me. Your brother is going as well, and for that reason, I will not leave you alone."

"Roger is going?" I will admit I am a little surprised that he agreed to go.

"He made a logical point. He is afraid that the children have been without adequate food and water for several days, and their health may not be good, and his services may be needed."

Now I understand, and he is correct; it is a very logical point.

"One of the children's fathers," he stumbles, "Mr. Ske.."

"Mr. Skelov," I add.

"Yes," he says, "he wants to go. Your brother convinced him to stay behind because I guess he, too, is a medicine man."

"Umm. I reckon you could say that. He is a very smart man and is very familiar with science and medicine, but he is not a doctor. I assume Roger told him that so he would stay back and, if needed, tend to very simple matters. Mr. Skelov is a nice man but wouldn't be able to take the ride for he has a bad back."

"I see," he says. He tilts his head and looks across at me. "And you?"

"What about me?" I ask.

"Can you handle the ride?" he asks.

"Who me?" I joke. "Absolutely," I confirm.

I hear him sigh as he leans forward and takes my hand.

"Carrie, there is something bothering me that I feel like I need to ask you?"

"Yes," I answer.

"Today when I was riding into town, I saw you coming out of the clinic in your nightwear," he begins, "you had been sleeping there correct?"

"Yes," I answer.

"Roger told me that you both were staying at the big boarding house in town, so why are you sleeping there?"

I sigh deeply. This is my opportunity to tell him that I am with his child. I look into his eyes. He is going through so much and I need him to focus on himself and stay alive. I told myself earlier when I knew I was pregnant that I would tell him when we were back with his people. By telling him now could do more harm than good. At least for a while longer I must keep it to myself.

"I have been feeling very nervous and not sleeping well. Roger believes it is from all that is going on. I went there because it is quiet, so I can sleep."

It wasn't all a lie. There was some truth in there somewhere.

"And how are you now?" he asks.

"I am feeling great," I smile.

He sits straight up again, deeply sighs, and rests back on his hands again. I am not certain, but I think he believes me.

"Today," he starts again, "when we were in the street, and you held out a gun to the sheriff, you told him he owed you. What does he owe you?"

Now, it was my turn to sigh. "Alright, I will tell you, because I we are traveling with him and you need to know the kind of man he is."

I stop a moment to think of my words because I know when I tell White Horse what Carl had done to me, it most likely won't go over well with him, and with Carl being on the same trail with us, it could be a disaster.

"About a year ago, when I was walking to the saloon to meet up with my ride home, I was attacked by Carl."

White Horse lifted his eyebrow, clearly not happy with what I just said.

"He had too much to drink, and he pulled me behind the saloon alley and tried to rape me."

White Horse said something on his tongue under his breath. Whatever it was, I knew by his posture that he was agitated. I continue.

"Stella was with me, and she ran to get Hank. Hank came to my rescue and beaten the tar out of Carl."

"I would have killed him," he spats. I faintly smile, as no one wishes that man dead more than I do.

"My father tried to have Carl arrested and sent away. It wasn't until recently that I believed the reason why the sheriff did nothing and tore my name down was that he was being blackmailed by Carl. I believe Carl helped the sheriff dispose of the Pawnee Squaw and kept quiet on that he raped Anna."

White Horse says nothing but is definitely interested in what I was saying and wants to hear more. "I told the sheriff he owes me for what he allowed Carl to get away with and degrading me."

White Horse curls his bottom lip and takes a few deep breaths. I know he is angry. After several moments, he leans forward, taking my hand as he gently caresses the side of my face.

"I now understand, and I promise you, he and no one else, will ever hurt you again. Because of what you shared with me today, there is absolutely no way that you will leave my sight. I will say nothing to this man unless he comes near you, and then he better hope I don't catch him because if I do, I will kill him."

I have no doubt in my mind that he can and he will.

The rest of the evening that we have together we do not talk about the attacks. We make no comment about the children and not once was Carl's name brought up. We spend the rest of the night together as a couple. The makeshift bed that he made earlier that day, he covered with a blanket from limb to limb, so we have privacy. With that privacy, White Horse and I made love.

Lying beside each other, with our fingers entwined, White Horse comes up on his elbow. He leans in and kisses me.

"My Prairie Dawn," he huskily says, "I have grown to love you so. I promise you many nights we will unite as one. I give you everything." he starts stroking my hair. "With you, I am weak because my heart is so strong for you. I am a Chief and a mighty warrior, but to my love, I am soft and full of more love than there is water in the ocean. Higher than any eagle can fly. Stronger than any current. With you, I am whole. I love you, Carrie, and don't you ever forget that."

I could have cried. That was the sweetest thing that anyone has ever said to me. I know I just witnessed a very weak and tender moment in the mighty Chief.

As with all the other nights that we have shared lately, it had to come to an end. White Horse lifts me up onto Sugar Foot's back, and Koawa escorts me back to meet up with Hank and Stella under the great apple tree.

Chapter Nineteen

The Journey

Morning arrives. I returned to my room late last night. I haven't received much sleep but am up and ready to leave. My morning sickness is rough again this morning and I have already made two trips to the outhouse. Breakfast is downstairs cooking and just the smell of it is making my mouth sour. I make my appearance downstairs to say good morning and kindly decline the breakfast, before making my way down to the stables to meet up with Roger.

"Couldn't eat Mrs. Forbes breakfast either, huh?" he jokes.

"Stomach is rough this morning," I comment.

"I have some medicine in my bag that will calm it down."

"Thank you."

Roger finishes saddling his horse and is working on mine.

"Have you seen father this morning?" I ask him.

"No, I haven't," he says. "He has been very distant since yesterday."

"Why?" I ask.

"He does not like the idea of you going along. He feels that the Chief has other ideas when it comes to you, and that makes him nervous."

"Understandable but not necessary. White Horse would never harm me."

He pulls the strap hard around Sugar Foot's big belly. He then loops it through the buckle.

"As much as it pains me to say this, I believe you."

"Oh, Roger," I grin. "Why the change of heart?"

"In the saloon yesterday, White Horse was asked by the sheriff why he is doing this. His response was that he was doing this because he, too, had a thirst for revenge, and he was concerned for his people's safety. Afterward, when the sheriff left, I overheard him tell Hank that his people were safe and that the only reason he was doing this was for you. I saw the sincerity in his eyes. Later, when we were walking into the clinic, he asked me about you and was concerned that you were ill. I again saw his sincerity and realized that he truly does love you but is keeping it inside and not allowing it to be seen by others. I know without a doubt, Carrie, you need to tell him that you are with his child before it comes out because I worry about what will happen to anyone who crosses him when it comes to you."

"You mean Carl."

"Yes. The sheriff became suspicious when White Horse was adamant that you come along. His excuse was that he needed you to be there when we got to the children because they would need someone to care for them. Later that day, when all the men were gathering for drinks, Carl made the comment that the only thing you are useful for is if your legs are spread and that no one should waste their time on you unless it is for a cheap thrill. White Horse was furious."

"What did he do?" I ask.

"He told the sheriff that Carl would go along as well as you, and if he is crossed in any way, Carl would be the first killed. He made it very clear to all of us that he holds the ticket to our freedom. If we want to be free of all of this and want to ever see the children again, then he must have complete control over everything and every decision, and he is not going to be asked why he has made the decision he has. I believe it is because you are going, and he is not going to explain the real reason why he wants you there."

"What did Carl say?" I wondered.

"Nothing, but you know him as well as I do. He is already suspicious and will be watching you. I, for one, think White Horse is playing a very dangerous game and both of you need to be very careful that you do not get caught. I do not worry too much for White Horse, although I do not trust Carl not to do something stupid; I worry for you when White Horse isn't there to protect you. I told White Horse this, and I assured him that I would stay with you on the trip, and you and Carl will remain as far away as we possibly can."

"So, what is the plan?" I ask.

"We are leaving just to locate the children. The sheriff will then make the arrangements for their return through the immigrants. Mr. Skelov is taking some of his men to Cedar Brook, where they will stay at the Orphanage. The children will be taken there because it is closer, and the terrain is not as rugged."

"Sounds like this has really been planned out."

"Yes," he says. "It has and in great detail."

It is not much longer after that than we see Carl, Hank, the sheriff, Koawa, and White Horse riding up.

"Morning," Hank says as he tips his hat to me.

"Morning," we greet.

My horse is saddled and ready to go. I hoist myself up onto my saddle. Roger secures his bag before getting on his horse. We then make our way out of town. We see a rider running hard across the bridge. It is Father.

"I am so glad I have not missed you," he says.

"Is there a problem, Pa?" Roger asks.

"Not at all, son," he says." I am coming along as well."

"Pa, we have been through this already. It has been agreed that you will stay behind with Mr. Skelov and meet us with the children in Cedar Brook."

"Mr. Skelov has enough people riding with him. I am not needed with them. I refuse to leave my children behind. I will go," he argues.

"This ride is for real men, Reverend," Carl snaps.

"You are going," Father snaps back. It is all we can do for none of us to chuckle. "Besides, Carrie will need my assistance when it comes to feeding all of you men because I am certain none of you will help her."

"Thank you, Father," I grin.

"I still do not feel you should be coming along, Pa," Roger argues.

"He will go," White Horse huskily says.

"Then enough said."

Father turns his horse around and follows us out of town. I catch Roger looking over at father and father just nodding his head. I am not sure what it is about or what secret they may be hiding.

We leave Willow Creek, and our riding order is as follows. White Horse and Hank are in the front. To the right of Hank, in the middle, is the sheriff with Carl on his distance right. Behind White Horse is Roger; to the left of him is my father and then me. Koawa is holding the back dead center. Many hours pass without any conversations. The scamper of a squirrel or the squawk of a hawk will occasionally be heard, which will bring a halt to the echoes of the hooves on the prairie ground. The high afternoon sun is beaming down, making it incredibly warm. My face is flushed, and I am perspiring. My canteen is almost empty of water. I swallow what is left. Roger looks over at me. He mumbles under his breath, asking me if I am alright. I nodded yes. Roger is no fool.

"Chief," he says. White Horse looks back at him. "We have been riding for hours. Our canteens are low. Would it be possible to stop for a break and water the horses and ourselves?"

"I know of a place not far," he says.

"Thank you, Chief," Roger says.

We soon reach a stream. Everyone dismounts and scatters. Roger helps my father off his horse. I am the last to dismount. When my feet hit the ground below, I become extremely dizzy and stumble. Roger rushes to grab my arm. I hear my father yell out my name. Hank wastes no time, scoops me up in his arms, and gently carries me under a tree, where I am put down. Both Roger and my father are by my side.

"I told you the bitch can't handle the ride," Carl snarls. I look over at White Horse, who is a good distance behind Roger, looking on. His eyes pierced through Carl. The sheriff mumbles to Carl, pulling him away, and they disappear to the far end of the stream.

"You stay here with her father," Roger says. "I am going to fill up her canteen."

"Oh, certainly, son," he says.

I watch Roger go to the stream. Roger squats down and starts filling the canteens. White Horse comes down beside him, cupping his hand in the water, and takes a drink.

"Is she alright?" he asks.

Roger continues filling the canteens, not looking his way.

"She is just overheated. She will be fine," he says.

"I saw her come out of your clinic when I came into town. Was I wrong to make her come along? Is my Prairie Dawn ill?"

Roger screws the lid onto my canteen and then starts to fill his own. He has never been a man to speak lies, but it not his business to tell the Chief that he is going to be a father. He gave his sister his word and he have every intention on keeping it.

"I assure you my sister is fine."

Roger comes to his feet, walks over, and hands me my canteen. I spot White Horse watching. Koawa comes to his side and speaks his tongue to him. White Horse shakes his head as both men look over at me.

"What's going on?" he asks.

"Not sure, keep an eye on her," White Horse says.

We continue our journey again in silence. The riding order remains the same, except for Koawa. Instead of him taking the center rear he moves and rides directly behind me. I am not sure on why the change, but I am suspicious it has to do with White Horse keeping an eye on me.

By late afternoon, the sun shifts, bringing us more shade and making the ride more bearable for me. Although we have been riding all day, and I am getting tired, I am feeling better, and my morning sickness has gone away. Koawa is still riding behind me and watching my every move. Although I do not know him, like I do White Horse, it is clear to me that there is very little that he does not see.

The silence of the ride is broken when I hear White Horse tell Hank,

"We will stop for the night on the other side of that ridge."

I look over at father, he is looking exhausted. Although he travels a great deal to Cedar Brook and back, he takes his time and allows himself two days. We are riding much harder and have only stopped once to get water. I am certain he is hungry. He has only eaten an apple all day. I hand him over a few berries to eat.

"Thank you, child," he smiles.

I sit back up in my saddle and put a berry in my mouth. I glance over to Koawa, who moves up and is riding alongside me. I offer him a berry. He refuses.

The terrain is becoming rockier, and we are close to our riding pattern. Koawa's horse's nose nearly touches Sugar Foot's tail, and he helps guide my horse up. We ride single file as we climb up the steep ridge. When I hit the top, I saw White Horse sitting in his stead, making sure everyone got up. I smile at him as I pass. I hear him speak his tongue to Koawa, and then Koawa gets off his horse. I see him pick up a large branch and start to rake the ground.

"What is he doing?" I hear father ask White Horse.

"He is covering our tracks," he answers.

"Why?" Father asks.

"I do not want to change our tracks being seen. We are crossing into Crow territory. I feel we are safe, but I do not wish to change it."

"Oh dear," Father says.

Just before sundown, we set up camp. White Horse and Koawa make their separate fire and cook their separate food. Another much larger fire is brewing on the other side of the camp. That is where our men are settled. My father helps me prepare a meal that is simple but filling. I hate the fact of having to waste perfectly good food on Carl, but what am I to do. With bellies full, soon, boredom hits Carl, and the whiskey comes out. Carl is a very loud and obnoxious drunk. I overhear White Horse tell the sheriff.

"You may want to quiet his mouth and calm down your fire, or the Crows will come in your sleep and slice your throats."

The fire calms down, but as for Carl's mouth, forget it. That is an endless battle, and until the whiskey is gone or he passes out, it is pointless. Roger makes the kind jester that he is going to sit with the Chief and Koawa while Father, and I clean up the dinner.

"May I have the honor to sit with you?" he asks White Horse.

White Horse offers him a seat.

"I cannot stand another moment with that man," Roger growls.

"Is he like this all the time?" White Horse asks.

"He is worse when he is drunk, which isn't too far away."

"I, too, like fire water, but I do not drink it in large amounts. It is forbidden and poison to the body."

"I wish he felt that way."

Carl lets out a loud laugh, followed by a rude jester.

"See what I mean?" Roger says.

"He is a small man with a big ego."

"That he is," Roger agrees.

"I don't know about you child," Father states, as he hands me the last of the plates to dry, "I am exhausted and short tempered right now."

"Oh, Father," I smile. "You are one of the most patient men that I know."

"Not tonight, child. Carl is really starting to make my blood boil."

"He is not any different than any other night," I comment.

"Hey bitch," we hear.

"Alright, so I am wrong," I say.

"How about coming over here and drying me with that towel?" he then cackles.

Roger looks across the fire at White Horse. He sees the flame in his eyes and is certain he is nearing the end of his patience.

"Relax," he mumbles. "Let our father handle it."

"Hank, you should have brought Rachel, we could have had a four some," he cackles.

White Horse's patience is near its end.

"That does it," my father roars.

He slaps his towel down and storms over to Carl. Roger comes to his feet.

"Come here, you filthy bitch," Carl slurs as he makes his way over to me. Hank comes to his feet, as does White Horse.

"Carl!" Hank warns. "Leave her alone."

When Carl is drunk, he is one of the boldest, cockiest sons of bitches around. Hank is a very big guy, well over six feet, and with a chest size that is just as large. He can usually just intimate people by his size, but with a drunken Carl, it doesn't faze him.

"I told you to come over here," Carl snaps. "Now damn it, woman, come over here!"

"I have had all I am going to take with you," Father snaps. "You come any closer to her, and I will see you to hell."

"Go ahead, you old geezer, show me what you have." Carl slurs.

"I will not tolerate any more of your..."

Suddenly, I see Father grabbing his chest and start gasping for air. He then wobbles, falling to the ground. I let out a scream.

Roger makes his way to Father, but he falls on his knees. "Pa!" He loosens my father's shirt. I see Father gasping for air, his forehead perspiring.

"Easy, Pa," Roger says. "Slow and easy breaths."

Roger looks up at Hank. "In my saddle bag is a tonic. Go get it for me." Hank does as he is told.

"Pa," Roger says. "Did you bring your medicine?"

"What medicine?" I ask. "Father does not take any medicine," I conclude.

"Yes, Carrie, he does," Roger says. "For his heart, Pa," he repeats. "Did you bring your medicine?"

"I. I took it before we left," he gasps.

Hank returns with the tonic, handing it to Roger.

"I want you to take this." Roger opens the bottle.

"No, I am...." Father gasps.

"You will take this with no arguments."

Roger lifts his head and brings the tonic to his lips. He then allows him to sip. My mind is racing. I never knew that Father had a bad heart. Why didn't he tell me? I feel betrayed. I glare over at Carl. This is all his fault. He stands there arrogantly, feeling untouchable. I am livid. I hate this man with a passion. My emotions are high, and my anger is uncontrollable.

"You heathen!" I yell at him. "I should have killed you when I had the chance."

I pushed past Hank, stormed over to Carl, and slapped him.

"You filthy bastard!" I scream.

Before Hank can stop it, Carl slaps me back, and I fall to the ground. Like a bolt of lightning, White Horse tackles Carl to the ground and is on top of him with fierce and hard blows. With his brute strength, he begins punching Carl in the face. Koawa rushes over to pull White Horse off. Hank, seeing the challenge of Koawa attempting to pull White Horse off, goes to give him a hand. It takes the full strength of both men to pull White Horse off. Koawa holds White Horse back as he tries to break free. Carl staggers to his feet, as cocky and arrogant as ever.

"You want the filthy cunt Chief?" he spats.

"You son of a bitch!" White Horse growls.

He then pulls himself free from Koawa's grip, charging after Carl. He head-butts him to the ground, nearly knocking the wind out of Carl. The fight is back on. Carl is no match for a raging White Horse. He is taking jabs to the head, chest, and groin. All Carl can do is shield himself, and he hopes White Horse will let up soon.

I am in a state of panic. I fear White Horse is going to kill him. I look over at Koawa. I know he is thinking the same thing. He races over and attempts again to pull White Horse off Carl. Hank comes to Koawa's aide. Both men attempt to pull White Horse off. White Horse is full of rage and remarkably strong. It is taking everything from each man to pull White Horse off. I see the sheriff, who has been still this entire time, remove his gun and shoot it in the air. The tactic works, and White Horse backs off. Koawa quickly moves in, holding White Horse back around his chest. He speaks his tongue to him. I can see the veins in White Horse's neck pulsating from rage. Koawa gently pats White Horse on his chest, speaking his tongue to calm him down. A bruised and battered-up Carl cowers to White Horse's feet. A slightly winded White Horse glares down at Carl and growls.

"If you ever lay another hand on her again, I will kill you."

When Koawa feels certain that White Horse is done, he lets him go. Both men turn to head back to their area of the camp. White Horse nudges me with his shoulder when he passes. I follow suit behind him. It is then that he notices my bloody lip. White Horse lunges at Carl. Koawa again calms him down. I can literally hear White Horse rapidly breathing as he attempts to calm his rage down.

Attention focuses once again on Father. His breathing seems less shallow, and he is regaining his color.

"He needs to rest," Roger tells me.

He places the blanket over him, and we allow the Father to sleep. I am just beside myself. My emotions are high. I cup my mouth to hold back my tears and start to pace. Roger comes up behind me to check my lip.

"How dare you keep this from me!" I spat.

"Carrie, it was Pa's wish. He knew you would worry."

"Of course I will. He never would have taken this trip if I would have known."

"That is why he didn't want to tell you. He knows you will carry on and baby him. He is not going to live his life having us care for him."

I wipe away a tear that is strolling down my cheek.

"How bad is it?" I ask.

Hank walks over with a wet towel, handing it to Roger to put on my lip.

"If Pa takes his medicine like I have asked and remains calm, he can live for many years."

I sniff and wipe another tear. Roger finishes cleaning my lips. He puts his hand on my shoulder.

"Carrie, I am doing everything that I can to help him, but a heart is a very delicate thing, and I am sorry to say that his heart will not get any better."

I can't hold it in any longer. Roger takes me into his arms and holds me as I weep.

White Horse just watches on as his Prairie Dawn cries in her brother's arms. It should be him who is holding her, washing away her tears. He glares over at Carl, his blood still boiling. Carl can count his blessings that he is still standing. White Horse's love for his Prairie Dawn is strong, and after tonight, he is certain everyone knows his love for her, but he doesn't care. Let this be a lesson to the one named Carl of what he will do if his Prairie Dawn is ever touched again.

Chapter Twenty

The Protector

Slumber is among the camp. Roger gives their father medicine that will allow him to sleep comfortably. Two watches are formed for the night. White Horse and Roger are taking the first, while Koawa and Hank take the second. It is unclear as to why White Horse won't allow the Sheriff to take a watch. I cannot help but wonder if it is because White Horse does not trust that the Sheriff will try something when we are all asleep. Whatever the reason, the Sheriff is enjoying a full night's sleep next to a snoring Carl.

I am finding it difficult to sleep. I feel obligated to keep an eye on Father, although Roger is awake. I tuck his blanket more under his chin and feel his chest to make sure he is breathing. Usually, Father is a snorer but tonight is he very still. I roll over and try to fall asleep again.

The second time I woke up, I noticed Roger sitting under a tree. Further on the other end of the camp I see White Horse. I wasn't asleep long as the first watch is still going on. I roll over to face Father. I touch his chest to see if he is still breathing. He looks so peaceful just lying there sleeping. I pull my blanket further over me and close my eyes.

I woke up again and looked over at father. He has not moved his position for several hours. I notice Roger sleeping on the other side of him. I spot Hank under a tree. Second watch has begun. I roll over to see that White Horse is continuing his watch. Did Roger fall asleep, I wonder? I then saw Koawa perched in a tree. Why was White Horse still awake?

He notices that I am awake and makes his way over to me. I come up on my elbows. I watch him as he walks at a slow pace toward me. He looks tired. I watch him squat down beside me. For a moment, he says not a word as he gazes into my eyes, stroking the side of my face.

"The sun will be rising in a few hours," he finally whispers. "Try to sleep, my love, as I will myself very shortly."

"I just worry for Father," I say.

"Yes, I realize this. I, too, have been watching him. Koawa will keep an eye on him. You rest."

How can I ever tell this man no? He is the most amazing man I have ever met. I place my hand on his cheek and give it a gentle stroke.

"I love you," I whisper. He faintly grins.

"As I do you," he huskily says. "Now please Love, try to sleep we leave at first light."

I quickly do as I am asked and within a few minutes I fall asleep again. I am awakened at first light with a sudden strong urge to vomit. I quickly toss my blanket off and run to the stream, passing a sleeping White Horse who is under a tree. Little am I aware that he opens his eyes just as I pass. He gets to his feet, glances over at Koawa and hastens into the woods.

White Horse quietly slithers through the trees to find his Prairie Dawn. He has a hunch where she is. He sneaks his way through the thickets. She shouldn't be too much further ahead. He then sees the stream. He hastens his stride as he hears her in the distance. He steps out of the cluster of trees to find her hunched over the water gushing out of her mouth. She is sick, he thinks. His poor, beautiful Prairie Dawn is ill.

He makes his way to his Blossom and crunches down beside her. He holds her hair back as she finishes gushing out. He rubs her back as she finishes and continues rubbing it while she sips some water. He is now clear why his Prairie Dawn is ill.

"I am sorry you had to witness that," I say.

White Horse comes down on the ground beside me. I feel him stroke my hair. I turned my head and looked at him.

"Carrie," he huskily says. "Are you with child?"

The cat is out of the bag, and there is no way I can hide it any longer.

I nodded. "Yes," I finally say. "I'm pregnant."

"When were you going to tell me this?" he asks.

"When everything is done, and I am living at your camp."

"How long have you known?"

"Not very long," I assure.

"The day I came into town..." he begins.

"I had found out the day prior."

"That is two days. Why didn't you tell me?"

"Please, White Horse, do not be angry with me. I wanted to tell you, but I was afraid about what you would say. You already have so much to think about. I don't want to add to your problems."

He lifts me up and scoots me into his lap. "You listen to me," he says, "never have you been a problem. You are the reason that I am here. I am doing this for you. I love you, Carrie, and I am at the point where I really do not care who finds out about us. You are my life." He cups my face. "I would die for you."

"So, you are alright with this?"

"Sweetheart. I am more than fine with this. I couldn't be happier."

I am relieved. "I have more reason now than ever to keep you close to me. For the remainder of the trip and until the attacks are stopped, I will not cause any harm to you. You will ride behind me, and when we get back to Willow Creek, I will need to find a place where you will be safe, even if it means that I will take you back to my camp."

"And leave my father?"

"I wouldn't dream of you leaving your father the way he is. He will come with you if need be."

I could have cried. "I love you," I tell him.

He holds me tightly. "As I do, too," he says.

I pull free from his arms and scoot off his lap.

"White Horse," I say, "I am worried about my father, and when he finds out that I am carrying your child. I fear he will not take it well, and his heart is so fragile right now."

"Relax my Love. As difficult as it will be for me, I will keep quiet for a while longer on our child, but after last night I do not believe there is not a one person, including your father, who does not see what you mean to me."

"The only one that I worry about is Carl."

Just the sound of his name made White Horse's blood boil.

"I have dealt with bigger and tougher men. He is no match for me. After last night, I do not believe we will be having any more conflicts with him, but when we return, if he starts anything with you, I meant what I said. I will kill him."

I have no doubt he would. Just then, we hear a whistle. White Horse looks out in the distance.

"It is Koawa," White Horse says. "Camp is waking. We must return."

"You got all that in a whistle?" I tease.

White Horse smiles as we come to our feet.

"I have known this man all my life. We think the same way."

"That is kind of like Roger and me."

We make our way just to the breaking of our camp. I start to step out of the woods; White Horse grabs my hand and swings me around. He then pulls me back into the woods, whisking me in his arms, and we kiss.

"You go first," he says after our lips part. "I will follow shortly."

I get back to camp and immediately head to my father. The horses are being packed up and morning tobacco is being inhaled. I greet Hank who is packing up his horse. I spot Carl who has one nasty shiner on him and a swollen lip. I am surprised he is even standing. He says not a word as I cross his path to my father. My father is sitting on a log as Roger is listening to his heart.

"Good morning, child," he greets. Roger removes the stethoscope from his chest.

"How are you feeling, father?" I ask him.

"As I was telling your brother," he begins. "I am feeling much better today. Thank you, Lord." I look over at Roger.

"His heart is at a better rhythm than last night." he says. "But Pa, I feel this trip has been too stressful for you and that you need to go to Cedar Brook as originally planned and wait for us there."

"I will do no such thing. We are nearly there. Going to Cedar Brook now is not even sensible."

"That is not true, Pa. We are closer to Cedar Brook than to Willow Creek."

White Horse sneaks back into camp, arriving on a different path so as not to raise suspicion that we were together. He comes up next to Roger.

"Is there a problem here?" he asks.

"It appears my children are concerned that I will not be able to handle the rest of the trip and asking me to leave and meet them at Cedar Brook."

"How are you feeling?" he asks.

"I am feeling wonderful," Father says.

"Then what is the problem?" he wonders.

"I feel the stress of the ride and facing Carl was too much for him, and he needs to rest," Roger says.

"Umm. Now I understand." White Horse looks over at Roger. "May I recommend a travois. I can drag him behind my horse."

"A travois?" Roger asks.

"They are very simple to make and quite comfortable. I have traveled in one myself when I was wounded as a boy."

"What a marvelous idea," Father says.

Roger thinks a moment.

"You said they are comfortable, so he will not move around much?"

"Yes, very much so."

"Alright. I will agree to it."

"I will go make one."

I follow White Horse as he walks away to begin getting what he needs to make the travois.

"White Horse, I am very concerned that he will not make the journey and that he is too weak to continue."

"Sweetheart, I will promise you that if he is too weak to continue, then I will carry him on my shoulders. I will not allow any harm to him."

All I can do is smile. Damn, I love this man more and more every moment. Roger watches as White Horse quickly assembles a travois and ties it up to his horse.

After Father lays down, White Horse covers him up, and we are ready to go.

"I will be right behind you, Father," I tell him before hoisting myself up onto Sugar Foot's back.

I kept to my word and rode directly behind the travois. Roger is riding to the left of it. Father seems comfortable and content. The attitude with everyone is different today. Hank, Roger, and I are remaining close to the warriors as Carl and the Sheriff are hanging back. This makes Koawa nervous. He turns his horse around and gallops back, coming right behind the Sheriff and Carl where he will remain for the duration of the ride.

After nearly three hours into the ride, Hank turns around and joins Koawa in the rear. I see White Horse glance back at me and motion for me to come up beside him.

"We are approaching the canyon. The ground will be steep and very narrow. We will have to get off and walk the horses up. Let your father know that the ride may be bumpy."

"I will tell him." I come over to my father.

"We are getting to a narrow and steep rocky area. We will have to guide the horses up by their leads. The ride may be bumpy, so hold on."

"I will be fine, child. You and Roger, just be careful going up."

We continued our ride in silence. We reach the area where the terrain turns rockier and narrower. We then form a single file formation as we begin to climb. I see Koawa come up behind me, followed by Roger. We continue our climb until the ground becomes too steep and unstable for the horses to climb on their own. Roger and I get off and start guiding our horse up the rocky incline. I see Koawa pull ahead of me, guiding his horse and my father's horse up the incline. I look up to see White Horse guiding his horse and travois the last few feet to the top. Hank is not far behind me and is quickly catching up with me. Carl and the Sheriff are a good distance below.

Sugar Foot starts to stumble, taking me with him.

"Carrie," I hear Roger yell.

I see White Horse slide down the rocks to me. He grabs Sugar Foot's lead and my hand and helps us up. Roger is right behind me. Koawa has made it to the top and is waiting with my father for everyone else to get up. Roger and I are both at the top of the hill. Father is sitting on the travois, anxiously waiting for our arrival. I see the look of relief on his face when he sees that both of his children are safe on top.

White Horse waits for everyone else to safely make it up the hill. Hank is the next to come up. Then, the Sheriff. He is winded from the steep incline and glares over at White Horse.

"You could have killed us," he growls.

"It is not my fault you eat too much," he snaps back.

White Horse walks back to his horse. The Sheriff looks down the hill. Carl is struggling to get up. White Horse gets back on horse.

"What, you are not going to help him?" the sheriff barks.

"If everyone else can make it, then so can he," White Horse says.

"He is injured, so no thanks to you. The least you can do is help him."

"He is injured because of the hole in his mouth and his inability to shut it," White Horse states. "You want him up, then go get him yourself."

White Horse waits for the rest of us to mount back up, and we move again. White Horse motions for Roger to come to him.

"When we get to the cave, you will need to ride very tight behind Carrie. Give your father's horse to Koawa. He has the skill to get both horses through."

"Sounds very dangerous," Roger says.

"It is very dark, and there is no room for error. The path is narrow and has a very big drop straight down. I will have to guide the travois through very slowly as we wind around."

"Perhaps, Chief, if I go in front of Carrie and put Hank behind her. My Mare and Sugar Foot were raised together. Sugar Foot will follow her."

"That will be fine. Just don't let Carrie slip."

"I promise you, with Hank behind her and myself in front, she will be fine."

Roger rides back and tells both Hank and I the plan. Carl and the Sheriff have caught up to us and are taking up the rear. With in a few minutes, we come to a bluff and White Horse stops in front of it.

"We are here," he says.

We all just look around. We see nothing but woods and mountains. We all watch as White Horse comes to an opening no wider than his horse and steps inside into the darkness.

"Come," he says.

Roger guides his horse in with no issue. Sugar Foot, on the other hand, wants nothing to do with it. I have a feeling this is going to be more difficult than planned. Hank has an idea. "You won't have an issue with mine. Let's trade horses."

We holler up at Roger to stop for a moment while we make the trade.

"Chief, stop for a moment. Carrie is having issues with her horse. Hank and her are trading."

Sugar Foot is particular about who rides him. Hank is a big guy and is refusing to let Sugar Foot win. After a few snorts from my beloved horse, Sugar Foot enters the cavern.

The immediate stench of bat guano is making my already queasy stomach even worse. I removed my scarf and covered my nose with it in hopes of stopping some of the odor and settling my stomach down. I look up to where we are going and to where White Horse is already climbing. Unbelievable, I think. Despite the odor, this place is beautiful. Over my head, there are stalactites making the cave glisten. There are bats flying around between them, giving the cave an eerie feeling. Everyone seems to be holding their breaths as we slowly make the twisting turns through the cave. There are so many dark places for one to hide and one careless step, and you and your horse could fall to your death.

Hank is nudging close to the rear of my horse. Hank's horse's tail is tickling Sugar Foot's nose. We are in complete silence as we all make our way to the top, with only the occasional squeak from a bat or the dragging of the travois across the rocks.

Chapter Twenty-One

The Secret Passage

A light appears, indicating the end of the cave. I hear White A light appears, indicating the end of the cave. I hear White Horse speak his tongue. Koawa is behind us, and I wonder who he is talking to. I heard him tell my father that we are here. Roger is the first behind White Horse to step out.

"Whoa." I hear him say. I then heard my father chuckle. I am the next out. I adjust my eyes to the sun. When I focus, I see why Roger is startled. Standing in the corner of the opening of the cave is an Indian dressed in warrior paint on his face and arms. He startles us all as we exit.

White Horse helps my father to his feet. Everyone dismounts. The sheriff wastes no time asking White Horse where the children are.

"I will show you," he begins, "but first, I need to be sure we have not had any unwelcome company when we were gone."

A man who appears in power comes up to White Horse. The men converse. We all look around with our eyes as we wait for the conversation to end. There are about four dozen warriors all around, and many are paying no mind to us.

"This place is amazing," Roger says.

"I visualize the Garden of Eden like this," Father says.

I must agree with him. This place is green, peaceful, untouched, and pure, a true virgin of nature. A magnitude waterfall flows powerfully over the bluff, spilling its multitude of clear blue water into a huge puddle of a spring below. The incredible height of the canopies above swallows you whole and several birds are seen in flight, disappearing over the mountains and into the great blue skies above. This place is truly one of God's great wonders. The conversation stops, and White Horse comes up to us.

"I will take you to the children," he says.

"Any problems?" Hank asks.

"None that Running Bear could not handle. The old woman returned to feed the children. She did not come alone. As I suspected, they are getting anxious and want to move the children soon. I believe this is the time to remove the children as enough food was left for several days. Meaning they will not return for some time. Follow me," White Horse says.

He takes us to the waterfall and walks us behind it. He then removes a small rock from the side of the mountain. We all hear a rumble, and the wall opens.

"Son of a bitch," Hank mumbles. Everyone is amazed.

"This place is bad," Running Bear says. "Mountains do not just open on their own. Bad spirits live here."

It is obvious that Running Bear is not alone in his belief of bad spirits being here, White Horse reluctantly walks in. He looks over at me.

"You stay away," he orders.

Whatever his beliefs are, I accept and stay out. The sheriff, Roger, and others follow White Horse in. The air is still as I wait patiently for a sign of the children. I glance around at all eyes on me. My skin begins to crawl as I am being sized up by the other Lakota warriors. I am certain my name has gotten out as the woman who will soon marry their Chief. Just then, the one named Running Bear stops his stillness when he speaks.

"You are Prairie Dawn?" he says.

"Yes. I am her." I shyly say.

"When I received word that my cousin was to wed a White Woman, I could not understand his crazy thinking. What I failed to be told is how beautiful you are," I blushed.

I was not expecting such a compliment from another Chief.

"You are his cousin?" I ask.

"Yes, and Chief of a neighboring band."

"White Horse never told me about you."

Running Bear faintly grins. "There will be many things that my dear cousin will not tell you, but fear not. He is a good man and will treat you very well."

"Thank you."

Our conversation stops, and yet again, I wait patiently for the children. My wait does not last long as I see the first sign of a child coming out from behind the waterfall, holding my father's hand. He is carrying a young boy in his arms. I quickly approach them as I see another child brought out, followed by the sheriff and Carl. Although the children are not of Willow Creek, I am so excited to see them and quickly give them all a hug. Sarah, the oldest of seven years old, and Mr. Slekov's daughter are the only ones who speak English.

"I am so proud of you," I tell her, "For taking care of the others when all hope appeared gone. Your father will be proud of you."

"When we were taken," she begins, "by bad men, I was scared that I would never see my family again. The Chief found us and told me not to cry anymore. I cry no more. I knew we would be home very soon. He promised me."

I look up at White Horse as he grins down at Sarah.

"They all seem well," Father grins widely. "Praise God."

One by one, Roger examines each child. He assures us that despite all the children needing a good bath and a well-deserved hot meal, that every one of them is well and considering what they have been through, their attitudes are good.

There is no time to waste on getting the children home and as far away from here as possible. The first part of White Horse's plan is set into motion. Roger insists that for health reasons, Father joins the others in getting the children to Cedar Brook, and fortunately, he provides no arguments and agrees. Carl is going with the sheriff, and for that reason, Hank is going with my father. White Horse is going to have to get Roger and me home. We say our goodbyes and quickly go our separate ways. Running Bear and his band of warriors are going to see the children part of the way to Cedar Brook. We make our way back through the cave and then split up. If everything goes according to plan, everyone will meet back up in two to three days.

Evening is upon us. We have traveled nearly half of our destination. Storm clouds are high above us, and very soon, a heavy amount of rain will fall across the land. Koawa knows of a den that once belonged to a mountain lion. It is a little cramped, but it will work for the night. We make our way through the Great Canyon and to the den. A fire is lit just as the rain begins to pour outside. Father has taken most of our supplies with him as he will be the one to have to feed the children, leaving Roger and I to fend for ourselves. Koawa makes a kill. The four of us sit around the fire and get our fill.

A loud roar of thunder followed by a bright light shakes the ground outside.

"I hope Father is alright," I say.

"He is fine. Running Bear will not leave him until tomorrow morning," White Horse assures.

"Those children have been through so much already. I just worry for them. I know the sheriff, and Carl will be no help to him."

"Do not worry, Hank is with him. I would not have left father alone if I did not think he would be alright."

"I do not know this Hank well," White Horse begins, "But by what I have seen of him, your father is in good hands. Running Bear will not allow Carl to drink too much fire water. I assure you. Your father will be fine."

Roger looks across the fire at White Horse.

"What makes you so sure that they do not realize the children are missing already and are looking for them?" he asks.

"The children were fed yesterday. There was enough food left for them for at least four days. It is clear they want the children alive. They are growing tired of the children and want to dispose of them. Therefore, they travel to a place where they are going to be sold, and my guess is that they bring parties to the children. This will take a few days; by then, the children will be safe, and you will be home."

"No one is watching the children?" I ask.

"One Eye cannot afford to have any of his men stay there. The woman that was seen, I believe, is riding with them and will return when they return."

"So, there are no Pawnee or Crow anywhere around here right now?" Roger asks.

"No, my friend, they are here. I assure you they are around us."

"Do they know we are here?" I ask.

"The Lakota are very strong right now. We outnumber them greatly at this moment. They realize that we are here, but they will let us pass because we are too great in number."

"But there are only two of you," Roger says.

"Only two that can be seen, but I assure you, my friend, if we are attacked when we sleep, my scouts will have an arrow in their backs before the first hit."

"So, we are being watched right now?" I say.

"Sweetheart, my men have been following us for days."

"I thought you were here in peace," Roger says.

"I am; my men just want to watch what your sheriff calls peace."

Roger just grins. I think it's pretty sneaky of White Horse.

"I have one more thing that is bothering me," Roger begins.

"Then I suggest you ask me?" White Horse says.

"Father is not aware that Carrie is with child. I want to know what your plans are with that child and how you plan on telling her father?"

"Roger!" I snap.

White Horse holds his hand out to me, telling me that it is all right and that he has taken no offense.

"It is alright, Carrie." He looks over at Roger.

"You are her protector and I respect that. I love your sister dearly and I am proud that she is with my child. I will treat her well. After what I saw last night, I agree with Carrie and feel that the truth may hurt her father so therefore, I will keep it between us until after she is with me and we are married. Then we can share our joy with everyone. I believe that your father will accept me and allow me to marry his daughter."

"And if he doesn't?" Roger wonders.

White Horse grew still a moment. "Then I will take her by force."

Both Roger and I sigh. I know he is capable of it and I too think the same. I know White Horse will not walk away without me. I truly am hoping it will not come to that, but if it does, I am ready to leave Father and take off with White Horse. Roger gives him no response. I am uncertain what he is thinking and honestly, I don't want to know. The conversation grows light after that until we call it a night.

It is deep into the night, and I am unable to sleep. I crawl to the opening of the den and gaze out. The storm has passed, leaving a gentle breeze in the night air. I begin to think about the child that I am bearing, my father, and White Horse. What if Roger is right? What if the father refuses to accept the situation? What will happen? Could I really bear the pain of walking away from him with such hostility and animosity? I can't bear the thought of losing the two men I love the most or the thought of having to choose between them. I feel a hand caress my cheek, interrupting my thoughts. I turn my head and see White Horse.

"Such deep thoughts," he says.

"I was just thinking."

"What brings such heaviness to that beautiful mind," he says.

"It's just silly thoughts that are not important," I say.

He is not fooled. He stands up and steps out of the den. He takes my hand and helps me to my feet and outside.

"Let us walk," he says.

"Are we safe?" I ask.

"We will not be far," he says.

We begin our short walk hand in hand.

"Now tell me what is on your mind?" he asks.

"I am just thinking of the baby and my father," I say.

"Ah, the conversation with your brother tonight is heavy on your mind?" he concludes.

"Yes," I admit.

"Carrie. I want a peaceful outcome as well as you do. However, I meant what I said. I will fight for you and our baby."

"That is what is worrying me," I say.

"Sweetheart, I assure you I will never physically hurt your father, for I completely understand his will to protect you. It is for that reason that I will remain patient with him and convince him that we are meant to be together."

"I love both of you so much and do not want to choose."

He abruptly stops and turns my shoulders around to face him.

"I do not want you to worry about this. Everything will be fine," he says, stroking my cheek. "I love you, Prairie Dawn, and I do not care how long it takes; we will be together. This I promise you."

I wrapped my arms around him, and we embraced.

"I love you, White Horse. I love you so much." He gently lifts my head with his finger, and we kiss passionately. Under the brightness of the moon and the dampness of the recent rain, White Horse and I remain in a kiss that tingles my inside. I know in my heart that White Horse is the one for me, and somehow, in some way, I must get my father to understand that.

Chapter Twenty-Two

The Soul Sisters

Preparations are being made for the pending attack. It has been four days since our return to Willow Creek. Today's challenge is finding a place where women and children can stay safe and away from any potential harm. White Horse finds a place that he feels will be ideal, but the issue is it is the Johnson home. Both Roger and I feel Mr. Johnson will not allow us anywhere near it, but White Horse is persistent and requests that we try again. Roger and I make our way to the Johnson home, stopping the wagon just outside the gate.

"Well, here goes nothing," Roger says.

We make our way to the porch and knock on the door.

"Go away!" we hear. Neither one of us was surprised, as we both knew we were not going to be welcomed.

"Mr. Johnson," Roger starts. "We just need to talk to you."

"I said go away!"

Roger presses on. "Fine, then I will say what I have to say through the door."

He waits in the hope of hearing the door unlock. When he hears nothing, he presses on again.

"As you may be aware, the immigration children have been found and are safely in Cedar Brook. The town is preparing for the attack that we are certain will happen very shortly. As you may be aware, there were two attacks yesterday, and only one family was home. They were tending to their fields when they were killed. Perhaps you know them." Roger knew he would. "The Websters."

"Remember them, Mr. Johnson?" I say. "Anna and I went to school with Elizabeth."

"Mr. Johnson," Roger begins again. "We need a place that is large enough to hold all the women and children so when the attack comes, they are safe."

"I am not a hotel," he barks.

"Mr. Johnson, I can assure you that your place will be taken care of and no expenses will be on you. I will even be willing to pay you for your hospitality."

"I said Go AWAY!"

Roger and I look at each other. This is not going as well as we had hoped. I have an idea. I came in closer to the door.

"Mr. Johnson, please, for Anna's sake, help us."

"You people killed my Anna!" he screams. "Why should I help?"

"Mr. Johnson, Anna was my friend. I miss her too."

I paused for a moment, hoping he would open the door. When he doesn't, I press on.

"Do you remember the time when Anna and I went fishing? She caught the tiniest fish. The line was bigger than the fish." I smile at myself, remembering it like it was yesterday. "She came running home to you to show you. You were so proud of her. Then what about the time when she and I ran our horses in the town race. No one thought we would win, but with your training, we won and brought home the trophy. You placed it on your mantel. I imagine it is still there." I smile again as I remember the times. "When Anna left, we were all so upset, and then when word got out that she died, a part of me died with her. Mr. Johnson, don't you want to see justice for the ones who hurt Anna and have brought all this despair to the town? I beg of you to allow us to enter your home and bring back the love to us that you gave to Anna."

The silence is thick. A gentle breeze glides through my hair as we finally hear the doorknob turn. Mr. Johnson steps out. His eyes are red and swollen from crying. My heart went out for him. How lonely and depressed he must feel.

"I will allow," he finally says. "For Anna, I will allow."

"Thank you, Mr. Johnson, thank you."

We entered the home. Mr. Johnson closes the big heavy door to reveal a dark and musty home. I have been in this home many times as a child when Anna and I were young. It had at one time been beautiful and so elegant. It is sad to see how untidy and lonely this big house looks.

"The only thing that I ask," Mr. Johnson states, "is that Anna's room is left as is, and no one is allowed to enter."

"I will take full responsibility for it," I say.

"We promise you, Mr. Johnson, nothing will be disturbed," Roger assures.

"I am ashamed to say that the place is very untidy, and if children will be in here, some cleaning up will need to be done."

"Not a problem," I tell him. "There will be plenty of us to clean it up for you."

Mr. Johnson gives us the tour. We quickly plan on what is needed to get this place ready for the children. When our tour is over, we gather in the parlor, and Roger begins to fill Mr. Johnson in on what he knows. It is a touchy conversation when Anna's name comes up as a victim of what we believe to be a serial rapist.

"I knew he hurt my Anna. He was way too fond of her," he grumbles.

"What we are unclear about is if the sheriff is the one who hurt Anna or if it is Carl. But what we do know is Carl is blackmailing the sheriff," Roger says.

"And because the sheriff killed this Pawnee woman, Willow Creek is being attacked?" Mr. Johnson asks.

"As farfetched as that sounds, Yes," Roger answers.

Mr. Johnson walks over to the mantel and picks up a locket that I know belonged to Anna.

"Did I ever tell you, Doc, how Anna really died?"

"No, Mr. Johnson, you did not. We all just thought she left town."

"She did. The sheriff found out she was pregnant and asked Hank if he knew someone who would terminate it. I was afraid for Anna's life, so I made the arrangements for her to go to Minneapolis to stay with my sister until the baby was born, and then she was going to give the baby up to a family there who was unable to have any children of their own. The sheriff escorted the stage couch out of town."

"What happened then?" Roger asks. "She delivered the baby just fine and gave it away as planned. She developed an infection just a few days after delivery. Even the best big city doctors couldn't save her."

"I remember now," I say. "Father came home one night very upset. He said he had just left your place. He wouldn't tell us anything. He said he couldn't." Mr. Johnson nodded his head.

"Yes, that is true. When I found out about Anna, I went into town with my rifle and was going to kill the sheriff. Your father stopped me. I wish he hadn't. Perhaps if I had followed through, Willow Creek would not be in the state it is now, and all these families would still be alive."

"You cannot blame yourself for this," Roger says.

"If only I had not allowed her to leave by herself to ride that day, she may still be here."

"Mr. Johnson, sometimes it helps the healing process if one talks about it. It has been so many years. Don't you think it is time to heal?" Roger suggests.

Mr. Johnson sits down in the chair next to the mantel and lowers his head. "I let her go take her horse, Molly, out for a run," I remember Molly, I thought. She loved that horse. "I told her to return home in one hour and to go no further than the Webster place. Anna was a good girl and always did as I asked her, so when she returned late, I was worried.

When she returned, she was hysterically crying. She told me that she was riding along the creek and stopped to get Molly and herself some water when she was jumped from behind. She said there were three of them, but only one had jumped her. I asked her who they were, and she told me they were wearing hoods over their heads, but I recognized one of the voices of the sheriff. She made the mistake of calling his name. She said when he heard her say his name that, they quickly ran off, but the damage was already done, and she had already been raped.

"Did she say who raped her?" Roger asked.

"Not at first. She kept saying he had a hood on. When I took Anna to see you, we met up with the sheriff. I told him what happened. I didn't realize then why Anna was so scared of him. I promised Anna I wouldn't tell you the real reason for what had happened. She was so scared, and I truly felt the sheriff would help us. I now understand why Anna did not want to tell her story to the sheriff. He was so cooperative when Anna became pregnant and was fast at getting her out of town. He made it sound like he truly cared about her wellbeing. It was the month that I went to see Anna in Minneapolis for the birth of the baby when she told me the truth about who the father was. I left her after the funeral. When I came back to Willow Creek, I wanted him dead. That was when your father came and stopped me."

I can tell he is trying to keep his anger under control. I had to give him credit. He is doing a remarkable job.

"Mr. Johnson, Chief White Horse has come up with a plan that will bring an end to all of this and finally allow your Anna to rest. Thank you for allowing us to use your home. I know that this cannot be easy for you," Roger says.

"You can do me one thing," Mr. Johnson says.

"What?"

"I would like to talk to the Chief. Can you bring him here? Invite him to dinner. I really need to speak with him."

"I can try," Roger says.

"You must," he pleads. "If Anna is going to rest, I must talk to him."

"Mr. Johnson, if it is alright with you," I say. "I would like to get started in cleaning up the place and getting the parlor ready for your dinner guest."

"Yes, of course. Whatever you need."

"I would like to bring Stella Miller here to help me."

"Yes, Stella. She, too, has suffered greatly. She is welcome."

I look over at Roger. "I will send her here."

Later that morning, Stella and I begin the daunting task of cleaning the big manor. Mr. Johnson excuses himself, leaving Stella and I alone. We concentrated downstairs, starting with the kitchen. We make it functional, then move on to the parlor. Stella opens the curtains allowing instant light to the dark and musky room.

"I cannot understand why Mr. Johnson would keep these old curtains closed," Stella says. "This room is beautiful."

"Yes, it is. It is a shame how he has let this place go for so many years," I state.

I begin the never-ending task of removing the dust that has accumulated over the years of neglect.

"When his Anna died, he just completely shut down."

"I know how easy that is to do," Stella says. "I wanted to do the same thing when my parents died."

"I was so young when my parents died that I do not remember them much. Sometimes I am glad it is that way," I conclude.

"I just hope that when this is done, Mr. Johnson will get the closure he deserves."

"You need a closure too, Stella," I say.

She looks over at me from across the room and stops the polishing of the table.

"Carrie, look," she gasps.

I walk over to where she is and look down at the table. I smile widely.

"Well, I will be."

When Anna was alive, she had many sleepovers, and although her room was huge, we always slept in the parlor. One night it was Stella, Elizabeth, Anna and me. Anna wanted to become a blood sister. Stella and I were all for it and were ready to cut our wrists to exchange our souls. Elizabeth was not as sure and did not want to do it. So, instead, we came up with the idea of each of us scratching our names on the side of a table where only we would know where it was. Anna scratched in a heart, and around the heart was our initials, and under the heart, it said friends forever. Stella and I are looking at the engraving. Elizabeth moved away when she got married. Anna passed on, leaving only Stella and myself, the two remaining in our pack.

"After all these years, it is still here," I smile.

"Amazing," Stella says. "I remember it like it was yesterday."

"Stella," I say, "let's finish what we started all those years ago."

"You mean become soul sisters?"

"Yes, we only did this because Elizabeth was too chicken to cut herself, but you and I are not. In Anna's memory, let's do it."

"Let's do it," she laughs.

We find a clean knife in the kitchen and come to the floor next to the table. Stella picked up Anna's picture on the mantel and joined me on the floor.

"Ready?" I ask.

"I am ready," she says, holding out her wrist.

I slice a slit on her wrist. She filches. Blood slowly begins to seep from her wrist. I then cut mine. A good flow begins to roll from my wrist. I tip it over and rub my wrist on Stella's.

"Friends forever," she says.

"Friends forever," I smile.

We both look at Anna's picture.

"We will never forget you," Stella says.

"Awe, Stella, I don't mean to come between you and a tender moment, but I am really bleeding here."

"My word," Stella gasps as she sees the blood running down my arm.

She quickly races to the kitchen and grabs some water and a towel.

"How deep did you go?" she asks as she starts applying pressure.

"Not any deeper than yours," I say.

"I have already stopped bleeding," she comments.

She takes another rag and ties it around my wrist to slow down the bleeding.

"My word," I say. After nearly ten minutes of pressure, the blood slows down to a trickle. "I reckon I won't do that again," I laugh.

"Carrie, you never do anything halfway," she teases.

"I reckon you are correct," I laugh.

Stella comes to her feet. When I started to come to mine, I became dizzy. Stella grabs my arm.

"Come sit down on the couch. I am going to go get Roger."

"No, Stella, I am fine; just let me sit here for a little bit."

"Well, if you are sure."

"Yes, I am sure," I say.

Stella picked up her dust cloth again and finished the table. As I watched her dust, I began to think.

"You know there is one thing I cannot figure out about Anna's rape."

"What?" Stella asks.

"Mr. Johnson told Roger and I that Anna told him that there were three men in hoods. We know that one is the sheriff. I assume the other one is Carl. But who was the third one?"

"Hmm, that is a good question," she thought.

"I have been thinking about it, and I think I may know who it was."

She stops dusting and sits down next to me.

"Who?" she asks.

"Sid," I answer.

"Sid?" she shakes her head. "I cannot see Sid doing something like that."

"I cannot either, but it makes sense. Sid would most likely be riding with them; after all, he works for the sheriff, and they are related."

"But Sid would never hurt anyone."

"Stella, I courted him for some time. Trust me, I know him; at least, I thought I did."

Stella stands back up and walks over to pick up her dust cloth.

"Towards the end of our relationship, Sid grew very distant. I can remember one night when he came to pick me up; he was very agitated. When I asked him what was wrong, he clammed up and said he couldn't talk about it. I cannot help but wonder if that was the day that Anna was raped."

"You think?"

"The timeline does not match the Pawnee squaw, but it does Anna."

"You may be right," she agrees.

Our conversation is interrupted by a knock on the door.

Chapter Twenty-Three

The Dinner

"Roger," I hear Stella say, "come in."

"I just came to tell Mr. Johnson that the Chief agrees to meet with him, and we will be here for dinner at seven tonight."

"We will be ready," Stella says.

After Roger leaves, I share the word with Mr. Johnson, who I found in the cellar. Immediate plans for dinner are made. I assure Mr. Johnson that he is not going to need to do anything and that Stella and I will cook it all. He told me that he was the one who had invited the Chief for dinner, so he would at least provide the food and the cider. The meal is prepared, and after an hour until the clock hits seven, Mr. Johnson allows Stella and I to wash up and provides each of us with one of Anna's dresses to change into for dinner.

We both know that this is a big step for him, allowing us to wear something that belonged to his precious Anna. We both are so honored to be allowed to wear them. Her taste in clothing was exquisite. Mr. Johnson gave her the best of everything. Stella and I both look fabulous.

The table is set with the best china and drinks are being prepared by Mr. Johnson for the arrival of our guests. Stella and I make our way down the grand staircase. Mr. Johnson pauses momentarily from pouring the drinks when he hears us coming down the stairs. Upon seeing us with his daughter's dresses on, Mr. Johnson's eyes welled up with tears.

"You both look absolutely beautiful," he finally says.

"Perhaps we should change," I tell him.

"Nonsense," he argues. "I want you both to have these dresses, as Anna would too."

"That is so generous of you," I tell him. "But only if you are certain you are ready to part with them," I caution.

"Yes, I am certain. Your brother is right; it is time I heal."

"Then we accept," I smile. Stella and I make our way to the dining room.

"The table looks beautiful," I tell him. "Stella and I would have set it, though."

"I wanted to do it. I have never entertained a Chief before." Mr. Johnson says. "I do hope he is pleased."

"Oh, I am sure he will be," I say. "He seems very easy to please," I say, playing dumb.

Finally, the moment we had all been waiting for had arrived. We hear a knock on the door. Mr. Johnson answers it.

"Doctor Briggs," he greets with a handshake. The men step in. It is then that I see my father as well. He shakes hands with Mr. Johnson.

"Chief White Horse, this is Theodore Johnson," Roger introduces.

Both men shake hands. "It is an honor, Chief. Please come in," Mr. Johnson says.

White Horse is very quiet, only giving him a nod. When the men enter the parlor, it is then that White Horse sees me. He faintly grins. I feel like a child as I twill my dress when White Horse walks by.

"Please have a seat," Mr. Johnson says, giving White Horse the best seat in the room. "I have made up some drinks. Would you care for one?" he offers him.

"That would be nice," Roger chimes in.

"Allow me to get them," I tell him.

Mr. Johnson sits down across from White Horse.

"First, I must thank you for all you have done and all you are continuing to do. Finally, my Anna will be able to rest in peace knowing the men who hurt her will be punished."

"You have suffered dearly," White Horse huskily says.

"Yes," Roger says. "When I told Chief White Horse about your Anna and that you requested to see him, he was more than eager to come."

I return with the drinks. One by one I pass them out. White Horse glances up at me as I hand him his drink. We exchange a smile.

"You look very lovely tonight, child," Father says.

"Yes indeed," Roger agrees.

"That is one of Anna's dresses," Mr. Johnson says. "I must admit your daughter looks very nice in it."

I know I am turning red. I handed Roger his drink from the tray.

"Put an old farmer's shirt with holes and overalls on her, and Carrie would make it look good."

"Roger," I blush.

All the men, including White Horse, agree and chuckle at my redness.

"I am going to go help Stella with the serving," I say, quickly getting out of the way of the ambush.

Dinner is on the table, and everyone gathers around. Bellies are well on their way to being filled. Lately, I have not had much of an appetite and am picking at my plate. Mr. Johnson starts the conversation.

"I do hope the meal is to your liking, Chief White Horse," he says.

"Yes, it is very good," White Horse smiles.

"I must admit I only purchased the ingredients. Carrie and Stella did the cooking."

"That explains it," Roger says. "Both women know their way around a kitchen."

"Thank you, Roger," I grin.

I glance over White Horse's way and catch a grin. It makes me wonder why, suddenly, Roger is full of compliments? Is he just making himself look good because of the company, or is he sucking up to White Horse?

"Chief White Horse," Mr. Johnson begins, "I must admit I am a bit surprised at how young you are. I have always assumed Chiefs were much older."

"Many are," he answers. "My father died at an early age. It is customary for the oldest child to be next to the Chief. I was barely a man myself."

"It must be very trying at times," Father says.

"Yes, it is, but I enjoy it. I love my people. They are my family. They make the task easier."

"Are you married?" Mr. Johnson asks.

White Horse grew still a moment and briefly glanced my way.

"I was," he finally answers, "for four years. She died when our camp was attacked by Pawnee. It was the same attack that killed my father and made me Chief."

"I am sorry," he says. "I lost my wife as well. I understand your pain."

"Thank you," White Horse says.

"The loss of my wife was more bearable because I had Anna. She brightened up my darkest days."

"Mr. Johnson," Roger begins, "your days will be bright once again when all these attacks have stopped, and the men who hurt your Anna are brought to justice."

"That is why I have asked the Chief here," Mr. Johnson states. "I want to have a significant part in your plan. I want to put all my burdens and sorrow behind me and move forward, not only for myself but for Anna as well. I ask of you, Chief Chief, to please allow me to be a part of this."

"There are many areas of his plan," Roger says, "that requires everyone's help. I am sure there will not be a problem. Am I right, Chief?"

"How close do you want to be?" White Horse asks.

"I want to be alongside you," Mr. Johnson says.

White Horse thinks a moment before he speaks. "I will show you in detail all that will be done, and then you can tell me what you want, and we will go from there."

"That sounds fair," Mr. Johnson says.

"Their leader, One Eye, is very smart and not easily fooled. I will need everyone's help to pull this off, including the women."

"What are we going to do?" I ask him.

"You will have many things," he vaguely answers.

"This man, One Eye, who is he?" Mr. Johnson asks.

"He is the son of a Pawnee Chief. The Pawnee Squaw was his sister."

"It would be most appreciated, Chief, if you would allow me to ask you more questions that my heart needs answers to."

"I will do what I can," White Horse says.

"Well," Father says, "I say we all sit down in the parlor and discuss this further then."

"That sounds like a marvelous idea," Mr. Johnson agrees. "Shall we?"

As I stand up to join the others, it is then that my father sees my cut wrist.

"Child, what happened?" he asks.

"Oh, I cut myself with a knife. Stella and I became blood sisters."

"You did what!" Roger barks. "Let me see that." Roger quickly comes to my side.

White Horse stops short and turns around along with Mr. Johnson.

"Why on earth would you become blood sisters?" Father asks.

"We had to. We had to finish what we started."

"Carrie, what are you talking about?" Roger huffs.

"Come, I will show you."

I walk to the parlor and over to the table, where I come down on my knees.

"Look." Mr. Johnson and Roger both look at the engravings on the side of the table.

"Well, I'll be," Mr. Johnson says. "I had forgotten all about that."

He chuckles to himself. "I remember when I found out how my precious expensive table was vandalized by four rambunctious girls, how angry I was," he smiles. "You four were definitely anything but dainty little girls," he jokes.

"How long did you bleed?" Roger asks me as I come to my feet.

"It was a rascal to control, but after applying pressure for about ten minutes, I got it to stop."

Both Roger and Father look at each other. "What?" I whine. "Oh, come on, it was just a little blood; it didn't even hurt much."

Mr. Johnson hands my father a drink.

"Shall we sit down?" he jesters.

"I am a man of the cloth. I do not drink," he says.

"It is only ours that is filled with whiskey. Yours is cider," Mr. Johnson smiles.

"In that case, I will accept." Father takes a sip and makes his way to his chair.

"Chief White Horse," Mr. Johnson says, "may I offer you a drink? I made it myself."

"Thank you," he says as he sits down in the fancy chair.

The men begin their discussion as Stella and I begin the dishes.

"I think the dinner went well," I comment to Stella.

"How would you know you were too busy looking at the Chief," she jokes.

"No, I wasn't," I defend. "Was I?"

"Yes," she laughs. I, too, laugh along with her.

"I can't say I blame you," Stella says. "He is very handsome."

"That he is," I agree, as I start to dry the plates.

"He is very smitten with you," she says.

"Is it that obvious?" I ask.

"It is pretty obvious that he is very fond of you."

"I hope Father doesn't see it."

"Oh, that wouldn't be good," she says.

"Father has seen many men flirt with me. He has never said a word. He trusts me."

"This isn't any man, Carrie," she argues. "This is an Indian Chief. Your father accepts him because he is a man of peace and love, but I honestly do not feel he will accept him or feel he is good enough for his daughter."

I can't argue with her because I, too, have the same thought.

"For now, Stella, I must keep our relationship quiet. I cannot change any further problems until these attacks are over. We need White Horse."

"His motives are already being questioned," she says.

"What do you mean?" I ask her.

"When I was in town today to check on the post office, I overheard Carl tell Sid that he is certain something else is bringing the Chief here and he is still behind these attacks. Carl is digging for the truth, and if he finds out, I fear what will happen to you."

"It is not our courting that I am worried about. God forbid if the truth comes out of me being with a child. I am not only worried for myself. I worry for my father."

"Carrie, you did the correct thing by telling Hank," she says. "He will make sure that Carl doesn't find out anything."

"Carl knows better than to mess with White Horse. He learned his lesson on that."

"Yes. He is rather upset about that as well," she chuckles. "Sure, wish I could have seen that. That had to have been a sight."

"It was. No one was expecting him to act that way, especially Carl."

"I don't know, Carrie, just be careful. I do not trust Carl."

Before I can respond, the kitchen door swings open, and Mr. Johnson steps in.

"Come, ladies. The Chief is just about ready to reveal what is necessary from us on his plan."

Chapter Twenty-Four

The Dummies

Two days have passed since the dinner at Mr. Johnson's. All the children and their mothers moved into their temporary shelter. Per Father's request, Stella and I moved in as well and her and I share a room. Father is refusing to leave the church. He is like a soldier protecting his Fort. The doors to the church remain open for anyone who needs rest, food, and prayer.

I have seen very little of White Horse or any of the Lakota. Many fear that they have left. Hank is assuring us that they are here and that their distance is all part of their plan and soon we will see them again. Stella and I are in town to grab what supplies we can from the general store. With no stagecoaches coming in to deliver, the store's shelves are picked over. We purchase what supplies we can and then make our way back to the Johnson home.

The streets to Willow Creek are eerie and bear, with only a few being seen on the street. I spot Hank just outside the saloon, sweeping the entrance free from dust. Stella and I both wave over to him before making our way across the bridge. As we are nearing the end of the bridge, we see Roger and my Father walking across. As I watch the men come across the bridge, I immediately sense something is wrong.

"What is wrong?" I question them when they stop in front of us.

"There was another attack last night," Roger says.

"Who got attacked?" I questioned.

"We did," Roger answers.

"Oh my God," I gasp.

"We just came back from there. Three bodies were found."

"What?" I am confused. "How could that be?"

"That is what we are asking ourselves as well." Chief White Horse and some of his men were there, along with the sheriff and Sid. They are just as puzzled."

"Where is the Chief?" I ask.

"He is in the saloon." I look over at my Father.

"Please allow me to see him?" I ask him.

"Yes, child, but now that the topic has surfaced, I must tell you I do not like the way that the Chief admires you. I forbid you from being alone with him, but I will allow this for now because of the circumstances, and Hank will be there. Do you understand me?"

"Yes, Father."

I quickly excuse myself and rush to the saloon. I literally bump into Carl when I swing the door open. I step back as he glares at me. Hank quickly makes his way to the door and holds it open. Carl briefly stops, towers over me, and nudges past me. I look over at Hank and step into the saloon. I immediately see White Horse standing not far from the window, and I am certain he saw it all. Hank swings the door closed and stands in front of it. I rush into White Horse's arms, and we embrace. During our embrace, I see Koawa sitting in a chair at the back of the saloon. He watches us embrace.

"How have you been?" he asks me. He takes my hand into his.

"I am a little baffled," I say.

"About what Love?" he asks.

"Roger just told me about our homestead being attacked. He said they found three bodies. How can that be?"

"Very simple. Hank and I put them there yesterday." Now I am really confused. I look over at Hank.

"They were the Websters," he says. I gasp.

"You mean they were already dead?" White Horse just nods. "That is sick," I snap." You degraded them."

White Horse holds my hand, thumbing his finger across the top of it. "I understand why you would think that, and I, too, feel the same, but allow me to explain."

He walks me over to the corner of the saloon to a table that has several drinks on it and a map of Willow Creek. We sit down across from each other.

"Remember what I told you about the fork?" he says.

"Yes," I answer.

"After looking at the map in detail, I concluded that your home was the next to be attacked." White Horse pushes the map in front of me and points.

"Here is the fork," he points. "These X's are the homes that have been attacked. If you watch closely, you begin to see a pattern." He is right. "When you get to the fork, you notice clearly on the map that your home is on the path towards Willow Creek. The other end of the fork leads you away from Willow Creek. When I showed this to Hank, he told your Father. That is why he was so adamant that you stay at the big house on the hill."

"Oh, I see," I say.

"Your Father had access to the Webster's bodies. If you remember correctly, they were killed during the day as they worked in their field. None of them were burned. Except for the holes in their back by the arrows that killed them, they were unscarred. We placed their bodies in your home and left a lantern on to make it appear that someone was home."

"That is just sick," I say.

"Oh, I assure you, Beautiful, your father gave them a ceremony that would have made you proud."

I feel horrible. The Websters were good people and didn't deserve to die and definitely didn't deserve to be used as a sacrifice. I am surprised that my Father agreed. White Horse reaches across the table and takes my hand.

"I understand that this is a lot for you to take in, but sweetheart, it is necessary. It is crucial that we not raise suspicion, as I am sure Willow Creek is being watched. That is why I must stay hidden from the town. If any of my warriors or I were to be seen, it could be devastating."

I sighed deeply as I began to understand the severity of the matter.

"I just saw my Roger. He did not seem to know it was the Websters in our home."

"Your father did not want to tell your brother, for he thought he would not understand, just as he did not tell you."

"What is the next target?" I ask.

White Horse points to the map.

"One of these two buildings." He points to the saloon and the church.

"Why do you think that?" I wonder.

"They are the two largest buildings, and, in their eyes, if they are big, then they must be important."

"I need to warn Father," I say.

"He is aware," White Horse assures.

"He is a stubborn old fool," I say, shaking my head. "He needs to get out of there."

"Your brother and Hank already had this conversation with him. He refuses to leave."

I could cry. I am terrified for my Father. White Horse, seeing my sadness, squeezes my hand.

"They will attack at night. This I am sure of. My scouts are stationed, and we will be ready for when they do."

I lower my head and sniff. White Horse leans forward across the table, cupping my hands. He comes directly into my face and looks at me with his dark, mysterious, handsome eyes.

"He will be alright. I will not allow any harm to him." He kisses my hand. "I give you my word."

"Do you think they realize that the children are missing yet?"

"I am suspicious they do, as they are moving in very close."

"How much time do we have?" I ask him.

"You had two attacks last night. The second one was minor as the home had been abandoned. They are working in threes. You have one more and then Willow Creek will be hit. Now let me warn you, I am not sure if the third one is one of these buildings or if that is separate. It could be yet tonight."

"What is your hunch?" I ask him.

"My hunch is telling me that tonight, one of these two buildings will be hit."

"Which one would you hit?" Hank asks. White Horse thinks a moment.

"Your saloon holds many people at night. As your church doesn't, for that reason, I would hit the church."

Both Hank and I are confused. Hitting a building where more lives could be lost would seem logical. White Horse sees our confusion and explains.

"By hitting the church, you are making a statement."

"Then I need to get my father out of there," I say.

"Now you listen to me," White Horse says. "You are carrying my child, and I will not risk anything happening to you or our child.

Let Hank and I handle your Father. You stay in the house on the hill. That way, I know you are safe."

"Alright," I reluctantly say. White Horse smiles.

"That's my girl. How are you doing on the project that I assigned you?"

"Stella and I came for the materials today. We will start on them right away."

"Good," he says as he sits back. "I have Mr. Johnson working on a project for me. It should make him feel involved without having to fight."

"Good," I mumble.

I am glad to hear that White Horse is not asking him to fight and keeping him behind the scenes, where he can still feel he is useful but not getting hurt.

"I hate to break this up," Hank says. "But if you do not want to raise any more suspicion, then Carrie needs to leave. Rachel will walk out with her to make it appear that she was here to see her and not you."

"Thank you," White Horse says as Rachel walks up.

He glances her way as I stand up. I look down at him and we exchange a smile. I then left the saloon with Rachel. We spot Carl across the street looking at the door of the saloon. Rachel and I start a casual conversation as we walk out of the saloon and down the walkway.

I know very little about Rachel, and we are not friends. Personally, she has always been nice to me. However, she and Stella have a history from the time Stella worked as one of

Hank's girls. It was a never-ending love triangle that Stella won, and Rachel never got over it. I unfortunately got caught in the middle and had to take sides when, one day, their fight became physical over Hank. Stella, being my best friend, won the fight and my support, but it hurt my friendship with Rachel. Now, we all just tolerate each other and have no special bond. When we make our way to the post office, Rachel and I part.

It is there where I find Stella. For the remainder of the day, I will gather the women who remain to begin our project. One would think that this is the time when everyone would work together, but unfortunately, several of the women are refusing to be in the same room with Stella. Seems her history cannot be forgotten. Those women choose to do the second part of the project in another room at the other end of the house. Esther, Beth, Rachel, and Priscilla, another one of Hank's girls, join Stella and me in the parlor.

"Tell me again why we are doing this?" Stella asks as she pulls her thread through the buttonhole.

"Chief White Horse," I begin, "is wanting these dummies made, as they will be set up throughout the town to make it appear as if the town is not deserted."

"These are the ugliest townspeople I have ever seen," Esther jokes as she lays her finished dummy down on the ground with the others.

The room fills with laughter. Stella jumps up with hers and begins to play with the arms. She then mimics. "Hello. I am the sheriff."

We burst into laughter again as her replica of the sheriff is priceless. I then showed off mine. "I am Carl," I tease.

Again, laughter fills the air. The dummy is perfect, down to the bottle of whiskey he holds in his hand. It takes us nearly all day to finish our dummies. By the time we finished, there wasn't a dry eye in the room from all the laughter and stories we shared.

"Well, we are done," I say. "It is up to the rest of the ladies to finish them with the clothing."

"I wonder how they are doing?" Stella asks. "It has been very quiet in there."

"They are too stiff to have any fun," Rachel says.

Just then, there is a knock on the door. Jimmy, one of the boys, comes running down the stairs and takes the honor of answering the door. It is Roger. He steps into the parlor and chuckles when he sees the dummies.

"Where am I?" he wonders.

"Relax, brother," I tease. "Esther, did you."

"Good," he answers. "I have come because Father has planned a dinner for us. He says he has something important to tell us and requests that I come and get you. He wants Stella there as well."

"Is he alright?" I ask.

"I think everything is just starting to get to him, and he wants his family close by."

"Just let me change."

I turn to head towards the stairs that head up to the room that I share with Stella.

"He requested that you bring your sleepwear," Roger states. "He says he made arrangements for all of us at the boarding house for the night."

"Alright," I say. "Give me a few minutes."

Chapter Twenty-Five

The Inferno

BOARDING HOUSE CLOSED UNTIL FURTHER NOTICE DUE TO INDIAN ATTACKS, is the note that is nailed on the front door of the boarding house. The three of us walk into the once full and vibrant home. The aroma of dinner fills the air as Roger closes the door behind us.

"Hello," we hear Father say.

"Hello, Father," I greet.

Father is not man who has ever been good in a kitchen, for him to prepare a meal for the family, something is heavy on his mind.

"Dinner is almost ready," he says. "Shall we sit while it finishes?"

"Father, is there anything I can do to help you?" I suggest.

"No child," he smiles. "Tonight is my treat."

We each come to the table and find a seat. Father wastes little time as to his reason for wanting us here.

"I am certain everyone is wondering why the secrecy," he says.

"I will admit, Pa," Roger says, "I am a little curious."

"I have brought you all here for some very important issues that give me much grief but are necessary."

Father reaches for some papers he has on the side table.

"I have in my hand here your parent's Will Stella." Stella looks surprised.

"They never told me they had a Will," she says.

"They didn't until just a few years ago, shortly after you left Hank."

Stella is dumbfounded. Her parents were not rich and did not have much to their name. The post office barely made ends meet.

"Your parents loved you so much and wanted to make sure you were taken care of properly after their death so you would not have to feel like you need to go back to Hank and your old life to make ends meet."

She shyly smiles. There was no mistake that the Millers did not like Hank, and Hank did not like them. Stella is very aware of this, as it causes a lot of friction between them.

"I was made their beneficiary," Father continues. "I can either read it to you, or you can read it yourself at your leisure."

He hands it to Stella. Stella is not well educated and a very poor reader. Father is aware of this, but to spare her the humiliation, he pretends not to know and instead highlights the areas that were the most important to her with a big red star beside them. I thought this was very subtle and sweet.

"There are a few things that you need to be aware of. One is that your Father left the post office with you. I will be happy to help you in any way with any decisions you may come across. Second, he left you the home; however, if you note in the clause just below it, it states if the homestead is lost due to fire or any natural disaster, that enough money is held back for your relocation or rebuilding." Father slightly grins. "It is almost as if they knew that both would be taken together in a fire. Strange how the Lord works."

"Reverend," Stella says.

"Yes, my child."

"I do not know the first thing about running a business or building a home."

"I understand, child, and I will help you in any way."

"Me too, Stella," Roger adds.

"And until you decide on what you want to do about your home, you are welcome to stay here with me, as I have rented this home out for a few months."

"Really, Father?" I say.

"Yes, it is unclear if Mrs. Phillips will return."

Mrs. Phillips is a spinster and next to Mrs. Forbes, she was the worse at spreading gossip especially when it came to me, however she had a good eye for business and her boarding house was always full. Her revenue here will be missed.

"Now, children," Father continues, "for the next matter at hand. With all these attacks going on, it got my old mind to thinking on my own Will in the event of my death."

Both Roger and I shake our heads. Neither one of us wants to hear what he is about to say.

"Now, children, I clearly understand how difficult it is for you both to sit here and hear me talking about my death, but I am getting up there in years, and, as Carrie is now aware, my heart is not in good condition."

"Father, you can go on like this for years with proper care. Roger even said so," I argue.

"Yes, this is true my child, however it is not up to me, it is up to our Maker on when he chooses to take me home."

I do not want to hear this. I come to my feet.

"I need to go check on dinner," I say.

I then walk out and leave them sitting there. Stella, in an awkward position, quickly joins me.

"Can you believe that?" I huff to Stella, "Talking about his Will like that, I tell you, sometimes I wonder about him."

"Carrie, he is only looking out for his children," she says.

"He is talking foolishly, and I will not listen to it," I snap.

Stella dropped the subject and helped me bring the food out to the table. We all gather around and dinner is served.

"Oh, Father, it looks and smells delicious," I say.

He removes the cover from the tray, revealing a Thanksgiving feast.

"Oh, my Father," I say. "This had to have taken you hours."

Father sits at the head of the table and opens his napkin, tucking it on his lap.

"Very well," he blushes. "I must confess. I did not cook it. Esther did. I was just keeping it warm."

We all laugh. I knew it was too good to be true. The dinner is delicious, and as much as Stella and I give Father a hard time for not actually cooking the meal and thinking he should clean it up, we give in and do the dishes anyway.

As the sun goes down and the dinner is cleaned, we all gather again in the front room for yet another serious talk. The three of us group together, trying to convince Father not to sleep in the church. Now that he has rented the boarding house and no one is using the church to sleep in, we feel there is no reason for him to either. He finally agrees. There is relief on everyone's face as Father finally agrees to stop being so stubborn. We all call it a night and head upstairs. Stella and I share a room. Roger is just down the hall, Father to his right. Stella and I lay in our beds and talked about tonight's event and her parents' Will. From my bedroom window, I have a perfect view of the top of the church, where I am told sentries are guarding. Confident that Father was safe in his bed, I fell asleep.

Across the street, Hank stands guard on top of the saloon. He lights his tobacco and looks across at Howard on the roof of the church. Inhaling a puff, he steps away from view and looks towards the dark silhouette on the hill of the Johnson house. Taking a few more puffs, he glances over at the church. He notices that Howard is no longer standing there. Assuming he moved to the back of the church, he looked away, concentrating on the street below. He briefly catches a quick movement in the alley below him. He looks back over to the church, still not seeing Howard.

Something doesn't sit right with him. The hair starts to stand up on his neck. He jumps down on the balcony below and whistles for Sid. Sid steps out of his post and looks up at Hank.

"Stay here, I am going to check on Howard," Hank says.

Although Sid is deputy, he does as requested and walks over to the saloon to relieve Hank. Hank makes his way to the trellis and climbs down when, out of nowhere, he is hit by an arrow that grazes his side. Sid hears him bellow in pain and runs to his aid just when the renegades appear in sight. Suddenly, the church is hit with a flaming arrow through the glass window. The deathly thunder of the racing hooves, followed by chilling war calls, awakes the slumber of the town.

I jolted awake. My heart is racing. I push off my blankets and race to the window. I look out and see the top of the church in flames. I yell at Stella.

"The church is on fire!" I yell.

She quickly comes to her feet and looks out the window. Roger bursts in.

"The church is on fire," he yells.

"We know," Stella cries.

"I will go wake Father," I say.

I raced down the hallway and to my Father's room. Roger and Stella approach the stairs when I scream, "Father."

Roger stops and runs towards me as I come rushing down the hall.

"His bed has not been slept in," I say.

"Where could he be?" Stella asks.

"I bet I know," Roger says. Roger runs down the steps.

"   You don't think he is at the church, do you?" I ask.

"I would bet on it."

"I am going with you."

"No, Carrie. You stay here."

"If Father is in that church, then I am going with you."

Roger knows better than to argue. As we make our way across the street, we see Hank holding his side, stumbling his way to the church. Stella runs up to him, wrapping her arm around his waist to help him along. Roger stops to render aid. Hank brushes him off.

"I'm fine," he growls. "Just go."

The street is buzzing with fear. The cries of angry warriors fill the air. Gunshots are heard as Roger and I make our way to the church. The renegades start to retreat just as the Lakota come into view. A renegade is hit in the back with a tomahawk that was tossed by a Lakota warrior. The renegade falls to his death. Roger and I gasped in horror as we saw our beautiful church engulfed in flames.

"Father!" I scream as I rush to enter the burning building. Roger holds me back.

"Carrie, no!" he yells. I squirm to break free just as White Horse jumps off his horse.

"Hold her!" Roger yells and races into the burning building. The tears are rolling down my face as I fear the worst.

"Get the buckets!" someone yells as Stella puts her arm around me.

Roger covers his mouth from inhaling the smoke as he makes his way through the foyer.

He yells. "Pa!" He then hears a cough. He repeats. "Pa!" Another cough is heard.

"Get out of here, son," he hears.

Roger then sees his Pa at the other end of the church, cowering in a corner.

"I am coming to you, Pa!" he yells.

"No, son. It is too late for me. Save yourself."

"I will not leave you!" Roger yells.

Roger pays no mind to the flames over his head as he inches his way to his Father. He bolts through the flames that are between him and his Father. He finds his Pa curled up in a ball. Roger removes his jacket and covers his Pa's head to stop the smoke from slowly suffocating him. He looks back at where he came in and sees it is blocked with high flames. He looks around for something to break the window with. He finds a chair and tosses it through. The glass shatters and brings in a sudden, quick breeze of fresh air, but it is only temporary and adds more fuel to the fire.

The sound of the broken glass is heard as an assembly line is being formed to,ssing buckets of water into the flames. A moment of relief comes over me when I see Roger by the window. Sid runs to the window but is quickly overcome by flames and retreats. I am refusing to sit back and do nothing. I jolt free from Stella and make a run towards the church. Hank, paying no mind that he is injured, quickly grabs me from behind, lifting me up off my feet and holding me back.

"Let me go!" I holler.

"Carrie, it is too late. The flames are too high."

"No!" I scream as I try to break free from his stronghold. "Let me go!"

No sooner have I said that when part of the roof collapses. I scream.

"No!" I bellow as I come down to my knees in despair and begin to sob uncontrollably.

I see White Horse motion to Koawa. Both men run to the window where Roger was just seen. White Horse grabs a bucket of water, tossing it on the flames by the window. When he sees a break in the flames, he jumps through it. I then see Hank and Sid grab two buckets of water and race over to join Koawa and two other Lakota warriors. White Horse pulls himself up and crawls through the window. Koawa tosses another bucket of water in. The assembly line moves and joins Hank and the others in tossing water at the window to keep it from closing. I wait and watch in dismay. The thought of the three men that I love the most may all perish together is more than I can bear.

Suddenly, through the smoke and flames, a figure is seen. Koawa and Sid rush to the window and grab Roger's arm. I watch them pull him free. I rush to him and come down beside him as Koawa places him on the ground.

"Oh my God, Roger," I cry out.

He rolls on his side and violently starts to cough. I rub his back and hug him. so relieved to see him alive.

"Where is Father?" I ask.

He points to the church.

"We were nearly out," he coughs again. "The roof fell in and I lost him."

"Oh my God," I cry out.

"White Horse pulled me out and told me he was going for him."

There is a deathly silence in the air as everyone waits in horror. Koawa grows extremely anxious as he begins to worry about his brother and Chief. The flames are growing higher; all hope is starting to fade. Koawa yells in his tongue. Another Lakota warrior runs up to the window. Just as he is getting ready to jump in, a gust of flames rushes through the window. I cry out in agony as I am certain that all is lost.

We then hear another window break from the back of the church, the only side that has yet to be engulfed. A rush is made to the back of the church, and White Horse is seen coming out with

Father hunched over his shoulders. Hank, who is joined by Sid and several Lakota's, helps White Horse and Father out of the window and to safety. I fell to my knees at my Father's side. The moments feel like hours as Roger works on Father to breathe. I am sobbing uncontrollably. Stella is doing everything she can to calm me down. The air is still as onlookers watch and pray that their beloved Reverend, who is loved by everyone, will survive.

Suddenly, I hear Father gasp for air and cough. My tears of despair now change to tears of joy. I take my Father's hand into mine as I lay my head down on his chest and weep with joy. Stella and a few other onlookers join Father by his side as they cry with joy that he is alive. Roger looks over at White Horse, who is covered with ash and coughing himself. He mumbles so only White Horse can hear.

"Thank you," he says.

White Horse faintly nods as Koawa makes sure he is all right. Attention is drawn back to the church. There is nothing left that can be done. Our beautiful church is gone. Sadness again is felt by everyone as everyone watches it burn to the ground.

Chapter Twenty-Six

The Joined Forces

The aftermath of last night's fire on the church leaves Willow Creek in a somber mood. Everyone knows the inevitable is coming, and you can see the fear in everyone's eyes. Phase two of White Horse's plan is set into motion. The dummies that we made earlier are set throughout the town. All the women and children are safely tucked away in the big house on the hill with strict orders not to come into town under any circumstances. There has been no sign of the sheriff for nearly two days, and with everything going on, no one is willing to go and search for him. Sid is the only one who is concerned about him and has left on his own to find him. Many are calling the sheriff a coward and are angry that he is not leading his town at a time when he is needed the most. Hank has delegated himself to lead the men who have remained back to help fight, carefully following every detail of White Horse's plan.

After several long hours, Stella, Roger, and I have all the dummies in their place. We begin our quiet walk across the bridge to the big house on the hill. Many thoughts are racing through our minds. Our fears and anxiety are high. The uncertainty of the next few days weighs heavy on all of us. We were near the house when I saw White Horse and a few of his warriors standing on a hill. White Horse stops what he is doing and makes his way down the hill to meet us.

"How is it going?" he asks.

"All the dummies are in position," Roger says. "Supplies have been taken to the Johnson house. We are ready."

"Good," White Horse says. "It will not be long."

We all sigh deeply. Although everything is prepared and the town is ready for the attack, I know I am not alone in thinking that none of us are ready for such an ordeal.

"How much more time do you think we have?" Roger asks.

"If we are lucky, two days," White Horse says.

"And if we are unlucky?" he wonders.

"First daylight," he answers.

His words are chilling and hit us all to the core. I sigh deeply, harder than the rest.

"I need to get Stella back to the house," Roger says. "I trust you will get Carrie there safely."

White Horse nods his head. When they are out of sight, White Horse takes my hand and walks me up the hill and out of sight from his warriors. He then strokes my cheek.

"I see fear in your eyes," he says.

"There is."

"Do not fear, my love."

"I do not fear for me," I answer.

"Then do not fear for me either, for I will be fine."

White Horse sees my hesitation.

"Sweetheart. You need to trust me," he says.

"I do White Horse, but...maybe...."

"Maybe what?" he asks me.

"Well...maybe they were just scaring us, and they have moved on." White Horse chuckles to himself.

"Not only are you beautiful, but you are very naive," he says. "My precious one, these men have a mission, and they will not stop until that mission is done. It won't be much longer."

"How can you be so sure?" I ask him.

He crosses his arms and stands erect. "I thought I asked you to trust me," he huskily says.

"Is there a chance you are wrong?" I ask.

"No!" he states firmly. "Willow Creek will be attacked very soon."

I lower my head in despair. White Horse relaxes his stance, lifting my chin. "I will share something with you that, up until now, I have kept to myself."

"What?" I ask. "The time when I left with my warriors to find out what was going on, I came face to face with One Eye." I gasp. "We stared each other down, and then he left. Koawa spotted one of his warriors, whom he knew very well. His name is Running Dog. He is Chippewa."

"What does that mean?"

"Chippewa and Pawnee do not get along."

"I am not following you, White Horse."

"For a Pawnee to recruit a Chippewa warrior, he is out for blood."

"I see."

"Running Dog is an excellent warrior. One Eye needs the best to attack Willow Creek, but that is not what bothers me."

"Then what?"

"Running Dog is the son of their Chief and is making his way up to a higher rank within his tribe. Why would he leave his tribe to help his arch-enemy, a Pawnee?"

"Why?" I, too, wonder.

"Pawnee are not the only ones with whom the Chippewa are at war; so are we." I gasp again.

"What better way to move up your rank with your Chief than by collecting scalps of a few White people and a Lakota Chief."

"That is just more reason why you shouldn't do this."

"No, sweetheart, if I was the target that day, weapons would have been drawn, but none were. It is clear that day was not the day they wanted to fight. They only wanted us to know that we are being watched."

"The sheriff has not been seen for two days. Perhaps they have found what they came for and left."

"Your sheriff is here. I saw him this morning under a weeping willow. He made himself a tent. I saw him, but he did not see me."

"Maybe the Pawnee will find him, get what they came for and leave."

"No, sweetheart. They are coming."

"I am so scared for you," I cry.

He faintly smiles, taking me into his arms.

"I need you to trust me. I am safe. My men will not allow any harm to come to me. But you must promise me that you will not leave the big house until I come for you."

"I promise."

Darkness comes to the Lakota camp. Blue Thunder brought in a kill, and all the warriors are getting their fill. White Horse is sitting under a tree a short distance away. He starts to think of his people back at home. He left the women and children unprotected, as most of his warriors were with him. Moving them to a safer place was a wise choice, and he feels confident that they are safe. He thinks of his Prairie Dawn and how upset she was this afternoon. He thinks perhaps he should not have shared with her what he knows in her delicate condition. His mind circles as he runs his plan repeatedly. He wonders if he has thought of everything. Is everyone ready? Too many lives are at stake if just one thing is overlooked. He wishes he could have told his Prairie Dawn everything, but he knows it will only scare her more. He has grown to love her so much that he cannot wait to make her his bride.

He thinks of the mother of his six-year-old son. Would she approve of Prairie Dawn? He feels in his heart that she would. His thoughts wander as he sees his Prairie Dawn in his eyes. He can smell her sweet aroma. How his body aches for her. How deeply he loves her. How he cannot imagine his life without her. He questions if his people will accept her as his wife because of her skin color? He feels certain that they will. He then thinks of the child that she is nesting in her womb. How delicate and fragile they both are. He worries about her and their child and about whether something should happen to him. What would she do? Where would she go? He is certain that she would not be accepted in her own life anymore as she is carrying a half-breed. Would her brother take her in? Would her Father understand? Would they fight for her to their death as he would?

His thoughts are interrupted when he feels a presence in front of him. He opens his eyes to see his best warrior and brother, Koawa, looking at him.

"You are quiet tonight, my brother," he says. "What touches your

heart?"

"My Prairie Dawn," he answers. "It is she that keeps me quiet."

"Why would women touch you so hard?"

"It is your woman as well that you lust for tonight, my brother. Am I right?"

"Yes, you are," Koawa grins. "I have thought of her tonight as well."

"Then you will understand what I am about to tell you."

"You are not only my Chief, but you are my brother. We have shared much together. Surely, whatever is heavy in your heart, you understand you can tell me as your brother, and it will stay with me."

"Yes," White Horse says. "You have always been loyal to me. I know I can trust you to take care of my Prairie Dawn if something happens to me."

"Why are you talking nonsense?" Koawa barks. "What is really bothering you?"

"There will be many warriors that I am certain of. Chippewa are excellent warriors."

"But we are better. Our many battle coups have shown that," Koawa reassures.

"I do not feel comfortable about the attack. My mind will not rest."

"Why not? Koawa wonders. "We have everything prepared. We are ready."

"My spirits have been talking to me. They warn me of danger."

"Ahh," Koawa ticks. "You worry for nothing. I have your back."

White Horse just looks at Koawa. "Look, if you are worried, then we can change positions," Koawa says.

"No. We keep the positions the same. That is not what concerns me."

"Then what?" Koawa wonders.

"I am not afraid to die. I worry about my Prairie Dawn if I do. She is carrying a half-breed. Her people will not accept her or the child."

"She is carrying a Lakota heir," Koawa says. "I will not allow her to stay with her people. She will come with me. I will raise the child as my own. I will care for them both."

White Horse grins. "Thank you, my brother. Your offer is very kind."

"You would do it for me."

"Yes, I would."

"Then rest assured, Prairie Dawn will be taken care of."

White Horse rests his hand on Koawa's shoulder. "You are a good man," he says.

"Only one problem?" Koawa says.

"What would that be?" White Horse asks.

"That woman of yours is filled with fire. She will not come easily."

White Horse grins. He knows all too well the fire that grows in his Prairie Dawn's bones. "I will talk to her. I will make her understand that this is the right decision. She will come."

"When will you tell her?"

"Tonight, but first, I rest my eyes." White Horse leans his head back against the trunk of the tree and closes his eyes.

Koawa comes to his feet and walks over to join the rest of the warriors. He sits down across the fire, his Chief in total view.

"Rest, my Chief. Your woman is safe," he mumbles.

Evening is on the big house on the hill. Dinner has been cleaned up and it is time to put the children down for the night. My Father rounds up all the restless bodies and sits them down in a circle in the middle of the room. My Father is a great storyteller and everyone gathers around, anticipating yet another great story.

"Are you going to tell us about Adam and Eve, Reverend," Jenny asks.

"Forget about Adam and Eve," Jimmy says. "I want to hear a story about Indians."

Jimmy is fascinated with Indians. He thinks Chief White Horse is out of sight. I for one completely agree.

"Jimmy, please," his mother begs. She looks over at my Father.

"Forgive him, Reverend. Seeing all these Indians around has got his mind thinking strange things."

"No worries, sister. I believe it is good for a child's mind to be open, but I think tonight I will tell a story about a very courageous boy and a lion." He tosses his hands around like he is growling. The children laugh. He then begins his story.

"Once upon a time in a land far away..." Just then, there is a knock on the door. Roger quietly gets up and goes to the door. He opens it up to White Horse.

"I need to see Carrie," White Horse says.

Roger says nothing and calls me to the door. I see White Horse standing there. "Is everything alright?" I ask him.

"We need to talk," he looks over at Roger who is still standing in the doorway. "Alone," he growls.

I look over at Roger. He stands for a few moments and then backs away. I step outside, closing the door behind me. White Horse takes me off the porch and leads me to the side of the house, away from view. It is there that he kisses me. "I do not think you came all this way just to kiss me," I tease him.

He grins. "No, I did not, but I must admit I enjoyed it," he teases back.

He entwines his long fingers into mine. "Prairie Dawn, you are with my child, whom we conceived out of love, and I must make you understand how important it is to our people that our child remains a Lakota." I nodded my head. Where is this leading? "In the event that I die tomorrow, you are to go with Koawa and live with him and raise our child."

I quickly removed my hands from his.

"You are not going to die!" I spat.

"Carrie, there is a chance with any battle of death."

"Then don't do it," I yell. He reaches for my hand, and I pull it away.

"Carrie, listen to me."

"No White Horse, I will not! I will not stand here and listen to you talk about dying."

I turn to walk away. He quickly grabs my wrist and turns me around. He grasps my shoulders firmly, looking at me squarely in the eyes.

"Do not turn away from me. You must understand what I am telling you."

"I can't," I cry. "I won't." I hear him sigh as I lower my eyes.

"My Love, please, I must be able to fight with a clear mind. I cannot fight without knowing that my child and the woman I love will be alright."

I am sobbing. "I need you not to fight me or Koawa on this," he wipes a tear. "Promise me you will go with Koawa if something happens to me."

I look at him through my tearful eyes. The thought of losing him is ripping me apart. I cannot stop him from fighting; it is in his blood. It is something I am going to have to accept. I know this child is important, not only to him, but to his people as well. If I love White Horse and Lord how I do, then I must grant his wish and accept.

"I will go," I sob.

He pulls me into his arms, and we embrace. It gives me such pain in my heart to think that this may be the last time I get to hold him. I let the embrace linger.

Father finishes up his story as I enter the house. I am too upset to join the others and start my way up the grand staircase.

"Carrie," I hear from Roger. I stop and turn to him. He sees my weeping eyes and makes his way up the stairs where I have stopped.

"What is it?" he asks. I rushed into his arms and cried.

Chapter Twenty-Seven

Tears of Fear

The morning sun peaks though the big pane window. I let a sleeping Stella lie and get myself dressed before heading downstairs. I make my way to the kitchen and start the morning coffee. My morning sickness, along with shattered nerves, is making my stomach turn circles. I quickly make my way to the outhouse to vomit. Roger is pouring himself some coffee when I return.

"Good morning," he greets.

"Morning," I mumble.

Roger comes up beside me, pushing a tonic bottle to me.

"Take a teaspoon twice a day," he says. "It will help calm down your stomach." I put the bottle in my apron pocket.

"I am sure it is just my nerves. I hardly slept a wink last night."

"Me too," Roger says.

"I wish I could say the same thing about Father. When I went to check on him, he was sleeping like a baby."

"Yes, I went to check on him as well. He was sound asleep, strange though," Roger says.

"What?" I ask him.

"When I was on my way back to my room, I saw Mr. Johnson standing outside of Anna's room just staring at the door."

"Hmm," I add. "Come to think of it, the day Stella and I were cleaning the home, I went looking for him to tell him about the dinner. I found him in the cellar, sitting under the stairs. He appeared very distraught and teary-eyed."

"I believe all this talk about Anna and her rape has opened up some wounds that were not yet healed."

"Poor guy. I wish I knew how to help him?" I say.

"Bringing the people to justice who hurt his daughter, I believe, will help."

"I just hope White Horse can stop it. I am so worried about him."

"He does not seem to be worried about it all."

"Roger, you didn't see White Horse last night. He is just as nervous as we are," I argue.

"In what way?"

"He told me if he was to die, I was supposed to go with Koawa back to their camp and live with him."

Roger seems a little surprised as he sips my coffee.

"What did you tell him?"

"That I would go."

"You wouldn't stay here and let me help you?" Roger asks.

"Roger, I am carrying a half breed. I cannot stay here. Think of what it will do to father."

I reach for a lemon in the bowl and begin to slice it half with the knife that is beside it.

"Besides, I don't think I will have much of a choice in the matter. Koawa would kidnap me. I know he would."

"Carrie," he cautions, "if you are at all scared about going with either one of them, I can make it where they cannot come around."

"Roger. I am not scared to be around them. Everyone has a calling, and I believe I have found mine."

"What do you mean?"

"Father is a reverend, and you are a doctor. Me, I have no purpose here. Maybe my calling is living with them."

"Oh, Come on, Carrie," Roger huffs. "You have a purpose here. I will take care of you and that child. Father will as well."

"Roger I am happy. I love White Horse. I am carrying his heir and if God forbid White Horse dies, I will willing go with Koawa."

Roger takes my hand. "I will not stop you. I can tell you are happy. You will be alright." I faintly grin.

I take a suck of the lemon.

"I wish I knew what was going on," I whine. "They could be fighting now, and we would never know."

"No," Roger says, "we would hear the gunfire and the bridge being blown up."

"That is right. That is when we all go to the basement."

"Yes," he answers.

"I am so nervous, Roger."

"We all are," he says, raising his cup to take another sip.

"I am so glad that Pa agreed to stay here and not try to fight."

"Amen to that!" I agree.

We hear the kitchen door swing open. It is Beth Jenkins.

"Good morning, Mrs. Jenkins," Roger greets. "Good morning. Have either one of you seen Jimmy?" she asks.

"No," we say.

"Well, where could that boy be?" she asks.

"Did you check the grounds?" Roger asks.

"Maybe he is in the outhouse," she says as she goes for the door.

"I was just out there, and I didn't see him," I say.

"I am worried. Jenny overheard him say last night that he was going to find the Indian camp."

Roger and I just look at each other.

"You don't think he...?"

Roger puts his cup down and goes to grab his coat.

"I would bet my money on it," he says.

"I am going with you," I say. "We can cover more ground."

"I will go too," Beth says.

"No, you stay here with Jenny. We will find him and bring him back," Roger says.

Roger and I quickly make our way out the door and down the big hill.

"He could be anywhere," I cry.

"No," Roger assures," he went to find the Indians, and they are all in town. He's down there. We just have to find him, and we must hurry."

Although there is no guarantee that we are going to be attacked today, both Roger and I can feel it in our guts that today is the day. This makes it even more urgent to find Jimmy and hurry back.

There is an eerie feeling as we cross the bridge. Willow Creek is deathly still. From a distance, the dummies look so life-like in the windows and in the chairs. They almost appear as ghosts trying to tell their story. Roger and I each take different sides of the walkway, looking through windows and down the street in hopes of finding Jimmy. We both turn down Main Street, where the Saloon stands and split up. Roger turns left towards the school as I continue straight. After several minutes of peering through the windows and searching down alleys, I spotted Jimmy at the end of the street just past the general store.

"Jimmy," I call out. I rush down the walkway to scold him. "James Jenkins," I huff. "I reckon you have caused enough trouble for one day. What in tar nations are you doing down here?"

"I just want to give my lucky rabbit foot to the Chief." He holds it up to me. "See?"

"That is a nice jester, Jimmy, but you had strict orders not to come down that hill."

"I know...but..." he squirms.

Just then, his eyes lit up like saucers. I turn around just as White Horse jumps off the roof.

"Whoa," Jimmy says. "Awesome!"

White Horse is dressed for battle. His face is partially painted, with several stripes going down it. His hair is free with several feathers looped in a small braid on one side of his head. He is shirtless and wears red paint across his chest in a geometrical design and looped over his shoulder he wears all the gear that is necessary for a battle. I can completely understand Jimmy's response, as White Horse look breathtaking.

"I told you to stay up at the house," he huskily says.

"Jimmy ran off. Roger and I came looking for him. I am sorry, White Horse," I say.

"Do not be angry with her Chief," Jimmy says. "It is all my fault. I wanted to find you." Jimmy pulls out his lucky rabbit foot and dangles it in front of White Horse.

"I wanted to bring you this for good luck." White Horse looks down at Jimmy. "You should not have come," he says.

I can see the disappointment in Jimmy's eyes. Feeling ashamed for upsetting the boy, White Horse comes down on one knee in front of Jimmy. He allows Jimmy to put the rabbit foot necklace over his head. White Horse looks down at it and grins.

"I will wear this with pride," he says. Jimmy smiles. "You are now one of my braves. Would you like that?" White Horse asks.

"Yes, Chief, very much," Jimmy smiles.

"Good. I will give you your first assignment as my bravery."

"What!" Jimmy wonders.

"I need you to escort this lovely woman back up the hill and protect her until I return. Can you do that for me?"

"Oh, yes, Chief. I will protect her with my life." White Horse grins and rubs the top of Jimmy's head.

"You must hurry. Go."

No sooner had White Horse said that when we heard a whistle. White Horse stands up and looks.

"There is no time. They are here."

He quickly takes me by the hand as I grab Jimmy's, and we are being rushed to safety. We ran down the street and into the Saloon. He pushes us down behind the bar.

"Stay down," he orders.

"Roger is out there," I cry.

"I will find him. You both stay down."

I watched him run out the door. I quickly take cover next to Jimmy when we hear the explosion of the bridge being blown up. The battle has begun.

The windows at the Johnson house shake upon the explosion. Everyone quickly runs to the basement door. Father reaches for Beth's hand.

"Come along, my child. We need to take cover."

"No, my boy is still out there," she cries.

"Beth, there is nothing we can do but pray that my children have found him," he coaxes her to the door. "Lord be with them." He says as he closes the door and walks down the steps to the basement floor. He quickly reaches for the lantern and lights it. Taking it with him, he joins the others under the steps and huddles in with them.

"Where is Theodore Johnson?" he asks.

"I saw him leave early this morning. I don't know where he went," Beth answers.

"Oh heavens," Father says. Another blast is heard.

"I'm scared, Mother," Jenny says.

"Me too, darling," Beth answers.

"Let us all pray," Father says. "Our Father who is in heaven." everyone joins in. "Hallow will be thy name. Thy kingdom come; thy will be done on earth as it is in heaven. Give us this daily bread and forgive us our trespasses as we forgive those who trespass against us. For thy is the kingdom, thy power, and the glory forever. Amen!"

The windows of the Saloon shatter, causing both Jimmy and I to scream. The noise of the explosions and gunfire fills the air. I hold my ears as the noise is deafening. The mirror above our head is shot, and glass comes pouring down. Jimmy and I scream as we scoot for better cover. Suddenly, we hear movement from the stairs above us. Jimmy and I both panicked as to whoever it was upstairs would come down and attack us. I grab a whiskey bottle under the bar. I hold it in my hand and am ready to strike. I hear footsteps coming down the stairs. Jimmy finds himself a weapon as well, and we are ready to strike. I then see that Roger followed White Horse. Another bullet flies through the window. We all take cover.

"Stay down," White Horse tells Roger before running back up the stairs.

Our hearts are racing as the battle rages on. A flaming arrow flies into the Saloon, igniting the wooden floor. Roger grabs a pitcher of water on top of the counter. He rushes over to it, pouring the water over the flames. The flames persist. He takes his jacket off and begins beating the fire out. Jimmy and I rush to his aid and help. Finally, the fire is extinguished. Another arrow is shot through the window, just missing Roger. We quickly take our cover behind the bar.

The last few days have been a blur for Theodore Johnson as his daughter's senseless death runs through his mind. He promised the Chief he would remain with the others in the big house on the hill and even promised him to keep a watchful eye on the young woman that he was fond of. He feels bad that he will break his promise, but right now, he has more important matters he must attend to. He hears the fighting going on in Willow Creek, more than a mile away. He knows everyone is busy, and he will not be missed. Theodore saw the sheriff yesterday under the big willow tree by Rosy Peak. He finds him again cowering in the grass. He sneaks up behind him, drawing his gun. He cocks it and watches the coward jump to his feet.

"I should have killed you all those years ago," he growls.

"Go ahead," the sheriff cries, "I don't care anymore."

"You filthy bastard," Mr. Johnson says. "You are nothing but a coward.

You were sworn to protect our town and to serve our needs. You do not deserve to live."

"I never meant to hurt that Squaw. I never meant for any of this to happen. You must believe me, Theodore."

"And my Anna, you never meant to hurt her?"

"It was not like that. I swear. It was not like that."

"You liar!" he screams. "You killed my Anna."

"No, I would never have killed her. What happened to her was not my doing."

"You took my daughter against her wishes. You killed her!"

"I can understand why you would think that. I really do. I only wanted to be with her. I loved her."

Theodore turns his gun around, hitting the sheriff with the butt. He falls to the ground with an open cut to his skull.

"You son of a bitch! Anna would still be alive if she never conceived. You killed her," he yells. He turns his gun back on him. "Now you will pay for what you did to my Anna." He cocks his gun. The sheriff comes to his feet, putting his hands in the air.

"No...Stop. Please!" he begs.

"Is that what Anna said as you were raping her?"

"No…No…!"

A quick cock of the gun and shot to the head, and the sheriff falls dead to the ground.

"Now it is over," he says.

Theodore looks down at the sheriff's lifeless body. He picks up the sheriff's gun and places it in his hand. He then repositions his body, making it appear as if the sheriff took his own life. He then casually walks to his horse and hoists himself up, feeling at peace and that justice has been served.

Minutes seem like hours as the battle is brewing outside. Jimmy is nestled in my arms, and both of us are too scared to move. Suddenly, the ground grows still. Has the battle stopped? We are too frightened to look. We remain where we are. After a few moments, Roger picks up his head.

"I think it is done." He jumps when he hears hollering. "They are cheering," he says. He smiles widely. "They are cheering!" Roger comes to his feet and steps around the bar. Jimmy and I slowly follow him out. He walks to the window. "Yes, Carrie! They are leaving." He hugs me. "We did it, Carrie, they are leaving." Roger swings me. "Thank you, Jesus."

"White Horse, I have to find White Horse," I say excitedly.

"Yes, let us go find him."

We make our way out to the grizzly sight. There are dead bodies lying everywhere. Some are Indian, and some are not. Some have been shot, some have arrows coming out of them, and some have been blown up.

"Oh, dear God," Roger says.

I cover my mouth in despair. None of it is fazing Jimmy, and he runs over to one of our men and pulls out an arrow.

"Jimmy, don't do that," I scold.

"Ms. Sims, look," he points.

I follow his eyes and see White Horse. With no hesitation I ran towards him. He grabs my shoulders. "It's over sweetheart. We did it."

He looks so happy. I am so proud of him and so thankful to see him alive.

"Is it really over, White Horse?"

"Yes, my love it is really over." I squeezed his hand. I am so happy and relieved. I walk with him down the street.

"Did you lose any men?" I ask him.

"I fear I did as I fear you did as well; we will know soon enough."

"I am sorry, White Horse."

"It does bring me sadness, but we will be alright. I need for you to go get the women and children and let them know it is safe to come out."

"I will," I say excitedly. "I most definitely will."

My insides are jumping for joy as I make my way in front of the livery to climb the hill to the big house. White Horse watches me as I pass by. His eyes widen. His face grows white, for he sees in horror the danger lurking in his Prairie Dawn. He takes off in a dead-heated run. Jimmy sees it as well and screams.

"Watch out!" Jimmy yells.

His scream makes all eyes turn. I turned my head to the livery, and I, too, then screamed, as not more than a few feet from me was the warrior they call One Eye aiming a gun right at me.

White Horse catches up to me, lunges forward, and pushes me down to the ground just as the shot is fired. I hear him bellow out as we both land hard on the ground. Another shot is heard, and One Eye is hit. He falls to the ground dead. I hear the shuffle of feet as I gaze up at White Horse, who is lying on top of me.

"White Horse," I say, giving him a gentle shake when he fails to move. I then feel a warm trickle on my hand. I called out his name again.

"White Horse," I say. I removed my hand from underneath me. A sudden moment of sheer panic comes over me as I realize the warmness that I am feeling is White Horse's blood. I roll White Horse over. His body is limp, and a huge flow of blood is seeping from his side.

"Oh my God, No!" I scream.

A flood of people, both of our own and Lakota, have come to his side.

Koawa plops down onto the ground beside White Horse.

"Let me by," I hear from Roger as he pushes his way through.

My body is trembling and tears are rolling down my face. Hank comes up behind me wrapping his arms around my waist and pulling me aside, allowing Roger to work.

"Is he dead?" Koawa asks.

Roger feels for a pulse and puts his ear to White Horse's chest.

"No," he answers. "But he is barely breathing."

"Roger, do something!" I scream.

Roger continues to assess White Horse. He shakes his head.

"This is bad, this is really bad." Roger comes to his feet. "We need to get him back to the clinic so I can stop this bleeding."

Koawa is quick to react and takes charge ordering his warriors to help in lifting their Chief to the clinic. White Horse is carried a short distance down the street and placed on the table in the clinic. Roger is quick to get what supplies he needs.

"I will need to remove the bullet and stop the bleeding," he says out loud. "Hank, I will need your help," he says. "Go wash up." Hank is quick to obey. Roger pushes me out of the way.

"I want to help," I cry.

"No, Carrie, you are too close to this," he says as he starts his work.

"But I know what to do."

"Carrie, I do not have time to argue." He looks over at Koawa. "Get her out of here."

Roger looks at the full room filled with Lakota's. "I want everyone except for Hank out of here."

Koawa hears the urgency in Roger's voice and obeys. I take one final look at White Horse. I leaned down and kissed his forehead.

"I love you," I whisper.

Koawa takes my arm and pulls me towards the door. I hear him tell White Horse, "Hang in there. Fight my brother, Fight."

He then leaves the clinic, closing the door behind him. Roger comes on top of White Horse with his scalpel.

"Come on, White Horse," he tells him. "You told me you would take care of her. Don't you die on me?"

Chapter Twenty-Eight

Shattered Dreams

The cleanup on the streets from the attack is underway. Koawa and I are sitting on a bench outside the clinic door. We have been sitting here for nearly two hours. The remaining Lakota warriors are gathering up their dead. So far, the death toll has included thirty-six Pawnee, ten Lakota, and twelve townsmen.

Blue Thunder, along with several other warriors, are refusing to leave and will remain at their nearby camp until word is known about their Chief. Koawa sends the other remaining warriors back home to bury their dead and spread the word about White Horse.

My heart is heavy with emotion. I am just beside myself with grief as I wait for any news on White Horse's condition. I notice Carl across the street in front of the Saloon. He has been standing there watching me since White Horse was brought in. I am unclear as to what he is so interested in, but knowing Carl, it cannot be good. The minutes are slowly passing by, and Koawa has not moved. The concern and love for his brother and Chief are deeply sketched on his face. He is taking this just as hard as I am.

I know very little about this man. He is very quiet and keeps to himself, not at all like White Horse. My heart goes out for him, as so much lies in his hands with White Horse being down and him next in rank. I can only imagine what he must be feeling.

"Roger is a good doctor," I tell him. He looks over at me.

"He really is. If anyone can pull White Horse through this, it is him."

"White Horse will not die."

He says it as if he is almost reassuring himself.

"I love him too, Koawa, and if God forbid he does not survive, I want you to know I will go with you. I will give you no problems." He does not say a word but simply nods his head.

Another hour will pass. Koawa and I sit in silence and wait for the clinic door to open. Our hearts grow more and more weary the longer we go without any word. Finally, our silence is broken when Stella comes walking down the walkway carrying a basket.

"I just heard," she says. "How is he?"

"No word yet," I mumble. Lowering my eyes. She sits down on the bench beside me when Koawa stands.

"It has been so long," I cry.

"These things take time, Carrie. Roger is doing everything he can. White Horse could not be in better hands."

"I know."

"I brought you something," she says. She opens her basket revealing some fruit. "For later. It may be a wait."

"Thank you, Stella," I faintly grin.

She truly is a great friend, and right now, I need one.

"I brought some for your friend as well."

Koawa looks over at her as she offers him an apple. He briefly hesitates before taking it. We then watch him bite into it, as he sits down on the top step looking out at the street.

"Doesn't say much, does he?" she says.

"No, he doesn't," I answer.

My anxiety about waiting for any news on White Horse is great. The thought of losing him is heavy on my mind. I sigh deeply.

"I cannot lose him, Stella," I cry. "I cannot raise this child on my own."

"Carrie. Don't lose your faith. White Horse loves you. His love for you will give him the strength to survive."

I wiped a tear and looked out to see Carl not more than three feet away from me. I jumped. I cannot believe not one of us had seen him approach. I am uncertain what he may have overheard. Koawa is quickly on his feet and in his face. He is making it very clear that at least for now I am his and he better back off.

"Relax," Carl smirks over at him. "I am only here to see how the Chief is doing?"

"Like you really care," I smart off.

"Now, Carrie, that was not nice. Here I am trying to be a gentleman, and you go and say something so mean."

I know Carl well enough he is up to something.

"See what I get. I come all this way over here from across the street and wait patiently for Stella to stop flapping her lips about your lover."

I grew still. Carl overheard. Koawa is quick to my defense. He folds his arms across his chest, planting himself between Carl and me. As little as I know about Koawa, I can tell that he is not nearly as patient as White Horse. I, for one, would not want to piss him off.

"You are not welcome here. Now Leave!" he snarls. Carl sizes him up.

"Don't be stupid, Carl," I warn. "The Chief is much nicer than he is."

Carl gets the point and, giving Koawa a glare, he walks away.

"Do you think he overheard?" Stella asks.

"Lord, I hope not."

"He better stay away from you," Koawa warns, "or I will finish what White Horse started."

It is a warning that gives both Stella and I chills. Koawa is not a man who will waste his breath on empty threats. He is the man who means what he says. I truly pity Carl if he is stupid enough to take him on. Stella remains by our side as the hours go by and still the clinic door remains closed. I take this as a good sign that White Horse is still alive. I know if he isn't we would have heard by now.

Roger's words start haunting me. "This is bad," he said, "This is really bad." Just how bad is White Horse hurt? The thought that he is lying in there fighting for his life because of me is heavy on my heart. How could I ever face his people if he died? How could I ever expect them to forgive me? I have no intention of going back on my word to White Horse. I will go with Koawa. I will live my life as a Lakota. I then think of Koawa; what are his intentions? What does he have planned for me? I ask myself, can I trust him? Do I even have a choice? My thoughts are interrupted when Koawa comes up beside me.

"This is all my fault," I mumble.

"You must not think like this," he says.

"The only reason White Horse did this was because of me. I got him shot." Koawa shakes his head no as he sits down beside me.

"White Horse did not only do this for you. He had a score to settle with One Eye."

"That is not what I was told."

"You believe what you wish. I know differently." He glances over at me.

"It is not your fault that White Horse is in there. I, too, would have done the same thing for the woman I love."

"How can you be so strong, Koawa?" I ask.

"One does not have to show on the outside the pain they feel on the inside." Koawa's inner strength is incredible. He never shows any emotion and never loses his focus. He is as solid as a rock through and through. Before I can respond, I see Beth and Jimmy approaching.

"Charles just told me. I am sorry," she says.

"Thank you."

"He will be alright, Ms. Sims. He is wearing the lucky rabbit foot," Jimmy assures me. I faintly grin.

"I hope you are right, Jimmy."

"The town is talking about him," Beth starts. "Many are grateful for what he has done. They are talking about you as well, but I do not believe what they are saying."

I didn't ask, and I don't care what is being said. It just doesn't matter to me. All I care about right now is White Horse.

"Thank you, Beth."

"Beth, come on," her husband Charles calls from across the street.

"Oh, he is so impatient," she huffs. "I must leave. We need to see if our home is still standing."

"Thank you, Beth."

"Please know I am praying for you and the Chief."

That means a great deal to me. I don't consider Beth, a good friend of mine. She is in our congregation and works a great deal with my father, but besides that association, we have nothing in common. I think it sweet to even come my way and express her concern. We watch as Charles helps his pregnant wife on the wagon. I glance over at Carl, who has returned to his usual spot outside the saloon door and is looking my way. He then appears as if something clicks, and he arrogantly makes his way across the street to me. He does not get far. Koawa is quick on his feet and has the bottom step blocked. Carl holds up his hands, easing Koawa back.

"Calm down," he growls. "I ain't gonna do nothing."

Neither Koawa nor I believe him.

"I want to share with you, Carrie, what I just figured out."

"Careful, Carl, don't think too much. You may hurt yourself," I spat.

"Very funny, Carrie," he teases, "but I believe I am the one who will get the last laugh."

"What are you talking about?" I whine.

"It all came clear to me when I saw Charles with Beth and her belly being so big with a runt. It got me thinking about you." I grew still. "I will admit it took me a while, with you being a whore and everything."

That strikes a nerve, and Koawa comes off the bottom step. Carl continues, "When the Chief viciously attacked me, it became clear how protective he is of his asset. That is being you. You are his asset, ain't you Carrie?"

Koawa steps forward and is in Carl's face.

"I will not repeat myself again," he growls. "You leave her alone."

"Touchy! Touchy," Carl boldly spats. "I can understand why you are so protective. Guarding your Chief's whore and everything, or are you just upset that you didn't get to her first?"

Koawa's patience is gone. He grabs Carl by his shirt, lifting him off the ground. Carl's eyes grow huge. He was not expecting Koawa to be so strong.

"You are a foolish, arrogant man whose hole in his face will get him killed. I will not warn you again. You leave her alone, or I will close that hole forever."

He then puts him down. I am not sure if Carl is intimidated by his threat, but I know Koawa means it. We watch Carl as he begins to walk back across the street. He then abruptly stops, snapping his fingers.

"Oh, I nearly forgot. When were you planning on telling everyone your dirty little secret? Oh, wait," he puts his hand out, "allow me." He clears his throat, throws his hands up in the air, and yells. "The bitch is pregnant!"

The gasps and whispers are heard throughout the street. I could have crawled into a hole and died. Carl is quick to disappear into the Saloon before Koawa can go after him. He gazes out the window, satisfied that he got the last laugh. I bury my head in my lap and cry. I have never felt so humiliated in my life. Stella puts her arm around me.

"Ignore him, Carrie."

"Oh my God. Why does that man hate me so much?"

"Shh, dry your tears. Your father is coming."

I quickly compose myself and come to my feet as he steps on the porch.

"My dear child. I got here as fast as I could."

"Thank you, Father."

"Sid told me what happened."

"It is bad, Father. It is really bad."

"There, there, it will be alright. He is a man that has a will to survive."

"I love him, Father," I blurt out.

"I know you do," he smiles.

"You do?"

"My child, I may be a man of the cloth, but I am not blind. I see how you look at each other. I have seen the man protect you. He is a man who loves you."

"I can't lose him, Father."

"It is alright," he consoles. "Any word yet?"

"No, Father, and it has been hours."

"I will go check on him," he gives me a hug. "Now go dry your tears. I will be right back."

He turns to go inside, briefly giving Koawa a pat on the back. No sooner has Father reached the door than Hank steps out. We all rush over to him.

"How is he?" I ask.

"He is alive. You can go in."

Just as we are ready to step in, Carl comes out of the woodwork, cutting in front of us. He takes my father's hand and shakes it.

"Allow me to be the first to congratulate you on your grandchild," he boasts.

Father quickly turns his head to me.

"Carrie, what is he talking about?"

Hank wastes no time getting Carl out of there. No further conversation is needed.

321

My father knows by my expression that what Carl has said is true. He shakes his head and walks away. Damn you, Carl, I say under my breath. I should run after Father. I owe him that much, but a gentle nudge by Koawa for me to go in kept me from doing it.

Chapter Twenty-Nine

Lakota Blood

Roger was washing his hands when we entered the room. A very pale and sick-looking White Horse lies on the table. I take his hand into mine.

"How is he?" I ask Roger.

"Very weak. He has lost a lot of blood. I was able to remove the bullet and stop the bleeding."

I stroked his cheek. He is so pale and cold.

"But he will live, yes?" Koawa asks.

"I will be honest with you. Most men who receive this kind of injury would not have survived. For him to still be alive is promising. He is very strong and has a will to live. That will help him, but he has a long road ahead of him. The next few hours will decide."

He puts his towel in the basin. "I will stay here with him tonight to keep an eye on him. You are both welcome to stay here as well."

"Thank you, Roger," I say. "I will leave you both alone with him. I will return very shortly with some food for tonight. We are going to need it."

I pull up a chair next to the table and sit down. I cup White Horse's hands into mine and kiss them.

"I am here, honey. I will not leave you."

I look over at Koawa. He comes to the other side of me and looks down at his Chief.

He then begins a very deep and slow chant. I light some candles and start my own vigil. Evening falls upon us, and Roger remains by White Horse's side, keeping a careful watch over him. It is a long night, and no one sleeps.

The first light arrives, and Roger is pleased. White Horse has survived the night.

"It is a good sign, but it is still too early to tell. Infection can still set in."

Midafternoon is on us and Roger feels confident enough to move White Horse to a more comfortable area. Graciously, Hank offers a bed over the Saloon. It is close and will give us access to everything we need to care for White Horse. White Horse is placed on a board and with the brute strength of both Hank and Koawa, he is carried across the street to the Saloon.

Hank moved a cot from the boarding house for me to sleep on. Koawa insists that he will sleep on the floor or in the chair. The room is set up very nicely and is quite large. There is plenty of room for everything we need. A big bay window lights up the room that looks down onto Main Street. The window opens, giving us access to a trellis that goes down to the alley below or on the overhang that we can access by climbing out the window. The back stairs are easily accessible from the room and lead down to the kitchen and outhouse. Hank gives us free access to the Saloon's kitchen from the backstairs and says that he will keep this end of the hallway clear so it will be quiet.

Roger remains another night with White Horse. Koawa and I continue our vigils. In the early hours of the morning, Roger gave us the news we were dreading. White Horse's left lung is filling up with fluid, a sign of infection.

"What do we do?" I ask him.

"There really is not a whole lot I can do as long as he is asleep," he says.

"I can keep the wound as clean as possible, and we can try to prevent fever from arising, but other than that, I am afraid it is up to him."

"How do we prevent fever?" I ask Roger.

"It is a wild card, but I have seen it done before and it works. We can rub him down with cool water every few hours, if a fever is coming and I suspect it is, we may be able to get ahead of it. We can also try packing him in ice."

"We have to try," I argue." He has come so far already. I am not going to lose him now."

"Alright, I will go get some supplies and ask Hank to bring up some ice from the icehouse." Roger turns to leave when Koawa grabs his arm.

"I know of an herb that we use," he says. "The forest is full of it. I will go get some."

"It couldn't hurt," Roger declares.

The remainder of the night we take turns rubbing White Horse down and packing him with ice. Roger is growing more and more concerned with every passing hour when White Horse does develop a fever and the ice is not keeping it down. I take it upon myself to rub White Horse down every hour on the hour. Koawa uses his herbs as well, about every two hours.

Another morning comes; White Horse is still with fever. Roger is confident it will not get any higher and that our persistence is paying off. An exhausted Roger is finishing up his exam on White Horse.

"We have done all we can," he says, coming to his feet. "I am going to leave for a little while and check on some other patients, but I will return later this morning." He looks over at me. "I know you are concerned about White Horse, but you need to take care of yourself and that child."

"I will."

"I will have Stella bring you both some food, and I want you to eat it," he stresses to me. "If you need more tonic for your stomach, just tell me," he says.

He then kisses my cheek and heads for the door. To my amazement, Koawa shakes his hand. It even takes Roger by surprise.

"I speak for my people, thank you," he says.

Roger pats his shoulder and walks out the door. A few hours later, Stella shows up with breakfast. She made it herself, and she went all out. We each had a piece of steak, two eggs, a hash brown, two pieces of toast, and juice, and she put two lemons on my plate. There is a lot of food, and it is greatly appreciated. She remains with us throughout our breakfast and watches everything I put in my mouth. I am certain Roger put her up to it. I am forced to eat something by both her and Koawa. They accept that I will not eat it all, so I get away with one piece of toast, all my juice, half an egg, and two bites of my meat. I am stuffed and have an already upset stomach, so it doesn't help. Koawa's plate is empty. He looks over at mine, eyeing the piece of meat.

"Take it," Stella says. "I know she won't eat it." Koawa smiles, takes it off my plate, and then sits back down on the floor beside the window.

"I thought Father would come," I say.

"Oh, Carrie," she consoles, "he just needs time."

"Have you seen him?" I ask her.

"Yesterday morning briefly. He is very busy with all the funerals."

"At least I know he is alright."

"He looked a little down, but he is alright. Roger is with him now."

"Roger is with him?" I ask.

"Yes, I saw him enter the boarding house when I came over."

"I will talk to Roger when he returns."

"Willow Creek is slowly returning to normal."

"That's good," I cover my mouth as my stomach turns. "Forgive me," I tell her and make a run to the door. Stella follows behind me.

"Are you alright in there?" she asks through the outhouse door. I open the door. "I guess I fed you too much," she empathizes.

"That's alright."

We make our way to the back of the Saloon. Carl is standing in front of the door, blocking our way in.

"Aw, did the little Indian whore get sick?" he mocks.

"Just ignore him, Carrie. We will go through the front."

Carl is quick and has us blocked in. In a flash, Stella gives him a low blow. Carl bellows over, allowing us to break free and run to the door. He ignores his groin pain and comes after us into the kitchen. He quickly halts when he sees Koawa standing at the foot of the steps. Stella and I slid past him and made our way up the stairs. Carl scowls and walks away.

Upon entering the room, Koawa closes the door behind us and glares over at me. "You are not to leave this room without me. Understand?"

I would be a fool not to. I nodded my head in agreement.

"I should be leaving," Stella says. "I will come check on you later."

"Thank you, Stella."

She looks over at Koawa, who is standing over White Horse with his arms crossed over his chest. She picks up the plates and leaves the room. I close the door behind her. Koawa fixes his eyes on his brother as he speaks.

"That man is still alive because White Horse lies in this bed, but his days are numbered if he doesn't leave you alone."

He glances at my way. It is almost as if he is warning me. There is nothing I can say. I, for one, would pity the soul who pushes Koawa over the edge.

For the rest of the day, I will remain by White Horse's side. Koawa climbed down the trellis a few hours ago. I am unsure where he went. I can only assume that with White Horse down, he is checking on his people. On his return, I found out my assumption was correct, as he told me that he had gone to meet up with Blue Thunder and gave him an update on White Horse. He then tells me that Running Bear and Flying Hawk are keeping an eye on the camp. The security, both at his camp and around Willow Creek, is high, as Koawa fears that with White Horse down, he is extremely vulnerable, and although we cannot see them, Lakota warriors are watching Willow Creek.

Two more days have passed. There is still no change in White Horse's condition. Roger is concerned but remains optimist. I still have not heard from my father. When I ask Roger about him, he vaguely says he is fine and quickly changes the subject. It has become clear to me that Father has not accepted my condition and is refusing any contact with me. Stella continues bringing our meals and today she brought me a change in clothes and a hairbrush.

Hank has been a wonderful host and is taking a liking to Koawa. He has offered him all the whiskey he can drink in the house. Koawa refuses and spends most of his evenings sitting outside on the overhang. My hourly routine of sponging down White Horse is finished. I crawl out the window and join Koawa outside on the overhang.

"Mind if I join you?" I ask him.

"I do not mind," he mumbles.

I crawl the short distance over to him and sit down. I hear the laughter and music of the Saloon below me. I am glad to see that the Saloon was not hit too hard during the attack, and Hank has reopened for business.

"It is a beautiful night," I comment, looking out.

"Yes, it is," he answers.

"White Horse would like this," I say. Koawa nods his head.

"Yes, and so would Running Water."

I slightly grin over at him. I am sure I interrupted his thoughts about her.

"You miss her, don't you?" I ask him.

"Yes," he answers.

I know very little about Koawa, for he is always short on words. White Horse says he is not. Perhaps it is just because of me. I want to know more about him, especially because we are going to be a family with or without White Horse. Feeling brave, I will try to open Koawa up and start talking about something that I know is dear to him, his wife.

"How long have you two been married?" I ask.

"Two springs," he answers.

"She is very pretty." He nods his head. "Have you known her all your life?"

"Yes, but it wasn't until after my father died that we became close."

"White Horse told me about that day. I am truly sorry. That had to have been rough."

"It was. It hit White Horse the hardest."

"He told me," I say.

"Running Water lost both her parents that day as well."

"Oh dear," I gasp.

"She had no one, and we had both lost. We consoled each other."

What a truly beautiful love story, I think.

"Is this your first child?" I ask.

"Yes," he answers. "Finally, our spirits provide us with a child after many months of trying," He looks over at me. "My brother's child will have a little one to play alongside with, as only a few months will be between them."

I grin, rubbing my belly. "Oh, dear Lord, I cannot lose him." I cry.

"White Horse will always be within you no matter what happens. For it his blood that flows through that child."

"I do not know how I can look into your people's eyes knowing that I am the reason why their Chief is dead."

"You must not think that way, for none of this is your fault."

"I just want to make him happy. Nothing else matters if I don't have him." Koawa faintly grins.

"When White Horse told me about you, I told him you were no good. Nothing good would come from loving a White Woman. He told me you were different. I called him a fool. It is I who was the fool."

I smile. I have a feeling I just found Koawa's heart. "You are not as mean as you make people think," I say.

"Silence, woman! Someone may hear you," he jokes.

We both chuckle. Koawa decides it is time to go back in and we make our way to the window and crawl in. Sitting next to White Horse I feel confident that I broke the ice with Koawa. Things can only get better now. Or so I thought.

Chapter Thirty

The Outsider

Today, I awakened with the worst case of morning sickness yet. It is all I can do to lift my head off the pillow. Three times, I have gone to the outhouse to vomit in less than two hours. Koawa is watching me like a hawk from the upstairs bay window. Roger gave me a stronger tonic and advised me to rest and allow it to pass. White Horse is still holding his own with very little change, and Roger is concerned about this. He is worried because it has been four days, and White Horse is still in a coma. He was hoping for some sign by now that he was starting to wake up, but still nothing. My efforts to keep his fever down and his wound clean are working, as it doesn't appear the infection is spreading. Roger changes his bandages and starts to leave.

"Roger," I say, as he reaches for the doorknob, "how is Father?"

He sighs deeply. "I'm sorry, Carrie, but he refuses to talk to you."

I lower my head and sit back down next to White Horse. Koawa spends most of his day either looking out the window at the street down below or crawling down the trellis and escaping the madness. I try to take Roger's advice and rest. Although I did not sleep, I do feel better when I come to my feet. The days have been very long, and Koawa and I both are becoming bored.

Earlier in the day, when Koawa did his morning routine, he brought back some wood. He has started to whittle to help pass the time. I asked Stella on her last visit to bring me something to sew. She returned with the quilt that I had started after her parents died and left it in her old room. I never got around to finishing it. I am now going to make it for White Horse and me to lay on our pelts when we return home. Suddenly, Koawa and I heard someone running up the back stairs, and the door was swung open. Koawa jumps to his feet and is ready to pounce. We are both relieved to see that it is Hank.

"You have company. Come quick," he says.

Koawa quickly follows Hank down the steps. I go to the bay window and look down at the street below. I follow the heads of the onlookers. I then see what the commotion is. Coming into town over the newly built bridge. Perched high on their horses, and a dozen or so Lakota rode in. I recognize many of them being in White Horse's band, but there are a few I do not recognize. I notice an older woman in the middle. I believe it is White Fawn. I open the window to get a better look. I see Hank and Koawa come out of the Saloon and down to the street. The Lakota stop in front of Koawa. I then see Sid, still wearing his arm in a sling from being hit by an arrow during the attack, come out to the street. He is followed by Roger. Our visitors do not appear as a threat, and one warrior, who I believe is the Red Hawk, begins a conversation with Koawa.

"What do they want?" Hank asks.

"They want to take the Chief home. They are angry with me that he is still here."

"He cannot be moved," Roger says.

"They say your medicine is poison to him. They want to take him to their camp where their medicine man can treat him properly."

"Their camp?" Hank questions. "These men are not with you?"

"They are from a neighboring tribe. This is Chief Running Bear. The woman in the middle is my mother, White Fawn. She asked Chief Running Bear to bring her here so she can bring her son home."

"You need to assure Chief Running Bear," Roger begins, "that Chief White Horse is in good hands, and if we were to move him, he could die."

Koawa turns to speak his tongue to Chief Running Bear. The conversation is quick, as Koawa translates. I see Koawa walk over to White Fawn and softly speak to her. She reaches down and takes his hand. Koawa gently rubs it as he speaks. I see her nodding her head. Koawa then walks back over to Roger.

"They are requesting that they see him. I suggest you allow it."

Roger thinks a moment. "I will allow it," he reluctantly says, "but only the Chief and the woman."

I watch the transaction take place, and Chief Running Bear and White Fawn Walk into the Saloon. I stand next to White Horse when I hear the door open.

White Fawn is the first to step in and immediately she is at White Horse's side. This very strong and powerful woman is nearing tears upon seeing her son. She leans over and takes his hand. She speaks her tongue softly in his ear. The moment is tender as you can imagine any mothers would be. Besides being her Chief, he is also her oldest son and that makes her bond even tighter.

Koawa places his hand on her shoulder and gives it a gentle squeeze. She stands erect and grabs hold of his arm. I am unsure how old White Fawn is, as White Horse has never said. The deep-set wrinkles and grayness of her hair make me think that she is well into her sixties. It is apparent that she has a close bond with both her sons, and I can only imagine how hard this must be for her.

The one called Running Bear is a cousin and is very close to the tribe. I know nothing about this man. He, in my mind, is what I picture a Chief to look like. He is considerably older than White Horse and carries himself very well. I watch him as he opens his medicine bundle and pulls out a rattle and some sort of oil. He pours a little of the oil onto White Horse's forehead. He then begins to chant a similar chant to what I heard Koawa do earlier. As he is chanting, he waves the rattle over White Horse's head. Koawa and White Fawn join along. Roger and I step away and allow the Lakota to perform some kind of healing ritual over White Horse.

When they have finished, the rattle and oil are returned to the medicine bag, and they are ready to leave. Brief words are spoken between White Fawn and Koawa; she then makes her way over to me. She smiles and takes my hands, placing them between her palms. She spoke her tongue and then let go. I looked over Koawa for translation but got no results. We watch her go to the door, where Hank is waiting outside. Through the great bay window, I watch her leave with the others.

"She is alright now," Koawa says. "She had to see with her own eyes that he is still alive."

"He has to be alright, Koawa; he just has to be."

Another night, Koawa and I are sitting outside on the overhang. Once again, Hank offers him whiskey at the house;

although Koawa does not usually drink fire water, he accepts it, and he enjoys some of it on the overhang. Tonight's conversation is lighthearted and, at times, even comical. I am not sure if it is the fire water talking, but I am truly enjoying Koawa taking me down memory road when he and White Horse were little boys. I started to realize, after the third story, how close the two really are and how much Koawa looks up to his brother and Chief. It reminds me a lot of Roger and me.

After he had his fill of stories, I started sharing with him some of the mischievous things I did when I was growing up, like the time I taught Roger and Stella to spit.

"Show me," he chuckles.

"Alright."

I come up on my knees and find a target below. Looking out I chuckle at myself when I see a drunken Carl stagger out of the Saloon and into the street. Koawa looks down and chuckles. I then let it hurl. I tilt my head back, cough it up and let it go. It goes flying below, landing on the top of Carl's head. We quickly duck when he turns to look up. It is all we can do not to blow our cover by laughter.

Another day is upon us. Although my morning queasiness is still a nuisance today, it is more bearable. I only ran to the outhouse once early this morning. Roger is like clockwork, always coming around the same time every day to check on White Horse, today is no exception. He performs his regular examination. When he is done, he finally gives us some good news. White Horse is showing improvement and finally Roger is feeling more optimist. Koawa and I are very pleased.

As our day goes by, Koawa is doing his whittling, and I am sewing my quilt when we hear movement outside the door. I go to the door with Koawa close behind me. I open it up. I immediately smiled ear to ear when I saw that it was my father. He doesn't speak a word. I looked down at the foot of the door and saw my suitcase.

"Father," I say.

He turns around to walk away. I stepped over my suitcase and rushed to him, grabbing the back of his coat. He turns around and pulls himself free. I can see the void in his eyes, a look I have never seen before. It is a look of hate, a look of disgust and betrayal.

"Father," I began to cry.

He steps back, avoiding a long look, and quickly makes his way to the grand staircase.

"Father!" I yell as I run after him.

Koawa is quickly on my heels and pulls me back down the hall as I watch my father go down the stairs. He pulls me back into the room and closes the door. My heart is torn in pieces. I never thought my father would disown me. He is a peaceful man, a man of the cloth, a man who would never turn his back on anyone, and yet he tossed me out like yesterday's trash. It is too unbearable for me to take. I come to my knees and sob uncontrollably.

Koawa comes down with me and takes me into his arms, allowing me to cry. Darkness is upon us. I lie on the cot as Koawa sleeps by the window. I curled myself up into a ball. Feeling alone and isolated from the world I have known all my life, I cry myself into a sleep.

Chapter Thirty-One

The Awakening

I am up before daybreak. My depression is deep. Feeling I am up before daybreak. My depression is deep. Feeling isolated and alone, the only thing that keeps me going is the child within me and the hope of its father making a full recovery. I find myself in prayer at White Horse's side as the sun just begins to rise. I whisper tender thoughts in his ear, unsure whether he hears me or not. I want him to know that I am here. Koawa is whittling next to the bay window when he hears a knock on the door, and Rachel steps in with our breakfast trays.

"Where is Stella," I ask.

"I am not sure," she answers. "Hank asked me to bring your trays."

Odd, I think and do pray that she is alright. It is after nine when Koawa and I finish our breakfast. We both find it strange that Roger has not shown up. I take it upon myself to redress White Horse's wound, but first, I must refill the water pitcher. I tell Koawa before making my way down the narrow back stairs that lead to the kitchen, where I will refill it.

I fill my pitcher and head my way back up the stairs. I jump when I turn around and bump into Carl, who quickly pins me against the wall. I smell his foul breath as he brings his face into mine. He is ready to speak when we both become startled when a tomahawk flies over our heads and lands hard in the wall behind us. Carl quickly turns around and sees Koawa standing on the bottom step. I grab the pitcher of water and make my way to the stairs. I watch as Koawa steps off the last step.

I see the anger in Koawa as he stares Carl down. He starts inching his way over to him. Carl is too frightened to move. I am frozen in fear as I anticipate Koawa's next move. The men are face-to-face. Carl is taller than Koawa, but Koawa could easily take him down, and Carl knows it. For several moments, only glares are exchanged as if Koawa is sending him a message. What happens next scares the hell out of me.

In a flash, Koawa grips Carl by the throat and squeezes. Carl fights to break free but is unable to as Koawa's grip becomes firmer. I hear Carl gasp for air as he is being lifted off his feet. I fear at any moment that Koawa will kill him.

I call out. "Koawa, White Horse!"

Koawa hears me and lets him go. Carl falls to the ground, welcoming the fresh air. Koawa arrogantly goes down to Carl's face.

"If you ever come near her again, I will kill you," he growls.

He then stands up, removing his tomahawk from the wall. Keeping a constant glare down at Carl, Koawa gives me a gentle push, and we disappear up the stairs. Finally, I do believe Carl got the message, and at least for the time being, I will be left alone.

It is late morning, and Roger finally appears. Roger is a man who is always well groomed, but today, his hair is askew, and his clothes are wrinkled as if he has slept in them all night. I ask him if he is alright, and he tells me yes, that he has just returned from Cedar Brook picking up supplies.

"I thought you always get your supplies from the stage?" I ask him.

"I do, but I am running very low due to the stagecoaches not running, so I picked them up myself."

"Hmm," I wonder.

Cedar Brook is a good day's ride there and back. I do not see how that could be possible. Roger's mind seems distracted as he hurries through White Horse's exam. I can tell something is weighing heavy on his mind. I have never seen him like this, and it concerns me. I give him a hug as he walks to the door. He holds on to me longer than usual.

"Roger, are you alright?" I ask again.

"Yes, Carrie. Send it to me if you need anything. Hank knows where I am at."

Early evening approaches, Koawa is whittling, and I am tending to my quilt when there is a knock on the door. I open it to Stella.

"I brought you your dinner," she says.

"I didn't think you would make it today," I tell her.

She hands a plate to Koawa. He smiles at her, takes his usual corner under the window, and begins to eat.

"I do apologize," she says. "I went to Cedar Brook with Mr. Johnson to sign the paperwork. I sold him the post office."

"Stella, that is wonderful," I say.

"He is also allowing me to stay there and work."

"I am so happy for you."

In her hand, she is also carrying a bag. She placed the bag down on the bureau.

"I bought you something," she says as she reaches inside the bag.

"You did not have to do that."

"I wanted to," she holds it up. It is a lovely maternity dress.

"Stella, it is beautiful," I say, holding it up to me.

"You are going to need one very soon. You are already starting to show."

"I am not," I argue.

"Yes, you are," she smiles. "Mr. Johnson sure was happy today. He said he has finally found peace with Anna's death."

"Oh, that is wonderful," I say.

"Oh, did I tell you the sheriff's body was found near Rosy Peak?"

"No, really," I gasp.

"Yes, Sid found him. He said he shot himself in the head. I guess he could not take all the pressure. Rumors are going around that he would have been hung if he was still alive."

"I do not believe in hanging. However, I do believe he deserved it. I only wish we could prove Carl was involved. I would love to see him dangling from a noose."

"I heard what Koawa did to him. Hank told me that Carl had told him. Man, I wish I had seen that."

I glance over at Koawa, who is sitting by the window eating his dinner. He is paying no mind to us.

"I am sure he would have killed him if I had not stopped him."

"As much as I love you, Carrie, you need to get out of here. I am afraid for you. Carl knows about the baby, as does the town. Carrie, they are speaking God-awful things about you. I truly fear for you."

"That is why I only leave this room when I need to."

"Oh, I almost forgot. I have another surprise for you."

"What?" I ask, confused.

"Rachel offered us her room where you can take a bath, wash your hair, and pretty yourself up."

"Do I really look that bad?" I ask.

I turn and look at myself in the mirror. "Don't answer that," I joke.

She was right, I looked rough.

"Finish your dinner." Stella looks over at Koawa. "You think he will let you go?"

"I don't know, let me ask him."

Koawa knows I am talking about him and looks my way.

"I am asking if you will allow me to go next door and take a bath? Stella will be with me."

He hesitates for a moment and agrees if only he can stand outside the door. Stella prepares my bath with everything one would need. I let myself soak in a desperately needed bathtub, cleaning every inch of my body. Stella sat on the bed across the room as we talked.

"Thank you, Stella. I didn't realize how bad I needed this."

"It is nothing."

"Stella, it is everything. I have been looked down upon for so long by so many people. Even my father, but you have always been there for me. You have never looked away."

"Carrie, you are my best friend. I am always here. Nothing will ever change that," she says.

"I just want to get out of this town," I mumble.

"You mean you want to be with White Horse."

"Meeting White Horse was the best moment in my life. I do not know what I would do without him. I am terrified of losing him."

"Koawa will take care of you. I see the way he looks at you," she grins.

"Koawa is a married man. He is taking me in because of the child and his brother. I do not believe there are any other reasons than that. He feels like he owes it to his brother to protect me and the baby. That is how his custom is. It is for the best. He will take care of me."

"I will miss you, Carrie, but I do understand."

"So, have you seen Blue Thunder lately?" I tease her.

"The day after the attack, I went to the apple tree to put flowers on my parent's grave. He was there. He seemed very upset. I understood it probably had to do with his Chief. We sat under the tree together."

"And....?" I coax.

"What?"

Stella stands up and goes for the towel. She walks it over to me, holding it open. I come out of the water and wrap the towel around me.

"I know what sitting under a tree with a handsome man means. Remember, I, too, have been in the arms of a Lakota." She shyly giggles.

I am feeling refreshed from my long-deserved bath. I got myself dressed in the new clothes that Stella bought for me. The waist of the dress is expandable for the baby growing inside me, and upon examining it, I realize Stella is correct, and I am getting a little bump. After nearly two hours, I am anxious to get back to White Horse. Thanking Stella for everything, I head back to the corner room where Koawa is waiting outside the door.

It is late evening, and Roger returns to check on White Horse. Although he still looks incredibly tired, he has changed his clothes and appears in a better mood. He redresses White Horse's wound and examines him for any indication that he is any closer to waking up.

"I still don't like how his lungs sound," he says. "I have put a post into Boston, asking a doctor there that I am familiar with for his opinion. My main concern is he is still in a coma, and I am concerned that there may be more fragments in there, although when I removed the bullet, it looked solid."

"What does this all mean?" Koawa asks.

"I cannot treat him with the medicine I wish until he wakes up. The longer he stays in the coma, the less likely he is to come out of it."

"So, he could still die?" I ask.

"Yes," he finally answers, "he could."

Both Koawa and I refuse to hear it. I fought back my tears.

"He will not die!" Koawa snaps.

"I really wish I had better news." Roger closes his medicine bag. "As soon as I hear from Boston, I will let you know."

He squeezes my hand before walking out the door. My heart is heavy when I sit down beside White Horse. I take his hand into mine. I bury my head into his chest and weep.

The remainder of the next day, I remain in my own world, lost in my thoughts. I look out the bay window at the street below, a place where I have been for quite some time. Willow Creek is back to normal, with the only exception of the church, which is just starting to be rebuilt. I look for any signs of my father but see none. How I wish I could see him and try to make him understand that I never meant to bring shame to him.

I think of a life without White Horse. I am ready to move on and put my life and my ways behind me to be with the man I love, but will I be able to do it without him? Will I have the will to survive? I think of the child inside me. I rub my bump to confirm that it is not a dream. Will I be able to raise the child outside of the tribe? Will it be ridiculed and scorned for being a half-breed? Can I trust the Lakota if their Chief is gone? Will they think it is my fault? Will they take the child, what belongs to them, and toss me to the wolves? Can I trust Koawa? Do I even have a choice? Deep in thought, I fail to hear Koawa come up beside me until he touches my shoulder.

"I have caused so much pain to so many people?" I mumble.

"This self-pity in yourself has to stop," he snorts.

I folded my arms over my chest and walked over to White Horse.

"Self-pity?" I snap. "Look at him. It is him I pity, not myself."

"That is where you are wrong. Do not ever pity White Horse. He did what he did because he wanted to fight. He knew the risk." He makes his way over to me and continues his lecture. "We are Lakota. Fighting is in our blood. Without it, we will grow weak and restless. We are not afraid to die, for we understand the great circle of life. The life you knew before is gone. You are a Lakota now. You are strong and proud, and you allow no one to take that away from you."

White Horse could not have said it better. I knew Koawa was right; from this day forward, I will not look back. I will make White Horse proud. I will put my head up and face forward. I will not look back. I AM LAKOTA!

Chapter Thirty-Two

The Reunion

The sun has fallen, and yet another night we spend in the upstairs corner room above the saloon. Koawa and I both ask ourselves if this will ever end. It has been seven days since the attack. Seven very hard and very long days. The nightlife below us is booming. Koawa and I again find our usual spot on the overhang and enjoy the evening air. After about an hour, the wind picks up, and we rush inside just as the rain begins to fall. The rolling of thunder mixed with the crackling of lightning makes for a horrific storm. Koawa and I watch outside the window as it falls.

"Many nights," Koawa begins, "when I was a boy, my father would tell White Horse and me stories to calm our restless spirits as the skies would open up."

"What sort of stories?" I wonder.

"Stories for only restless souls like White Horse and I had," he smiles.

"One day," he continues. "Your children will be told the same stories when they are restless."

"I do hope so," I say as I turn to White Horse.

"You will. Lakota's have many children to keep our tribe strong."

"Koawa, what if White Horse doesn't make it? What am I going to do?"

"It is custom for our people to have more than one wife if they choose, especially a man of high power like White Horse."

Oh, like hell he will, I think. I would never forgive him. "If something should happen to him when you are done grieving, then I will make you my wife. When you are ready, then we will mate."

"So, you do not necessarily have to love someone to make them your wife?" I ask him.

"No, although in your case, White Horse is in love with you. I realized that the night he fought with Carl."

I grin. How I will never forget that night.

"I do not believe you have to worry about that. He will never take another woman to his pelt. His love for you is too deep. I see it in his eyes when you walk into his view. It is a look I have never seen before. It is that love that gives him the strength to survive."

"Why are you telling me this?" I ask him.

"Because you are losing hope."

He goes to his usual spot, picks up his wood, and starts to whittle. I am not sure if that is the only reason why he is telling me this, and it makes me wonder if he, too, is losing his hope that White Horse will survive.

I woke up with a start from a horrific nightmare. I dreamt that I was running and stones were being thrown at me as I ran. I fell into a ravine, and crows began to pick at me and scratch out my eyes. I screamed for help, but all I hear is laughter circling me as the crows continued picking my skin. The dream felt so real. I toss the blankets back, get up from the cot, and sit down next to White Horse. It is only a dream. Thank God it is only a dream.

I looked over at the window and saw Koawa asleep. I hear the pattering of the rain as it hits the window. A streak of lightning flashes, lighting up the room. I sigh deeply. Oh, dear God, I mumble. I lay my head down on the edge of the bed and close my eyes. I slowly nodded back off to sleep. I then feel a soft touch on my hand. Startled, I sat up and looked down, I gasped. White Horse's hand is resting on mine. I look at him and let out a cry. Gazing back at me are the darkest, most beautiful eyes I have ever seen. I stroked his face as a small tear escaped.

"Hi," I cry. I call out to Koawa. "Koawa," I say louder.

He jolts awake, and I flag him over. He rushes to the other side of the bed and chuckles. I take Koawa's hand and squeeze it. We are both ecstatic. I kiss White Horse's forehead.

"I will be right back. I am going to get Hank."

I quickly make my way to the top of the grand staircase. All eyes turn on me as I call out Hank's name.

"Go find Roger, hurry!" I say and rush back to the room.

Roger is quick to arrive. He removes his wet trench coat and hat and rushes to our side.

"What happened?" he asks.

"He opened his eyes and held my hand."

Roger brings the candle closer to White Horse's face. He forces one of his eyes open, quickly looking into it and then allows it to close.

"White Horse," he says, "It's Roger."

Slowly, White Horse opens his eyes. Roger smiles.

"Welcome back," he says.

"Where am I?" he says in a low audible voice.

"You were shot. You are above the saloon."

White Horse faintly nods his head. "I remember...Carrie."

"I am right here, sweetheart, and so is Koawa."

White Horse is still very weak but seems to relax when he hears my voice.

"So thirsty," he mumbles.

Roger reaches for the cup of water on the table. He looks over at Koawa.

"Help me lift his head so he can drink." Koawa is eager to help.

I hear him faintly speak his tongue as he reaches behind White Horse's head and lifts him up. White Horse is anxious to get the water.

"Take it slow," Roger says.

Little by little, Roger helps him drink. When finished, White Horse limply lies back down. I pull Roger aside.

"Is he alright?"

"He is just very weak. He lost a lot of blood."

Koawa joins us to hear what Roger is saying.

"This is great news," Roger says. "I am feeling much better about his survival. I will bring some medicine when I return first thing in the morning. Until then, let him rest." Both Koawa and I agree.

I watch White Horse as he sleeps. When he opens his eyes again, I want to be the first thing he sees. Daylight breaks, and I briefly do off. When I lift my head up from the edge of the bed, White Horse is looking at me. I take his hand and kiss it before coming to the side of the bed to sit beside him.

"How are you feeling?" I ask, stroking his cheek.

He raises his hand, placing it on my cheek. I nestle my cheek firmly in the palm of his hand. How I miss his touch.

"My Prairie Dawn," he mumbles.

I lean forward and kiss his dry lips. I reach for the pitcher and start filling the cup with water. Koawa comes to the other side of White Horse and speaks his tongue to him. White Horse only nods.

"Let's try to get some more water down you."

White Horse tries to sit up. He groans and quickly lies back down.

"No, sweetheart. You must lie still," I say.

Koawa takes the cup from my hand and lifts White Horse's head. He then helps him sip.

"How bad is it?" he asks after he finishes and is laid back down.

"It was bad. Roger removed the bullet and stopped the bleeding. You have lost a lot of blood," I say.

"You were not hit?" he asks.

"No. You pushed me out of the way, and that is when you got shot."

"One Eye. I saw One Eye."

"He is dead," Koawa says. "I shot him." White Horse seems relieved

"Roger, he did all this?" he asks, pertaining to the bandages that he is now aware he has.

"Yes," I answer. "White Horse, he saved your life."

"I will be sure to thank him."

"You will get your chance. He should be here soon."

"I want to sit up." I look over at Koawa. He is thinking what I am.

"If the medicine man says it is alright, then I will help," Koawa says.

"I need to sit up. I want to see where I am at."

Koawa finally gave in and helped White Horse into a sitting position. White Horse endures a great deal of pain, but his stubbornness to get his way prevails, and he is sitting up. I fluff the pillows as Koawa gently helps him get comfortable. It is then when, like clockwork, my morning sickness hits.

"Koawa..." I whine.

He is all too familiar with the look. I rush to my feet.

"I am sorry, love, but our child is calling me."

Koawa watches me from the big bay window as I enter the outhouse.

"Why do you watch my Prairie Dawn so closely? She is with her people," White Horse wonders.

Koawa chuckles. If only he knew.

"There is something you are not telling me?" White Horse says.

"When you are stronger, I will tell you," he answers.

"You will tell me now," he demands.

Koawa turns and looks at White Horse. "You are very bold lying in that bed," Koawa spats.

"I may be lying in this bed, but I am still your Chief."

Koawa just shook his head. "I am glad you are back, my brother," he smiles. "I will tell you."

Koawa tells White Horse everything. When he finishes White Horse, he is remorseful for me but severely livid by everything else.

"That does it," White Horse snaps.

He attempts to get out of bed. Koawa is quickly beside him, coaxing him down as White Horse utters in pain. He plops back down in horrendous agony.

"No, my brother, you are not ready to move."

"I will not tolerate this any longer. I want my Prairie Dawn out of here," he grunts.

"I understand your anger. Give yourself a few more days. I will keep your Prairie Dawn safe."

White Horse is steaming and is out for blood. He vows to himself that Carl will pay. No one makes a fool of him, and no one hurts his Prairie Dawn. Make no mistake this time, all will know what will happen when you push White Horse too far. Carl will be taught a lesson for all to see, and he will pay with his life. Against his wishes, he listens to Koawa, and for the moment, Carl will see another day.

I make a quick stop to the kitchen for some fresh water before heading upstairs. Upon entering the room, it is clear to see that I walked in on a deep conversation. I come to the table, putting the clean pitcher down. White Horse tilts his head, motioning for Koawa to leave. Koawa quietly sneaks out the window and down the trellis. I pour a fresh glass of water for White Horse and reach for the applesauce that I didn't earlier.

"You haven't eaten anything for nearly seven days. You must be starving."

I pick up the spoon and dip it into the applesauce. White Horse's eyes are on me. He reaches for my hand. "Leave it," he says.

"We have other fruit, pears, grapes, ah," I hold up the lemon. "This one is mine," I tease. "Helps my stomach." White Horse slightly grins.

"I do not want any fruit. What I want right now is you."

I shyly grin. He gently places his hand on my face to caress my cheek.

"Koawa told me about your father." I lower my eyes.

"I knew he would."

"I am sorry, for I did not want him to find out that way."

"Damn that, Carl. He is just not happy unless he makes me miserable."

"His time on badgering you is done. I will get out of this bed, and when I do, he better run because I am coming after him."

"It is not Carl that bothers me, it is my father. He won't even talk to me."

"He is still sore. I do not blame him, for I would be too."

Just thinking of my father was opening a wound, I am trying to forget. I feel a tear coming to my eyes.

"Oh, Beautiful," he says, catching my tears. "I understand your pain."

"I never should have kept it from my father. I just wanted to shield him from the shame."

"What shame?" he asks.

He lifts my chin when I fail to answer him. "The shame of conceiving a child out of wedlock or the shame of its father?" he wonders.

"No!" I argue. "Don't ever think that. I am not ashamed of you, and I don't care what anyone thinks."

"Except your father."

"He is such a good man, and I love him so much."

It is then that I begin to cry. "I have lost him, White Horse. I lost him."

He opens the one good arm he has, and I crawl in.

"When I get out of here and before we move on. We will go together and talk with your father."

"It will do no good. He won't even talk to me."

"We must try."

"How? I can't even get close to him." White Horse thinks a moment.

"When I had taken you home the time you were at my camp, you mentioned to me that you expected to see a letter when you went inside. You speak to your brother with words on a paper, perhaps you can do the same to your father."

"You really think so?" I wonder.

"I am a man who believes in speaking face to face, but in your situation, I believe you should at least try."

I lean in and kiss him. "I will start right now before Roger gets here. He should be here anytime." I come to my feet, handing him the applesauce.

"Please try to eat," I say. Smiling, he takes the bowl and begins to eat. I then find a pen, ink, and paper and begin to write.

Dear Father.

I am writing you this letter in hopes you will take a few minutes out of your day to read it. I was hoping to see you in person, but Roger has made it clear to me that you wish not to see me. Therefore, I respect your wishes and hope this last desperate attempt will give me the satisfaction and peace of mind I have been searching for.

Due to situations beyond our control, White Horse and I dread that the news of our child was not shared by us. He has asked me to marry him, and I have accepted. We only wish it would have included your blessing. I understand the shame I have caused you, as not only did I conceive a child out of wedlock, but I laid willingly with an Indian. When I look into White Horse's eyes, I see the man under the skin. I see the honesty, the integrity, the philosopher, a man very similar to you. Our child was conceived out of love, a love that holds no boundaries and sees no prejudices.

I owe this to you, Father, for you taught me to see people for who they are and not the color of their skin. The only regret I have is not telling you sooner, but the thought of hurting you is what held me back from the truth. I am not asking your forgiveness. I am only asking for your acceptance. As soon as White Horse is well enough to travel, I will be leaving with him to start my life as a Lakota Sioux. I do not know if I will ever see you again, so I wanted to tell you I love you and thank you for making me the proud woman I am today. I will think of you often.

Carrie

I then folded the letter up and put it in the envelope. I am not sure what it will accomplish, but I feel good in my heart and at peace. I come over to White Horse and hold his hand. I look into his eyes and smile. Yes, I tell myself. Everything I said to Father is true. I now have no regrets. I can start clean. I can be the woman that White Horse deserves.

Chapter Thirty-Three

The Memories

It is early the next day when we hear a usual knock on the door with the turn of the handle.

"Good morning," Roger says.

He removes his hat and coat, looking over at White Horse.

"If you are not a sight for sore eyes," he smiles. "How are you feeling?"

"I will feel better if I am home," White Horse answers.

Roger joins White Horse next to the bed.

I see Carrie has been giving you water." He sees the applesauce. "And some fruit, that is good."

"I want to thank you for saving my life," White Horse says.

"You are welcome." Roger reaches into his medicine bag and pulls out some supplies. "I need to examine you if I may?" Roger asks.

"You do as need be to get me out of here."

White Horse remains still as Roger does what is needed. Koawa returns to the room and joins me alongside Roger.

"I would like to give you some medicine," Roger states, "that will help infection, and I also have something for pain if you need it."

"When can I go home?" he asks.

"Let us see how the medicine works first, and we will go from there."

Roger closes his medical bag and makes his way to the door. "I will be back this evening," he says before turning the knob to open the door.

"Roger, wait," I say. "Can you please give this to Father for me?" I handed him the envelope.

"Carrie...I."

"Roger, I have to try. I must know that when I leave here, I at least tried to make peace with him. Will you give it to him please?"

"Carrie, I will give it to him, but I need to tell you something."

"What?"

"I should have told you sooner, but with everything going on with White Horse, I decided to wait."

"Tell me what?" I ask.

"I lied to you about going to Cedar Brook. The reason I was late that day to see White Horse was because I was with another patient."

"Why didn't you just tell me that?"

"Because the other patient was Pa."

"What?" I gasp. "What happened?"

Roger looks over at White Horse and deeply sighs.

"Roger! What is wrong with Father?" I snap.

"He had a heart attack," he says.

I gasp. "He is better now. I am making him rest."

I am in complete despair. I walk over to White Horse's side and sit down in the chair. He reaches for my hand as I fight my tears.

"Carrie," Roger begins. "I must tell you that Pa's heart is weakening. I do not know how much more it can take before it will give out."

A lonely tear escapes down my cheek.

"He must keep his activity to a minimum. Another outburst like he had with Carl could kill him."

"What did Carl do?" I glare. Roger gave me no answer. I bolt out of my chair and into Roger's face.

"What did Carl do!" I yell.

"Pa was very upset when he found out that you are with child. Sunday Service was held outside, and few attended, and it was because of you."

I close my eyes with grief. Roger continues as I sit back down next to White Horse. He reaches for my hand.

"He was devastated, and as much as I tried to talk to him, he would not listen. That was when he packed your bags and came here. After he left here, he went to Esther's to get something to eat. Carl walked in. He started badgering Pa. Pa got in his face, and Carl hit him."

"That son of a bitch," I spat through my teeth.

"That evening, Pa went into a deep depression and later had a heart attack."

My sadness immediately turns to rage. The room is still, and all eyes are on me. I attempt to calm myself down by pacing but to no avail. I rush to the door. Roger is quick and stands in front of it.

"Get out of my way," I bark.

"Carrie!" I deeply hear.

I turn to look across at White Horse. He holds his hand out, gesturing for me to come. I obey and come to his side. He takes my hand, coaxing me down to the chair.

"This man will no longer torment my Prairie Dawn," he says, stroking my hand. White Horse looks up at Roger. "We leave tomorrow," he tells him.

"White Horse, you cannot ride," Roger argues.

"I can and I will," he spats.

"No, honey," I say. "I will not take the chance. I just got you back."

"This is not the time to think of me. I must consider you and our child. I will not sacrifice either one of you again."

"Sweetheart, it is just a few more days. I am fine."

White Horse is not taking no for an answer. He adamantly shakes his head back and forth.

"White Horse, you are filled with stitches. If you tear, you could bleed to death," Roger cautions.

"White Horse, please," I beg.

White Horse holds up his hand. I hear him grunt as he moves.

"I will hear no more. My mind is set. We leave tomorrow."

Neither Roger nor I are happy, but at this point, there is little that we can do to change his mind. White Horse is refusing to back down.

"I know of a way to get him home where he won't have to ride," Koawa says. "We take him on a travois..."

"No!" White Horse interrupts.

Koawa spats off something in his tongue for only White Horse to understand. When he spoke his peace, he continued in a language we all understood.

"You are not only my Chief, but you are my brother, and I will take care of you and Prairie Dawn. You will go."

"I will not let my people see me on a travois looking like a fool."

"Your people need you to guide them and to lead them to great places. You are no fool, and we all know that. Stop being stubborn and listen to what I have to say."

White Horse grows still. I am certain no other man or woman has ever spoken to White Horse in that manner. The conversation is over, and at least for the moment, Koawa won.

"Explain to me what a travois is?" Roger asks.

"It is a means of transportation that our people use to carry our belongings or injured across the prairie," Koawa answers.

"Remember Roger, Father was on one."

"This one will be stronger and more secure. White Horse will not move," Koawa says. Roger thinks a moment.

"I will insist on coming in case I am needed. Will this be a problem?"

"As you wish," Koawa answers.

Our last evening above the saloon is upon us. Koawa left several hours ago to meet up with Blue Thunder and spread the word that their Chief is returning home. The rain is pattering outside the window. I am gazing out at the town below as White Horse sleeps. A streak of lightning lights up the sky, revealing the huge willow tree in the schoolyard. A faint smile appears on my face as I remember all the times when I was a child climbing that tree. Despite me being a girl, I was always the one who could outclimb any boy. It was also used as a sweetheart tree. I think of my first crush and wonder if my initials are still there that I carved in the bark. I remember how upset I was when his family moved away. It makes me wonder what he is doing now.

I remember back to the first day I arrived in Willow Creek, how I was all shy and scared. Stella and Anna were my first friends. Those were the good days, the innocent days. I think of the fun times when Roger and I would fish in the pond after school. He could never catch as much as me. "Don't let the skirt fool you," he would tell boys. "She can outfish anyone." And I did. I remember the hot summer days swimming in the river. Anna and I coaxed Stella to jump off the rope into the water. She had never been a good swimmer, but it was a good sport, and one day, she took the leap. There are many memories in this town; some are good, and some are not, but Willow Creek was home, and I am really going to miss it.

"What are you thinking, my Love?" I hear.

I turn to see White Horse wide awake.

"It is really coming down out there, and Koawa is out in this."

"Koawa can take care of himself," he says. "I am sure he has found shelter."

I walk over·to his side, sitting down on the bed. I stroked his cheek.

"I was so frightened that I was going to lose you."

"I live for you," he says.

"I so much want to make you happy."

"With you in my arms, I am always happy," he says.

I grin. He is so tender and so sweet, a side of him that I am sure that few see. I lean in, and we kiss. We are interrupted by a knock on the door.

"Are you expecting anyone?" he asks.

"No," I answer.

"Hand me the rifle," he mumbles. I go for the rifle and hand it to White Horse.

"Who is it?" I ask through the door.

"Sid." I faintly hear.

Sid, I think, what does he want? I open the door as he removes his hat.

"May I come in?" he asks. I glanced at White Horse's. He nods his head.

"You may come in, but be warned, there is a rifle pointing to your head," I say.

"I will not take much of your time." He glances over at White Horse. "I am sure glad you are doing better." White Horse fails to move as he points the rifle at Sid.

"I have not come to start any problems." I can tell there is something heavy on Sid's mind.

"Then why are you here?" I ask him.

"My brother died because he could not face the truth. The truth has been kept secret for far too long. It is time I be a man and face the truth of what I have done."

"And what is that?"

"The day that Anna was raped, we were out looking for some horse thieves. We got thirsty and found a river to get some water. We came across an Indian squaw bathing. Carl wanted to have some fun with her and went into the water. She got scared and ran out of the water. She tried to get her clothes when Carl attacked her. The squaw was fighting him. The Sheriff came to the squaw's aid, trying to pull Carl off. He then tried to console the woman and went to hand her her clothes. I suspect the woman thought that the Sheriff was going to hurt her because she started hitting his chest with her fists. He gripped her wrists to stop her from fighting, and the woman spit in his face. Carl was causing havoc and would not shut his mouth. The Sheriff got mad at Carl and turned to shut him up when the squaw kicked the Sheriff in the groin. He became angry and started yelling at the squaw, asking her why she did that, that he was only trying to help her. He was finally able to calm her down. He gave her back her clothes and turned to walk away. That is when the squaw picked up a big rock and was going to hit him with it. The Sheriff blocked the blow by pushing the squaw. She tripped over some rocks and fell, hitting her head and killing her.

That is when we panicked. We all knew that whoever she belonged to would be looking for her, so we got the hell out of there. Carl and the Sheriff were fighting all the way home, each blaming each other. On our way to Willow Creek, we see Anna at the river. It was like a nightmare all over again. Carl saw her swimming. He knew she was naked and an easy target. He came up with the idea of the hoods. The Sheriff and I wanted nothing to do with it, but he said if we didn't go along with him, he would tell everyone what the Sheriff did, and he would drag my name into it as well. I knew he meant it. We had to go along with it. Carl got to her first."

I closed my eyes. That sick bastard, I thought.

"He had her out of the water and onto the shore. She was screaming, and Carl was afraid that we would be heard, so he started slapping her around to silence her. The Sheriff was always fond of Anna, and many times, he would fantasize about her to me. He would never hurt her, so when Carl started hitting her, he was very upset and yelled at him to get off her. When he did this, Anna recognized his voice. He knew he was caught, so he took off his hood and ordered us to do the same. It was his idea to take Anna to Doctor Briggs.

He scared her enough to keep her quiet. When she became pregnant, he was afraid everything would resurface again, so he paid her off and convinced Mr. Johnson that her leaving out of town would be the best for her. We had no idea she would die."

I am speechless. My heart went out to Anna and the squaw. Sid lowers his head in shame.

"Carl was boasting that he finally got Anna, and now he was going after you." My ears perked up, as well as White Horse's. "I told him to leave you alone, but he went after you anyway. I knew you were telling the truth, and I was ready to back you up."

"Why didn't you?" I wonder.

"He brought up the squaw and Anna. He blackmailed me to keep me quiet. He reminded me we were kin and that we should stick together."

"So, you sold your soul to the devil and allowed me to be drug through the mud." I spat. I walk to the door and open it. "Get out!" I yell.

Sid looks over at White Horse and quickly turns to leave when White Horse cocks the rifle. Burying his head, he turns to walk out.

"I am sorry, Carrie," he mumbles.

"I don't need your pity," I snap.

"Please, Carrie. Forgive me."

"My name is Prairie Dawn, and I am Lakota."

I then slam the door in his face. I look over at White Horse and see him smile. No words were spoken. They did not need to be. I know I have made him proud.

The night is dwindling away. The soft pitter-patter of rain is heard on the window. I lie on the cot with the blankets curled around me and attempt to sleep. Sid's words are hitting me hard. He is more of a coward than I ever imagined, and Carl is a pig. All this time, we were led to believe it was the Sheriff who raped Anna when all along, it was Carl. How it made me hate him even more. The thought that he is still out there as a free man is sickening. How thankful I am to be leaving and never have to deal with that pig again.

Roger turns in for the night. Frustrated and exhausted, he welcomes the sleep. He gave his Pa the letter that his sister wrote but is doubtful that it will get read. He has a long day ahead of him tomorrow, and he needs his rest. He has no idea what to expect but needs to see for himself that his sister will be alright. So much has changed so quickly in his life. He is thankful that he can adjust well. He thinks of his sister as he slowly doses off. He is going to miss her but understands it is for the best. He falls asleep, remembering the good times.

In the room across the hall, his Pa lies. He finishes reading his bible and closes the cover. He picks up the envelope, looking at the words addressed across. He always thought that his daughter's handwriting fit her looks, beautiful and curvy. He debates if he wants to read what is inside. He is compelled to open it. He feels bad for what he did. He knows it hurts her, but he is hurt, too. He is a Christian man and practices what he preaches. Therefore, he knows what he must do. He leans closer to the lantern and opens the envelope. He then begins to read what is inside it.

Chapter Thirty-Four

Across the Great Plains

Morning arrives. I follow my daily routine of finding the outhouse to get sick before returning to White Horse. I opened the door to our room, bringing in our breakfast trays that were left outside our door by Stella. White Horse is awake when I enter.

"I was starting to get concerned," he says.

"Sorry, darling," I say, putting the tray down on the bureau. I lift the lid on my plate and get a good smell of scrambled eggs and bacon. My stomach curls, and I quickly put it down. I come over to White Horse, putting the tray on the table beside him. I lean over and give him a kiss.

"How are you feeling?" I ask.

"I should be asking you the same," he says.

"I am fine," I answer.

"You are not a good liar," he jokes. "Come," he says, opening his arms for me to climb in beside him.

"I don't think that is a good idea," I argue.

"You look exhausted. You have a long ride ahead of you. Come."

It is pointless to argue with him, so I pull back the blankets and slowly crawl into bed beside him.

"There, is that not better?" he asks.

"Yes," I say, snuggling into him.

I am unaware of how true his words are when I close my eyes, and in no time, I am asleep. White Horse is nearly asleep himself when he hears Koawa crawl through the window.

"Shh," White Horse says. "She is sleeping."

"Finally," Koawa states. "She has not slept much. She needs it."

"When I get her home, she will rest. I will see to it."

"Everything is ready for your return."

"Excellent," White Horse says. "The sooner I get her out of this poisonous town, the better."

"You are making her a better home," Koawa states, "you need not worry; Running Water will show her our ways."

"You can forget about that foolish travois. I am going to ride," White Horse says.

"Your horse has a tall back. You will not be able to get on it."

"Then I will walk," he argues.

Koawa chuckles. "I think you fell too hard and hurt your head. You are talking nonsense."

"You know how I feel about this."

"Yes, I do, and it is my responsibility to get you home, and that is what I am doing. There will be no more arguments. You go home on a travois, or you wait a few days and ride home. Those are your choices."

"I will not leave her here another day," White Horse argues.

"And I will not leave you alone to take her back, so you are going on a travois."

Yet again, Koawa wins the argument. White Horse is not happy but has no choice. Koawa and him are so much alike that it is like arguing with himself. The conversation stops when I stir awake.

"Good morning, Love," White Horse says.

Suddenly, there is a familiar knock on the door by Roger.

"Good morning," he smiles when he enters the room.

"Good morning," we greet back.

"How is the patient?"

"Restless," White Horse says. "I want out of here."

"As your doctor, I want to go on the record that I do not agree with this and feel it is too soon to move you, but as Carrie's brother, I feel the sooner she gets out of here, the better."

"Then we go," White Horse says.

"One more thing. There is something I need to get off my chest."

"Go ahead."

"We started off on the wrong foot with each other. I will admit I felt Carrie was too good for you. I questioned your motives, and until just recently, I felt she was in great danger being with you. My Pa befriended you and felt as if he was betrayed. I am here to tell you that I feel he is wrong, and I honestly believe you only want what is best for her, and I accept you as a part of my family."

White Horse grins. I could have cried. I watch as both men exchange a handshake. The tender moment passes, and with a quick exam by Roger, White Horse is prepared for the trip home.

Roger is planning on keeping White Horse heavily sedated, making the trip more bearable. The first obstacle is getting White Horse down the stairs. Since the travois is too large and the staircase is too narrow, White Horse will have to be carried down, or he will have to walk. Stubborn as he is, he chooses the second. With Hank's help, and along with the strength of Koawa, White Horse slowly makes it down the grand staircase.

When he reaches the bottom, White Horse has to rest. While he is catching his breath, he looks across the saloon and sees Carl at a back table smoking. He arrogantly smirks. I can literally see the hair standing up on the back of White Horse's neck. His eyes immediately turn to ice. White Horse wants him bad but is in no shape to even try, making him even more annoyed. Carl's days are numbered. This I am sure of. It is just a matter of time before White Horse kills him. Getting all of us out of Willow Creek is for the best. When White Horse catches his breath, we continue outside, where his ride is waiting. Carefully, he is laid down by Koawa and covered up. Roger address Koawa.

"I have given him medicine for the pain, but he may need more."

"If we need to stop, you tell me, and we will." Koawa then goes to his horse. Hank squats down next to White Horse.

"You take care of yourself," he tells him.

"Thank you for everything."

Hank pats his shoulder and stands up. He then walks over to me. Hank and I have always been close. I consider him another brother. I am going to miss him very much. I threw my arms around him and gave him a huge hug. He returns it.

"I am going to miss you," I cry.

"You are going to be fine. But if ever need anything, you know where I am at."

It is hard to let him go. I never realized how hard it was going to be. I wipe my tears and reach up to get on my horse. Hank holds the reins, helping me up.

"Do tell Stella I will miss her."

"I tried to convince her to come and tell you goodbye, but she will not leave her room."

"It is alright. I understand."

Stella is a very emotional person and does not handle goodbyes very well. It is probably for the best, as I don't want to cry anymore myself. Hank then goes to Koawa. The men shake hands.

"You will always have a place with the Lakota," Koawa says.

"Take care, my friend, and if you ever need anything, you let me know."

"Thank you."

"I will keep any followers away." Koawa nods. He then gives the signal, and we are off. When we head up the hill just past the cemetery, I look back at one final glimpse of Willow Creek.

Watching from the parlor window, he sees his daughter ride by. He wants to wave. He wants to stop her, but his stubbornness keeps him away. He will never see his Carrie again, maybe it is for the best. She looks happy, and her happiness is all he ever wants in her. He did his job. He raised her the best he could. But how he misses her already. He closes the curtain and walks away.

From an upstairs saloon window, Stella watches her best friend ride off. How she wishes she had the strength to tell her goodbye. She knows she will be fine and will be happy in her new life. She closes the curtain when she sees her best friend disappear over the hill.

The journey leads us to the open plains. Willow Creek is just a shadow in the dust. We have been riding for about two hours, and White Horse has slept most of the way. Koawa motions for me to come forward.

"We are safely out of Willow Creek," he says.

"Alright."

"Soon, we will meet up with Blue Thunder and more warriors."

"Alright."

"You need to tell your brother that there will be many of them, not to be alarmed. They are here to protect their Chief in the event we are ambushed by your people."

Koawa is smart not to trust Carl or Sid, even though Hank told him he would keep them away. There is also the threat of Blue Coats that are rumored to be around. It is no secret how intense feelings are between the two cultures. I am certain the word of White Horse and what he did will be twisted around, and what has happened has spread all the way to Washington. I completely understand where Koawa is coming from and how vulnerable White Horse is.

"In the event that we are ambushed, you and Roger need to run to that canyon." I look across the landscape at the huge silhouette of rocks called Bear Canyon.

"And White Horse?" I ask him.

"We will protect him."

Roger is aware of the plan and, surprisingly enough, has thought of the same thing. Carl has had enough time to notify Washington of the Chief's whereabouts. I also know Carl is slimy enough to do it. There is no secret that he does not like me or White Horse, which makes Carl very dangerous. Roger is concerned at how calm Carl was when White Horse came down the stairs back to the saloon. Does Carl have something up his sleeve, or is he simply just afraid of Koawa.

It was not very long after that when we saw a swarm of warriors come down the ridge. They ride up alongside White Horse and look down at him before taking their position. The magnitude of warriors makes me realize that not all of them are White Horses and that Running Bear has joined forces. It showed me the love and the unity that the Lakota have with each other, and I am now part of this unity. It is well known the Sioux are one of the biggest tribes in the nation. How proud I am to be one of them.

We continued our ride in silence, moving further and further along the plains. I removed my canteen wrapped around the saddle horn. I look down at White Horse, who is awake as I take a sip. He looks uncomfortable.

"Are you alright, honey?" I ask.

My question is heard by Roger and two other warriors riding beside me.

"Do you need something for the pain, White Horse?" Roger asks.

Koawa glances back but continues. We see White Horse move his hand under the blanket. Suddenly, he grows very white and removes his hand. It is filled with blood. I screamed out for Koawa to stop and quickly jumped off Sugar Foot's back, rushing to White Horse's side. Roger is right behind me.

"He's bleeding," I yell.

Koawa jumps down and joins us. All horses stop, and concern grows with every warrior as they watch on. Roger removes the blanket to reveal the blood on his bandages. He then starts to unwrap him. White Horse flinches with the pain.

"Carrie, grab my bag," Roger says. I quickly obey.

"How bad is it?" Koawa asks.

"He has opened part of the wound. I knew we should not have moved him."

I returned with Roger's bag. He quickly reaches in and gets what he needs. We all watch on as Roger works.

"You alright, White Horse?" Roger asks.

White Horse inaudibly mumbles what I believe is his tongue.

"He looks pale," I observe.

"Yeah, he does," Roger agrees. "How much further do we have, Koawa?"

"After we cross the river, it is very close."

We both know that the river is nearly four hours away. I am growing even more concerned.

"Can he make it?" I ask.

"I will make it," White Horse groans.

Koawa squats down, speaking his tongue to White Horse. The conversation is brief. Koawa nods his head and stands up.

"Instead of following the river around, we can cross in the shallows. It will take less time."

"With these rains, that river will be high," Roger says.

"There are enough strong men here we will be able to carry him across."

Roger just looks at him, as skeptical as he can be.

"I trusted you," Koawa says. "Now, it is your turn to trust me."

Roger smiles and agrees. Roger finishes stitching up White Horse the best he can with the limited supplies he has.

"It is going to have to do," he states. "I am out of sutures."

Blue Thunder hands Roger a strand of horsetail. He looks at Koawa, confused.

"We use horsetail when we need to sew someone up," Koawa says.

"Really?" Roger says. He looks impressed. "I will have to remember that."

Roger goes down to White Horse and finishes sewing him up. It wasn't the most pleasant thing that White Horse ever felt, but he handled it like a true warrior. With White Horse comfortable and another dose of Morphine, we continue our journey home.

The view of the river is faintly seen. The scout that was sent ahead of us has returned to Koawa with word. I watch the men talk for a few minutes. The scout then turns and rides off in the direction he came. Koawa motions for Roger and me to come up beside him.

"The river is very high," Koawa says, "and running very swiftly."

"What do we do?" Roger asks.

"Find a low part and cross. The horses will have to be walked across. The men will help with this. You two are going to have to cross on foot."

We both agree that we will do what we must do to get White Horse home safely. When we approach the river, Koawa sizes it up. Not only is it high, but it is flowing at an incredible speed. Koawa points out.

"We will cross here," he says.

Everyone dismounts, and White Horse is prepared to cross. On Koawa's command, a six-man team of three on each side then lifted White Horse's travois onto their shoulders and made their way into the river. It is a carefully and meticulously organized effort, with each step across the river being calculated in unison. Roger and I follow in carefully behind Koawa, stepping where he does. The remainder of the warriors gather the horses and come up behind us. The ground below me is slippery. Even though I am stepping in Koawa's path, the undercurrent is strong, and I am having trouble keeping my balance. My misery is not alone. Roger is having the same issue.

We quickly realize that this isn't as easy as it looks. I held onto Roger's hand for extra support. This turns out to be a bad move. Roger loses his footing and starts to teeter back and forth. He is caught by the warrior behind him and is quickly stabilized. I, on the other hand, am not as lucky and go under. Roger rushes to reach me before my head goes under but to no avail. As I realize I am going down, I struggle to stand up. The unfriendly current has trapped me. I see a hand reach down and pull me up. I come to the surface. I look up to see Koawa. He doesn't miss a step. With his part of White Horse still resting on his shoulder, he reaches down and pulls me out of the water. It became clear to me at this moment how incredibly strong he really is.

"Hold on to my tunic," he says.

I do as he says, and the rest of the journey across is unremarkable. Reaching dry land has never felt so good. Little do I know our problems are just beginning. As White Horse is laid back down on the ground, another scout appears. Koawa can't believe what he is hearing.

"Are you alright, darling?" I ask White Horse as I come down beside him.

"I heard you fall. Are you alright?" he asks me. I stroked his cheek.

"I am fine, darling, just a little wet."

Koawa squats down beside me. He looks at his Chief and brother.

"What is wrong?" White Horse faintly asks.

"The high water has made the rocks fall. Our path is not as smooth as I had hoped. We will have to carry you."

I could tell by the shock in White Horse's eyes that this must be a great distance.

"How far?" I ask.

"A few miles."

"Can you get the horses through?" White Horse asks.

"The horses are able to walk through, but I cannot drag you; it is too narrow."

"You do what must be done to get me home," he states.

Koawa nods and stands up. The last few miles are hard. The land is unsteady, narrow, and rocky as hell. I am clueless about where we are or how much further we must go. But it is Koawa and the other five warriors who are carrying White Horse that my heart goes out for, as their strength is being tested. Several of the warriors will trade on and off, taking turns carrying their Chief, but Koawa never takes a rest. He is determined to make it the entire way.

Word comes out that we are near the home stretch with less than half a mile to go. We are starting to be joined by women and children who wish to greet their husbands and chiefs. Running Water is one of them. She walks alongside Koawa as we head into the home stretch. Very soon, the camp is seen ahead of us, tucked around a lake. Finally, we are home.

Chapter Thirty-Five

The Homecoming

The camp is buzzing with all eyes on their Chief when we enter. There is much happiness, and many smiles are seen throughout. Everyone is excited and so grateful to see their Chief. Blue Thunder and Yellow Hawk work on the crowd as White Horse is brought into his lodge with the aid of several warriors. I come to White Horse's side, taking his hand into mine.

"You are home, sweetheart," I whisper.

"No, we are home," he says.

Roger is by White Horse's side, making sure everything is alright. Flying Hawk, along with Koawa, are beside us.

"If you need anything," Koawa tells Roger. "You tell me."

"I need you to get some of these people out of here."

Koawa is quick to obey, kicking everyone out.

"My people are glad I am home," White Horse says.

"I understand their joy," Roger says. "But you need to rest."

"My people need me," he argues.

"That is why you need to rest," Koawa argues back. He looks over at Roger. "Your lodge is ready if you need to rest."

"My lodge?" Roger questions.

"Yes, you do not think you will be leaving tonight, do you?"

"Well...I really do not wish to cross that river again in the dark."

"When you are ready to leave. I will show you an easier way to get here. It is only because of us dragging him that we came the way we did."

"I thank you, but I do not wish to be a bother."

"You are famous with my people," White Horse says.

"My Chief is correct," Koawa states. "Everyone wants to meet the White Great Healer who saved their Chief's life."

"Great Healer?" boasts Roger. "Who would have thought." He chuckles to himself.

Roger rarely ever takes credit for what he does. It is humorous to see him gloat.

"Then you will stay?" asks Koawa.

"Yes, I will be honored."

The festivities are grand. Everyone is celebrating White Horse's return. The flap of our lodge is opened, exposing the celebration outdoors. Roger and I watch in awe at the dancers around the fire. Koawa is among them. Our lodge is busy with many guests of all ages anxious to see their Chief. White Horse enjoys each and every one of them. Roger met Kikimo, who spent most of the evening tucked in his father's arms. It is a joyous time shared by everyone. The evening festivities end when White Horse becomes too tired and sore to continue.

Roger blushes as Minoke loops her arm through his and escorts him to his lodge. Kikimo goes with White Fawn. I slip in beside White Horse. I leaned over and kissed him.

"I love you," I tell him.

He caresses my cheek and grins. To be exhausted for much more, he dozes off.

My first day as a Lakota woman has finally arrived. Roger left to go back to Willow Creek. He will return in a week to check on White Horse sooner if we need him. Koawa and Blue Thunder help White Horse to his feet, moving him to shelter under an overhang, looking out at the camp. This way, White Horse can see everything going on and slowly be able to build up his strength. I come down on my knees and hand him his plate of food that I prepared myself. I also change my clothes to look like a squaw.

"I made it myself. I hope you like it," I tell him.

"If it is from you, I will like it," he grins.

"I am going to go with Running Water today if that is alright with you?" I ask.

"She will teach you well," he says.

"I want to learn everything. I want to make you proud."

"Sweetheart, our ways are very different from yours. It will take you time to understand it all. You will always make me proud just by being you."

He is so sweet and so magnificent in so many ways. How can I not love him?

"I have a reputation to live up to, and I promise you I will not disappoint you," I say.

"I have no doubts that you won't." I watch him as he bites and swallows his food.

"White Horse," I begin, "how does a wedding go in your culture?"

"Most of the time, it is very simple. Take us, for example; by Lakota law, we are already married."

"We are?" I ask, confused.

"Yes, but I understand how you may wish a more formal wedding as you are not accustomed to our ways. Therefore, it is as you wish."

"But that does not seem fair to you."

"Sweetheart, you as my wife is what is fair. How you wish for that to happen, I do not care."

"Then I want something simple in front of the water and mountains."

"As you wish."

"Who will perform the ceremony?" I ask.

"Who performs it in your culture?" he wonders.

"Usually my father, sometimes Roger."

"That will be fine."

"I have an idea," I say as he takes another bite.

"And what would that be?" he asks after he swallows.

"We can combine the two cultures. It will be beautiful."

He places his hand on mine.

"No, my Love, you are beautiful."

He is being no help. I know it is going to be up to me. I am hoping Running Water or White Fawn will be able to help.

"I want to invite Stella and Roger. Is that alright?"

"I told you as you wish."

I lean in and kiss him. I then stood up to leave. He pulls my hand for me to stop. I turned and looked down at him. He motions for me to come forward. He then looks at my stomach, placing his hand on the bump.

"Our child is going to be big," he smiles.

I lay my hand on his and grin.

"How are you feeling?" he asks.

"Fine, except for the morning sickness. Roger gave me some medicine to take, but it doesn't seem to help."

"That is because our child is Lakota. He does not like Whiteman's medicine," he teases. I chuckle. "Promise me you do not work too hard on your first day," he cautions.

"I promise, but it is Running Water I worry more about. She is nearing her time and pushes herself way too much."

"Koawa is a good husband to her. He will keep an eye on her," he says. "Now go and do what you need to do, but keep in mind, I, too, am watching you."

His point is taken. I leave to go find Running Water. I will spend the rest of the day with her. For the next three days, Running Water and I are rarely apart from each other. I follow her and watch her every move. Learning everything I can and as fast as I can. I learned how to stretch a hide, sew a tunic, put up a tepee, skin a hide, and prepare wild food. I am astonished at how hard these women work and how knowledgeable they are with the land. There is not anything that we need that the land cannot provide for us, you just need to know how to do it.

I am starting to learn the language. White Horse is taking the honor of teaching me. I am selective about who I will practice with as it is quite comical when I mess up, especially with Kikimo, who I am growing to love tremendously. Preparations for the wedding are almost done, with the help of Running Water and White Fawn. It is scheduled for two weeks. I figure this will give Roger time to come and White Horse to get on his feet. Since my arrival, I have had no problems whatsoever with Minoke. She and Running Water are very close, and this is helping. I will not say that we are friends, but we are learning to respect each other. I am sure she has little choice, as I am marrying her Chief.

Another week has passed. White Horse is on his feet but moving very slowly. He is becoming bored and anxious to get well. I spend what time with him I can. The times I am away from him, he is either in the lodge whittling or in the smokehouse. It has been hard on him, as White Horse is not a man to stay still for very long.

Roger is due at any time. I am eager to see him. I am not feeling homesick at all, but I do miss picking on him. When I see the scouts come in with Roger beside them, I run to greet him. When he gets off his horse, I throw my arms around him.

"Hello, sis," he greets. He seems just as happy to see me.

"How is the patient?" he asks as he pats the top of Kikimo's head and hands him his reins.

"See for yourself," I point.

Roger looks a short distance and sees White Horse under the overhang. We walk the distance together, coming to White Horse. Roger shakes his hand.

"You are looking good," he says.

"I am feeling good."

"Walking much yet?" Roger asks.

"Short distances," he answers.

"Tolerating it well?"

"Yes."

"He is just not used to sitting around," I add.

"Understandable," Roger adds. "Just do what you can. It will come."

"Did Carrie tell you the news?" White Horse grins.

"What news?" Roger asks.

"We are getting married next week," I tell him.

"That is great," Roger says. "I really am happy for both of you."

"You are coming?" White Horse asks.

"Me...oh, you are damn right I am. I would not miss it."

"I want Stella to be here as well," I say.

"Sure, I can bring her."

"How is father?" I finally ask.

"He is good. Honestly, he is looking good."

"Good," I say.

I really am happy that he is feeling better and think that perhaps my leaving when I did was the best thing for him.

"Well," Roger says, coming down on his knees. "Let me look at those stitches. They may be ready to come out."

"That would be nice," White Horse says.

Roger finishes what is necessary with White Horse, removing his stitches and wrapping him back up. After giving him a good bill of health and predicting a full recovery, he closes his medical bag and stands up.

"I am afraid I must tell you both something that I believe White Horse, you will find interest in," Roger says.

"Go ahead," he says.

"Sid Barnes stepped down as Sheriff of Willow Creek and is moving out of town. Hank was offered the position by Sid, but the Marshall of the territory refused to give it to Hank."

I was almost afraid to ask but did anyway.

"Who did he give it to?"

"Carl."

Neither White Horse nor I could believe it.

"Why?" White Horse asks.

"Carl made him a promise."

"What sort of promise?" wonders White Horse.

"That he could find and kill you."

White Horse just smirks, chuckling under his breath.

"Alright. Carl wants to play cat and mouse. I'm game."

"White Horse, this could be serious," I say.

"Only for the new Sheriff, my dear. Not for me." White Horse looks up at Roger. "He will learn very quickly what happens when you mess with me." Roger grins. I, on the other hand, am more nervous.

"There is something else you both may find interesting."

"What?" I ask.

"I examined the Sheriff's body when it was brought in, and I am certain he did not kill himself. I think he was murdered."

"By a Pawnee?" I ask.

"I do not think so. The position on the way he was found and the entry of the bullet, I believe he was on his knees when he was shot. The reason I believe this is his trousers showed a lot of dirt on his knees."

"Roger, maybe he was just on his knees praying just before he shot himself," I say.

"I would believe that if it wasn't that he was shot in the head in the front, and although I cannot be certain, I do not believe his gun was ever shot off."

"What makes you think that?" I wonder.

"The Sheriff was very particular about his gun. He always kept it clean and polished. When I looked at the gun, it was spotless, even the chamber. He did not shoot that gun off. I would bet my money on it."

"So, someone killed him, big deal. He was a scum."

"He did not rape Anna or kill that Indian squaw. Carl did. The wrong man was killed," Roger argues.

"But he knew what was going on. He accepted the blackmailing. He accepted Carl to walk free. He refused to stop him. Willow Creek was attacked because of him and his inability to stop his own brother. White Horse was shot because of him, and I, for one, would praise the man who shot him."

"I agree with you, and the person who killed him by now has realized he killed the wrong man."

"How can you be so sure?" I ask.

"Because I know who killed him."

"How?"

"A few nights ago, Pa and I were talking about the attack, and he mentioned to me on that day when everyone gathered in the basement that Theodore Johnson was nowhere to be found. Several hours later, after the attack, he was seen coming into his home. Pa asked him where he was, and he said he had to finish something. When Pa asked him what he meant by that, he would not say."

"So, you think he killed the sheriff?"

"Yes, I do, and when he finds out who the real killer is, it is not only White Horse who wants Carl dead."

"Have you told him?" I ask Roger.

"No, I am not planning on it. I do not blame Theodore for killing the Sheriff, and he got away with it. I refuse to see a good-hearted man hang for this. That is why I will not tell him about Carl, because I do not want to chance him killing again and this time not being so lucky."

"Oh, I will not say a word, but Roger, you have another problem on your hands. You now have a sheriff who is a murderer and rapist, who will probably strike again."

I know it is a thought he is thinking as well, and right now, I am so glad I am not there because I most likely would be a target. Roger does not stay with us for the night. He says he has business in Cedar Brook and will go as far as he can tonight. White Horse assures him that he will be safe in Lakota territory if he needs to camp out for the night, as he is going to send several of his warriors to spread the word. Roger seems pleased with this and soon leaves.

With the evening winding down, I come down on the pelt beside White Horse. The week has been eventful, and I have learned so much. My mind is weary, and my body is tired, I am welcoming the sleep. I curl myself up next to White Horse with no cares at all. I will not let myself worry about Carl. I need to hold White Horse. I need to feel his touch and hear his heartbeat. He is all that matters. I know if I have everything with him, everything else will be fine. I close my eyes and fall asleep.

Chapter Thirty-Six

Morning Dove

A beautiful day has arrived. I find myself at the lake freshening up for the start of the day. The water is cool and remarkably clear, allowing me to see my reflection. I start to reach to take one final splash of water on my face when I notice that I am not alone in my reflection. I quickly jumped up. I sighed with a deep relief when I noticed it was Koawa.

"Don't do that," I say, catching my breath. "You gave me a start."

Koawa is still with a blank look on his face.

"What is wrong?" I questioned him.

"Have you seen Running Water?" he asks.

"Not since last evening," I answer.

"I have been up before the sun looking for her."

"She will show up," I reassure.

"She is angry with me," he says. "She speaks of foolish things. She runs off and hides when she is upset."

"I see."

"I must find her. I fear our child is coming."

"What makes you think that?" I wonder.

"She kept holding her stomach last night. When I asked her to let me help her, she became very angry with me."

I know from helping Roger deliver babies that some women will get very agitated when they are in labor. Koawa is right, we must find her.

"Do you have any idea where she may have gone?" I ask him.

"She has to be close, as if not, the scouts would have seen her leave and had stopped her."

"Alright then, we just need to search the area for her."

"I told you I have been!" he snaps.

"Alright, Koawa, calm down. She must be around here somewhere."

"This place is new to us," Koawa says. "We came here to be close to our Chief when he lay injured. We will be leaving soon when he is strong enough to travel on his own horse. There are many caves and hollows here. She could have gone into one of those and now is unable to move because the child is coming. There are many big cats out here, and she is unprotected."

I can hear the frustration and concern in his voice.

"Have you told White Horse?" I wonder.

"Yes, a search is being started. He asked me to come get you. He said you would want to join us."

I rush behind Koawa into the camp. White Horse is on his feet, supporting himself on a cane that one of his warriors made for him. He is standing near our lodge. Other warriors on horseback have left in their search for Running Water. I rush up to White Horse's side.

"What can I do, Dear?" I ask him.

"I not only fear big cats for her, but I also know Carl is looking for us and may have found her." I gulp. I had never thought of that. "For that reason, I do not want you to stray far."

"Alright."

"I want you to join the other women in the berry patch."

White Horse grabs my arm as I turn to leave. "Carrie, do not leave any further than the berry patch," he sternly warns. "I will have to sit this search out and cannot protect you. Do not be foolish by traveling further than the camp boundaries."

"Alright," I reassure. "I won't"

I quickly find the others in the waist-high berry patch. The wild berry patch is quite large. The largest one I have personally ever seen. The women split up. Her name is being called out to no avail. After an exhausting search done by all, we decided to move on. I am near the edge of the trees when I hear a cry. I call out for one of the women to stop and make my way into the trees. Pushing a large tree limb aside, I found Running Water. I rushed to her side, finding her in hard labor.

Songbird steps behind me. She gasps. In one of the few phrases I have learned in Lakota, I tell her to find Koawa. Songbird runs off, and Minoke steps in. I quickly act and look under Running Water's dress. She is crowning. There is no time. Running Water is going to have her baby right here. Minoke rushes to Running Water's side and starts talking her through it. With the best Lakota I know how, I tell her when to push and after several hard pushes, the baby is born. Minoke hands me her knife and the cord is cut. I clean the baby the best I can with my dress and coax it to cry. Joy fills the air when a soft cry is heard. Songbird returns with a blanket. She steps inside along with Koawa. I wrap the baby up gently, placing it in Running Water's arms,

"It is a girl, Koawa," I smile.

Koawa squats down in front of his wife. A tender moment is seen as they both gawk over their child. Koawa stands.

"I need to get her back to our lodge. Will you carry the infant back?"

"I will be honored," I say.

Word of the baby's birth and me delivering it has quickly spread throughout. I am greeted with praises and joy as I enter the camp. White Horse has slowly made part of the trip and waits for me to arrive. A smile ear to ear is seen on his face when I stop in front of him; my attention on the baby is momentarily paused as I look up at White Horse.

"I am proud of you, my Love," he says.

He looks down at the baby, grasping her little finger.

"I used to help Roger all the time deliver. It is nothing."

"No Love, this is everything for our people. Few can do this. You are looked at differently now. You are considered as a gift to our people."

"Here, I thought they were being nice just because of you," I tease.

"Not anymore. You earned their respect, and you got it."

I look down at the beautiful baby in my arms. I grasp her little fingers around my pinky. "Did you hear that sunshine?"

White Horse smiles. "You look beautiful holding that child."

I grin up at him. "I can't wait to hold ours," I comment.

"Our child will be very fortunate to have you as a mother. This I am certain of."

I hope he is right. "Tomorrow, mother and child will be taken to the river to be blessed, but for the moment, they will rest. I suggest you do the same."

I do as he suggests, returning the baby to her proud parents before going back to our lodge to rest.

Three days have passed. This evening, at a naming ceremony, Koawa and Running Water announce their daughter's name. Many speculations on what the name will be are all around. Even White Horse has an opinion, although he refuses to tell me what it is. Whatever the name may be, one thing is for sure, White Horse and I are the Godparents. When the ceremony begins, which is led by White Horse, I am allowed to stand by his side when her name is announced. Morning Dove is then welcomed by the tribe. Around the centerfire, many warriors dance in celebration of their new arrival. When both mother and child are ready for bed, it is then that White Horse and I leave the celebration and head to our own lodge.

"That was just beautiful," I comment.

"Yes, it was," he says as he comes down on the pelt.

"Will there be one for our child, too?" I wonder.

"Yes, but bigger, for our child belongs to their Chief."

I watch White Horse as he removes his tunic. A once painful task is now virtually effortless.

"How do you choose a name?" I ask as he covers himself up and lays down.

"Many times, you will receive a vision. This was the case for Kikimo and Running Water."

"What if I do not receive one?"

"I will not be surprised if you do."

"Don't you have to be Indian to receive one?" I ask, confused.

"No, my Love. Anyone can get one. The reason your people do not is because they do not believe in its existence."

"The name we give our child will that be their name for life?"

"Only the boys will change names when they become a man."

"Will Kikimo change his name?"

"If he receives his vision, then yes."

"Was your name changed?"

"Yes, when I became a man. I was given a name suited for a Chief."

"And what was your name when you were a boy?"

"Once you receive your new name, your old name is no longer spoken."

"Oh, come on," I whine. He chuckles.

"It is not important," he turns to his side and strokes my cheek. "What is important is what I have here, right at this moment."

"Oh, White Horse," I blush. He leans in, and we passionately kiss. I fall asleep in his arms and count the days until I become his wife.

Chapter Thirty-Seven

The Vision

Two weeks have passed. I woke up in White Fawn's lodge. Keeping to the tradition of it being bad luck to see the groom the night before the wedding, I came in here last night, much to White Horse's dismay, who is having problems understanding the tradition. It has been a game ever since with the Warriors on keeping White Horse away. He managed to attempt a sneak last night by slipping under the flap, only to be greeted by White Fawn, who slapped his hand with the back of a spoon. It was quite amusing to hear him yelp.

I hold up the dress as the finishing touches are being made by White Fawn. She has been working on the dress for over a week. The dress is breathtaking. It is made from a doe hide that is tanned white. It is then carefully crafted all the way down to the beads. I watch her as she adjusts the length to make a perfect fit. My leggings are made from buffalo hide and match the dress to perfection. A loop of flowers will be placed in my hair that will match the flowers that lay on Sugar Foot's back, that I will ride when I am led up to the altar. To replace the rings that we will not exchange, White Horse will place a necklace, made specifically by him, around my neck that will tie our unity.

The ceremony will be given by our Sharman, Flying Hawk. With everything in place, I make my way to a secluded place at the lake to take a bath. Disrobing, I make my way into the chest-high water. I allow my body to adjust to the temperature of the lake. Several minutes passed before I warmed up enough to dip under the water to wet my hair. White Fawn gave me some soap made from buffalo blubber to wash my hair and body. As I lather up, I hear rustling across the lake in the trees. I lower into the water and look around. Seeing nothing and not hearing it again, I assume it is a deer grazing and continue with my bath. I dip again under the water to rinse off.

I resurface and see White Horse stepping into the water. I am certain it was him I heard hiding in the bushes.

"White Horse," I yell. "Stop right there."

He ignores me and continues his way with a childish grin.

"White Horse, please. It is bad luck."

"Stop speaking foolishness," he smirks as he inches in closer.

I splashed water in his direction. "I mean it, stop!"

He has the smirk of an evil child who is ready to do something that they know is wrong. When he is inches from me, I splash him again and giggle.

"White Horse stop." He splashes me back.

"You give up this foolishness, and I will stop."

"It is not foolish to me," I spat.

"It is hard to listen to your reasoning when your nakedness reflects so beautifully in the water," he grins. I splashed him again.

"Stop it," I blush.

With a devilish grin, he dips his arms in the water and tosses me a huge splash at the same moment he has me in his arms. I feel his lips on my cheek.

"Next time we meet, our naked souls will be one."

He then releases me and walks out of the water.

The time for the wedding arrives. I start to wonder if Roger and Stella are going to make it. Running water, who is carrying Morning Dove in her papoose, helps me with my hair as White Fawn straightens my dress. There is much laughter in White Fawn's lodge as I am helped in getting ready, most of it being stories about White Horse. White Fawn, being his mother, has loads of them that I am certain if White Horse knew she was telling, he would not approve.

Our laughter is interrupted when riders are heard coming in. Opening the flap, I notice Yellow Hawk and Blue Thunder riding in; with them, they have brought three visitors. I strain to get a better look. I knew two of them had to be Roger and Stella, but who was the third? I gasp when I notice it is my Father.

Koawa looks out the flap of White Horse's lodge.

"Who is it?" White Horse asks.

"Our guests have arrived," he answers.

Just then, Koawa develops a huge smile.

"What is it?" White Horse asks as he starts to put on his wedding gear.

Koawa watches me as I run to meet the riders and greet my Father.

"Answer me," White Horse says.

"It is her father," he says. White Horse looks surprised and must see for himself. He comes to the flap. Koawa pushes him away.

"You know you can't see her," he spats.

White Horse jokingly pushes back. "She will never know."

From the flap entrance, White Horse watches on. Koawa takes it upon himself and makes his way to me and our guests.

I rush into my Father's arms and weep. Our embrace is tight.

"I am so sorry, Father," I cry.

"Hush, my child, it is I who needs to apologize. I let my foolish pride and beliefs come between us."

"I did not think you would come."

"What, and miss my daughter's wedding?"

He pushes away to look at me. "My, you look radiant."

"Thank you, Father."

Koawa joins us. Roger shakes his hand.

"Father, you remember Koawa?" he says.

"Yes, I do," he shakes his hand. "You kept my daughter safe when I could not. Thank you."

Koawa motions for Eagle Scout to take the horses of our guests and put them in the corral.

"Please join us by the lake. The ceremony will be starting very soon," Koawa states.

"I would like to see the groom," Father says. "If I may?"

"I will take you to him."

White Horse, who has just finished putting on his headdress, is standing at the back of the lodge when both men enter.

"It is very good to see you up and moving around, Chief," the Father says as he shakes White Horse's hand.

"It is good to be around," he answers.

He returns the handshake and offers Father a seat. It is then that Koawa leaves to give them their moment.

"Thank you for coming," White Horse says. "This means a great deal to Carrie."

"I need to talk to you about Carrie," Father quickly says.

"We will pass the pipe, and then we will talk."

The exchange back and forth of the pipe goes on for several passes. Father has never been a smoker but continues for White Horse's sake.

"What do you wish to speak to me about regarding your daughter?" he asks after he puts the pipe down.

"I wish to know why you have chosen her?" Father asks.

"Your daughter is not only very beautiful, but she is like no one I have ever seen before."

"In what way?"

"Your daughter has a spirit in her that most women do not have."

"I will agree with that," Father smiles.

"Your daughter is unique."

"Do you love her?" Father asks.

"Yes, with every beat of my heart."

"When you took my daughter's innocence away, I was very angry."

"I understand why you would be, but let me assure you when I did, it was out of Love. Love I have seen in a vision, love I have had for her for many years."

"Explain."

"You are a man of the cloth, so I feel you may understand. I had a vision several moons ago of a woman whose hair was the color of the prairie and whose skin was as bright as the morning sun. In my vision, I was told we would meet, and I was to go to her, that she was going to need my help. In return, she would bring great joy to myself and our people."

"You love Carrie because you were told to from a dream?"

"No, I love Carrie because we are meant to be. You see, Father, I did not help Willow Creek because I was told to or because I had a taste for revenge; I helped Willow Creek because I love your daughter, and her happiness means everything to me."

"Then, my son, you have my blessing," Father says. White Horse smiles.

"I promise you I will do good by her. I will shower her with great Love."

"I am certain of that now."

"In our culture, it is necessary to offer gifts to the bride's family. You may take as many horses as you see fit."

"The only gift I need from you is the assurance that you will treat her well and make her happy."

"I want nothing more than to see her happy, and I promise you, no harm will ever come to her. I would give her my life."

"Well, you have proven that," Father says.

White Horse smiles and helps Father to his feet.

"These rickety old knees will get the best of me yet," he jokes as he comes to his feet.

"The ceremony is soon approaching. Will you walk with me to the lake? It is there where we will meet the woman we both love."

Chapter Thirty-Eight

Gifts from the Past

Sugar Foot is walked up to White Fawn's lodge. I am lifted on the back of an even layered bed of flowers. Koawa then walks me through the camp and down to the lake to meet White Horse. Running water on one side and Stella on the other are keeping even strides with us. When White Horse is in view, we both smile at each other. He has never looked more handsome. He is dressed in buckskin that is heavy with fringe, and his headdress is filled with feathers that nearly touch the ground.

The radiant view of the mountains overlooks the lake when Koawa stops Sugar Foot. White Horse walks up, lifting me off his back. He pauses a moment, gazing heavily at my eyes before putting me down. Flying Hawk begins the ceremony, speaking words that neither White Horse nor I are paying any mind to. We continue a constant gaze into each other's eyes, each speaking our own words to each other. White Horse receives a nudge from Koawa, telling him to pay attention. He then hands White Horse the necklace. More words are spoken from Flying Hawk, and then finally, White Horse puts the necklace over my head. Roger leans into White Horse.

"I think that is your cue to kiss her," he says.

You did not have to tell him twice. Paying no mind that this sort of affection is highly unusual with mixed company, White Horse leans in, and we kiss. Laughter is heard throughout the camp as our lips remain locked. Koawa puts his arm between us.

"That is enough, her father is here," he jokes.

"Oh, by all means," Father says. "Don't let me stop you."

For the ones who understand and even too many who don't, the laughter is hard. The celebration of our wedding goes well into the evening. A feast has been made, and everyone gets their fill. Dancers form around the fire. Stella is drawn to Blue Thunder, watching him as he glides around the prairie. White Horse and I take Roger and Father to the overhang overlooking the camp.

"Son, will you please go get the gifts from my bag," Father says.

"Oh, Father, you did not need to bring gifts," I say.

White Horse removes his headdress and carefully places it behind him.

"Yes, you did not have to, but we thank you," he says.

"Nonsense," Father says. "It isn't every day my daughter marries a Chief." White Horse, and I smile as he rubs my shoulders.

"Marrying your daughter is all the gift I need."

"Oh, White Horse," I blush.

Roger returns with the bag. "I just brought the whole thing, there are too many to carry."

"I imagine I may have gone overboard," Father teases.

We watch as he opens the bag. "This is for the Chief," he says.

White Horse looks a little surprised that he is first or even that he gets anything. He reaches for it.

"I must admit it is not easy finding a gift for a Chief," my Father says.

White Horse unwraps it to reveal a tobacco bag and a pipe.

"This is a very nice gift for a Chief. Thank you," he says.

"You are welcome." My Father then reaches back into the bag.

"This is for you, dear," he hands me a shoe-size box. "Go ahead, dear, open it."

I open the box. Inside are several items, each carefully wrapped with paper. I open the first one. It is a brooch. "Oh, Father, this is beautiful."

"Do you recognize it?" he asks.

"No."

"That was your mother's."

"Oh my." I nearly cried.

"She told your Father that she always wanted her daughter to have it on her wedding day. I am doing as she asked."

I could feel the tears. "Now, don't get mushy eyes; there is still more," he teases.

I reached in, grabbed the next item, and unwrapped it. This one I recognize.

"This is the doll I used to play with when I was a child."

"Yes, now your child can play with it." I reached in again. It is a necklace with a ring around it.

"That was your father's wedding ring." I started to cry. White Horse rubs my shoulders.

"Do not cry, Love. You have a part of them now."

"He is right," Father says. "You have one more from me in that box. Open it, child."

I removed the last thing from the box. It is a small jewelry box. I open it up and find a key.

"What is this, Father?" I ask.

I then see him start to tear up and reach down into his pocket, removing a chain with a key at the end of it.

"That, my child, is the key to my heart," he cries.

I couldn't hold it in any longer. I began to cry. I rushed into his arms, and we tightly embraced.

"I am so sorry I hurt you, Father," I sob.

"No child, it is I who am sorry. I was wrong for leaving you."

"When you dropped off my suitcase and wouldn't talk to me, I thought I lost you forever."

"Shh," he consoles. "I know. I know." He releases his embrace to look at me. "My child, all my life, I have always wanted what was best for you. I always thought of you as my little girl. I just couldn't bear the thought of you growing up and one day leaving me alone."

"Father, I would never leave you."

"But child, you are, and that is alright with me because that is what makes you happy, and there is nothing more I want than to see you happy. That is why I gave you the key. I have one, too. So, whenever we need each other, we only hold the key, and it will feel as if we are still near to each other."

"Oh, Father," I embrace him again.

"Alright, I am feeling a little left out here," Roger teases. "Can we get to my gifts?"

We all laugh. Roger reaches inside the bag and pulls out two packages. He hands White Horse his. It is a bullet. Confused, he looks at Roger.

"That, my friend, is the bullet I removed from you when you damn near died on me."

"Wow, that is really amazing," I say.

White Horse nods in agreement.

"I will tell you this now, I honestly did not think you were going to make it."

"I am so relieved he did," I chime in.

"I will wear the reminder all my life," he says, pointing to his side where a scar will remain forever, "and how you saved my life. I will never forget it. Never." He reaches across and shakes Roger's hand. "Thank you."

"Your turn, Carrie," Roger says. I unwrap the gift that is carefully tucked around a baby blanket. "The blanket is for the baby," Roger says. "It can get pretty cold on the prairie."

"It is beautiful." Tucked away inside the blanket is everything one may need to deliver a baby.

"Oh, Roger, this is perfect."

"If you need me to explain anything, I can."

"I could have used this a few weeks ago," I say.

"I saw the beautiful bundle. She looks good. I'm proud of you."

"You taught me well."

"By the way, Mrs. Simpson's baby is thriving and doing very well."

"Good." Suddenly, my Father yawns.

"Pardon me," he blushes.

"It is late. Carrie will show you to your lodge," White Horse says.

"I will be there shortly, Pa," Roger says, helping Father to his feet. Arm and arm, we make our way to the lodge.

"What can you tell me about Carl?" White Horse asks as he watches his wife and her Father disappear into the lodge.

"Hank and I are trying to tell him that you have moved on."

"Does he believe you?"

"I don't believe so. He is vowed to find you and destroy you."

"Find is the word."

"I honestly do not think he will be able to. This place is hard to get to."

"Maybe I need to make it easier for him."

"You want him to find you?"

"I see him as no threat. My main concern is for my wife."

"I understand that. He is obsessed with her."

"That is why this needs to end, so Carrie can roam freely."

"He will not come alone."

"Is he calling in the Blue Coats?"

"I would not put it past him. He is trying to form a posse, but no one in Willow Creek is willing to join because they remember how you helped them. He has found a few from Cedar Brook, but I do not see a great threat."

"That is what I mean. My warriors can take care of them."

"How much longer are you planning on staying here? Roger asks.

"Not much longer. We will go to our winter camp as soon as I can ride."

Roger knows that will be soon as White Horse is getting stronger every day. He is moving around virtually pain-free with no aid at all. It is just a matter of days before he is certain White Horse will be on the back of a horse.

"I was just asking," Roger begins, "for the sake of seeing my sister off."

"I understand. When we go, I will be certain that you will get the word. Just keep in mind that I will not allow Carrie to be too close to Willow Creek for her own protection, but Blue Thunder and Koawa know their way around without being seen. Are you still at the big house in town?"

"Yes," Roger answers.

"Good; when we leave, I will send them there to find you, and you can come to her."

"Thank you."

"You stay and join the festivities as long as you wish," White Horse says. "I am going to find my wife and have my own festivities in our lodge." Roger chuckles as White Horse comes to his feet.

"Hey, Chief," he says as White Horse turns to walk away. "Go gentle," he grins. White Horse smiles and walks away.

The evening is brought to a close. White Horse rolls over on his side, scooping me up in his arms. His kisses quickly tell me he has one thing on his mind.

"White Horse, the baby."

"What about it?" he huskily says between his advances.

"I don't want to hurt the baby."

"It is our wedding night."

"I know, but the baby doesn't know that."

"It is alright." I push his hands away as he lowers them.

"I don't think it is a good idea," I argue.

"I do," he says.

He rolls on top of me and kisses my bump. "You sleep, my little one," he says. "Your mother and I are busy."

I giggle and quickly fall into his trap with his lovemaking.

Stella follows Roger to the lodge that is set up for them for the night. Blue Thunder comes to her side. A flirtatious grin was exchanged between them. Blue Thunder nods his head for her to follow him. She glances over at Roger. What could he do? He has no control over her, and besides, he sort of likes the guy. He just shakes his head, yes. Stella then follows Blue Thunder into his lodge and into his arms.

Chapter Thirty-Nine

The Loss

One week has passed, and my life as a Lakota bride is phenomenal. I am quickly getting into a routine and learning what my duties are every day. White Horse is up and moving around on his horse. He is now able to go out and hunt and scout among his warriors. He has moved his scouts out farther in the event of locating Carl. It is a game for him of cat and mouse, with us being the mouse. He spotted Carl and his posse several times and is leading them in circles all around us. White Horse is obsessed with this, and for that reason, he decides to stay here, at least for the moment, or until he and his warriors become bored with the chase.

I know White Horse well enough that when he becomes bored with the chase, he will go in for the kill, and Carl will be dead, but for now, White Horse and his men are enjoying the game. I, for one, am becoming very nervous and feel White Horse should be less arrogant and move us on. As they are out today scouting around, White Horse spots a familiar-looking horse. He knows it to be his brother-in-law. Odd, he thinks, as he knows of no further reason why he would take such a long ride. Except for the scar, which he will wear for the rest of his life, he is feeling great, and the wedding is behind them. The circle in the sky is still low, which he finds peculiar, as it must mean that Roger has been riding before sunrise to get here. Although he is always happy to see his new friend, he concludes that it must only mean one thing, something is wrong. He wonders if it is Blue Coats. Along with his warriors, he rides down the slope to meet up with him. He greets him with his tongue. It does not take him long, upon seeing his long face, that, indeed, something is very wrong.

"Your face is long, my brother," he says. "What is so heavy to bring you all this way?"

"I need to see Carrie," he says.

"She is back at camp," White Horse says. "What is wrong?"

"Pa died two days ago."

For a few moments, all that is heard is the wind whipping through White Horse's hair. A deep sigh is heard both from White Horse and Koawa.

"This brings me great sadness," he finally says. "He was a good man.

My Prairie Dawn will not handle this news well."

Roger, so grief-stricken himself, faintly nods.

"I am sorry, my brother, for your loss."

"Thank you," he mumbles.

"I will take you to her. Come."

I come out of the lodge when I see the riders return. The shock I receive when I see Roger among them. I quickly make my way to the edge of the camp as they stop and jump off their horses. I immediately rushed to give Roger a hug. I didn't get the welcome I was hoping for. Looking up at Roger, I see great sadness in his eyes. I look over at White Horse and get the same void.

"What's the matter?" I ask them.

Roger takes my hand into his. "There is no easy way of telling you this," he somberly says.

"Tell me what? What is it, Roger?"

I hear him sigh as if he is getting the courage to tell me. I look over at White Horse. The expression on his face said it all.

"It is Father, isn't it?" I ask. Roger nods.

"Carrie, Pa died a few days ago. I have only now been able to get away to tell you."

I gasped, and immediately, my eyes teared up. I now become angry.

"You're lying," I glare.

"No. Carrie. He's gone." I whip my hand free from Roger's.

"This is some crude joke," I snap.

"I wish it was." He attempts to hold my hand again. I pushed him away.

"You said he would be alright!" I push him again and yell. "You lied to me. You told me he would be alright!"

White Horse grabs me from around my waist.

"Carrie, stop it," he spats.

He turns me around to face him, and grabbing my shoulders, he gently shakes me. I look up at him. I knew it was true. White Horse would never lie to me, and he would never play such an awful joke.

"Oh, dear God," I cry. Putting my hands over my mouth, I became weak in my legs and plopped to the ground on my knees. I then begin to sob uncontrollably. Roger joins me on his knees, placing his arms around me. We then sob together. After a few moments of weakness, Roger pulls himself together and stands up.

"I want you to know he did not suffer. He went to lie down. He told me he was tired. When he didn't come to dinner, I went to check on him. I found him on his back with his arms crossed, holding his bible."

I wipe some tears from my cheek and stand up.

"I found this in his bible." Roger hands me a piece of paper. I open it up. I read out loud.

To my dearest children,

If you are reading this, then you will already know that I have left this world for a better place. I am with my Maker and Creator. I lie in green pastures filled with my favorite flowers, as far as I can see. Do not cry over me, my children, as I am at peace and will be watching you both from above. No matter where your life may take you, I will never be too far. For there is only one sky filled with a million stars, and one of those stars will be me looking down on you.

Father.

I folded up the letter and handed it back to Roger.

"He knew he was dying," Roger says. "I found something else under his mattress when they took his body."

He pulls out the key identical to mine.

"Father's key.... I don't understand."

"Carrie, this key is a key to a lock box at the Orphanage. I was with Pa when he bought the box. It takes two keys to open. You have the second key."

"Why would he give me the key?"

"Whatever is in that box, he wanted to be sure you could get into it no matter where you were. He left me his key because he knew he had no use for it. One key for me and one key for you."

I pulled out the necklace that held the key on it from under my dress.

"He told you that key is the key to his heart. He literally meant it was the key to his heart."

I gasp. "Are you thinking what I'm thinking?" Roger nods.

"That inside that box there will be a Will."

I remove the necklace from around my neck and hand it to Roger.

"Take it. See what it opens. Whatever it is, you keep it."

Roger looked shocked. "Are you sure?" he asks.

"Yes. I have no use for it here. If it is money, give it to the Orphanage. They need it more than I do."

Roger looks over at White Horse. "I will go to Cedar Brook yet today to visit Sister Ann. I will ask her about the box and tell her about Pa. How much longer will you be here?"

"Only for a few more days. Soon, the ground will turn hard."

"I will return by then." I grabbed Roger's hand.

"I'm sorry I was curt with you." He leans in and kisses my cheek.

"I love you," he says.

"Me too."

Evening is upon us. I lie entwined in White Horse's arms on our pelt, my Father's death still heavy on my mind. White Horse has been wonderful during my grieving as I try to make sense of his death. The philosophical side of my husband emerges.

"With our people," he begins, "we are taught that dying is a complete circle of life. When one life is taken, another one emerges. It is when the one who dies has not yet lived is when you ask yourself why? Your Father has lived and has taught others how to live as well."

"That does not make it any easier," I protest.

"Death is never easy, no matter what age. You cannot look at death as the end, you must look at death as a beginning."

"So, my Father's death is the start of a new. Like our child?"

"Could be a child. It could be a marriage. It could be anything that is fresh."

White Horse has a point, and his words made a lot of sense. I lift my head to briefly kiss his lips.

"I love you," I say. He grins.

Seven days have passed. I am well into my fifth month with morning sickness behind me. I am feeling gentle movements from the child within. There are no signs of Carl anywhere, but White Horse is almost certain that he will be back. My gut instinct is telling me the same. Roger has yet to return. Certain that my Father's funeral is over, I am sure he is just busy tying up his estate and will return when he can. I only hope White Horse will wait around long enough, as very soon, the ground will get hard. Although White Horse promised Roger he would wait or send word of our departing, he too is feeling restless about Carl and wanting to move on for fear I will get hurt if Roger is followed here in some way.

White Horse is in our lodge sharpening his knives on a stone, and I am finishing the quilt that I was hoping would have been done by now when Kikimo runs in. He speaks his tongue to his Father and runs off.

"Your brother is here," he says.

Putting down my quilt, I join White Horse at the flap. After being greeted by many and handing his reins off to Minoke, he walks over. I give him a hug as he steps in, unaware of all the danger that lurks ahead.

Chapter Forty

The Stranger in the Woods

"Don't leave me in suspense, Roger," I anxiously say after we all make ourselves comfortable in our lodge. "What did you find out?"

Roger reaches into his coat pocket, pulling out an envelope. "It was indeed his Will, along with other interesting items."

I open the envelope to unfold the papers. "Like what?" I ask him.

"Sister Ann took me to the basement to another box on the top of a shelf that belonged to our father."

"That doesn't surprise me, the Orphanage was his second home." I pause a moment to read the Will.

"Wait a minute, Roger, there must be a mistake here. Father left everything to me."

"That is no mistake."

"You knew that?" I question.

"Yes, he told me what he was going to do, and I was fine with it."

"Why would you be?"

"Pa knew financially I would be fine. I make do as a physician. However, Pa knew you were unwed and would need it."

I was about to drop my teeth when I saw the amount. Father left me a considerable amount of money that would have secured me for many years.

"He must have been saving all his life," I comment.

"He was. Every penny."

"He left me real estate as well. I did not know he owned any real estate."

"Father was loved by a lot of people who would leave him things when they had no other family to care for them."

"I don't need this. I have everything I need right here."

"I knew you were going to say that. So, I went to see Pa's lawyer, who drew up the Will and asked him what we could do. He gave me this paper for you to sign." He reaches into his pocket again. "You tell him what you want done, and he will do it."

"I want you to have it," I say.

"That is generous but not necessary. It is yours." I think for a moment.

"Then I will sign it all to you, with the stipulation that a third of the money goes to the Orphanage with a plaque of Father's name on the front, naming the Orphanage after him."

"Alright," he agrees.

He then hands me a pre-inked pen. I sign the paper, make the changes, and hand it back to Roger.

"I will take it back to him as soon as I can." He folds it up and puts it back in his pocket.

"Now tell me about the other box," I ask.

"There were only two things that I thought meant anything. One of them was this."

He opens his medical bag, pulling out a picture. He then hands it to me.

"It is a picture of my mother," I say.

White Horse, curious, leans in and looks at the picture.

"You look just like her," he says.

"The resemblance is stunning," I comment.

"Flip it over, Carrie, and look at the date," Roger says.

I flipped it over and read the date. I faintly smiled. This picture was taken three months before I was born.

"I thought that ironic," Roger said. "In that picture, she is pregnant with you, and by the date, she is about the same distance along as you are."

"May I keep this?" I ask him.

"By all means." Tickled to have a picture of my mother put me on cloud nine. I carefully lay the picture beside me.

"There is one more thing that you both need to know."

We set our eyes on him.

"Carrie, did Pa ever tell you how your mother died?"

"Yes, she died in childbirth," I answer.

"Did he tell you how it came to be?"

"No."

"When you were born, your father had a very difficult time stopping your mother from bleeding to death."

"I didn't know that. How did he?"

"Your Father was a brilliant man. He did a lot of research on his own on herbal medicine." That perked up White Horse's ears. "According to Pa, he even spent some time with the Cheyenne researching different plants and what they are used for." White Horse is finding this very interesting.

"Wow," I state. "I never knew that."

"When your parents were courting, your mother cut herself on a dish and could not get it to stop bleeding. It was not a very deep cut and should not have bled as much as it did. After some time, your Father was able to stop it. It got him to think that something may be wrong. Living in Boston at that time, he had the resources to do some research and came up with a diagnosis of Hemophilia."

"I have never heard of that."

"It is a blood disease that causes severe bleeding. Your blood is unable to clot, and therefore, you continue to bleed."

"Oh," I say.

"It is hereditary." My eyes widen.

"You think I may have this?" I wonder.

"Do you remember the time you and Stella became blood sisters, and you both cut your wrists?"

"Yes, it bled like a dickens."

"Yes, and the time we went fishing and your leg got caught on the hook?"

"Yes, it bled a lot too." Roger looks over at White Horse.

"When you brought her back to your camp after she was attacked by that bear, did you have trouble stopping the bleeding?"

"Come to think about it, yes," he answers.

"Carrie, I believe you have this disease, and this is what concerns me when you give birth."

"What can we do?" asks White Horse.

"Your Father found a plant that when the root is boiled and drank, it will stop the bleeding. The forest is full of them. I found one on my way here. I will show you."

He reaches again into his medical bag, pulling out the plant. He hands it to White Horse.

"Yes, I am familiar with this. We use the flower. We have never used the root."

"A Cheyenne Sharman showed your father how to use it but never showed him how to grow it or keep it alive in the cold."

"I do not know of a way either. It is a flower, and it dies off when hard water crosses the land," White Horse says.

"This is what your Father was researching. When you were born, the forest was filled with this, and he could easily access it, and he believes, as I do, that it saved your mother's life."

"So, I just take this after I have our child," I conclude.

"Carrie, your brother was born in the winter when the plant is dormant."

"Just pick a whole bunch of them."

"No, my Love," White Horse says. "The root has to be alive."

"Exactly," Roger says. "Pa knew this but never told you. When he realized when the child was going to be born, it was then that he told me."

White Horse is extremely concerned, and with good reason.

"Is there a chance that she will not bleed?" he asks.

"It is normal to have some sort of bleeding in childbirth. So no, she will bleed." Roger assures. White Horse grows still.

"There may be a way," Roger says hopefully, "but it will take a great deal of patience and time."

"Tell me," White Horse says.

"Carrie's Father was working on the greenhouse effect of preserving the root during the cold climate. I have his diagram here that was in that box of what he was working on."

He removes it from his bag and hands it to White Horse.

"Unfortunately, her father died before he ever knew if it really works."

"I will speak to Flying Hawk. He is very knowledgeable about this sort of stuff. I will see what he thinks." His dark-set eyes grow stern. "I will find a way. I will not lose my wife or my child."

"I would like to see what it looks like in the wild?" I tell Roger.

"I saw a whole bunch within walking distance from here. I can show you."

"May I White Horse?"

"It is just over the ridge," Roger adds.

"You go no further," he warns.

"I won't."

"I am going to speak with Flying Hawk. Don't be gone long."

The walk to the ridge is not necessarily far but a little hilly. When you get to the top of the ridge, there is a beautiful view of the prairie below and the forest behind you. To the right of that, tucked in the valley, is our camp. White Horse comes here often just to screen the area around us. I know exactly where we are.

"It is not much further," Roger says. "I remember that big boulder."

"Roger, why don't you go to the city where you can make more money?" I ask.

"Being a doctor is all I have ever wanted to be. It has nothing to do with the money."

"Are you going to stay in Willow Creek?"

"I am not sure. There isn't really anything keeping me around here once you leave."

"You make it sound so bad."

"Don't feel that way. I knew one day someone would sweep you off your feet," he grins. "I just never imagined this."

"I don't know why you seem surprised. I have always been the black sheep of the family."

"That's not true," Roger states.

"Yes, it is. Even Sister Ann thought so. Many times, she told Father that I was too wild for a little girl just because I liked to play in the dirt and mud. I guess I wasn't dainty enough."

"Pa knew differently, Carrie. He always said you were one of a kind."

"White Horse tells me that."

"See," he grins. "I don't think too many people would argue with him." I chuckle. "Sometimes I admire you, Carrie," he says.

"Me? What forever for?"

"You are not afraid to get in and stand up for yourself. Many women do not talk out of turn. You are a very strong woman, Carrie."

"Oh, heavens no," I argue. "Look at Carl, for instance."

"You are correct to be cautious of him. He is made from bad blood."

"And poor Anna, she was just another victim of his sexual games."

"That could have been you."

"I know."

Just then, we hear a rustle in the trees beside us. We both stop for a moment and look.

"Huh," Roger says after seeing nothing. "Most of been an animal."

We ignore it and keep going. We make our way to the boulder. I sit down on it as Roger picks the flower. He walks over to me and sits down beside me.

"Here you go," he says, handing it to me.

"Sure, it is a pretty thing," I comment.

We then hear the rustling again. I can tell it is bothering Roger.

"I wouldn't put it past White Horse if he has one of his scouts following us," I conclude.

"You think so?" he asks.

"Wouldn't surprise me." He seems somewhat relieved.

He grins. "He sure is protective of you."

"Yes, he is. Sometimes too protective."

"At least I know I will not need to worry about you," he jokes.

"No, you don't. White Horse will rip the head off anyone who tries to hurt me." We both giggle.

Suddenly, the movement is closer. Roger picks up a rock and tosses it in the direction of the noise.

"Get out of here," Roger says.

"White Horse did tell me that there are big cats around here. You don't think?"

Just then, the rock that Roger tossed is tossed back at us. I quickly jumped to my feet.

"That is no cat," I utter. Roger removes his gun from his holster and pulls me behind him.

"Who's there?" Roger bravely says. "Show yourself."

"What are you two doing?" We hear behind us. We turned around to see Koawa perched high on his horse. We both sighed in relief. Roger, feeling foolish, puts his gun back into his holster.

"You know you really should not scare people like that!" I snap.

"Like what?" Koawa says.

"Tossing that rock back at us like you did."

"I do not understand this foolishness you are speaking of."

"You didn't just toss that rock back at us?" Roger asked.

"No," he answers, "I just got here." Roger and I gulp. "Someone tell me what all this means. I only came because White Horse sent me here to check on you."

"Carrie and I heard movement. We thought maybe it was a deer or maybe a big cat. I tossed a rock at it, and it tossed it back."

Koawa looked out into the woods. "You two stay here," he says.

I glanced out towards the prairie below us. Out a short distance, I see a large trail of dust blowing around. It had to be Carl and his posse. We have been found.

"Koawa, look," I point.

Koawa looks out to where I am pointing.

"Both of you run back to camp and tell White Horse. I am going to hold them off."

He then rides quickly down the ridge. Roger and I waste no time and, as fast as we can, we run back to camp. When we get down the hill, Roger stops.

"You go ahead. I am going back to help Koawa."

"Be careful, Roger," I say.

We then split in our directions. Roger, by no means, is a warrior and knows Koawa can probably hold his own, but he can't just leave him. He runs as fast as he can, sliding down a rocky incline to the prairie below.

Chapter Forty-One

The Farewell

The dust is seen by the Lakota scouts. Immediate action is taken to back them off. Blue Thunder is fast on his horse, approaching the camp. He gives word to his Chief of the pending attack. White Horse is quick to react, ordering his men to charge in.

"Carl is his," he says, "I want him alive."

He jumps on his horse, running as fast as he can to fight alongside his men. Roger reaches the top of the boulders and looks out at the prairie below him. He can see the Lakota warriors charging in. He is confident that Koawa does not need his assistance, so he heads back to meet up with his sister.

I am rushing back to camp across the rocky terrain. The steepness and the unsettled ground are making for a slow run. For fear of slipping and possibly injuring myself or my unborn child, I slow to a fast walk. I carefully and meticulously watch my every step. I glance down at the ground below me and cautiously continue, being mindful of my footing as any wrong movement could take me to my death. I abruptly stop when Carl jumps in front of me. I gasp in horror.

"Well, look here," he smirks. He glances down at my stomach. "Well, ain't that cute." He pulls out his gun. "Too bad it has to go."

The warriors are charging in. The posse comes to a stop.

"Son of a bitch," one of the men says.

"Carl never said that there would be so many," said another one.

"No wonder why he bailed."

"Fuck this shit, I'm out of here," one hollers.

The men then retreat. The warriors keep coming, not allowing any of them to get away. White Horse is thirsty for revenge and is scoping with his eyes for the one named Carl. One by one, he watches them fall. Where is the snake, he wonders, the only blood he can taste. He is nowhere to be found. Fear then enters his soul, Prairie Dawn.

Stella is quick at getting Hank's attention. She saw the posse come into town. She heard what they had to say, kill the Chief and steal the bride. She saw Theodore Johnson quickly following behind. She slipped and told him that Carl had raped Anna. She was sworn not to tell and is angry with herself for not keeping quiet. She is riding hard with Hank by her side. She only prays she can remember the way. The river, yes, she was almost there. She is praying she isn't too late. She must warn them. She must try.

Roger enters the camp and notices that his sister has not returned. She should have been here by now, he thinks. He ran to get on his horse. He knows something is wrong. He makes his way to the boulders as fast as his horse goes.

Carl is aiming his gun at my stomach. I started pacing in circles around him, looking for a place to run. His eyes are full of hate as he follows my every move.

"It was you following us. Wasn't it?" I ask.

"Yes. Your brother is weak at covering his trail. I knew he was up to something. That is why I followed him, and I was right. He led us right to you."

"You were the one who tossed the rock back?"

"Yes. I was going to come out then when I saw the savage who tried to kill me in Willow Creek. I decided against it."

"Give it up, Carl. You will not get away."

"I have already gotten away," he growls. "I saw you both walking up to the ridge. I left the men and came to you instead." He cocks his gun. "By the time they realize I am not there, you will be dead, and I will be gone."

"Why kill me? What could you possibly gain by killing me?"

"You have been a thorn in my side for years, you and your brother." He tilts his head out of frustration. "I never knew a woman could be so much trouble," he shakes his head vigorously. "No more. I will get the last laugh."

"Is that how it was with Anna? Did you get the last laugh with her?"

"Anna killed herself by getting pregnant. It was not my fault."

"Because of what you did to her and that Pawnee squaw."

"That squaw got what was coming to her. She slipped and fell. I didn't kill her."

"No, you just raped her."

"That is where you are wrong. I never raped her. My brother did."

"That is not what Sid told me." Carl faintly smirks.

"Is that what he told you? Sid lied."

"Why would he?"

"Because he is just as guilty as I am. Sid found the squaw in the river. The sheriff came to her as she tried to run off. It was Sid who caught her and tossed her down. I never laid a hand on her until she was buried."

I figured I would allow him to continue his blabbering on as I try to find my escape.

"And Anna?" I ask.

"It was the sheriff who came up with the hood idea. We had seen her a few minutes before when she went into the river. He wanted her, he had wanted her for years. I never raped her. I wanted someone else."

He steps closer to me.

"I only wanted you one time. I only wanted to touch you one time."

I coward my face away as he attempts to touch it.

"But now you are trash. Worthless, filthy trash. The Chief will die alongside you, and I will get the reward of being the sheriff who did it. I will finally get what I deserve."

I watch him step back as he cocks his gun. I find my escape and run just as Carl shoots. It hits a rock above my head. I slouch down behind some boulders.

"Damn you!" he hollers.

I hear the crackle of rocks below his feet as he comes down the hill.

"You can't hide," he cackles. "Come out. I know you are in there."

Remaining still, I look around for something I can use as a weapon. I found a stone and picked it up.

"Just show yourself," he says.

I hear the rocks stop moving, I know he is standing on the other side of the boulder. I tossed the rock, hitting him in the head. It was hard enough that he staggered with his balance. I then make a run. Another shot is fired. I tuck behind some more rocks as the bullet ricochets off the boulders.

"Now look what you did. You plum got me pissed off," he barks.

Roger hears the shot coming along the way of the rocks. He kicks his heels into the ribs of his horse and rushes off in the direction of the noise. White Horse abruptly stops upon hearing the second shot. It is near the big boulders. He turns his horse and, fiercely jabbing its side, pushes his horse to astonishing speed.

"You just wait until I find you," Carl roars.

Oblivious to where he is walking, he trips into a hole in the ground and curses. I take this opportunity to make another run. Carl sees me as I slip between some more boulders. He finds his gun and shoots. I scream in pain as I get hit in the leg and fall to the ground.

"I got you now," he cackles.

Unable to run any further, I try to crawl to hide. I spotted a good-sized stick within my reach. I place the stick under my arm and attempt to use it as a crutch. My first attempt at getting to my feet fails. I frantically attempt again as I see Carl rushing towards me. I wobble painfully to my feet. Dragging my leg, I stumble to get away. My efforts are in vain. Carl is within reach. I scream. It is heard throughout the valley.

White Horse is in a panic. He hears his Prairie Dawn scream. He knows she is in danger. He pushes his horse harder.

Falling to the ground, I hit Carl with the stick, knocking the gun out of his hand. It goes flying a few feet away. He makes a run for the gun when I trip him with the stick. We both start crawling to the gun. Carl is uninjured and not pregnant, allowing him to succeed. He grabs the gun and points. He cocks it. He sneers. All I can do is sit there, catching my breath, and pray for a miracle as I stare him down.

"Drop it," I hear.

It is Roger pointing his gun at Carl. "Put the gun down and back away," he says.

For a split second, it appears as if Carl is going to. Then I see his look. I watch him as he curls his lower lip. He has no intention of giving up. I now fear for Roger. In the blink of an eye, Carl quickly grabs me, using me as a human shield. He has his gun pointing at my head.

"Go ahead, Doc. Shoot me." Panic fills my eyes. "She will be dead before it leaves the chamber."

The standoff continues. Roger fears for his sister's life. There is only one thing he can do. He drops his gun and puts his hands in the air.

"Kick it over to me," Carl orders.

Roger does as he says. Carl then pushes me to the ground. Grabbing Roger, Carl pushes him down beside me. Roger sees me bleeding. We both look up to a barrel in our faces.

"I will kill you both," he growls. "The whore first."

He points the gun at me. Roger throws his body across mine to shield me. We both shudder, anticipating the painful death. Suddenly, Carl is hit in the head from behind and falls to the ground. Roger and I both look in amazement as we see it is Theodore Johnson.

Carl looks just as surprised as we are as he rubs the back of his head from the blow. I hear him growl. Theodore has his gun on him.

"I couldn't save Anna from you, but I will not allow you to hurt anyone else."

Carl is fierce and extremely heartless, and quickly, a battle between the two is on. Carl has Mr. Johnson on the ground and starts strangling him. Mr. Johnson is putting up a good fight, but both Roger and I are fearing for his life. Roger jumps up to come to his defense when we both see White Horse jumping over a boulder and onto Carl's back. Carl is immediately tossed around like a rag doll. He struggles to find his gun and cocks it. White Horse is quick and kicks it out of his hand. Carl tries to take a swing, but White Horse is fast and moves out of the way.

Carl then tries to run for his gun when White Horse grabs his legs, pulling him down to the ground. He then gives him a swift kick in the jaw. A tooth is seen flying out of his mouth, and Carl comes to his knees. He glares up at White Horse and lunges forward to fight him. White Horse sees the stick that I am using as a crutch and picks it up. He slams the end of it into Carl's stomach. I hear him holler as more blood comes out of his mouth.

The rage in White Horse is extraordinary, and poor Carl is no match for his brute strength. Carl looks up at him. I have no doubt that his jaw is broken. Carl is unable to speak. His eyes plead. He knows White Horse is going to kill him. The air is deathly still as White Horse glares down at Carl. Suddenly, we gasp in horror as Mr. Johnson lunges into Carl. The men begin to wrestle. I am amazed that Carl has anything left.

I see Carl turn Mr. Johnson over and tower on top of him. They start to fight for Theodore's gun. The gun goes off just as Carl receives a blow from behind from White Horse from a heavy rock. Carl falls to his death from a broken skull. Roger runs to Mr. Johnson, who has been shot just as White Horse drops the bloody rock. I hear Roger sigh.

"Oh, dear Lord."

Roger removes Mr. Johnson's hat and covers his face. It is then that I realize he is dead. I immediately shook hysterically. We are joined by many Lakota warriors running up the rocks. Koawa then sees Mr. Johnson dead with a gunshot. White Horse comes a short distance from me, falling on his knees. He takes me in his arms as the tears are rolling down my face.

"It's alright, Love. It's over."

I lay my hand down on his chest as he wraps his arms around me. It is then that White Horse sees my leg.

"Oh no," he mumbles.

His tone immediately changes. Roger joins us on the other side and is looking at my leg as he, too, tries to console me.

"Is it bad?" White Horse asks Roger.

"I don't believe so. I think it just grazed her."

I look out at Mr. Johnson. "He tried to save us. He didn't deserve to die." Roger rubs my shoulders.

"Carrie, he is with Anna now. He is happy. You must try to believe that. He was such a lonely man. He never would have healed. He is where he wants to be."

I wipe a tear. I know Roger is right, but he was such a sweet man and such a pointless death. Koawa joins us, speaking his tongue.

"She is alright," White Horse says.

Suddenly, I am hit with the most excruciating pain in my abdomen. I grab my stomach and wail.

"What is it?" White Horse asks concerned.

Roger sees the pain in my eyes. My tears intensify.

"Carrie, is it the baby?" he asks. I nodded my head yes as I tried to breathe.

"We need to get her back," rushes Roger.

"Oh God no," I wail.

White Horse wastes no time. He scoops me up in his arms and runs. He passes me off to Koawa long enough to jump on his horse. In his tongue, he commands. "Leave the snake where he lies. Take the other one back and get ready to move."

Back at camp, White Horse nervously waits outside with the others for any news on me. Suddenly, several warriors are seen rushing in, and they have brought company. White Horse recognizes them as Hank and Stella. Stella is quickly off her horse and rushes to White Horse.

"Thank God you are alright," she cries.

"Yes, we are fine."

"And Carrie?" she cries.

"I am confused why are you here." White Horse says.

"I overheard Carl; he said he's coming to kill you and steal Carrie."

Hank joins Stella by her side. It is then that they see Mr. Johnson's body slouched over Koawa's horse. She gasps and starts to cry. Hank walks over to Koawa's horse, lifting off the body. He then carries it over his shoulder and over to his own horse.

"I will take him back and bury him next to the Reverend."

"I am sorry for your loss. You must know he died a hero," White Horse says. Hank only nods.

"We saw the men on the way here dead on the grass. That is when Stella really got nervous."

"Yes, we stopped them quick."

"Where's Carl?" Hank asks.

"Among the dead," he states. "He shot Carrie."

Stella gasped. "How is she?"

"Roger is with her right now."

White Horse looks over at Hank. "You must understand. He came to us. We were defending ourselves."

"I do not doubt this, and I promise you, Chief, I will do whatever I can to clear you of this now that I have accepted the sheriff position."

This is music to White Horse's ears. He knows he can trust Hank. Just then, he sees the flap open, and Roger steps out.

"If you will excuse me. I need to check on my wife."

"How is she?" he asks when he approaches the outside of the lodge.

"Her and the baby are going to be fine." White Horse sighs in relief.

"May I see her?"

"Yes, but one thing."

"What?" he worries.

"She is very upset about what happened with Carl and very concerned about what will happen to all of you."

"She needs not to worry. We are leaving tonight."

Roger looks sad upon hearing the news. He knew the day would come when he would have to say goodbye to his sister. He must be strong. He chokes back any emotion.

"I will leave you two alone."

He then walks off. White Horse opens the flap and steps in.

"How are you feeling, my love?" he asks as he kneels beside me.

"Roger said the baby is alright, and my leg is only superficial."

"That is wonderful news," he grins. "You had me worried."

"I know. And I am worried." He strokes my hair.

"I do not want you to worry about anything ever again."

"White Horse, you killed a sheriff."

"He deserved what he got."

"I am not saying he didn't, but not everyone will see it that way. And what about his posse? Are they dead as well?"

"Sweetheart."

"Well, are they?"

"Yes," he finally answers.

"The Marshall will come for you. White Horse, you must get out of here." He places his finger over my lips.

"Everything will be alright. I do not want you to worry about it."

"White Horse, you don't understand."

"Sweetheart, I do. We will leave here very shortly." I am relieved. "But first, there are a few things we need to discuss."

"What?" I wonder.

"Where we are going is very far from here. You will not be able to see your brother."

"My life is with you, White Horse. I am aware I will not see Roger, perhaps never again. I do not care. I love you, White Horse, and I will follow you anywhere."

"You say that now, but you may change your thinking later."

"White Horse, I am your wife. When I married you, I gave up my life. You give me a better life. I don't care how hard it may be for me as long as I have you." He grins and kisses my forehead.

"Only take what you need. The other women will pack up our lodge."

"I want to help," I argue.

"Not this time, Love. You will not walk as most of the women do. You will ride alongside me."

"I love you, White Horse," I say.

"I love you too." He says and leans in to kiss me.

Our lips remain locked for several seconds. Hmm, we hear. We unlock our lips and look towards the flap to see Roger.

"I'm sorry. Koawa told me to come on in," he says. White Horse stands.

"I need to check on everything. Take your time."

"Roger." He holds his hand up.

"I know what you are going to say. I do not want any tears." He squats down in front of me.

"I am going to miss you," I cry.

"I will miss you too."

"What are you going to do?"

"I will stay in Willow Creek, at least for now."

The thought of leaving him and perhaps never seeing him again is sinking in. "I am sure if I ask White Horse, he will let you come with us." Roger chuckles.

"Thanks, but my life is being a doctor. I would miss it too much."

As much as it pains me to hear it, I know he is right. A doctor is all Roger has ever wanted out of life.

"Who knows, maybe I will settle down and find myself a wife."

"You settle down, Roger?"

"Yes, I have been thinking about it. I think it is about time."

"Then I am sure you will. Any woman would be lucky to have a man like you," I grin. "Who knows, you may even have little Rogers walking around."

He busts out laughing. Family is one thing Roger has never really thought of.

"I have a surprise for you," he smiles.

"What?" Just then, I see Stella and Hank walk in. Stella is quickly on her knees, giving me a hug.

"Oh, my goodness, what are you two doing here?"

Hank fills me in on everything, even him becoming a sheriff. Seems after much uproar with the town, the Marshal reconsidered. This is great news for White Horse. I, in return, filled them in on what Carl had told me. None of us are convinced it is the whole truth. We all agree that no one will ever really know the full truth about the Indian squaw and who indeed raped Anna. We can only hope that both women have received their justice and are able to rest in peace.

"The camp is nearly packed up. I reckon you will be leaving soon," Roger says.

"I am going to miss you all so much," I cry.

 "We will too," Stella cries back.

Dusk is on us, and everything is packed up. Our travois is loaded with what belongings I can bring. With everyone ready, it is time to leave. I come over to Roger with the aid of White Horse's old cane and give him a hug.

"Remember, no tears," he whispers in my ear.

"You take care of yourself," I say.

"You too."

Roger will not dwell on it any further and removes his embrace. He goes over to White Horse and shakes his hand.

"You take care, White Horse."

"You do the same, and thank you for everything." White Horse then gives him a hug. Roger is trying so hard to be strong, but I can tell it is tearing him up inside. Roger then goes to Koawa, who is already on his horse. He looks up at him and shakes his hand.

"You watch her for me."

"I will."

I go over to Hank and Stella. Hank gives me a bear hug and a kiss on the cheek. Stella and I hug and cry a tearful goodbye. Roger makes his way to his horse, briefly stopping by Running Water to kiss Morning Dove on her forehead.

Hank shakes White Horse's hand. "You take care of my girl," he tells him.

"I will," he reassures him. "And thank you again for everything."

"I will keep your passage clear. You will be safe."

"Thank you." He then goes to Koawa. Shaking his hand.

"You stay strong, my friend."

"You too," Koawa says.

"When we meet again, I will buy you that whiskey." Koawa just smiles.

We watch them as they get on their horses. Blue Thunder, high on his horse, comes up next to Stella. I can tell she is trying not to cry. I do believe she has fallen for him and has refused to follow him. I wonder if it is because of Hank. He gives one more plead with his eyes. She looks away as her tears begin to fall. I watch Blue Thunder glance over at Hank and then turn and ride off.

"I will never forget you all," I tell them.

Before anyone can respond and before Roger sheds a tear, they quickly run off. I wipe my eyes as White Horse comes up beside me.

"You ready?" he asks.

"Yes," I answer.

He then lifts me up and helps me on Sugar Foot's back. I look out to the horizon as White Horse jumps on his horse. Roger and the others are almost a blur. On his command, we begin our journey and my new life.

Chapter Forty-Two

The Footprints

Three months later. We are settled in our winter home. These past several months, White Horse and Flying Hawk have been working diligently on preserving the special root. It is not as easy as they had hoped. They have made many failed attempts, and evidently, all hopes of preserving are lost when the last one dies. We are beside ourselves but haven't lost hope. Anticipation of our new arrival is felt throughout, an heir to their Chief is nearly here. Rumors of a boy or girl are heard. I am carrying low, so it must be a boy. My face is shiny, so it must be a girl. I am carrying in the front with little weight on my hips, so therefore, it must be a boy. White Horse and I just laugh as we honestly do not care.

I have been nesting, as you may put it, preparing what a newborn baby may need. White Horse made a cradle that will lay beside us when our child is born. The gift I received from Roger is close at hand. The blanket lies in the cradle. Running water will be with me when our child is born. She said I delivered hers, so she wants to deliver mine. White Fawn will be there as well. On a very cold winter's day, the moment that everyone is waiting for arrives. I start having contractions very early in the morning, before sunrise. The contractions are getting stronger and closer together.

White Horse starts a fire just outside our lodge. Several of his warriors are keeping him company as he waits for any news. Many hours pass, and finally, it is time to push. I have gained a great deal of respect for Running Water as she never bellowed in pain when she had Morning Dove. This truly is the worst pain I have ever felt. I can't help but bellow out. White Horse is on edge with every scream he hears. The thought of me in this much pain is unbearable for him. Fortunately, Koawa and Night Owl are there to talk him down.

"Something is wrong!" he says.

"She is fine, my Chief," Night Owl says. "White Fawn is with her."

"Let's play," Koawa says, rolling the dice.

Running Water speaks her tongue. "I see the head," she says.

Good, I think I am almost done. Time comes to push again, then again, then again. Running water calls for White Fawn. I can tell by White Fawn's look something is wrong. I have no energy to think of the Lakota words.

"What's wrong? I ask.

Neither one responds, but I know something clearly is wrong. I scream.

"What's wrong with my baby!"

My scream gets White Horse's attention just outside the lodge. He jumps to his feet and looks at the lodge flap.

"I told you something is wrong!" he spats to his men. He then goes to the lodge. Koawa stops him.

"Let them be. Women talk crazy when they are having babies. It must hurt or something," he says.

Reluctantly, White Horse backs up and sits back down with his men.

White Fawn speaks her tongue to me. I don't understand what she is saying. Oh, dear Lord, how I wish Roger was here. Running water, in a panic, runs to the flap and yells for White

Horse. Like a bolt of lightning, he runs in and immediately is at my head.

"Something's wrong," I cry.

Running Water speaks her tongue. White Fawn argues that it is forbidden that White Horse be in here. White Horse snaps at her in a frantic voice. He doesn't care, and neither do I. Custom is being overlooked for the sake of our child.

"Honey, the baby's head is turning blue," he says.

The urge to push hits again. I arch my back in agony as I stop myself from pushing. Panting, I explain to White Horse.

"The cord is wrapped around the baby's neck. She will have to release it. Then the baby will come."

White Horse translates. A painful attempt is made. I have never seen White Horse so nervous. He takes my hand. Thank God he is strong because I squeeze it flat. She speaks her tongue.

"She can't get it," he says.

I catch my breath before I reply. "She is going to have to cut me."

White Horse has the most troublesome look on his face.

"Honey, no. You will bleed more."

"If she doesn't, the baby will die."

He grows still, trying to absorb what I am saying. There is no time to make him understand that every precious second counts if our child is going to live. I yell at him to snap him out of his trance and focus.

"White Horse!" He looks at me. "Tell her to cut me."

His face is motionless, and fear overwhelms him with the thought of cutting his wife. He knows the risk. Will he allow it? He cannot live his life without his Prairie Dawn. He reflects on how much he wants this baby. What great joy it will bring to them both. He looks at his wife's pleading eyes. She is so beautiful even in the state she is in. He cannot let her down. He reluctantly tells Running Water to cut me.

Unaware of White Horse, a conversation came up earlier with Running Water when I was explaining to her all the tools are used for that Roger gave me. I had drawn her a diagram, to the best of my ability, showing her where to cut if need be. I only hope she is calm enough to remember.

"Ask her if she remembers how I showed her?"

He just looks at me. I am sure he is asking himself why would she? He speaks his tongue to her.

"Yes," she answers.

It's one of the few English words that Running Water knows. Running water glances up at me. She speaks her tongue to White Horse. White Horse, in return, grips my hand. Then she snips. I bellow in pain. Tears form in my eyes. White Fawn lifts my head, supporting it over her arm. She reaches for her son's arm, pushing it under me to raise me up. She tells him to stay there. Another slit is felt. I then feel her inside, releasing the cord from around the baby's neck.

"Yes," she says.

"Alright. Now look out because here it comes." I lift on my elbows. I take a huge, deep breath and push. White Horse's eyes light up. A huge smile appears on his face when our child slides out and is born. The cord is then cut and saved. White Horse looks as if he is going to cry when White Fawn takes our child and cleans it up.

"It's a boy," I hear him say.

I am so relieved, so thrilled to give White Horse a son. I plop back down to catch my breath.

The cry of our son is heard outside the lodge. Koawa speaks outside the flap. Running water wipes her hands and opens the flap. She announces the birth. The immediate joy of whooping and hollers are heard throughout. Great joy fills the land. White Horse cannot stop staring at his son. He is truly the most amazing thing he has ever seen. He adores Kikimo and has received great pleasure watching him grow, but this is different, this child is from his Prairie Dawn. He is a part of her that they will share forever. He could not have asked for a better gift. How he vows from this day forward to never let her down. Never let their children down. He vows to raise them as mighty warriors, wise beyond their years. Oh yes, his sons are going to be well-known in the Lakota tribe. He watches White Fawn as she wraps the blanket around his son. He turns to his wife as the child is carried over to lie with his mother.

"Look, sweetheart, look what our love made."

There is no movement from his Prairie Dawn. The room is turning dark all around me.

"Carrie," White Horse says.

My stiffness and my pale face arouse him.

"No!" he shakes me to wake me up.

I faintly opened my eyes. He is only a blur moving farther and farther away. He rushes closer to me, touching my face. White Fawn places the baby in the cradle and comes to White Horse's side. White Horse fights to stay calm as he watches his Prairie Dawn fade away.

"No!" he yells as he shakes me harder to keep me awake. He barks at his mother to go get Koawa. He lifts his wife up into his arms.

"Don't you leave me," he cries.

He sits down, resting me in his lap. He cradles me in his arms, rocking me back and forth. Burying his head into his Prairie Dawn, he starts to weep.

"Don't leave me, Love, don't leave me."

Koawa rushes in alongside Running Water to see their Chief cradling his wife on the floor. His head is buried in her. They hear him cry. Running water, who has grown to love her so, starts to cry as well. Koawa, choking back his emotions, puts his arm around his wife to console her. He must remain strong. He must keep his emotions inside. His brother needs him. After several minutes, White Horse pulls himself together. He lifts his head, looking up at Koawa with tearful eyes.

"Get the circle ready," he sternly says.

He is refusing to give up without a fight, as long as there is still breath in his Prairie Dawn, he has hope. Grabbing a blanket and placing it over her, he rushes out the flap and to the circle.

The light is beautiful. The amount of peace that fills my soul is amazing. I watch it as it comes closer and closer. I reach out for it, wanting to be inhaled into its glory.

"Child," I hear.

"Father, is that you?" I ask.

I look around into the amazing light.

"Where are you, Father?" I ask. "I do not see you."

"I am on the other side of the light, child."

"I'm coming, Father. Please wait."

"No child. You must not come."

"But Father, it is so beautiful here and so peaceful."

"Yes, child, but it is not your time."

"But Father, I want to stay here in all this glory."

"Child, it is not your time. You must go back."

"Go back?" I question. "But I have come so far."

Suddenly, in front of me, next to the light, there appears the most beautiful Indian woman I have ever seen. She has long, beautiful hair that is blowing behind her.

"Go back to White Horse. My son and he need you," she says.

"Flowering Blossom?" I ask.

"Yes."

"I do not understand."

"Carrie, you are in the afterworld," Father says. "You do not belong here yet."

"You must go back, Carrie," Flowering Blossom says. "A great war will invade our Nation. Many will perish. You will bring comfort in a time of need. White Horse is going to need you. You must return."

"What can I do?" I ask her. She beautifully smiles.

"Look at him."

I look below where my body lies in a circle made of rocks. I see White Horse, Flying Hawk, Koawa, Blue Thunder, Yellow Hawk, and Night Owl, all dancing, performing healing over my body. I see the despair on White Horse's face.

"His Love for you is stronger than any other love he has ever had. It is that Love that cannot die. You must not leave him, for if you do, he will die, and my son will be alone."

I cannot believe what I am hearing. I stand there still, letting it all sink in. Am I dreaming? I can see myself in White Horse's arms. I can feel his pain and see his sorrow.

"Go take care of my grandson," Father says. "Do not let him stop you from giving him more children. For we are here."

"But the bleeding? There is so much," I say.

"If you have a child when there are many flowers, all will be fine."

Flowering Blossom watches from above as White Horse lifts my body from the circle. "You must hurry, Carrie. The ceremony is complete. You must hurry and go back before it is too late."

I turned to go back the way I came. The road is dark.

"How do I get back? The way I came is dark."

"Hurry, Carrie. You do not have much time," she warns.

"I can't get back." I cry out as the path is in total darkness. I turned around, and Flowering Blossom was gone.

"Father, I can't get back," I whine.

Slowly, he starts fading away. "Follow the footprints, Carrie. Follow the footprints." He is then gone.

"The footprints?"

I look around for any footprints. Magically, they start to appear. They appear large and gradually become smaller.

White Horse lays his Prairie Dawn on their pelt. He sits by her side, where he refuses to move. He takes her hand and prays to Mother Earth for his Prairie Dawn. The hours pass, and still, his Prairie Dawn does not move. Koawa comes down to his brother's side. He placed his hand on his shoulder. White Horse buries his head into his Prairie Dawn's side, holding her beautiful limp hand.

"Why Koawa? Why? What have I done to the Great Spirit to anger them so?" he cries.

"My brother, you must not ask yourself that. For no one is angry with you."

"Then why do they not want me to love? Every woman I have ever loved dies. Why my brother? What have I done?"

"Your heart is heavy and full of pain. What has happened to Prairie Dawn is not your fault. The only thing you are guilty of, my brother, is loving her."

"I cannot lose again, Koawa. I don't have the strength."

"My brother, you have not lost. Your Prairie Dawn is still alive."

Running Water brings the newborn baby in, laying the child in its cradle. Koawa comes to his feet.

"She will return in a few hours to feed again."

Evening is on the camp, and the snow begins to fall. White Horse is not moving from his wife's side. He sleeps little and prays to his Spirits often. He is sick with worry. His sorrow is deep. He is resting his eyes alongside his Prairie Dawn as he is heavy with sleep. He quickly wakes up when he hears his Prairie Dawn move. His insides get excited, and he crawls closer to her side. His smile widens when he sees his Prairie Dawn open her eyes. He strokes her hair, overjoyed beyond words.

"Hello beautiful," he greets.

"White Horse?"

"Yes, Love, I am here." He kisses her ever so gently. "I almost lost you."

"The baby?" I faintly say.

"He is just perfect," he grins.

"I want to see him."

"Of course," he says.

He stands up and walks over to the cradle, lifting his son into his arms. He walks him over to me, gently placing him down beside me. I open the blanket, counting all fingers and toes. I soon agree with White Horse that he is perfect.

"Running Water has been feeding him," he says. "She says he eats a lot."

"Oh, White Horse, he is perfect, just simply perfect," I smile.

"Look at his little feet," White Horse says, grabbing hold of his foot.

"That's it." I light up.

"What Love?"

I wasn't sure if White Horse would believe what I was going to tell him, but I must try.

"I saw my Father. He talked to me. He told me to go back to you. I couldn't find my way. I was so scared I wouldn't get back to you in time. He told me to follow the footprints. They started out very large and then went smaller."

White Horse is just looking at me, smiling ear to ear, happy that I am alive. "Don't you see White Horse? My Father was showing me the vision that I always wanted. We must name our child Little Foot."

He leans over and kisses me on the forehead.

"Then Little Foot it is," he whispers.

"I also saw someone else," I tell him.

"Who?" he asks.

"Flowering Blossom." This time, he looks surprised.

"No, I really did. I only saw her face. She was beautiful, her hair long and blowing free behind her."

He grows still, no doubt remembering her.

"White Horse, she told me of a great war on our Nation. Many lives will perish. She told me that I would be needed. She stressed so hard that I returned to you."

There is no doubt in my mind that White Horse loves me, but I am certain he still has so much Love for her.

"She is why I returned. She wants us to be together. She wants us to have many more children."

"No. There will be no more. I nearly lost you. I will not go through that again."

"She told me that as long as there are many flowers on the land when the child is born, I will be alright."

White Horse stands up. "We will discuss this later. For right now, you and our son need to rest."

All through the night, White Horse is diligent in giving me an herbal drink to help build up my strength. He helps with the baby so I can sleep. Running Water returns twice to help with the feedings. It is a long night for both, but neither one seems to mind. Especially White Horse, who watches me as I sleep, his eyes so full of Love and gratitude that I am alive.

The winter sunrises, reflecting its rays through the flap. I awake feeling so much stronger and revived. White Horse is nowhere to be seen. I see the cradle that lies not far away. I slowly come to my feet, ignoring my pain and walk over to my son's cradle. He is wide awake.

"Good morning," I greet. "Well, aren't you a ray of sunshine?"

I reach to pick him up when White Horse comes in.

"Honey, you shouldn't be on your feet," he says as he rushes over.

"Well, you were not here, and I am sure he is hungry."

"I went to get you food."

He puts down the bowl he is holding and comes for his son. He gently removes him from my arms.

"How is my little one?" he greets.

I walk my way over to the pelt with the aid of White Horse. I lie back down and take the baby from him.

"It is very cold out there."

"Is there any snow yet?" I ask him.

"Yes, it snowed last night."

"I want to see it."

"You speak foolishness, my Love," he smiles. "You cannot go out there, you could catch a chill."

"But I love the first snow."

"There will be other snows."

"Not first snow," I argue. I hear him giggle.

"I love you, woman, but I do not understand you sometimes. Eat your breakfast, I will be back in a little bit."

Both of our bellies are full, and Little Foot lies beside me asleep. I hear playing outside the lodge. Hmm, I pout. I want to play too. I remove my blankets and slowly come to my feet. I put on my moccasins and a heavy buffalo robe and go to the flap. The snow lying across the land is breathtaking. Oh, hell no, I am not passing this up. I step out into the snow. Kikimo is the first I see, then Blue Thunder. I hear him call out to White Horse. Little snitch, I think.

White Horse is quick on coming.

"I told you not to come out here," he scolds.

"It is so beautiful," I tell him.

"I realize that, but I am not going to chance you getting ill. Now, you go inside and keep our son."

"He is sleeping."

"It is not up for an argument. Now go!"

He points to the lodge. Fine, I think. I will go. I turn to head in. When his back is turned, the devil side of me comes out. I picked up a ball of snow and tossed it at him, hitting him in the back. I hear gasps throughout the camp. White Horse stops dead in his tracks and turns around. He tilts his head, pointing his finger.

"I am not playing. Now go inside!" he orders.

One thing White Horse is going to have to learn about me is my desire to play in fresh snow. I have never missed the first snowfall, and I am not planning on starting now.

"No," I argue.

White Horse was taken back. I don't think he is told no very often. He comes after me, his feet deep in the snow. I devilishly smirked, picking up another ball of snow and tossing it, hitting him in his chest. I hear the chuckle from nearby lodges. He can't believe it. For a moment, he pauses, and then, in a flash, I see him run.

"Alright, now you are going to get it," he teases.

The snowball fight is on. Laughter is heard as I manage a few solid throws. Soon, others are joining in, tossing at each other. My aim and throws are good, but soon, I grow tired, and White Horse is getting the best of me. Never have I quit a snowball fight. Mercy has always been on the other person, which was usually Roger. I am not giving up just yet. I walk the knee-high snow as fast as I can, ignoring the throbbing pain in my stomach as White Horse hits me with a ball.

I fall to my knees as if I were in pain and remain still. I hear him call.

"Carrie!" He runs.

The others cease their playing and watch on as White Horse falls on his knees to render to my needs. Unbeknownst to him, I grab a snowball and wait.

"Honey, are you alright?" he asks, lifting me off my stomach. I then tossed the ball, hitting him square in the chest.

"Gotcha," I tease.

"Why, you little thief," he says.

You could hear the laughter all around. White Horse was tricked. He, too, got a chuckle out of it. He reaches over to me.

"Come here, you."

He pulls me onto his lap and gazes down at me. "I love you," he says.

"I love you too, oh so very much." In front of everyone, deep in the snow, our lips lock. There is no care. We are together forever.

The End

~

Stay tuned for the next sequel, Lakota Blues. Follow Prairie Dawn as she lives her life as a Lakota woman. Walk alongside her as she enters a life of uncertainty and despair. She feels her emotions as she endures and goes to great lengths to keep peace with the Blue Coats while her husband, White Horse, leads his people through the Sioux War. Be touched by her strength and courage as she endures the unthinkable in order to ensure the safety of the people she has grown to love. Become involved as the lives of several characters are changed forever.

www.ingramcontent.com/pod-product-compliance
Lightning Source LLC
Chambersburg PA
CBHW051131300726
48978CB00011B/231